SCIENCE FICTION STORIES VOLUME 3

<hr>

SCIENCE FICTION STORIES VOLUME 3

<hr>

KEVIN J. ANDERSON

EBook ISBN: 978-1-68057-726-6
Trade Paperback ISBN: 978-1-68057-727-3
Dust Jacket Hardcover ISBN: 978-1-68057-728-0
Library of Congress Control Number: 2024937272
Cover design by Janet McDonald
Cover artwork by Tithi Luadthong "grandfailure"
Kevin J. Anderson, Art Director
Vellum layout by CJ Anaya
Published by
WordFire Press, LLC
PO Box 1840
Monument CO 80132
Kevin J. Anderson & Rebecca Moesta, Publishers
WordFire Press eBook Edition 2024
WordFire Press Trade Paperback Edition 2024
WordFire Press Dust Jacket Hardcover Edition 2024

Printed in the USA
Join our WordFire Press Readers Group for
sneak previews, updates, new projects, and giveaways.
Sign up at wordfirepress.com

CONTENTS

I'll just come right out and say it—I think this is one of my very best stories, influenced by a lot of baggage and experiences in my own life.

Not long ago, I recalled an old boyhood friend and realized I hadn't thought of him in decades. I'd completely lost touch. He didn't have many friends, and I didn't think he'd ever had a family. I wondered that if I forgot about him, then would he be completely forgotten? Vanished as if he'd never existed?

I've also known friends, colleagues, and family members who suffered from Alzheimer's or dementia. I watched their tragic decline, saw them lose everything they were, bit by bit, memory by memory, until literally nothing remained.

This is a poignant story about an old man suffering from a debilitating brain disease struggling to preserve the memory of his beloved long-lost wife, so that she isn't forgotten forever.

RUINS OF MEMORY

As he lay back in the transpod, waiting for his consciousness to be sent across the galaxy to his desperate destination, Arky held the photo in his shaky hands and focused on the picture of his wife one last time.

The actual photo would not travel with him, nor would his body, but he burned Etta's beautiful face into memory … as he had done so many times before. But the details kept slipping, slipping, disappearing.

He could not let her be forgotten, could not let *himself* forget, but his mind was riddled with holes like swiss cheese. Once he arrived on Lluxiv, he wouldn't have to worry about forgetting anymore. Etta would be preserved in his memory—his clean memory—like a fly in amber.

Beneath her sparkling brown eyes in the photo, her soft lips smiled at him. Yes, that was the perfect picture of her. Arky smiled back at the image.

Then the transpod activated, and he was gone.

Lluxiv was an abandoned world once home to a vanished alien race —like so many others in the Merge Archives. For a xeno-archaeologist, the Archives were a treasure trove of empty planets just waiting to be explored (or at least cataloged), whenever someone got around to it and whenever funding was available. He could have chosen any world, but Lluxiv would serve his purposes as well as any.

Arky had never thought he would go on an expedition again. He'd walked away from it all after he'd lost Etta, after Aan-00, but it was getting harder and harder to think every day, and this was his only solution. Taking the transpod through the Mass-O network, to whatever planet, would fix things. Arky would arrive at the other end in a fresh new skin created from the genetic record of his previous trip thirty-five years ago.

For weeks, he had scoured the Archives, overwhelmed by the countless choices of unexplored worlds. The terse listing for Lluxiv noted the planet's breathable atmosphere, temperate climate. The vanished people were called only "Inhabitants."

But the intriguing crystalline growths in the exotic ruins caught his attention. Etta had always liked crystals—he still remembered that much about her. On their fourth anniversary, he'd given her a beautiful refractive shard. The pendant hadn't cost much, but she'd loved it. She would gaze into the shiny surface, turning it this way and that in the light, looking at each facet. The happy fascination on her face was clear as a bell. Therefore, Lluxiv was his choice.

But while the solution was simple, the approvals were not, and bureaucracy was a difficult battle. He had to make his case to the Academy approvals bureau.

He did his homework, wrote down notes, marshaled his arguments. Before contacting the board, Arky took all of his meds and waited for them to reach full efficacy. His tremors were down, almost unnoticeable, and he could fake being normal, healthy. Then he gathered his courage and contacted Lucinda Bakira at the Academy administration.

Though he had known her predecessor well enough, this woman hadn't even been an undergrad at the time of Arky's last expedition. But she was now head of the exploration division, and she was the one he needed to convince.

He wore his nicest jacket, sat in his neat office in his Earth apartment. On the comm screen, Bakira brightened. "Why, Dr. Arky Sehar, this is unexpected! I thought you'd retired." He was glad that she at least recognized his name.

The woman had wiry blue-black hair that stuck out in strange shapes, making him think of a topiary on her head. Her soft round face suggested that she spent little time on rugged field expeditions, but rather dealt with bureaucratic matters.

That was fine. He needed a bureaucratic release now.

"Retirement isn't all it's cracked up to be," Arky replied. "I'd like to go back out into the field. I've found a planet that deserves to be cataloged."

Lucinda raised her eyebrows. "Oh? What's it been, twenty years?"

"Thirty-five." He watched her expression change as she considered his age, but he pressed on. "The planet is called Lluxiv. You can call it up in your database. The civilization there is long gone, but well preserved."

"Lots of planets in that category, Dr. Sehar," she said. "The Academy has to be selective. Why should we bother with this ... Lluxiv?"

"I've got a hunch about it. From markings found on the ruins and the distinctive appearance of the architecture, I think this race could be related to the Hithree, who left intriguing dimensional mathematics behind on several worlds, which the Merge has adapted. The place could be profitable, and I'd like to follow up on it." A completely fabricated reason, he knew, but he doubted she would dig deeper. "Just a small, preliminary recon, no need for a big expedition."

"We'd never fund a big expedition." Like all bureaucrats, she was skilled at saying no. "And you have been out of the game for a long time. Maybe I should put it on the list for consideration by one of the other candidates who's been waiting longer."

"I hope my reputation is still worth something." His earnestness was obvious. Maybe too obvious. "Lluxiv needs to be explored, and I'm the one to do it, Dr. Bakira." He put on a brave face.

She frowned, then mumbled, "It's just *Ms.* Bakira. Still intending to finish that doctorate." It sounded like an excuse she had given many times before. On the screen, her eyes wandered as she called up the data on Lluxiv. "Looks like a good candidate. You really think this race might be a Hithree derivative? No one else has shown interest in the place before."

"It's subtle, but definitely possible." He hoped she didn't ask him to prove it. "Or you can send me somewhere else, but I'm happy to go solo. Save costs."

She sighed. "There are so many worlds it would take decades and an army of explorers just to do a brief survey of them all. But there's no funding."

He nodded, showing he understood her dilemma. "That's why we should choose candidates with a good chance of applicable discoveries. The Academy certainly benefited from my previous work."

She looked up again. "People remember you positively around here, Dr. Sehar, and yes, you made the Merge plenty of profit. The Academy has a display case with some of the artifacts scanned from Aan-00." Her sepia eyes filled with real sincerity. "But … are you sure about this, sir? You retired for a reason—a very good reason. I know your story, even read your book back at the university. Didn't you vow you would never do xeno-archaeology again after … after, you know, what happened to your wife?"

"Yes, I know what happened to Etta." *I still remember* that, *at least*. He realized he sounded terse.

"Transpod travel is expensive, and many skilled researchers are, quite frankly, higher on the Academy's list. You've been out of the game a long time. Even with your impeccable credentials, it may take a while for the request to be approved."

But Arky didn't have "a while," not by any stretch.

"I understand your financial quandary." He played his last card, though he had intended to play it all along. "I did earn a fair amount of royalties from the Aan-00 discoveries, the pharmaceuticals, the alien music. I am willing to cover part of the cost with my own funds, but I need the Academy to cut through the red tape so I can leave quickly."

He would sell every possession, liquidate his accounts. What was he going to use the money for anyway? Some days he even forgot how to hold a toothbrush.

He crossed his arms in front of the screen. "I've made up my mind, Ms. Bakira."

"A very generous offer, sir, and that should make the difference." Bakira continued scanning information on her screen. "Ah, here it is. Your earlier body map is still in the Mass-O database from your prior travel, so that makes it easier. When you emerge from the transpod on Lluxiv, you'll be in a forty-year-old body." She smiled again. "I doubt you'll mind that."

"Not at all," Arky said. A clean slate for his consciousness, and that was the most important thing. Pristine brain tissue that wouldn't forget everything … "Please be sure to use the genetic map from my original outbound transit to Aan-00, not the return body."

"We usually use the most recent one. It's only a few months' difference."

A few vital months. "It is important to me," he insisted. Very important. "And the cost is the same."

"Very well." Bakira shrugged. "I'll authorize the mission, provided you bear half the costs of transportation. We can't afford a team to go with you, though. This will be a solo field expedition."

Even though this was exactly what he wanted, the idea was still daunting—going to an uninhabited, unstudied world without any support other than what the ancient Discovery Lander provided. But he was more frightened of losing his memories forever. "That's fine."

She ticked off the final points on her fingers. "Go see if you can find more Hithree mathematics, or anything else of value. Send the Academy regular updates. Let's hope Lluxiv is as fascinating and as profitable as your previous expedition was."

Now, when he woke in the Lluxiv transpod he braced himself for the nausea of transfer sickness, which he remembered from the previous expedition, though it had been decades. Nevertheless, when he emerged inside a clone of his forty-year-old body, even the physical sickness and mental confusion did not diminish his joy.

His head pounded like the worst hangover he'd had in college, but the thoughts were *there*, the memories clear in an uncorrupted brain. Alas, he would never know how many poignant experiences and conversations had been lost forever as his old mind deteriorated, but any memories that were just inaccessible due to ruined neural pathways were now there again.

He could print a new copy of Etta's photo if he wanted, but he didn't need it. He didn't need it! Now she was there in his mind, so bright and clear. He could picture her as if he had just seen her yesterday.

Arky was already smiling as he climbed out of the pod and set foot inside the ancient Lander. In wonder, he brushed his hands down his durable travel shirt and trousers—the same clothes he had worn when he'd arrived on Aan-00 as a younger man. It gave him a strange sense of déjà vu, and he glanced over his shoulder, as if Etta might emerge from the other pod, joining him as before.

But of course not.

Inside the Lander, Servitors moved about, tending him, monitoring the equipment. The quicksilver spiderlike robots remained unobtrusive, uninterested in him, but they weren't of interest to him either.

At the console, he programmed assemblers to generate the archaeological equipment he would need, exploration tools, recording apparatus, a translation database, even an old-school paper notepad and stylus. All the while, he recalled going through similar activities with Etta on Aan-00, savoring details that had been blurred by time and his own disability.

Back then, she had programmed the food synthesizer with some of her favorite recipes from Earth, and he suddenly recalled their first meal on Aan-00, a spicy vindaloo. His mouth watered now; he could almost taste it. He hadn't eaten vindaloo in years….

He already had what he had come here for. In fact, he could just sit back inside the Lander and reminisce, which he did for several hours, feeling the wet tears down his face. There was no hurry. He didn't have to explore this place immediately, but he would carry the memories along with him whatever he did. And Etta would have wanted to go out and have a look at Lluxiv, even sketch some of the things she found interesting.

Before long, he was ready. "All right, my dear. Let's see what this place has to offer."

He stepped outside, a new man on a new world, excited and alive again.

Ages ago, the Progenitors' Discovery Lander had settled near a complex of Inhabitant ruins, a hive-like city surrounded by a prairie of spiky grasses and flowering plants. He inhaled the odd air, caught an undertone of cinnamon and dust. Scarlet bird analogs flitted about.

He set out for the nearby city. The blue-white sun shone on the curves, arches, and pockmarked windows in the high structures. The tan, weathered architecture wasn't at all like the Hithree civilization, and he was glad Lucinda Bakira hadn't asked for too many justifications. Arky was sure he could find something worthwhile to earn his keep.

Most remarkable were the strange transparent growths that wound through the silent ruins—crystal vines, tubes of glass that branched out in all directions, like voracious weeds that had turned to silicon. Etta would have found them pretty. He didn't see any immediate purpose to the vines, could not tell if they were some kind of implanted infrastructure or wild crystalline growths.

Arky walked among the outer structures, feeling the oppressive grandeur of infinite age. How long ago had this exotic race fallen? What had destroyed them? And what had they left behind? This titanic civilization was now simply vanished from memory, from history. Ruins and memories—just like him.

Etta had been so excited when they'd first arrived in the jungles on Aan-00. And he felt just as much excitement to think of it now, the childlike smile on her face, the sparkle in her eyes. Yes, that was better than any xeno-archaeological treasure.

Occupying himself as he daydreamed, he spent the first day taking a general survey of the Inhabitant ruins, filing numerous images to send back to the Academy. He found no markings on the buildings, no writings or stelae or chiseled statues, and in his initial report he promised to continue his search for Hithree-inspired equations. He downplayed his excitement, so as not to intrigue other xeno-archaeologists, not that the Academy would send a second expedition here.

He would have the world to himself.

The intriguing crystalline growths were wild and random, like weeds, yet he suspected there was a pattern somewhere, one he simply couldn't see. Had the Inhabitants planted these glassy vines to adorn their structures, or were they natural growths, crystalline weeds that had taken over the long-forgotten ruins? Power conduits? Defensive systems?

He chipped away samples of the glassy nodules so that his analytical equipment could run tests. He took images, spectral analyses, thermal signatures, and brought everything back to his base camp at the ship. He spent each evening documenting his work and planning the next day's activities.

And all the while, he basked in his rediscovered memories of Etta.

He worked his way deeper into the ruins. Though all alone, he was surrounded by history, though he still had learned little about the vanished race, certainly nothing that would excite the Merge. Before the Great Fracture, the Progenitors had begun their extensive search for inhabited worlds. When a Lander had finally stumbled upon Lluxiv thousands of years ago, was the planet already a tomb? Had these extinct Inhabitants just barely missed being saved?

He didn't understand the curvature of the doors, the prominent towers and stubby lumps, all infested with crystal vines. He found no squiggles and lines that denoted language, no artwork or detailed carvings. It seemed the Inhabitants had left no written or visual language, no record of themselves at all.

Looking at the towers, he inhaled the faintly cinnamon air and shook his head. Back on Aan-00, he and Etta had been sounding boards for each other, bouncing ideas back and forth, the wilder the better.

Now, trying to imagine what the Inhabitants had been like, he mused aloud, "I wish I understood you."

Out of the corner of his eye, Arky caught a flicker of light, shades of color awakening within the crystal vines. The transparent stalks shimmered, and then they displayed images for him. He turned around amid the transparent stalks and saw ghostly holograms in the air, like whispers of the past struggling to be seen and heard again.

The crystal growths began to show him the Inhabitants at the height of their civilization! Locked inside the silicon matrix was a panoply of stories, like video records.

As he walked from vine to vine in wonder, each stalk displayed a new set of images. Arky stared at all the different stories as the Inhabitants flitted about. The creatures were like locusts with long wings and oval insectile heads, but they walked upright, with four arms and two legs.

The records showed Inhabitants building their cities, burrowing in the ground, flying in daredevil moves that were apparently mating dances. They participated in races across the sky or clashed in large groups—warfare, or perhaps just sporting events.

Next, the transparent vines began to hum, and then he heard actual music, atonal melodies created and recorded by the Inhabitants. He moved in awe, realizing that perhaps these glassy structures were how the aliens preserved their memories, keeping them intact, frozen in crystal. Just waiting for someone to remember them.

And Arky was here.

His pulse raced as he wandered through the structures, watching the lightshow inside the vines, but he could not absorb so many recordings at once. It would take him months and months just to sample them all.

As he experienced a sense of joy and discovery, how he wished Etta could be here with him, just as she had been on that glorious, and damnable, expedition to Aan-00. His mind was clear now, not addled by the rapid degeneration. She had been such a perfect partner back in those perfect days....

As that thought occurred to him, Arky gasped as Etta's image danced like a ghost inside the alien crystal growths. Her face, her slender body, her quick yet agile movements. She was there, as clear as any memory!

He moved from stalk to stalk, and Etta was reflected back, drawn from his memories, treasured there along with the alien history. The crystal vines recorded it all.

Arky reached out with trembling fingers to touch her embedded image—and he received another burst of memories.

All his life, Arky had dreamed of doing fieldwork for the Academy. The Mass-O Hub offered instantaneous transpod travel to so many worlds, vibrant cultural and business centers, members of the Merge. But he was more interested in the empty and untouched ones, the mysteries that were mere footnotes in a catalog.

Arky dreamed about the unexplored planets with once-grand civilizations that had fallen into the obscurity of time and history. What had happened to them? What went wrong? How many remarkable races had died out before the unification of the races, just missing what might have saved their people? A tragedy.

He wanted to see for himself.

Fascinated to fill in some of those blanks in the Archives, he got his certification in xeno-archaeology, and yet his expedition requests were declined seven times before he finally got approval to go to Aan-00. But the Academy couldn't afford a research team to go with him, except for a possible research assistant.

When he was an undergrad, he had met Etta, a shy history major studying the background of the First Cycle and the Great Fracture. She was also an artist who loved to sketch the plants, flowers, bugs, and birds around them on Earth. They had fallen in love, stuck together. Although she wasn't specifically trained in xeno-archaeology, Arky pulled strings to get her named his research assistant, and the two of them were off to a pristine world that had once been home to a powerful race.

Aan-00 was a lush, jungle world covered with sluggish mosses and towering fern groves, flowers and seeds and (inedible) fruits of all kinds and colors. The assemblers inside the Discovery Lander created anything they needed—tools, shelters, food, analytical devices.

He and Etta scanned the genetic profiles of native flowers and berries, uploading the data for possible Merge pharmaceutical uses. Despite the perfectly accurate and detailed images from their recording apparatus, Etta preferred to sketch the odd plants and fungi herself; she added her own flair, comparing herself to the intrepid historical naturalists Darwin or Audubon.

He and Etta slept in open tents; they made love in the fern groves. Whenever they didn't want to get soaked by the warm jungle rains, they could run back to the Lander and collate their notes, clean up, and sometimes make love again. Arky picked pretty bouquets and gave them to Etta. She drew sketches that featured him next to the alien flora. It had been a genuine honeymoon: Adam and Eve on an alien Eden. Aan-00 was idyllic, or so they'd both thought at the time.

The Aan aliens constructed ziggurat structures out of black rock quarried from jungle outcroppings. The identical buildings were spaced in geometric patterns like an extraterrestrial connect-the-dots, visible only when Arky dispatched drones to take images from high above.

Though the alien civilization had vanished millennia ago, the ruins were pristine, the edges still sharp. He and Etta cracked open chill vaults within the pyramids, where they found the cadavers, perfectly preserved Aan inhabitants. They were a race of salamander-like creatures, their dead spotted skin somehow still moist and covered with a protective slime. It took days for Etta to get up her nerve to sketch them in close detail, but eventually she did the lost race justice.

Inside other ziggurats, they found libraries, and the two of them settled in to scan the material, running images and words through translation approximators and sending data back to the Academy Archives.

Etta discovered pinecone-shaped objects, which proved to be alien music players, and she and Arky spent weeks recording the lost music of Aan-00. Now, in a perfectly sharp memory, he could hear her humming along in camp, trying to match the atonal melody with human vocal cords.

As the lead xeno-archaeologist, Arky narrated the reports dispatched to the Academy; naturally shy, Etta refused the attention, preferring just to be his assistant. After all, xeno-archaeology was *his* passion, although her sketches and paintings added something unique to each report.

When at last their allotted time was over and they had to say goodbye to their little slice of Eden, he and Etta returned home through the Hub. Rather than reusing their outbound clone map to create new skins, the Academy had paid for a fresh, up-to-date scan. Retaining every detail of their bodies after months working on the field expedition was considered a reward, a small pat on the back.

They were happy, even minor celebrities in their academic world. Merge pharma researchers found that the strange Aan-00 flora contained a unique chemical structure that led to new drug families. The music from the pinecone-shaped recorders became immensely popular across the inhabited worlds.

Although the Academy, and hence the Merge, retained the rights on all such discoveries, Arky earned a small fraction of royalties as lead researcher. That eventually became a significant source of income. He and Etta talked about the next expedition they would undertake.

He even wrote a book about their blissful expedition, playing up the mystery of Aan-00, including her artwork. He gave Etta every speck of credit she deserved, but she had been shy since the first moment he'd met her, and he respected her wishes to stay out of the limelight.

Six months later, Etta's first symptoms manifested—initially as forgetfulness, then piercing headaches. Her thoughts became more and more disorganized. He spotted the differences right away, but doctors weren't able to diagnose the cause until the damage was so extreme they couldn't help but notice it.

In addition to all those wondrous memories, Aan-00 had also given Etta a brain parasite, an insidious alien retrovirus that encoded itself into her DNA like a worm wrapped around her neurons. It began to flourish not long after they were back home, at which point the plaques and nodules appeared growing throughout her cerebrum like fern forests on the alien planet.

Etta had holes in her memory, holes in her mind. Whole sections of her past were eaten away until she couldn't remember the simplest things, couldn't remember her life … couldn't remember him. With astonishing rapidity, she couldn't even remember how to *live*.

Arky begged for medical help, called upon the Academy as well as those pharmaceutical companies that had benefited from his discoveries. But the news cycle had moved on, distracted by other incredible discoveries, other scandals, other political upheavals. Some news reports did mention Etta's plight, but she had never been the star of the expedition. A little-known "research assistant" did not fire the imaginations of the Merge, and the publicity generated nothing more than impotent "thoughts and prayers."

During that brief gray area when Etta understood what was happening to her and before she lost her capability to think, she worried that Arky was infected as well. He endured tests and scans, but the doctors found no sign of the parasite in him. Etta must have had the misfortune of catching the parasite from something in the air she breathed, the water she drank, from one of the odd fungi she sketched, maybe from contaminated dust or pollen in the tombs. Perhaps she'd just been unlucky, inhaling the virus while he did not.

His scans remained clear, and his heart was broken as he watched her fade.

The onset of the brain parasite was like a wrecking ball, and within months Etta was gone. Afterward, Arky simply didn't have the heart for his work anymore. With the success of his book and the tangential profits from the Aan discoveries, he could have gone on a new expedition, this time with a full research team. But he would undertake no more alien expeditions without her. Instead, Arky Sehar simply retired and vanished into obscurity.

After thirty-five years, though, he still had enough clout and enough money to force the expedition to Lluxiv. And now he had his memories back.

Arky spent his days surrounded by a wealth of history and memory. The crystal vines recognized his presence, and they were hungry to share the records they had cherished all these millennia, memories ready for an audience.

Walking through the crystal archives, he recorded the visual history of the Inhabitants, which he dutifully relayed to the Academy, where their linguists would spend years deciphering the records.

Some of the insectile words had a more singsong quality, and he imagined they were spoken by poets or religious figures. Other images showed incomprehensible designs that might have been art, might have been mathematics. Maybe Merge engineers could find something useful here. He just basked in what the vines showed him. His pristine mind had room for all of those stories.

And the crystal growths picked up on the memories—the history —that he brought with him. The alien crystals reflected his life and Etta's back at him, showing him images in the curved glassy surfaces. A new historical record. All day long, he walked through a magical forest of Etta.

Needing no further encouragement, Arky accessed his happy days. The memory vines showed flickers of his boyhood as the memories came back to mind, a dog he'd loved and also lost, because that was the way of pets. He saw his school days, the first girl he'd been infatuated with; he couldn't remember her name, but he knew she had long braids....

Arky shook his head and focused on what really mattered to him. He didn't care about other spots in his life. He had come here to reclaim the memories of Etta, and now this crystal forest on Lluxiv was preserving her in a way he had never dreamed—her beautiful face, her silly laugh. Once he remembered her life, she would be preserved forever here on Lluxiv.

An excellent cook, Etta would choose a specific planetary cuisine for a month, then switch to a new culinary adventure the next month. His mouth watered at the thoughts as they came back to him, and he made up his mind to have the Lander assemblers recreate some of those meals.

He recalled a rafting trip they had taken down a languid river in North America during the first year they had dated. Warm under the open sky, they'd drifted along in silence, satisfied with each other's company. They'd eaten sandwiches from the cooler— nothing fancy, just thick layers of sticky peanut butter and sweet raspberry jam, an old traditional recipe Etta had discovered. When they'd kissed, they had smeared the remnants over each other's faces, and then they'd dunked into the river water to wash off.

Another time, they went camping in the wilderness just to see how much they enjoyed the rugged experience. In his imagination, Arky had been preparing for an alien expedition someday. As if to test them, the skies turned gray, the temperature dropped, and a cold rain drenched them. He and Etta found shelter in a grove of trees, erected their tent, and waited it out. After nightfall, the clouds cleared, and the two emerged to see a midnight sky exploding with diamond stars ... countless worlds that were now connected by the Mass-O Hub.

Now, giving the memories to the crystal vines, he thought of when he and Etta at last traveled to Mars and the nearest Discovery Lander, the jumping-off point for transpod travel through the Hub. They were both excited and nervous, marveling at the Martian complex and the first Academy outpost there, the wonder of the ancient vessel that had opened the human race to a new age of exploration and galactic commerce. From there Arky and Etta had gone on their adventure to Aan-00....

In his new body, his new mind, the restored memories were

completely real to him, and even though they brought tears to his eyes, they were tears of joy. He considered the beauty of lost things, not the pain of the loss itself.

Unfortunately, with this newfound clarity of his past, he also began to see images of Etta that he wished he could forget for all time. The grayness of her skin in her last days, the glassy confusion in her eyes as they flicked back and forth, showing no knowledge of where she was or what had happened to her, or even who *he* was.

The brain parasites consumed her thoughts and memories. Etta had been lost to him one neuron at a time, one memory at a time, until all that remained was her heartbeat. And even that went away.

Now that clarified memory was a curse. Arky huddled in the crystalline grove watching the reflected images of her last moments babbling, incoherent, unaware. He squeezed his eyes shut.

After all this time, few people back home remembered Etta at all, not even her name. Her footnote in the Archives was even smaller than his. So, the responsibility of preserving her fell to Arky—because once he forgot her, then she would truly be gone forever. A veritable hermit in his apartment on Earth, he had clung to each of those memories.

Year by year, in his private journal he wrote down everything he could recall. He stared at the photos in his personal scrapbooks thousands of times, then he took up the hobby of digital art so he could create new images as he thought about her. By no means was he as talented as she had been, but love and longing blurred his critical vision anyway.

With no one to distract him at home, he would go back and reread the old journals he had written, embellishing events, adding details that occurred to him. One day, however, he was perplexed, and then concerned, as he read his own lengthy description about a surprise birthday party that Etta had thrown for him ... but he didn't remember the event at all! It was entirely gone from his memory.

Two days afterward, while using his art apps and digital paintbrush, he stopped halfway through painting Etta's profile, frozen with self-doubt because he couldn't recall exactly what her eyes looked like.

Once he noticed that, he began to connect the dots. He realized other instances in the previous months where he'd been uncharacteristically absent-minded. At first, he'd laughed it off as a symptom of growing older, but when he reread the journal entry about the birthday party, he understood that the memory wasn't just faded, but *gone.* That gave him a deep chill.

He knew those symptoms.

After copying Etta's old medical records, he hurried in for a full scan himself. No cure had ever been found for the Aan brain parasite, no treatment proposed. In fact, it had barely been studied. The Merge knew of only one case, one datapoint. A curiosity.

Even after so many discoveries and profitable materials had spun off from Aan-00, the Merge had interdicted the planet, placing it on a quarantine list. Arky and Etta's survey had been thorough, if not complete. No one needed to visit there again. There were so many other worlds to choose from.

The brain scan showed that Arky did indeed have the Aan parasite. He had been infected after all. Tied to his DNA, the retrovirus had hidden dormant within his neurons for decades, but now it activated at last, for whatever reason. Her symptoms had just manifested much sooner.

Arky knew exactly what was going to happen to him, and he knew how fast the brain burn would occur, like little novas going off in his mind, erasing or burying memories. Before it was too late for him, he had used up his remaining wealth and clout to book one more Academy field expedition. The Discovery Lander could rebuild his body cell by cell, neuron by neuron, DNA strand by DNA strand—from the original pattern when he had first traveled to Aan-00, not the infected one that had returned home. His consciousness could go into a pristine new skin.

Arky needed to hurry, because his memories were slipping away day by day. He would never return to the old deteriorating body left behind in storage. He didn't have the finances to jump into a new skin back home, to hopscotch from body to body for years as some wealthy people did. No, this trip had been his only chance not just to save himself, but to save Etta, to save her memories. He wouldn't lose her again.

Smiling now, though, Arky walked through the crystal forest of memories. These silicon vines, whether natural growths on Lluxiv or some exotic data-storage tech, were also remembering her, as eager to preserve Etta as he was. He could stay here and just reminisce about her for a long time. He had everything he needed.

Shared by the memory vines, the alien Inhabitant culture would interest him for the rest of his life, and the Merge would be satisfied with the data he kept sending them. The Academy could check off Lluxiv on their list, a world thoroughly cataloged.

Arky had a new life and a clarity of purpose, as well as a clarity of memories. Etta lived inside his mind again, and these crystal vines helped make her bright and clear, as if every event in their lives together had happened only yesterday. And it would now be stored forever.

He touched the cylindrical vines, the crystal offshoots that rose up through the ruins and held so much of the past, not just of an entire civilization but of Arky's own life. Like a fly caught in amber.

As he stood among the ruins of Lluxiv, he drew a long, satisfied breath. Now, Etta would last for millennia, just like the memories of the Inhabitants had.

Now let's journey to the universe of Frank Herbert's Dune, *where I've spent more than half of my writing career.*

The galactic empire revolves around the desert planet Arrakis and its vital spice melange, which is guarded by giant sandworms. Central to Dune's political conflicts is the feud between the Atreides and Harkonnen noble houses.

This tale is set more than 10,000 years before the events in the classic novel, at the very beginning of House Harkonnen. It is chronologically the very first Dune story in the series.

When Brian Herbert and I were preparing for the release of our epic Legends of Dune prequel trilogy, which chronicles the great war between humans and thinking machines, we wanted to introduce this new epoch in Dune history. The publisher, Tor Books suggested we write a teaser story to hook readers, to be distributed as a free chapbook available in bookstores around the country.

"Hunting Harkonnens" introduces an ancestor of the Harkonnens from Dune in a deadly encounter with thinking-machine warriors called cymeks.

The rest of the story is told in our novels The Butlerian Jihad, The Machine Crusade, *and* The Battle of Corrin.

HUNTING HARKONNENS: A TALE OF DUNE

(with Brian Herbert)

—I—

The Harkonnen space yacht left the family-held industries on Hagal and crossed the interstellar gulf toward Salusa Secundus. The streamlined vessel flew silently, in contrast to the fusillade of angry shouts inside the cockpit.

Stern, hardline Ulf Harkonnen piloted the yacht, concentrating on the hazards of space and the constant threat of thinking machines, though he kept lecturing his twenty-one-year-old son, Piers. Ulf's wife Katarina, too gentle a soul to be worthy of the Harkonnen name, asserted that the quarrel had gone on long enough. "Further criticism and shouting will serve no purpose, Ulf."

Vehemently, the elder Harkonnen disagreed.

Piers sat fuming, unrepentant; he was not cut out for the cutthroat practices his noble family expected, no matter how much his father tried to bully them into him. He knew Ulf would browbeat and humiliate him all the way home. The gruff older man refused to consider that his son's ideas for more humane methods might actually be more efficient than the inflexible, domineering ways.

Clutching the ship controls as if in a death grip, Ulf growled at his son, "*Thinking machines* are efficient. Humans, especially riffraff like our slaves on Hagal, are meant to be used. I doubt you'll ever get that through your skull." He shook his large, squarish head. "Sometimes, Piers, I think I should clean up the gene pool by eliminating you."

"Then why don't you?" Piers snapped, defiant. His father believed in forceful decisions, every question with a black-and-white answer, and that belittling his son would drive him to do better.

"I can't, because your brother Xavier is too young to be the Harkonnen heir, so you're the only choice I have ... for the time being. I keep hoping you'll understand your responsibility to our family. You're a noble, meant to command, not to show the workers how soft you can be."

Katarina pleaded, "Ulf, you may not agree with the changes Piers made on Hagal, but at least he thought it through and was trying a new process. Given time it might have led to improved productivity."

"And meanwhile the Harkonnen family goes bankrupt?" Ulf held a thick finger toward his son as if it were a weapon. "Piers, those people took terrible advantage of you, and you're lucky I arrived in time to stop the damage. When I provide you with detailed instructions on how our family holdings are to be run, I do not expect you to come up with a 'better' idea."

"Is your mind so fossilized that you can't accept new ideas?" Piers asked.

"Your instincts are faulty, and you have a very naive view of human nature." Ulf shook his head, growling in disappointment. "He takes after you, Katarina—that's his main problem." Like his mother, Piers had a narrow face, full lips, and a delicate expression ... quite different from Ulf's shaggy gray hair framing a blunt-featured face. "You would have been a better poet than a Harkonnen."

That was meant to be a grave insult, but Piers secretly agreed. The young man had always enjoyed reading histories of the Old Empire, days of decadence and ennui before the thinking machines had conquered many civilized solar systems. Piers would have fit into those times well as a writer, a storyteller.

"I gave you an opportunity, son, hoping that I could depend on you. But I have had my answer." The elder Harkonnen stood clenching his large, callused fists. "This whole trip has been a waste."

Katarina caressed her husband's broad back, trying to calm him. "Ulf, we're passing near the Caladan system. You talked about stopping there to investigate the possibility of new holdings ... maybe fishing operations?"

Ulf hunched his shoulders. "All right, we'll divert to Caladan and take a look." He snapped his head up. "But in the meantime, I want this disgrace of a son sealed in the lifepod chamber. It's the closest thing to a brig onboard. He needs to learn his lesson, take his responsibilities seriously, or he will never be a true Harkonnen."

—II—

As he sulked inside his improvised cell, with its cream-colored walls and silver instrument panels, Piers stared out the small porthole window. He hated arguments with his stubborn father. The rigid old ways of the Harkonnen family were not always best. Instead of imposing tough conditions and harsh punishments, why not try treating workers with respect?

Workers. He remembered how his father had reacted to the word. "Next you'll want to call them employees. They are *slaves*!" Ulf had thundered as they stood in the overseer's office back on Hagal. "They have no rights."

"But they deserve rights," Piers responded. "They're human beings, not machines."

Ulf had barely contained his violence. "Perhaps I should beat you the way my father beat me, pounding contrition and responsibility into you. This isn't a game. You're leaving now, boy. Get on the ship."

Like a scolded child, Piers had done as he was commanded....

He wished he could stand toe to toe with his father, just once. Every time he tried, though, Ulf made him feel that he had let the family down, as if he were a shirker who would waste their hard-won fortunes.

His father had entrusted him to manage the family holdings on Hagal, grooming him as the next head of the Harkonnen businesses. This assignment had been an important step for Piers, with complete authority over the sheet diamond operations. A chance, a test. The implicit understanding was that he would operate the mines as they had always been run.

Harkonnens held the mining rights to all sheet diamonds on sparsely populated Hagal. The largest mine filled an entire canyon. Piers recalled how sunlight played off the glassy cliffs, dancing on the prismatic surfaces. He had never seen anything so beautiful.

The cliff faces were diamond sheets with blue-green quartz marking the perimeters, like irregular picture frames. Human-operated mining machines crawled along the cliffs like fat, silver insects: no artificial intelligence, and therefore considered safe. History had shown that even the most innocuous types of AI could ultimately turn against humans. Entire star systems were now under the control of diabolically smart machines, and in those dark sectors of the universe, human slaves followed the commands of mechanized masters.

At optimal spots on the shimmering cliffs, the mining machines would lock onto the surface with suction devices and separate the diamond material with sound waves at natural points of fissure; holding diamond sheets in their grasp, the dumb machines would make their way back down the cliff to loading areas.

It was an efficient process, but sometimes the sonic cutting procedure shattered the diamond sheets. Once Piers gave the slaves a stake in the profits, though, such mishaps occurred much less frequently, as if they took greater care after they received a vested interest.

Overseeing the Hagal operation, Piers had come up with the idea of letting the captive gangs work without typical Harkonnen regulations and close oversight. While some slaves accepted the incentive program, a number of problems did surface. With reduced supervision, some slaves ran away; others were disorganized or lazy, just waiting for someone to tell them what to do. Initially, productivity dropped, but he was sure the output would eventually meet and even exceed previous levels.

Before that could happen, though, his father had made an unannounced visit to Hagal. And Ulf Harkonnen wasn't interested in creative ideas or humanitarian improvements if profits were down....

His parents had been forced to leave their younger son Xavier on Salusa with a pleasant old-school couple. "I shudder to think how the boy will turn out if *they* raise him. Emil and Lucille Tantor don't know how to be strict."

Eavesdropping, Piers knew why his manipulative father had left his little brother with the Tantors. Since the aging couple was childless, wily Ulf was working his way into their good graces. He hoped the Tantors might eventually leave their estate to their dear "godson" Xavier.

Piers hated the way his father used people, whether they were slaves, other nobles, or members of his own family. It was disgusting. But now, trapped inside the cramped lifepod chamber, he could do nothing about it.

—III—

Programming made the thinking machines relentless and determined, but only the cruelty of a human mind could generate enough ruthless hatred to feed a war of extermination for a thousand years.

Though they were kept in reluctant thrall by the pervasive computer mind Omnius, the cymeks—hybrid machines with human minds—often bided their time by hunting between the stars. They could capture feral humans, bring them back to slavery on the Synchronized Worlds, or just kill them for sport....

The leader of the cymeks, a general who had taken the imposing name of Agamemnon, had once led a group of tyrants to conquer the decaying Old Empire. As implacable soldiers in the cause, the tyrants had reprogrammed the subservient robots and computers to give them a thirst for conquest. When his mortal human body grew old and weak, Agamemnon had undergone a surgical process that removed his brain and implanted it within a preservation canister that he could install into varying mechanical bodies.

Agamemnon and his fellow tyrants had intended to rule for centuries ... but then the artificially aggressive computers stepped into power when they saw the chance, exploiting the tyrants' lack of diligence. The Omnius network then ruled the remnants of the Old Empire, subjugating the cymek tyrants along with the rest of already-downtrodden humanity.

For centuries, Agamemnon and his fellow conquerors had been forced to serve the computer evermind, with no chance of regaining their own rule. Their greatest source of amusement was in tracking down stray humans who had managed to maintain their independence from machine domination. Still, the cymek general found it a most unsatisfactory venting of his frustrations.

His brain canister had been installed inside a fast scout vessel that patrolled areas known to be inhabited by League humans. Six cymeks accompanied the general as their ships skirted the edge of a small solar system. They found little of interest, only one human-compatible world composed of mostly water.

Then Agamemnon's long-range sensors spotted another vessel. A *human* vessel.

He increased resolution and pointed out the target to his companions. Triangulating with their combined detection abilities, Agamemnon discerned that the lone ship was a small space yacht, its sophisticated configuration and style implying that its passengers were important members of the League, rich merchants ... perhaps even smug nobles, the most gratifying victims of all.

"Just what we've been waiting for," said Agamemnon.

The cymek ships adjusted course and accelerated. Connected through thoughtrodes, Agamemnon's brain flew his ship-body as if it were a large bird of prey, zeroing in on his helpless target. He also had a terrestrial walker stored aboard, a warrior form that could be used for planetary combat.

The first cymek shots took the League vessel completely by surprise. The doomed human pilot barely had time to take evasive maneuvers. Kinetic projectiles scraped the hull, pounding one of the engines, but the ship's defensive armor protected it against severe damage. Cymek ships swept past, strafing again with explosive projectiles, and the human yacht reeled, intact but disoriented.

"Careful, boys," Agamemnon said. "We don't want to destroy the prize."

Out on the outskirts of League space, far from the Synchronized Worlds, the feral humans obviously hadn't expected to encounter enemy predators, and the captain of this vessel had been particularly inattentive. Defeating him would be almost embarrassing. His cymek hunters would hope for a better challenge, a more entertaining pursuit....

The human pilot got his damaged engine back online and

increased speed down into the isolated system, fleeing toward the water world. In his wake, the human launched a flurry of intensely bright explosive shells that caused little physical damage, but sent pulses of confusing static through the machine sensors of the cymek ships. Agamemnon's cymek followers transmitted a series of imaginative curses. Surprisingly, the human victim responded in a gruff, defiant voice with equal venom and vigor.

Agamemnon chuckled to himself and sent a thought-command. This would be more fun. His attack ship burst forward like a wild and energetic horse, part of his imaginary body. "Give chase!" The cymeks, enjoying the game, swooped after the hapless human vessel.

The doomed pilot flew standard maneuvers to evade the pursuers. Agamemnon held back, trying to determine if the human was truly so inexperienced or just lulling the cymeks into an unwarranted sense of ease.

They plummeted toward the peaceful blue world—*Caladan*, according to the onboard database. The world reminded him of the blue irises his human eyes once had.... It had been so many centuries, the cymek general could recall few details of his original physical appearance.

Agamemnon could have transmitted an ultimatum to the pilot, but humans and cymeks knew the stakes in their long-simmering war. The space yacht opened fire, a few pathetically weak blasts designed for shoving troublesome meteoroids out of the way rather than defending against overt military action. If this was a noble ship, it should have had much more serious offensive and defensive weapons. The cymeks laughed and closed in, perceiving no threat.

As soon as they approached, though, the desperate human pilot launched another flurry of explosives, apparently the same as the gnat-bite bombs he had launched previously, but Agamemnon detected slight fluctuations. "Caution, I suspect—"

Four proximity mines, each a space charge ten times as powerful as the first artillery, detonated with huge shock waves. Two of the cymek hunters suffered external damage; one was completely destroyed.

Agamemnon lost his patience. "Back off! Engage ship defenses!"

But the yacht pilot fired no more explosives. With one of the surviving cymeks moving only sluggishly, the human could easily have taken him out. Since he did not, the human prey must have no further weapons available. Or was it another trick?

"Don't underestimate the vermin."

Agamemnon had hoped to take the feral humans captive, delivering them to Omnius for experiments or analysis, since "wild" specimens were considered different from those raised for generations in captivity. But, angry at the pointless loss of one of his over-eager companions, the general decided it was just too much trouble.

"Vaporize that ship," he transmitted to his five remaining followers. Without waiting for the other cymeks to join him, Agamemnon opened fire.

—IV—

Inside the lifepod, Piers could only watch in horror and wait to die.

The enemy cymeks pounded them again. In the cockpit, his father shouted curses, and his mother did her best at the weapons station. Their eyes betrayed no fear, only showed strong determination. Harkonnens did not die easily.

Ulf had insisted on installing the best armor and defensive systems available, always suspicious, always ready to fight against any threat. But this lone yacht could not withstand the concerted attack from seven fully armed and aggressive cymek marauders.

Sealed inside the dim compartment, Piers could do nothing to help. He watched the attacking machines through a porthole, sure they could not hold out long. Even his father, who refused to bow to defeat, looked as if he had no tricks remaining to him.

Sensing the imminent kill, the cymeks streaked closer. Piers heard repeated thumps reverberating in the vessel. Through the hatch porthole, Piers saw his mother and father gesturing desperately at one another.

Another cymek blast finally breached the protective plates and damaged the yacht's engines as the vessel careened toward the not-close-enough planet with broad blue seas and white lacings of clouds. Sparks flew on the bridge, and the wounded ship began to tumble.

Ulf Harkonnen shouted something at his wife, then lurched

toward the lifepod, trying to keep his balance. Katarina called after him. Piers couldn't figure out what they were arguing about; the ship was doomed.

Cymek weapons fire rocked the vessel with a dull concussion, sending Ulf skidding across the deck. Even the augmented hull armor could not withstand much more. The elder Harkonnen struggled to his feet at the lifepod hatch, and Piers suddenly realized that he wanted to unlock the chamber and get both of them inside with their son.

Piers read his mother's lips as she shouted, "No time!"

The lifepod's instrument panel flashed and began running through test cycles. Piers hammered on the hatch, but they had sealed him inside. He couldn't get out to help them.

While Ulf tried frantically to work the hatch controls, Katarina raced for the panel on the wall and slapped the activation switch. While Ulf turned to his wife in astonishment and dismay, Katarina mouthed a desperate farewell to her son.

With a lurch, the lifepod shot into space, away from the doomed space yacht.

Acceleration threw Piers to the deck, but he scrambled to his knees, to the observation port. Behind him, as the lifepod tumbled recklessly through space, the cymek marauders opened fire again and again, six angry thinking machines combining their destructive power.

The Harkonnen ship erupted in a sequence of explosions into a dazzling fireball, which dissipated into the cluttered vacuum ... snuffed out along with the lives of his parents.

Like a cannonball, the lifepod tore into the atmosphere of Caladan, spraying red sparks of reentry as it zoomed toward the blue oceans on the sunlit side of the planet.

Piers struggled with the crude emergency controls in an effort to maneuver, but the small ship didn't respond, as if it were a machine rebelling against its human master. At this rate of speed, he couldn't possibly survive.

The young Harkonnen heir took an agonized breath and tapped pressure pads to alter the thruster pattern. He had little experience in piloting, though his father had insisted that he learn; previously, the skill had not been a priority for Piers, but now he had to figure out the systems without delay.

Looking back, he saw he was being pursued by one of the cymek fighter ships. The spray of reentry sparks increased, like iron filings from a grinding stone. The pursuer's exploding projectiles rocked the atmosphere around him without making direct hits.

Piers sped low over an isolated landmass toward a snowy mountain ridge, with the vicious cymek on his tail, still shooting. Sparkling glaciers girdled the jagged peaks. One of the enemy's kinetic projectiles hit a high ridge, shattering ice and rock. Piers closed his eyes and boldly—without a choice—flew through the debris, heard it pummeling the lifepod. And he barely survived.

Just after he scraped over the ridge, he heard a tremendous explosion and saw the sky behind him light up in a flash of bright orange. The mechanical pursuer had gone out of control. Destroyed, just like his parents and their spacecraft ...

But Piers knew there were other enemies, and probably not far away.

—V—

Agamemnon and his cymeks clustered around the space yacht's wreckage in unstable orbit, while mapping the trajectory of the single ejected lifepod. They marked where it crossed the atmosphere, how fast it descended, and where it would probably land. The general was in no hurry—after all, where could the lone survivor go on this primitive world?

Without orders, though, the one cymek damaged by proximity mines shot after the lifepod, hungry for revenge. "General Agamemnon, I intend to make this kill on my own." Angrily, the cymek leader paused, then agreed. "Go, you get the first shot. But the rest of us won't wait for long." The cymek leader held the rest of them back until he could finish his analysis.

Agamemnon played the distress signal the noble pilot had transmitted shortly before his destruction. The words were encoded, but not with a very sophisticated cipher; the cymek's onboard AI systems translated it easily. "This is Lord Ulf Harkonnen, en route from our holdings at Hagal. We are under attack by thinking machines. There is not much chance we will survive."

Such amazing powers of prediction. Agamemnon assumed the

survivor aboard the lifepod must also be a member of the noble family, if not the lord himself.

A thousand years ago, when Agamemnon and his nineteen co-conspirators had overthrown the Old Empire, a group of outlying planets had banded together to form the League of Nobles. They had defended themselves against the tyrants, maintaining their defense against Omnius and his thinking machines. Computers did not hold grudges or gain vengeance ... but the cymeks had human minds and human emotions.

If the survivor in the lifepod down on Caladan was a member of the defiant League of Nobles, the cymek general wanted to participate personally in his interrogation, torture, and ultimate execution.

Within minutes, however, he received a last-second transmission just before the cymek pursuer crashed on the surface.

"A foolish mission. Next time I want it done right," Agamemnon said. "Go, find him before he can hide in the wilderness. I give the hunt to the four of you—and a challenge. A reward to the cymek who finds and kills the prey first."

The other cymek ships streaked away from the debris field, heading like hot bullets into the cloudy skies. The human escapee, unarmed in his barely maneuverable lifepod, certainly would not last long.

—VI—

Abruptly the lifepod shuddered, and a warning siren sounded. Digital and crystal instruments sparked on the panel. Piers tried to interpret them, adjusting the clumsy controls of the careening vessel, then looked up through the porthole to see brown-and-white slopes ahead, bleak frozen hillsides with patches of snow, dark forests. In the last instant, he pulled up, just enough—

The lifepod scraped tall, dark-needled trees and crashed into high tundra covered by only a thin blanket of snow. The impact bounced the pod back into the air, spinning it around for a second plunge into the patchy forest.

In his energy harness, Piers rolled and shouted, trying to survive but expecting the worst. Cushioning bubblefoam squirted all around him just before the first impact, padding his body from the worst injuries. Then the pod crashed again, ripping up snow and frozen dirt. The pod finally came to rest, groaning and hissing.

The bubblefoam dissolved as Piers picked himself up and wiped the fizzing slime from his clothes and hands and hair. He was too shaken to feel pain and couldn't take the time to evaluate his injuries.

He knew his parents were dead, their ship destroyed. He hoped his blurred vision was from blood in his eyes, not tears. He was a Harkonnen, after all. His father would have struck him across the cheek for showing cowardly emotion. Ulf had managed to damage the enemy in a fruitless attack, but there were still more cymeks up there. No doubt they would come hunting for him.

Piers fought down panic, turned it into a hard, instant assessment of his situation. If he had any hope of surviving, circumstances forced him to respond with decisiveness, even ruthlessness—the Harkonnen way. And he wouldn't have much time.

The lifepod contained a few survival supplies, but he couldn't stay here. The cymeks would zero in on the vessel and come to finish the job. Once he ran, he would have no chance to return.

Piers grabbed a medical kit and all the ration packs he could carry, stuffing them into a flexible sack. He popped the lifepod's hatch and crawled out, smelling the smoke and hearing the crackle of a few gasping fires ignited by the heat of impact. He took a deep breath of cold, biting air then, closing the hatch behind him, he staggered away from the smoking pod, crunching through slushy snow into the meager shelter of dark conifers. He wanted to get as far away as possible before pausing to consider his next step.

In a situation like this, his father would have been concerned about the family holdings, the Hagal mines. With Piers and his parents gone, who would run the business and keep the Harkonnen family strong? Right now, though, the young man was more worried for his own survival. He had never fit in with family business philosophies anyway.

Hearing a high-pitched roar, he gazed into the sky and saw four flaming white trails coming toward him like targeted munitions. Cymek landers. Hunters. The machines with human minds would track him down in the desolate wilderness.

As the danger suddenly came closer to home, Piers saw he was leaving deep tracks in the snow. Blood dripped from a nasty cut on his left wrist; more scarlet splashed from another injury on his forehead. He might as well be leaving a roadmap for the enemy to follow.

His father had said it in a stern, impatient voice, but the lesson was valuable nevertheless: *Be aware of all facets of a situation. Just because something is quiet does not mean it isn't dangerous. Do not trust your safety at any moment.*

Under the trees, listening to the roar as cymeks converged over his pod's crash-down coordinates, Piers slathered wound sealant on his injuries to stop the bleeding. *A moment's hurry can cause far more damage than a moment's delay to plan ahead.*

He abruptly changed direction, selecting a clear area where trees had sheltered the ground from the snow and rocks. He moved over the rocky surface in a deliberately chaotic course, hoping to throw off pursuit. He had no weapons, no knowledge of the terrain … and no intention of giving up.

Piers climbed higher up the sloping ground, and the snow grew thicker where the trees became sparse. When he reached a clearing, he caught his breath and looked back to see that cymek landers had converged at his lifepod. Still not far enough away, but still without any place to run.

Watching in horrified fascination, Piers saw mobile, resilient walker-forms emerge from the landed ships: adaptable mechanical bodies to carry cymek brain canisters across a variety of environments. Like angry crabs, the cymeks crawled over the sealed wreckage, using cutter claws and white-hot flamers to tear open the hull. When they found no one inside, they literally ripped the lifepod apart.

The walker-forms stalked around the pod, their optic threads gleaming with a variety of sensors. They scanned his footprints in the snow, moved to where their prey had paused to apply his medical pack. The cymek scanners could easily pick up his footprints in the dirt, thermal traces from his body heat, any number of clues. Unerringly, they set out across the bare ground toward where he had chosen to flee.

Chiding himself for the momentary panic that had made him leave such an obvious trail, Piers broke into a full run uphill, always looking for a place to hide, a weapon to use. He tried to ignore his hammering heart and his difficulty breathing in this cold, rugged environment of Caladan. He crashed into another thicket of the dark pines, always climbing. The slope became steeper, but because of the dense conifers, he couldn't see exactly where he was going or how close he might be to the top of a ridge.

He saw sticks, rocks, but nothing that would be an effective weapon against the mechanical monsters, no way to defend himself against the horrific machines. But Piers was, after all, a Harkonnen, and he would not give up. He would hurt them if he could. At the very least, he would offer them a fine chase.

Far to his rear, Piers heard crashing sounds, cracking trees, and imagined the cymeks clearing a path for their armored bodies. Judging from the smoke, they must be setting the forest on fire as well. Good—that way they would ruin the subtleties of his trail.

He kept running as the ground became rockier, with patches of ice spreading out on steep slopes. Precariously balanced snow clung to the mountain, ready to break loose at any moment. The trees at this elevation were bent and twisted, and he smelled a foul sulfurous taint in the air. At his feet he saw tiny bubbling puddles, suffused with yellow.

He furrowed his brows, pondering what this could mean. A thermal area. He had read about such places in his studies, esoteric geological anomalies that his father had forced him to learn before sending him to the mining operations on Hagal. This would be a region of volcanic activity with hot springs, geysers, fumaroles ... a dangerous place, but one that offered opportunities against large opponents.

Piers ran toward the strong smell and the thickening mist, hoping this would give him an advantage. Cymeks did not use eyes like humans did, and their sensors were delicate, sensitive to different parts of the spectrum. In some cases, it gave the machine pursuers an incredible advantage. Here, though, with the wild plumes of heat and the rocky, sterile ground, the cymeks could not use their scanners to pick up residual traces from his footprints.

He raced through the misty, humid no-man's-land of rocks, snow patches, crusty bare earth, trying to throw off pursuit and seeking a place to hide, or defend. After hours of headlong flight, he collapsed on a warm boulder encrusted with orange lichen next to a hissing steam vent. More than anything else, he wanted to curl up under a rocky overhang next to one of the hot springs, remaining hidden long enough to sleep for a few hours.

But cymeks did not require sleep. All of their life-support needs were taken care of with restorative electrafluid that kept them alive in their preservation canisters. They would keep pursuing him without pause.

Piers cracked open the food rations and gobbled two high-energy wafers, but he forced himself to set off again before he felt any resurgence of stamina. He had to press his advantage, not lose any ground.

Using his hands and feet now, Piers climbed steeper rocks. His fingers became powdery with yellow sulfur. He chose the steepest terrain, hoping it would prove difficult for the cymek walker bodies, but it also slowed him down.

The wind began to pick up, and Piers felt it against his face, alternate blasts of warm and cold. The mists cleared in patches, and suddenly the landscape was revealed around him. He looked back toward the last remnants of conifer forests, jutting rocks, and the bubbling mineral pools far beneath him.

Then he saw one of the cymek walker-forms, alone, stalking him. The other three must have separated, circling in their hunt, as if it were some sort of game. The mechanical body glistened silver in the sudden wash of afternoon light. Searching.

Piers knew he was exposed and unprotected on the rocky slope; he slammed his body tight against the rocks, hoping to remain unseen. But within seconds, the cymek had targeted its prey. The mechanical walker unleashed a fiery projectile, a splattering globule of flaming gel that missed Piers and struck the rock, clinging fire.

He scrambled up the rock, finding a new surge of energy. Scuttling rapidly, the cymek negotiated the rough slope, no longer wasting time on the tedious job of tracking the human.

Piers was trapped, with precipitous drop-offs and hot sulfurous pools on the left and right and a steep, smooth snowfield crusted with yellow contaminants above him. Once he got to the top of the ridge, perhaps he could throw rocks, somehow dislodge the cymek below him. He saw no other option.

Clawing with his hands and struggling for footholds, Piers worked his way up the slick glacier field. His shoes punched through the crust, sinking into cold snow up to his knees. His fingers soon grew numb and red. The frigid air seared his lungs, but he scrambled faster, farther. His domineering father would have sneered at him for worrying about mere physical discomfort in a time of such urgency. The glacier seemed to go on forever, though he could see the top, a sheer razor edge on the crest.

The machine hunters must have split up, and perhaps he had eluded the other three among the thermal plumes and crumbling rocks. Unable to find his tracks, they would be combing the ground ... relentless, as machines always were. Only one of the cymeks had found him, apparently by accident.

Even so, a single monstrous enemy was more than enough to kill him, and this one would be in radio contact with the others. Already they must be coming this way. But this one seemed eager to kill Piers all by itself.

Below, the cymek reached the base of the ice field, scanned for a moment, and then scuttled up. Its long legs stabbed into the snow, climbing faster than any human could hope to run.

The cymek paused, rocked back, then launched another gelfire projectile. Piers burrowed into the snow, and the hot explosive ripped a crater barely an arm's length away from him. The violent impact caused the steep and precarious snowfield to tremble and shift. Around him, the crust began to break apart like a peeling scab. Taking a chance, he kicked hard at one of the hard slabs of packed snow, hoping to send it tumbling down to strike his enemy, but the frozen surface jammed tight again, squeaking and groaning, then falling silent. With a deep breath, he climbed upward again.

As the cymek closed the gap, Piers noticed a rocky outcropping that protruded from the snow. He would scramble up there and make his stand. Maybe he could throw boulders at the machine, though he had no illusions about how effective that would be.

Only a fool leaves himself without options, Ulf Harkonnen would have said.

Piers grumbled at the memory. "At least I survived longer than you did, Father."

Then, to his astonishment, at the crest of the glacier he saw a group of figures that looked ... *human!* He counted dozens of people who stood at the top of the snowfield. They shouted incomprehensible curses at the cymek.

The silhouetted strangers lifted large cylinders—weapons of

some sort?—and began to beat on them. Loud booming sounds echoed across the mountains like thunderclaps, explosions. *Drums.*

The strangers pounded on their noisemakers. They had no apparent rhythm at first, but then the pulses combined into a resonance, an echoing boom that set the whole snowfield trembling.

Cracks widened atop the ice, and the glacier began to shift. The massive cymek walker struggled for purchase as the frozen ground began to slide.

Seeing what was about to happen, Piers dove for the rock outcropping, sheltering himself in a pocket walled off by thick stone on each side. He held on just as the snow broke free with a hissing, tumbling roar.

The avalanche struck the cymek like a white tidal wave, bowling over the walker-form, knocking and battering it against other rocks. As the enemy machine crashed down the slope, Piers closed his eyes and waited for the rumbling roar to reach its crescendo and then taper off.

When he finally emerged, amazed to be alive, the air itself sparkled with ice crystals thrown into the sky. While the snowpack undoubtedly remained unstable, the strange people charged pell-mell down the broken snow and ice, yelling excitedly like hunters who had just bagged an impressive quarry.

Still unable to believe what he was seeing, Piers stood atop the boulders. And then he spotted the twitching and battered cymek far down the slope, toppled onto its back. The avalanche had struck it with a destructive force equivalent to a heavy weapon. The cymek had been bashed, dented, and twisted, but still its mechanical limbs attempted to haul the walker-form upright.

Although the primitive humans wore drab survival garb made of scavenged materials, they carried sophisticated tools, more than just spears or clubs. Four young natives hurried to the edge of the broken icefield and the trees—scouts?—and they kept watch, wary of other cymeks.

The remaining humans fell like hyenas upon the crippled cymek, wielding cutters and grappling wrenches. Was the mechanical hunter calling for help from its three comrades? The natives quickly bashed the transmitter antennae on the walker body, then with startling efficiency they dismantled the walker's struggling legs. The cymek weapon arm flickered in an attempt to launch another flaming projectile, but the Caladan primitives quickly disconnected the components.

From the cymek's speaker patch came a volley of angry threats and curses, but the humans paid no attention, showing no fear. They worked diligently to disconnect the hydraulics, fiber cables, neurelectronics, setting each piece aside like valuable scrap material. They left the cymek's brain canister exposed, the traitorous human mind disembodied once again, though this time not by its own volition.

Numb, Piers looked at the oddly harmless-looking canister that held the cymek's mind. The natives did not destroy it immediately, but seemed to have other plans. They held it up like a trophy.

Full of questions, Piers made his way down the shifting surface of broken snow. The natives looked up at him as he approached, showing curiosity without threat. They spoke a gibberish language that he could not comprehend.

"Who are you?" Piers asked in standard Galach, hoping that someone here would understand him.

One of the men, a gaunt old fellow with a short reddish beard and lighter skin than his companions, gestured toward Piers in happy victory. He stood in front of Piers, pounded himself on the chest. "Tiddoc."

"Piers Harkonnen." He responded, then decided to simplify, "Piers."

"Good, Piers. Thank you," he said in recognizable Galach, but with a thick accent. Seeing the young man's surprise, Tiddoc spoke slowly, as if fishing the right words out of his memory. "Our tongue has Galach roots from the Zensunni Wanderers, who fled the League long ago. For years I worked in cities of the noblemen, performing menial tasks. I picked up words here and there."

Paralyzed and immobile, the captured enemy cymek continued to snarl insults through an integrated speakerpatch as the Caladan natives used two of the amputated walker legs as support rods, lashing the brain canister so that it dangled between the poles like some captured wild beast. Two of the strongest-looking natives put the metal rods over their shoulders and began to march back up the slope. The other natives gathered up the components they could carry and climbed the rough mountainside.

"Come with us," Tiddoc said.

Piers had no option but to follow them.

—VII—

As Piers followed the rugged men uphill, one of his knees throbbed with each step, and his back stiffened until it burned. He had not yet had time to accept the deaths of his parents. He missed his mother, for her kind attentions, her intelligence. Katarina had saved his life, launching the lifepod before the cymeks could destroy the space yacht.

In a way, Piers even missed his father. Despite Ulf's gruffness, he had only wanted the best for his sons, harshly focused on his responsibilities for Harkonnen holdings. Advancing the family fortunes was always paramount. Now it seemed that his little brother Xavier was all that remained of the Harkonnen bloodline. Piers had little hope that he would ever get away from Caladan ... but at least he had survived this long.

He limped up the steep slope, trying to keep pace with the agile natives. Inside its preservation canister, the evil cymek brain sloshed as the primitives carried it. Staticky shouts came from the canister's speakerpatch, first in standard Galach, then in other languages. Tiddoc and the natives seemed to find it amusing.

The natives paid little attention to the disembodied brain, except to glare at it and bare their teeth. The red-bearded old man was the most demonstrative. In addition to menacing facial expressions, he made threatening gestures with a cutting tool, swinging it close to the canister's sensors, which only served to agitate the captive brain more. Obviously they had encountered cymeks before and knew how to fight them.

But he was concerned about the other three mechanical hunters. They would not give up the pursuit—and once they found the avalanche site and the dismantled walker-form, the cymeks could track the natives here. Unless the captured one had not been able to signal for help before the avalanche had swept it away. Cymeks did not like to admit weakness.

Piers looked around for any fortifications the people had made. Ahead, overhanging ice formed a giant roof that sheltered a settlement. The primitives had made their camp in a large area melted out by thermal vents in the ground. Women and children bustled among rock huts, performing chores, pausing to look at the approaching party. The people wore thick clothing, boots, and hats lined with fur from unknown local animals. Piers heard the yelping of animals, saw furry white creatures near the dwellings.

Beyond the shelter of the overhang, steam roiled up through thick layers of ice and snow, accompanied by heat bubbles from mudpots and geysers. As Piers followed the tribe down narrow rock steps toward the settlement, he marveled at the stunning contrast of fire and ice. Occasional droplets rained down from the ceiling of the dome, slowly melting, but when Piers looked up at the blue ice overhead, he thought the glacier—and the settlement—had been here for a long time....

When abrupt darkness fell like a curtain drawn in front of the sun, the native Caladan women used jagged pieces of wood to build a large fire on a rocky area at the center of the settlement. Scouts went out on patrol to keep watch for other cymek hunters while the rest of the tribe settled down to celebrate. The men brought hunks of fresh meat from other hunts and speared them on long metal spits over the fire.

They placed the captive cymek's brain canister off to one side, in the ice, and ignored it.

Speaking to one another in their guttural tongue, the natives sat on furs around the fire and passed the food around, sharing with their visitor. Piers found the meat too gamey for his liking, but he finished a large hunk, not wanting to insult his hosts. He was famished, and supplemented his meal with part of a ration bar he had salvaged from the lifepod; he offered the rest of the packaged food to his rescuers, and they eagerly accepted.

Following the meal, Tiddoc and his people sat around the story fire, telling ancient parables and adventures in their native tongue. During the sharing, the tribesmen passed around gourds of a potent beverage. Wrapped in a fur to ward off the chill air, Piers drank, and felt warm in his belly. At intervals, the old man translated for Piers, relating tales of the downtrodden Zensunni who had fled the machine takeovers, as well as slavery in the League of Nobles.

A little tipsy, Piers defended the League and their continuing fight against the thinking machines, though he sympathized with the unpleasant plight of the Buddislamic slaves on Poritrin, Zanbar, and other League Worlds. While Tiddoc struggled to translate, Piers told of epic battles against the evil Omnius and his aggressive robots and cymeks.

And, with a thick voice, he told how his own ship had been destroyed, his parents killed …

Tiddoc gestured to the cymek brain canister. "Come. The feasting is done. Now we finish our machine war. The people have been looking forward to this." He shouted something in his own language, and two men lifted the canister by its improvised poles. The cymek grumbled from its speakerpatch, but it had run out of effective curses.

Several women lit torches from the central fire and led the way up a path from the dripping glacier overhang. Full of good cheer, the natives marched away, carrying the impotent enemy brain. The cymek hurled threats in every language it could think of, but the primitives only laughed at it.

"What are you doing?" the cymek demanded. Controlling his last functional thoughtrodes, the disembodied brain twisted in its container. "Stop! We will crush you all!"

Piers followed them over a ridge and down a slope to where the air reeked of sulfur and the porous rock grew warm underfoot. Carrying the helpless cymek, the group paused at a steaming hole in the rock and stood chattering and laughing. They held the brain canister over the ominous opening.

Piers bent closer to the hole, curious, but Tiddoc yanked him away. The red-bearded elder wore an eerie smile in the torchlight.

A rumble sounded deep below, and with a preliminary spurt of hot spray, a geyser erupted, a scalding jet that parboiled the cymek's brain. The enemy's curses turned to shrieks, followed by babbling sounds and disjointed pain that trickled out of the damaged speakerpatch.

When the geyser subsided, the delirious cymek cried and gibbered. Moments later the geyser erupted again, and the speakerpatch unleashed hideous howls that sent shudders down Piers's spine.

Even though this monster had tried to kill him, had taken part in the murder of his parents, Piers could not tolerate hearing its misery any more. When the boiling jet subsided again, he took a rock and smashed the speaker, disconnecting it.

But the natives continued to hold the agonized brain over the geyser hole, and when the scalding spray gushed out a third time, the cymek screamed in silence, until it was boiled alive in its electrafluid.

The natives then cracked the canister open on a rock and devoured the hot, cooked contents.

—VIII—

The rock hut was warm and marginally comfortable, but Piers slept poorly, unable to put the horrific images out of his mind. When he finally dreamed, he saw himself strapped to poles while the natives held him over the geyser hole. He heard boiling water rushing toward him, and he awoke with a scream caught in his throat.

Outside, he heard only the howl of an animal, then silence.

Then mechanical sounds.

He stumbled to the entrance of the hut and peered outside into the cold, sulfur-smelling air. Now the furry guard animals howled. The primitives shouted and stirred in their encampment. The scouts had been watching.

In a slit of grayish, misty sky between the ground and the icy overhang Piers saw four aircraft approaching with insect-machine noises, their engines glowing in the predawn sky. *Cymeks!*

Tiddoc and the natives fled their stone huts, grabbing torches, weapons. Piers ran out, anxious to help.

The cymek ships landed in the nearby rock field and opened hatches, each one disgorging an armed walker body. The crablike warrior machines marched downslope with alarming speed. Ahead, the primitives scattered, hooting, waving torches, taunting the enemy.

One of the cymeks launched a rocket of gelfire, which exploded and collapsed part of the arched, glacier ceiling. Shards of ice tumbled down, smashing the evacuated stone huts.

Tiddoc and the villagers scampered out of the way as if it were a game, gesturing for Piers to follow as they hurried along the path they had taken the night before, onto the geyser field. In daylight Piers saw that it was a broad, gently sloped area of boiling mudpots and hot springs. Fumaroles and geysers belched repeatedly, filling the air with foul steam and heat plumes. Shouting, cursing, the people split up, following instinctive routes across the crusty ground. The natives' supposed panic was a strangely organized action, like a cat-and-mouse game. Were they luring the enemy? They seemed to have a plan, a hunt of their own.

Piers ran along with them, ducking as the four cymek walkers shot projectiles into the hissing thermal area. Their mechanical bodies plodded forward like heavy spiders on the uncertain ground. For sophisticated machines, their aim was terrible. The cymeks' optic threads and thermal sensors must be nearly blinded in the chaos of heat signatures.

Tiddoc hurled a spear, which clanked on the head turret of the largest cymek walker. Agitated, the machine-creature bellowed through a speakerpatch, "You cannot escape Agamemnon!" The other three cymeks scrambled along behind it.

Piers shuddered. All free humans knew the famous general of Omnius's army, one of the brutal original tyrants.

With a lucky shot, one of the enemy machines blasted a young man who danced too close to the weapon arm, and his twitching, burning body writhed on the ground. The Caladan natives, looking angry and vengeful, tightened their ranks and worked harder against the cymeks.

Light-footed, the primitives raced across the volcanically active area. The cymeks, oblivious to the trap, charged after their prey, smashing salty encrustations, pursuing the natives into the reeking mists. They shot more blobs of gelfire, fired explosive projectiles.

Tiddoc and the natives kept hooting and shouting, defiant. Two of the smaller cymeks surged forward into a crater-pocked geyser field. The waving, taunting primitives stopped and turned, expectant.

The thin shell of hardened ground cracked, split. The two mechanical walker-forms tried to skitter backward, but the surface gave way beneath them, breaking apart. Both cymeks plunged through the dangerous ground and tumbled screaming into roiling sulfur cauldrons.

Piers joined Tiddoc and the other humans in their loud cheer.

Unexpectedly, a furious geyser blast rocketed out of the ground next to a third cymek attacker, scalding the brain canister. Its thoughtrodes damaged, the mechanical behemoth veered away and stumbled around in confusion. The cymek fell to its articulated knees, the electrafluid in its stained brain canister glowing blue as it focused its mental energy.

Tiddoc tossed a small, home-made explosive onto the ground, like a crude grenade. The detonation caused no further damage to the armored walker, but the ground crust fractured. While the wounded mechanical enemy reeled, disoriented, the surface gave way. The third cymek joined the others in the molten mud.

Agamemnon kept advancing toward the retreating humans, as if scorning his incompetent underlings. The lead cymek stalked unwavering toward old Tiddoc. The red-bearded man and his companions threw their spears and more crude explosives, but the mechanical general did not flinch. Behind them and on the sides lay superheated soil, while the immense cymek blocked their only avenue of escape.

On impulse, Piers ran in front of the lead cymek, shouting to distract it. He snatched up a discarded spear and thumped it against one of the tall walker legs. "Agamemnon! You murdered my parents!"

To his surprise, the cymek general swiveled its head turret, and thermal sensors locked onto the upstart human's form. "A feisty one!" the monster said with considerable amusement. "You are the vermin we have been chasing."

"I am a Harkonnen nobleman!" Piers shouted. He swung the spear like a cudgel at the brain canister. He struck the thick armor plaz with a blow hard enough to rattle his bones—but he left only a tiny nick on the protective canister.

The cymek bellowed a laugh. One of Agamemnon's clawed legs grabbed Piers, yanked away the spear. The young man felt the sharp claw tighten around his torso. He was dimly aware of Tiddoc howling—

Then suddenly the crust gave way beneath the heavy cymek walker. Frothing mud gushed upward, and Agamemnon tumbled into a boiling geyser pit, still clutching his human victim. Superheated steam blasted upward, eradicating all signs of Piers and the last machine invader.

—IX—

Alive and angry, Agamemnon reinstalled himself in an intact

spaceship lander and departed from the watery world. With his heavily protected walker body, he had clamped onto the edges of the fuming pit, endured the steam blasts without falling into the molten mud. The people had rallied, hurled more explosives at him, and Agamemnon despised himself for being forced to retreat. Already damaged, his walker-form limped back to the landed spacecraft. Systems onboard reconfigured his brain canister to the ship's controls; he discarded the ruined walker body, leaving it as scrap on the cursed surface of Caladan.

The only survivor of his cymek squad, Agamemnon left the unremarkable world behind. He would return to Earth, and the computer evermind Omnius, and make his report.

At this point, he was at liberty to create whatever explanation he chose. Omnius would never suspect him of lying: such things simply did not occur to the all-pervasive computer. But the cymek general had a human brain....

As Agamemnon flew out into open space, he would have a long time to think of appropriate explanations and shift the blame. He would include his version of the events in his ever-growing memoirs recorded in the machine database.

Fortunately, the all-powerful and all-seeing evermind simply wanted information and an accurate recounting of all events. Making excuses was a purely human weakness.

On the League capital world of Salusa Secundus, a young boy looked up at dark-skinned Emil Tantor, a wealthy and influential nobleman. They stood on the front lawn of the sprawling Tantor estate, with the tallest buildings of the city visible in the distance. It was early evening, with lights twinkling on in the palatial homes that dotted the hills.

Ulf Harkonnen's distress signal had finally been intercepted, and Emil Tantor had brought the boy the terrible news about his parents and brother. More casualties in the long-standing war against the thinking machines.

Young Xavier Harkonnen bowed his head, but refused to cry. The kindly nobleman touched his shoulder and spoke deep-throated, gentle words. "Will you have me, and Lucille, as your foster parents? I think it is what your father wanted, when he left you in our care."

Xavier looked into his brown eyes, nodded.

"You'll grow into a fine young man," Tantor said, "one to make your brother and parents proud. We will do our best to raise you right, to teach you honor and responsibility. You will make the Harkonnen name shine in the annals of history."

Xavier gazed beyond his foster father up to the faint stars glimmering through the dusk. He could identify some of those stars, and knew which systems were controlled by Omnius, which were League Worlds.

"I will also learn how to fight the thinking machines," he said. Emil Tantor squeezed his shoulder. "I will defeat them one day."

It is my purpose in life.

—XI—

On a dark night in the bright snowfield and dark pines, the Caladan primitives sat on furs around a roaring fire. Keeping their oral tradition alive, they repeated the ancient legends and stories of recent battles. The elder Tiddoc sat beside the foreigner accepted among them, a hero with bright eyes and waxy, horribly scarred skin. A man who had fought single-handedly against a cymek monster and fallen into a scalding hot opening ... but had crawled out alive, clinging to the battered cymek walker-form.

Piers gestured with one hand; the other—burned and twisted into uselessness—hung limp against his chest. He spoke passionately in the ancient Buddislamic tongue, halting as he struggled for words and then continuing when Tiddoc helped him.

Caladan was his home now, and he would live the rest of his life with these people, in obscurity. No escape seemed possible from such a remote place, except through the stories he told. Piers kept his audience enthralled as he spoke of great battles against the thinking machines, while he also learned the Songs of the Long Trek, chronicles of the many generations of Zensunni Wanderings.

As his father had realized, Piers Harkonnen had always wanted to be a storyteller.

The first two volumes of my SF stories introduced Alternitech, a multiverse with a lot of ideas and possibilities, prospectors who explore subtle changes in timelines, tiny events with big consequences.

What if a key piece of evidence was accidentally found in one timeline, but that unique coincidence had not happened in other nearby timelines? Would the identical crime go unsolved in that parallel universe? What about conspiracy theories? Do different timelines maybe have additional or unique evidence in, say, the John F. Kennedy assassination?

The possibilities were as endless as the multiverse.

AN INNOCENT PRESUMPTION

A freak accident. Never happen again in a million years.

Rain slicked the pavement like a black mirror, reflecting the amber lights of the tow truck and the squad car's scarlet and blue flashers. A Toyota SUV had stalled high on the span of the Oakland Bay Bridge, angled so that it disrupted two lanes of traffic. Cars slowed across the bridge, crawling forward like a slow but belligerent garden slug.

A cop stood in the cold drizzle, waving his arms and fruitlessly directing traffic while a tow truck backed up, aligning itself to remove the offending SUV. Its warning beeps sounded like high childish screams.

A placid-looking older man in a blue Mercury eased forward to change lanes and bypass the obstacle. The cop held up one hand and waved with the other. The blue Mercury lurched forward while cars in the adjacent lane struggled to stop.

A different driver jumped the gun and accelerated, then hit the brakes. He skidded forward on the slick road and crunched into the rear of the Mercury. With the impact, the older man's trunk popped open.

Disgusted, the cop walked forward, holding out both hands to stop traffic. The driver of the rear car rolled down his window to yell curses.

The older man in the Mercury opened his door, looked at the

railing of the bridge high above the gunmetal-gray water. Dazed. Determined.

The frowning cop saw the young woman's bloody body in the Mercury's trunk. Two deep and brutal slashes across her face, her cheeks sliced open to expose white teeth. Both eyes ruined by the blade. Her throat cut all the way to the windpipe and spine.

The cop yanked out his service revolver, holding it in a stance he had often practiced at the firing range but never used in the line of duty. The old man froze before he could make a run for the edge of the bridge. The drizzle continued, but everything else had fallen silent, a snapshot tableau.

After two years and seven victims, intensive manhunts and giant budgets from crack crime-solving agencies, "Slasher X" was caught because of a silly fender-bender, a mere coincidence.

⚛

Another day on the job exploring alternate timelines.

Heather Rheims shouldered her pack, looking like a nondescript student. She wore a loose flannel shirt and comfortable jeans, a look that was in style in virtually every parallel universe. Timeline prospectors had to be unobtrusive, finish their tasks without drawing attention to themselves, then slip back through the portal to the central complex of Alternitech.

With her long rusty-brown hair and large gray-blue eyes, she passed as a typical college sophomore. Only her sharp gaze and hard expression revealed that she had scars and concerns beyond looking for parties at the student union or picking up guys in her poly-sci class.

Now, inside the main control room, portal frames gleamed in the too-white light. The air was always frigid, overly air-conditioned to pamper the dimensional equipment. One of her fellow timeline prospectors, a tall crewcut blond who looked as if he belonged in an ROTC recruiting office, came up to her. Rod's normally stony face was a mixture of sympathy and victory. "Hey, I hear they caught the bastard last night."

Heather's lips formed a grim line. She took a moment before answering to make sure her voice was steady. "Better late than never, I guess. Although if they'd caught him after victim number three instead of number seven, then I could still go biking on the headlands with my sister."

Rod squeezed her shoulder, then turned away as the tech supervisor called his name and prepared the portal for his day's assignment.

Heather said, "Still looking for novel leukemia treatments?"

"No, just novels." Rod gave a foolish smile. "Maybe Mario Puzo's sequel to *The Godfather*, or another historical epic by James Clavell. Maybe I'll find a universe where Stephen King never did retire." He went over to the dimensional doorway as the air shimmered and crackled with a smell of ozone.

Alternitech explorers like Heather sidestepped into parallel universes nearly identical with the modern world but with subtle differences: timelines where the Beatles had not broken up, where James Dean had a long and successful film career, where scientific researchers had achieved useful medical or technological breakthroughs that, for whatever reason, had been stymied in this world. A timeline prospector's job was to identify these differences and bring them back home, where Alternitech would sell them to the highest bidder.

"Oh, Ms. Rheims?" called the tech supervisor in his thick British accent. "If you would grace us with your presence, we are ready to send you."

With the news of Slasher X in all the papers, the tech supervisor didn't give Heather his usual deprecating smirk about her "embarrassing" current quest; since her patron paid a generous fee for Heather's skills, Alternitech allowed him his eccentricities.

"Money-Is-No-Object" Feldman was obsessed with the John F. Kennedy assassination. For over a month now he had sent Heather on expeditions into parallel universes in order to secure evidence that proved or disproved the conspiracy theory.

Now she shouldered her backpack, taking several deep breaths to prepare herself. She exhaled all the air, then stepped forward into the ripple—

—Without moving, she found herself in another universe that seemed identical to her own. She had three hours here, enough time to ransack the archives in the university library.

The city maps were similar in every timeline, with only the most minor deviations of street names. She knew exactly how to get to the UC San Francisco library or, failing that, the main downtown branch. For her purposes, all she needed was a microfilm archive or public access computers with newspapers dating back to 1963. Despite all the differences, the Windows Operating System seemed ubiquitous across timelines.

The routine was familiar by now. Heather even had her favorite carrel picked out. Sometimes, she had found greater evidence for a conspiracy, various shooters other than Lee Harvey Oswald; in some timelines, no assassin had ever been caught or even accused. In others, no crusader or conspiracy theorist like Jim Garrison had even raised the possibility, and Kennedy's murder went quietly into the history books as the work of a single madman.

"Money-Is-No-Object" Feldman was delighted with each nuance, each deviation, although so far the clues added up to nothing more tantalizing than the blurry photos often used to "prove" the existence of Bigfoot or the Loch Ness monster.

In this timeline, though, Heather felt a thrill as she discovered a significant change in history: This universe's Kennedy had survived the shooting, living out his term in office paralyzed from the waist down. After the assassination attempt, however, he had no longer been a fiery leader, and his presidency was remembered as basically ineffective. No shooter had ever been caught.

She followed the history threads, surprised at how easily the timeline's broad strokes had shifted back to her version of "normal." Heather used her hand scanner to copy the documentation. Feldman would be ecstatic.

Since she had a little time remaining before she needed to find her way back to the Alternitech portal, she glanced at current events. When she stumbled on the headline of the morning edition of the San Francisco Chronicle, Heather sat frozen, gulping the details with her eyes.

"Slasher X Claims Eighth Victim."

Then, of course, she knew exactly what she had to do.

⚛

Parallel line after parallel line. Feldman's enthusiasm did not diminish as Heather continued to retrieve tantalizing nuggets that maintained the eccentric millionaire's funding. But she had another mission now. She no longer cared about the razzing from the tech supervisor or the other timeline prospectors who didn't consider her "tabloid work" to be worthy of Alternitech's potential.

Now, Heather was saving lives, innocent people just like her sister Jamie.

In each new parallel universe, her first action was to check the newspapers, then make an anonymous phone call to tip off the police. The story was always the same: her own parallel universe was the only one in which a bad-luck traffic accident had exposed the serial killer's identity.

When she delivered her bombshell of information, the detectives were sometimes skeptical, sometimes angry, other times mercifully grateful for any lead. Since the killer had been caught in her own timeline, Heather had followed the details of the case, and she could offer enough veracity to convince the investigating homicide detectives that she wasn't a crank.

She understood, for instance, that Slasher X—an older retired man with the unusual name of Eric Keric—used a fat black marker to draw an X on the faces of his victims before commencing the bloodier work. Keric slit the throats first so that the victims didn't struggle, and his thick carving knife could make precise strokes along the dark line he had marked, crossing out their faces. Many nightmares ago, Heather had been called in to identify Jamie's mutilated body—her face gashed with the terrible deadly X, her throat cut....

After a while, Heather stopped even checking the reports before she made her anonymous call. She simply tipped them off to Eric Keric and let the professionals handle it from there. It was so easy to be a good citizen, to get her revenge for Jamie ... and to make sure that Slasher X paid the price for his terrible crimes. She began to feel like a hit-and-run crusader for justice, almost like Jim Garrison tirelessly trying to track down JFK's killers.

In her work for Feldman, she also came back in triumph to Alternitech. At last, she found a parallel line where Lee Harvey Oswald had lived long enough after being shot by Jack Ruby to blurt out a confession. With his dying breath, Oswald had fingered a man named Francis Tarryall, a shifty Dallas businessman with ties to Cuba and the Soviet Union. He'd been in trouble with the law many times but had managed to hire the best lawyers, to get evidence dismissed, and he had always walked. But after Oswald's accusation, Tarryall's trial was swift and the outcome sure. Tarryall never confessed, but the investigations by that universe's Warren Commission yielded seemingly incontrovertible evidence.

Heather copied several months of news stories so Feldman could study the aftermath.

She was rushed at the end because this time her usual call to the police had taken an excessive amount of time. The detective—not one of the familiar names usually assigned to the Slasher X case— asked too many questions, wanted to know about the killer's victims, pumped her for even the most obvious details.

Frustrated, she insisted that he check out Eric Keric, even divulging the old man's address, which she had memorized. The fact that the detective knew Keric's name and where he lived was a good sign. Perhaps the police had already been following him....

Rushed and exhilarated with her new Oswald discovery, Heather hurried back to meet the Alternitech portal. She promised herself a nice restaurant meal to celebrate a productive and satisfying day.

Alternitech prospectors rarely returned to the same parallel universe, but Mr. Feldman offered a substantial bonus. He had discovered with great glee that Heather hadn't obtained the full story about Francis Tarryall.

She'd copied later articles without reading them, and one of her last wire-service transcripts cast extreme doubts on Oswald's dying confession. Other evidence came to light that Tarryall and Oswald had been very personal enemies, their philosophies close enough that minor differences led to shouting matches and hatreds. Some of the Warren Commission's conclusions had begun to unravel ... but Heather had not obtained the rest of the story.

She supposed that her patron wanted to seize any possibility that the conspiracy hadn't actually been solved. In his subconscious at least, Feldman perhaps needed something to hold onto. Her last mission had apparently given him the answer, but now he hoped she could cast doubt once again.

Heather stepped through the portal, backpack and equipment

slung on her shoulder, and went right to work. The answer was obvious as soon as she scrolled through newspapers a few months farther ahead in time. Francis Tarryall was proven innocent, much of the evidence found to be false or misleading, Oswald's confession dismissed as a dying man's last vendetta with no relevance to the JFK assassination.

As she copied the articles, she recalled that this was the parallel reality where she had spent so much time arguing with the skeptical detective about Slasher X. Heather flipped through recent newspapers in the library, looking for headlines proclaiming that the killer had been caught, that innocent victims had been saved. She could take credit for the justice, but she alone would know it. This was her quest ... just like Feldman's.

But she found no headline, no story whatsoever, no mention of Eric Keric or his arrest. The detective had ignored her! It was unbelievable.

With a fluttery dread, she flipped past several months and found no banner stories announcing the serial murders. Heather brushed her rusty-brown hair behind her ear, blinking in puzzlement. It didn't seem possible that Slasher X had managed to hide all of his victims, that people like poor Jamie were simply written off as missing persons, runaways, unexplained disappearances ... maybe even alien abductions.

What if, in this alternate timeline, Eric Keric himself didn't exist?

Breathing quickly, hoping that was the answer, she pawed through the residential phone book. In her own universe, Keric did not have an unlisted number. She found him right where she expected his name to be. The address listed was the same.

The bastard hadn't been caught. She had called the police, given her information—but the idiot detective had apparently done nothing, and the killer remained on the loose.

She looked at her watch. Still more than an hour left, since she had been so quick to get the answers Feldman needed.

Indignant, Heather thought about calling the detective again, demanding to know why he hadn't acted on her information. But she would not be coming back to this parallel universe, and if she didn't make sure that Slasher X was caught, then all his later victims would be on her conscience.

She could go there herself. She had never faced her sister's killer, never even seen the madman. Eric Keric had no idea who Heather Rheims was, despite the fact that she had turned him in timeline after timeline.

She made up her mind in an instant, even though in a horror movie this was probably a very bad decision. But Alternitech would sweep her away in an hour, no matter what happened. After all, Eric Keric had no reason to suspect her, or even recognize her. Heather decided to take the risk.

The murderer's house was repulsively charming and quaint. Neat bluechip junipers lined the walkway up to his little cottage. Flower boxes held green succulents and brown perennials that had died back for winter. Heather thought of the wicked crone's gingerbread house from the story of "Hansel and Gretel."

The front door was painted a slate gray with white trim. Obviously the old sociopath took time between killings to keep his house immaculate. She drew a deep breath and glanced at her watch again before knocking on the door. Only half an hour remained before the Alternitech portal would return. In her jacket pocket, she clasped a can of pepper spray.

Eric Keric had never seen her before in his life. She convinced herself she had nothing to worry about. Heather hoped that she looked like a newspaper salesperson or some other door-to-door annoyance. Then she rang the bell.

The old round-faced man pulled back the curtains beside the door and stared at her for an instant, then ducked away. Keric opened the door, and Heather stepped forward, tense and ready to lure him into a brief but incriminating conversation.

But his hand moved like a rattlesnake, snatching her long rusty-brown hair. "I'm not taking any more of this!" He yanked her head toward him. "And I've certainly had enough of you."

Before she could fumble the pepper spray out of her pocket, he swung the baseball bat that he kept beside the door, striking her a harsh sharp blow on the side of the head. Heather didn't even have time to cry out....

Pain hammered through the grogginess. She had been stunned into twilight for only a few minutes, but Eric Keric had had enough time to drag her into the kitchen and thrust her into a metal chair beside the dinette table. He had lashed her elbows and wrists with two rubbery bonds—extension cords, she realized as she fought her way back to full awareness. Her ears rang, and bright colors swam at the fringes of her vision.

Keric dragged a thin wooden easel across the linoleum floor, standing it in front of her. He was dressed in a checked shirt, partly unbuttoned so she could see his low-necked undershirt and wiry gray chest hair. His sleeves were rolled up on his forearms as if he was ready to get down to work.

The smells and appliances in his kitchen, speckled Formica countertops and stainless-steel sink, were the trappings she had come to associate with kindly grandfathers, but Eric Keric seemed anything but paternal as he glared at her with both fear and anger in his eyes. He pulled the easel in front of her, and Heather lifted her throbbing head to look at it.

"I don't know who you are," the old man growled, "or why you keep tormenting me. What have I done to you?"

She tried to make words, but only a groaning sound came from her slack mouth and thick tongue. The ringing in her ears grew louder. He pulled up the white cover sheet on the easel's large sketchpad, and Heather was astonished to see an accurate, painstakingly rendered pencil and charcoal sketch of her own face. Keric straightened the easel so that she was forced to look at herself. She wondered if she might be hallucinating.

"You ... killed my sister," Heather finally blurted.

The old man scowled at her. "I didn't kill anyone—no matter what you keep saying, no matter what the police accuse me of." Heather couldn't figure out what he was talking about. "You are an evil, spiteful woman. I know you won't tell me who hired you, or who is responsible for this conspiracy, but you've succeeded in ruining my life—if that was your purpose."

He drew a deep breath, and his eyes flickered shut as if he were composing himself, then he squared his shoulders. "But I cannot change other people. I must change myself. I must take control of my life."

He turned away from her as if he couldn't bear to look at Heather's face. She knew she'd been stunned for only a few minutes at best. He couldn't possibly have drawn the exquisite portrait in that amount of time.

"The police have come to my house five times, twice with search warrants. They ransacked my private possessions, everything I own, but they found nothing, won't even tell me what they think I've done or what they're looking for."

Then he pointed an accusing finger at her. Heather was so frightened she tried to squirm away. The chair screeched with her movement, but she could not break the extension cords.

"Because of your harassment, I've lost my job. It wasn't much, but I worked hard at it. They had no reason to fire me." Keric paced the kitchen floor, and his face had a pathetically desperate plea written across it. "Don't you think every day isn't enough of a struggle? I walk on the edge, but I have the strength. I know how to deal with this burden...."

His voice became a low growl, and his eyes lit up. "But you keep piling more and more stress. You're trying to drive me over the edge. You want to push me into some violent action. I don't know what you have to gain by making me go ... berserk."

He clenched his fists but then squeezed his eyes shut again, breathing deeply as if reciting a silent mantra to himself. "But I won't let you. You don't have the power. My life is under my control. You cannot force me to break the law or to hurt anyone."

He withdrew a fat black marker from his pocket and wrenched off the plastic cap with a squeak. She could smell the ink's pungent sour fumes, and her heart skipped a beat. Slasher X always scribbled his indelible mark on the faces of his victims before he cut with the heavy knife.

"You have no power over me," he said, and turned.

With a brutal swift stroke and then a backward slash, he made a black accusing mark across the picture he had drawn, crossing out her face, obliterating the sketched eyes as if he had eliminated her.

"There," he said, satisfied. "You can no longer bother me."

Keric tore the picture off of the easel and carried it, fluttering in his hands, over to a wooden closet door beside the refrigerator. On the back of the door, skewered on a long nail, hung a stack of sketches. Now, Keric stabbed Heather's portrait on top of the others, faces of men and woman, all of them X-ed out.

"Like all those others, you simply don't matter to me anymore."

Her thoughts spun with what he had said. Could it be true that in this parallel timeline Eric Keric had never become Slasher X? That he had found a way to divert his murderous rage and take it out symbolically on his sketches rather than using a knife? She felt sick.

And if this particular incarnation of Eric Keric also had deep psychological problems but retained his sanity by the thinnest of threads … then by making anonymous phone calls accusing him of crimes, had she driven the old man closer toward an edge he had so far managed to avoid?

He went behind her, and Heather was afraid he would strike her, cut her throat. But then she felt the extension cords tug at her elbows and wrists—and Heather found herself freed.

The old man tossed the cords onto the linoleum floor. "Go. Get out of here. You are erased from my life."

Heather stood, disoriented, still feeling the concussion. She looked at the old man, but couldn't say a word. Too many conflicting ideas clamored in her mind.

Bolting like a frightened rabbit, she ran for the front door. She had only a few moments before the Alternitech portal would appear. Keric stepped after her, not in pursuit, but eager to seal the door tight behind her. She looked over her shoulder. "I'm … sorry. I made an assumption, perhaps a wrong one."

She yanked open the door—and startled herself. She stood facing a carbon copy of Heather Rheims, another her. But this one held a handgun, drawn and ready to fire.

Heather's first absurd thought was that this version of herself had come more sensibly prepared than with a pocket can of pepper spray. She recovered and figured it out first. "Of course. There have to be Alternitechs in parallel timelines."

"Yes, and we both had the same idea," the other Heather said. "Did you kill him?"

Then Eric Keric stepped up, crestfallen and anguished. "Why won't you leave me alone?"

The other Heather's lip curled, and she swung up the handgun. She said accusingly to Heather, "Why did you let him live?"

"Because he … isn't guilty," she said. "Did you look for the headlines in this universe? Did you see any mention of Slasher X? Did the police react strangely when you called to turn him in?"

The alternate young woman kept the pistol aimed at Keric, but her expression wavered.

"This guy might be a brutal killer in most of the parallel universes we've visited, but not here. Oh, he's got plenty of mental problems, but so far he has managed to deal with them. He hasn't hurt anybody."

"That's ridiculous," said her counterpart.

"I know ... but it's still true."

Keric looked back and forth between the identical young women, resigned instead of surprised. Heather realized that an endless succession of parallel versions of herself had come here to accuse him.

"This one doesn't kill people," Heather insisted. "He just draws pictures."

"How can I accept that?" said her alternate. "I need to do something for Jamie. This was my only chance for revenge. How can I let that go?"

"Would I lie to you?" Heather looked at her with a deeply sincere expression. And then the other part of the puzzle slammed into place with thunderous force. "And in this timeline, Jamie must still be alive."

Before she could continue the argument, before she could hope to see her sister again, the Alternitech portal shimmered in the air. Heather looked at her counterpart, who wore a startled expression on her face probably identical to her own.

But she couldn't stay. The portal beckoned. She knew she was not likely to come back to this parallel universe ... and she had wasted her time here. Heather had no choice but to return, without seeing Jamie again.

But perhaps her counterpart would use her time for something more beneficial than useless revenge.

When she returned, blinking and disoriented, Heather stepped out of the portal into the Alternitech control room. Quickly, the tech supervisor and two security men came up to surround her. Heather didn't know what had gone wrong, why they were so intent on intercepting her.

"Ms. Rheims," said the tech supervisor, "kindly hand over all of your documentation on the John F. Kennedy assassination. Your investigation is now terminated, your information forfeit."

Heather shrugged off her backpack, her mind spinning in another direction. She hadn't even thought about Feldman and his obsessive quest. "What's wrong?" She removed all her scans and copies about the frame-up of Francis Tarryall, how the JFK conspiracy remained unresolved. "I found some interesting information, but—"

"Mr. Feldman apparently deceived us and has cost Alternitech a great deal of money. He defaulted on his last several payments, and we've just discovered that he's bankrupt."

"Bankrupt? Money-Is-No-Object Feldman has no money?" She tried to wrap her mind around that shift in reality.

With his sarcastic British reserve, the tech supervisor looked at her. "Mr. Feldman insists it's a conspiracy designed to prevent him from discovering the truth about the JFK murder."

Heather felt numb. Somewhere, in another universe, an alternate Heather Rheims was again accusing an alternate—innocent—Eric Keric of unspeakable crimes. Or maybe she was embracing a confused but warm-hearted Jamie.

Swallowing hard, she stepped away from the portal. Now she could hope for a reassignment, go exploring parallel universes for a more legitimate purpose, finding medical cures, scientific discoveries, even artistic works. Heather's vigilante streak made her a poor dispenser of justice. She would no longer solve crimes, not personal ones or political ones. The truth wasn't always clear-cut, even in her own timeline.

Instead, she would remember Jamie, keep the fond memories, maybe do some good things in her honor. She was alive, somewhere.

That was a truth Heather could hold on to.

Richard Matheson was a seminal, brilliant, and highly influential writer who deserves to be a household name along with Ray Bradbury or Isaac Asimov. Although he isn't as well known, you are familiar with his work, as the writer behind countless incredible films, such as I Am Legend, Somewhere in Time, Duel, The Incredible Shrinking Man, What Dreams May Come, A Stir of Echoes, Real Steel, The Legend of Hell House, *and many others. When a specialty press asked me to contribute to a Matheson tribute anthology about the human effects of war, I knew I had the perfect idea.*

I had wanted to write this story for more than a year, but never had the impetus to do so. The idea kept nagging at me, and it seemed to fit perfectly with the anthology.

After I delivered "Combat Experience," I received this letter from Matheson's son, Richard Christian Matheson—an extremely talented novelist and screenwriter in his own right—saying he loved the story, "Its dread about war's futility (even far tomorrows, sadly, immunizing none) resonates with quiet melancholy and it absolutely belongs in the anthology." I knew I had hit the mark.

COMBAT EXPERIENCE

They brought him back to consciousness, even though he had hoped, prayed, begged never to wake up again. He groaned, but he had no voice … not yet. The breathing tubes, pulse monitors, electrodes, and blood-pumping machines provided a flood of chemical and electrical stimulants that kept his biological house of cards functioning—all so that his brain remained capable of planning strategy.

Alliance Command would not let him die until the war was over, and the war would never be over.

"General Schaeffer," said a voice that remained disembodied because he hadn't yet been able to open his leaden eyes. "Sorry to disturb you, sir, but the Human Alliance needs you again. The Agrec are on the move. Alien ships have been spotted on the outskirts of Sector 7."

Schaeffer's thoughts became sharper, and he felt more alert— primarily because they had added more drugs that worked like a cattle prod on his mind. He opened his eyes.

It was the same as always. Each time he woke up he found himself in a hospital bed that was a nest of life-support systems, IV feeds, and tubes pumping him full of nutrients and pharmaceuticals. Most of his senses had faded long ago, but the smell remained as strong as ever. The place reeked of antiseptics, age, and death—his own death, much delayed.

But Alliance Command used heroic measures to keep General Liam Schaeffer alive because they considered him a hero. Apparently, their only one.

"We need your tactical advice, sir." Schaeffer's vision focused on a young, distraught-looking lieutenant next to a more stoic colonel. At least the colonel had the good sense to look ashamed to tap into Shaeffer's expertise again. The lieutenant said, "No one knows the Agrec the way you do."

Nurses increased the tempo of the beat on the medical monitors. Colors changed in the chemical fluids that traveled through tubes into his failing body. Schaeffer was no more than a skeleton with a parchment membrane of skin, a handful of still-functioning organs, as well as a large number of artificial ones.

"Let me be," he croaked. "Already ... done enough."

The colonel spoke in a hard voice. "You have to do your duty for humanity, General. You have more combat experience than any other commander." His name plate said ARLO; the nervous young lieutenant was DARVI.

A virtual screen appeared before Schaeffer's face. The medical displays were replaced with tactical projections, star charts, and symbols indicating the enemy Agrec ships. Lieutenant Darvi said, "If we had any other choice, sir, we would take it, but we need your assistance. If you can't provide us with tactical insight, then countless young soldiers will die—and when they fall, then so will millions of innocent colonists ..."

Schaeffer let the breathing pumps charge up his lungs before he gasped, "That's what you said the last five times."

The dour colonel didn't flinch. "And that's what we'll say the next five times until the Agrec invasion swarm is defeated."

Schaeffer felt a sad hopelessness press down at him with a weight greater than the medical machinery. The war with the Agrec had already lasted nearly a century, and he had been there at the beginning.

Defeated, Schaeffer managed to say, "Let me see the projections and tell me what's different this time."

⚛

He had been only eighteen, wet behind the ears, a mere colony outpost soldier when the Agrec first struck Farvin, the planet where he was stationed. Farvin was a hardscrabble place in its first decades of terraforming. Humans could breathe the air, and terrestrial crops could grow, if given considerable fertilizer and nurturing. The colonists lived in prefab huts, knowing it would be many hard decades before anyone could call the world comfortable. Only fifty outpost soldiers were assigned to watch over the five thousand settlers.

Up until then, the Human Alliance had needed nothing more than a token military presence against unlikely raiders. Farvin was a bleak colony planet with nothing anyone would want to take by force. Thus, they were entirely unprepared when the first alien expeditionary vessel arrived.

Young Liam Schaeffer had stared at the modular warship, a cluster of geometrical pods arranged around heavy engines. None of the Farvin colonists or soldiers had seen any vessel like it. Schaeffer and his comrades were intimidated and confused as the vessel landed on the outskirts of the settlement.

As they gathered around to stare at the sapphire-hulled ship, the vessel opened up and disgorged hundreds of bald, blue-skinned humanoids wearing slick uniforms. The Agrec moved as perfectly regimented soldiers, clustered into discrete groups that advanced with an impossible precision.

The Farvin colony leader came forward, hands upraised to welcome the strange visitors in a quavering voice. The Agrec gunned her down first, then opened fire with incandescent projectile weapons. The aliens didn't speak, merely wore stony expressions on their mannequin-like faces. Streams of deadly fireworks killed the panicked colonists and leveled the prefab huts as if they were clearing a forest.

Screaming orders to one another, Schaeffer and his companions fired their sidearms, while others raced to the armory to commandeer the colony's few larger weapons. Fifty soldiers would never be enough.

Young Schaeffer, untried Schaeffer, terrified Schaeffer was certain he would die that day as he watched the massacre. The fifty defenders tried to mount a futile defense, and the local commander howled, "Open fire! Open fire!"

The Agrec marched forward as if in a parade, grouped in units of exactly fifty-three alien soldiers. Even one of those combat swarms would have been a match for the Farvin defenders—and the aliens had a dozen of them. The colony soldiers learned quickly enough that their projectiles could not penetrate the slick armored jumpsuits.

The bald aliens had unprotected heads, however.

Scoring a head shot was much more difficult in the frenzy of combat, but Schaeffer took aim, steadied his trembling hands, and fired five times before he hit one of the aliens. The bullet burst the Agrec's skull, and the alien toppled to the ground. The other fifty-two members of the combat swarm paid no attention to the loss, but kept marching forward in lockstep, opening fire, killing colonists, killing soldiers, destroying structures. The invaders acted as if they were no more than a janitorial crew cleaning up an inconvenient settlement.

"Hit their heads!" Schaeffer shouted. More than twenty of the outpost soldiers had already been killed, and hundreds of colonists were dead. The Agrec kept flowing out from their ship. His battlefield focus narrowed around him, and his aim grew more precise as he kept shooting. But it was futile.

Tears streamed down his face, and he screamed in defiance with each shot. One more alien down, then another.

In the middle of each combat swarm, though, he noticed that one of the nearly identical alien soldiers looked slightly different. The Agrec's uniform was the same, the expression and physical build the same, but a rectangular patch on its face was a darker blue. Schaeffer took aim and killed the marked alien. The bullet splashed through its head, and the Agrec fighter collapsed.

To his astonishment, every one of the remaining members in its combat swarm also collapsed like puppets with severed strings. With one shot he had incapacitated the entire group!

At first, he couldn't find words, then he raised his voice to his surviving comrades. "Find the one with the mark on its face—in the center of the group. That's your target."

With concentrated fire, the remaining soldiers made their last stand. The Agrec pressed forward, slaughtering human soldiers and colonists, but Schaeffer remained focused and cool, firing and firing.

He took out another one of their "commanders," which neutralized another group of fifty-three aliens.

The invaders moved like automatons, showing no reaction to their losses, even when two combat swarms had been felled. Schaeffer's comrades chose their targets and began taking out other swarm commanders—but the aliens kept fighting, wiping out much of Farvin.

When all but three of their combat swarms had fallen, the Agrec finally acknowledged their peril and retreated to their main ship, leaving their dead behind. After they boarded, the modular ship sealed itself and roared upward into the smoke-smeared skies of Farvin.

More than five hundred dead alien bodies lay on the battlefield. The colony was destroyed. Fewer than a hundred settlers survived, and all of the fifty outpost soldiers were killed—except for Schaeffer.

Amidst the shocked moans and the crackle of burning buildings, Schaeffer collapsed onto the raw ground. He sat stunned, shell-shocked, but convinced he had to return to Earth and report what he had learned.

The invaders would surely attack again.

Alliance Command scientists discovered that the Agrec were a distributed hive mind, like a mosaic of components. Each combat swarm consisted of a group of exactly fifty-three units guided by one commander sub-brain. They theorized there were higher and higher orders of over-commanders back at their home world.

Human researchers dissected, probed, and studied the bodies left behind on Farvin, but the key realizations and the vital tactical knowledge came from young Schaeffer's reports. He was treated as a reluctant hero, given a battlefield promotion, and debriefed incessantly about the actions of the Agrecs.

He had time to repeat his story fourteen times before the aliens struck another human outpost. Unfortunately, his discovery about targeting the combat swarm subcommander was not distributed in time, and the world of Benesar IV was lost with no survivors.

All across the Human Alliance, Alliance Command geared up for a full-scale interstellar war, and Schaeffer was given a small command of his own. His superiors dispatched him with a group of eager soldiers who were pleased to be fighting alongside the hero of Farvin. Not long afterward, when Agrec forces struck a third human colony, Schaeffer was there, yelling at his men to target the lone alien with the discolored face.

Mowing down combat swarms, one after another, they turned the tide of the battle, and as Schaeffer's fighters charged forward, they were exuberant, victorious—until the Agrecs brought out a new sort of annihilation-wave weapon that sent shock ripples across the human soldiers. Brave troop leader Schaeffer and his men were scattered like leaves in the wind. Ninety percent of the soldiers under his command were killed outright, five percent were blinded, and the rest suffered major injuries....

Later, as Schaeffer recovered in a Human Alliance military hospital, the doctors told him he was among the lucky ones. Crowded around his hospital bedside, intense advisers debriefed him, wanting to know what he had seen of the new annihilation-wave weapon. They counted on him, extracting intelligence that they could share with their defense scientists.

Schaeffer painted a vivid picture of the new Agrec weapon, and his descriptions yielded details that none of the other survivors had been able to provide. The Alliance Command weapons developers insisted that Schaeffer's singular insights were key to developing fresh shields.

During the eight months that Schaeffer recovered in the planetary infirmary, military think tanks worked frantically. By the time the med specialists declared him fit for duty and dispatched him to the front again, all Human Alliance soldiers carried special shielding to face the Agrec annihilation-wave weapon. Upper command promoted Schaeffer again, giving him responsibility for an even larger group of faithful and wide-eyed young soldiers who believed he was good luck incarnate: a miracle survivor of two devastating Agrec attacks.

Schaeffer didn't feel lucky at all, but he went out to fight—and he did survive the next three horrific engagements on fringe colony worlds. He even led a surprise frontal assault that recaptured the devastated world of Benesar IV, site of the second Agrec assault. The image of his iconic raising of the Human Alliance flag in the rubble of the colony, with Agrec bodies strewn all around, made him even more famous than he already was....

It took the hive mind aliens two full years to adapt their combat methods and protect their distinctive swarm subcommanders. When the combat swarms marched out in lockstep to fight the human troops, the subcommanders wore enhanced helmet shielding—which also made the vital person far easier to identify. Captain Schaeffer directed all of his forces to target the helmeted subcommanders with a no-holds-barred onslaught, something he labeled "holy hell tactics."

Schaeffer won five more victories that way and showed all other Alliance commanders how similar victories could be won in future engagements. Word spread throughout the military, and the Human Alliance scored many wins against the Agrec before the aliens changed their tactics once more.

The aggressive race seemed inexhaustible and intent on taking over the colonized planets. For their next gambit, the Agrec added decoy subcommanders to their combat swarms, artificially tinting the blue faces of several normal drone soldiers, but Captain Schaeffer had seen enough of their up-close combat techniques that he could still recognize the real target by instinct. He won again.

And the war continued....

⚛

Now, the cobweb-and-muscle remnants of old General Schaeffer lay ensnared in medical safety nets and life-support systems, sustained by a flow of chemicals. He focused on the projections Colonel Arlo showed him.

"All of their new battleships are in a phalanx formation." The grim officer pointed to the screen. "They are due to penetrate Sector 7 within six weeks. We'll have enough time to prepare—if you can spot the weak point for us, sir."

Schaeffer's head pounded, and he had difficulty focusing his vision. Too much adrenaline mixed with other stimulants thrummed through his system. Eager Lieutenant Darvi—a man who reminded Schaeffer so much of himself when he had been gung-ho about the war—waved to a nurse. "Can't you give him something for more clarity of thought? We need his mind sharp!"

Schaeffer lifted a feeble hand to wave her away, but the nurse injected something into his IV, and he felt his thoughts grow clearer, more intense, when all he really wanted was to fade into the warm comforting blackness of sleep, release ... even death, if they would ever let him have it.

"Can't you learn for yourself?" Schaeffer asked. Forcing out that sentence seemed as difficult as winning a battle.

"We have you," said the colonel. "You're the greatest tactical mind in all matters regarding the Agrec. We don't need those other think tanks."

"I already debriefed you ..." he gasped. "How much more do I need to give?"

"Until we win, General. Until we win."

By the fourteenth year of the war, enough Human Alliance colonies had been devastated and enough battles fought that even a summary of the conflict would have filled volumes. The main fury of the war shifted to battles in space, and the tactics of fighting the Agrec changed entirely.

The commanders put Schaeffer—now a colonel—in command of a Behemoth-class warship leading a battle group of fifty destroyers, well-armed cruisers, fast recon vessels, and rammers. His soldiers were superstitiously pleased to serve under "Survivor Schaeffer's" command. They saw him as blessed, as indestructible—even though he had served as much time recovering in military hospitals as he had in actual combat.

When his battle group clashed with the first Agrec shipswarm, he recognized the imposing modular vessel design, the geometrical shapes studded around bulky starship engines and heavy weaponry. He would never forget what he had seen when the first alien invasion force had landed on Farvin. Now, he realized that the ship he had seen on the innocent colony was one of the smallest in the Agrec space fleet.

The first space clash was a free-for-all, a brawl of scraping hulls and weapons blasts, vented atmosphere, drifting bodies, exploding fuel tanks, wrecked engines. Schaeffer lost more than a third of his ships in three hours, but his battered Behemoth flagship survived.

He ordered his surviving vessels to retreat into lightspeed and leave both human and alien wreckage behind.

Schaeffer considered the engagement a debacle, but the soldiers serving under his command cheered, taking the very fact of their survival as proof of his tactical genius. When they got back to the nearest main base, Alliance Command debriefed him thoroughly and paid close attention to his personal impressions, but he had no insights to offer them.

They responded by giving Colonel Schaeffer another battle group, this time with three Behemoths and twice as many ships. They sent him out again.

During the flight to the outer fringe, beyond which—somewhere—lay the Agrec home world, his soldiers and pilots drilled and drilled. Colonel Schaeffer memorized the images of his first battle, trying to tease out which actions were effective and which ones weren't. Engrossed in the feed, he finally grasped a subtle pattern and thought he understood a familiar set of movements, a carefully uncoordinated dance.

The Agrec shipswarm was comprised of giant vessels and fast destroyers mixed among a large cloud of otherwise nondescript ships. Why carry so much deadwood along in a battle group? As Schaeffer enhanced and stared at the grainy images, he focused on one of those seemingly innocuous ships, enlarged it, and saw a familiar rectangular marking on its hull—a marking the others lacked. And he smiled....

During the next space engagement—eight months later—Colonel Schaeffer launched into the alien shipswarm with the same excessive, free-for-all battle tactics, but he gave one heavily armed squadron another assignment. Ten of his armored ships soared forward to take out one specific vessel.

When they did so, the Agrec ships in the entire swarm reeled, losing power and command integrity. At once, they drifted in space, aimless and confused. The higher-level subcommander was dead.

The rest of Schaeffer's battle group showed no mercy and obliterated the alien ships, except for the ones they captured intact for Alliance weapon scientists to study....

The war continued year after year, but no negotiations took place, no détente—no communication with the Agrec whatsoever. The Human Alliance didn't even know how the aliens communicated; if the Agrec were a segregated hive mind comprised of discrete smaller swarms, perhaps they didn't have any kind of language at all, any more than a human hand knew how to talk to a human foot.

If a main Agrec mind existed, it would be located on the alien home world, but no one knew where that was. Obsessive tacticians plotted course projections, back-calculating paths toward a presumed common point, but there was none.

After twenty-five years, the Human Alliance population had become accustomed to the war; the constant threat of alien invasion was their everyday existence. Colonists lived their lives, having long ago given up hope that the conflict would end soon; they couldn't waste decades just biting their fingernails and waiting.

Political leadership changed, and a pacifist president was elected. Since the outright conflict had resulted in neither victory nor the cessation of hostilities, the new Alliance president proposed sending an ambassador on a mission to track down some representative of the Agrec and conduct face-to-face talks.

The war-weary people applauded the thought, convinced the alien invaders must be as exhausted as the humans were. General Schaeffer—his last promotion because there were no higher ranks to give him—thought it was a terrible idea, so the president appointed him ambassador and sent him out.

Unconvinced, Schaeffer assembled an escort of eight warships as well as his flagship Behemoth. It wasn't a large enough battle group to bring into a prolonged space battle, but it was enough to put up a good fight, damage the enemy, and possibly escape—if diplomacy didn't work.

As they went beyond the boundaries of Human Alliance space hunting for enemy ships, the young soldiers in his crew grinned with confidence, sure that "Survivor Schaeffer" could talk some sense into the Agrec. Meanwhile, Schaeffer contemplated everything he had learned in fighting the deceptively human-looking enemy.

He had absolutely no idea how to negotiate with a race that didn't think in the way humans did, a race that might not even have a language.

Three weeks out, the diplomatic group encountered an Agrec shipswarm, an aggregation of ships five times as big as Schaeffer's fleet. Because it was his mission, Schaeffer opened a channel and broadcast. "This is General Liam Schaeffer, commander of this ... swarm of ships. Are you able to communicate?" He waited on the bridge, but heard no response from the looming alien ships. He glanced at his crew, then turned back to the blank screen. "I wish to speak with your overall hive mind. How can we achieve this?"

After ten tense seconds passed without a response, the Agrec ships opened fire, unleashing new weapons. Gouts of disintegrating energy ripped open the nearest Alliance ship like a high-pressure water hose striking gelatin.

"Open fire!" Schaeffer shouted, and his ships began to fight back, but the new alien weapons bombarded the diplomatic group, obliterating one vessel after another.

Minutes earlier, however, when the shipswarm initially surrounded his diplomatic group, Schaeffer had identified the one nondescript alien vessel that held the hive submind, and now he accelerated the Behemoth. If nothing else, he intended to get up enough speed to ram the one key vessel. From this distance, his artillery would not be sufficient.

His first officer shouted commands, howling at the weapons officers, who did their best to respond. Amidst the alarms and nearby explosions, Schaeffer yelled, "These are new weapons! The Human Alliance has to know about them. We've got to dispatch an emergency buoy, some kind of message—"

The first officer grabbed Schaeffer. "Absolutely right, sir. You can tell them everything yourself—get to the lifepod. We'll take it from here."

"I will not abandon my ship."

"It has been an honor serving with you, and I apologize for the mutiny, sir." The first officer looked around the bridge as the Behemoth picked up speed toward its target. "Crew, please help me assist General Schaeffer in his escape."

The flagship roared past the other Agrec ships, ignoring them. It outran the disintegrator waves, while the rest of his diplomatic escort ships tried to defend the General ... and died doing so.

Before he knew it, Schaeffer found himself unceremoniously thrown into the shielded lifepod and locked inside. The last-ditch interlock systems triggered an emergency backup dump of all records from the flagship's bridge console. He was able to yell one more time, pounding on the lifepod hatch before the first officer ejected it into space.

If the flagship did ram the key enemy vessel, the rest of the shipswarm would go dead, but Schaeffer already knew that the rest of his escort fleet had been destroyed; the battered and burning Behemoth was the only ship left. It careened headlong among the Agrec ships.

Inside the pod, Schaeffer was tumbled about in the explosive launch, and he grabbed a handhold to steady himself. He spun, disoriented, nauseated, unable to get his bearings, until stabilizers finally kicked in.

Clawing and gasping, he was able to look out the small windowscreen to see the Behemoth collide with the small but key Agrec vessel, decapitating the entire alien shipswarm. Even as the large group of enemy ships fell dead in space, the lifepod raced out into open space.

His locator beacon thrummed into the emptiness. He really had to get home and bring this vital intelligence to Alliance command.

But he was deep in Agrec space, with only minimal engines and life support that would keep him alive for a month ... but he doubted that would be enough to return to human-held territory. If he kept the course straight, this lifepod might arrive inside the Human Alliance in a year or so, carrying the data, and his lifeless body....

Not good enough.

General Schaeffer proved his military genius once again by extinguishing the lifepod engines, reorienting the clumsy vessel, and limping back *toward* the cluster of dead Agrec warships. He managed to maneuver the lifepod inside one of the alien vessels, where he disembarked. He worked his way among all the dead Agrec bodies until he reached the strange bridge. He spent a week figuring out how to use their star engines, although he had basic information derived from all the previous Agrec ships that had been dismantled and studied.

When he single-handedly flew a stolen alien warship back home —bringing not only the log records from his failed diplomatic mission but also an actual functional Agrec disintegrator weapon for the scientists to study—his legend grew tenfold. Alliance Command added more and more stars to his rank to the point where it became absurd.

And the war continued.

Fifty years after the initial attack on Farvin, General Schaeffer had accomplished everything he intended to do for humanity, and it was time to hand off the war to a new generation. He announced his retirement, and no one disputed that he had earned the right.

The Human Alliance celebrated his career and gave him a send-off attended by an estimated ten thousand people, including all of the still-living soldiers who had served under his command and the families of those soldiers who had died during his various battles.

As Schaeffer compiled his notes for a multi-volume set of memoirs, he looked back at the battles he had fought against the Agrec. Perhaps he was blessed, as the rumors said, or more lucky than anyone in history had ever been.

He was toasted, lionized, applauded; weepy women threw themselves at him, which he would have found delightful, if he had been decades younger and less scarred. Still, it reminded him that once retired, a wealthy and famous man like himself could surely find a suitable woman to settle down with and give him a few pleasant decades to counterbalance the decades of war.

The hours of his retirement celebration were more stressful and exhausting than any combat scenario, but it was the price he had to endure, after which he settled into a quiet and happy retirement.

Which lasted less than three weeks.

A frantic military commander arrived at Schaeffer's home, demanding to speak with him. Her face was flushed, and she could barely sputter out her words. "The Agrec attacked again, sir! Wiped out two of our worlds—one in Sector 3, one in Sector 6. It makes no sense. We see no pattern."

Schaeffer drew his brows together. "There's always a pattern. We just have to study it."

The officer was frantic. "General, we need your help! Would you come with me, sir? Please?"

Alliance Command refused to let him sail off into the sunset. For years, the Human Alliance used his life, his mind, and endless promises of "this is the last time" like a cat-and-mouse game. They brought him on as an adviser, then sent him to the front so he could see firsthand the unexpected difficulties faced by the beleaguered human troops.

Alliance Command think tanks relied on him for every emergency, even though they had their own tacticians, and by now there were many other experienced commanders. Regardless, the military always fell back on him. Decade after decade.

Schaeffer's luck finally ran out when he was eighty-seven years old, and he suffered severe burns over thirty percent of his body when his recon ship endured heavy enemy fire. But he was rescued, patched up, and kept alive, though severely injured. And the people still called him "lucky."

When Schaeffer was ninety-three and barely able to walk, unable to live by himself unless tended by a medical team, he had a massive heart failure. As he collapsed into the dark pain, he thought at least it would be quiet and restful there in death, and the Human Alliance would have to solve their own problems.

But he woke up resuscitated, on life support, to see another grinning officer. "General, sir, I'm glad to see you're recovering. There's been an incursion—the Agrecs are using new ships ..."

Decade after decade ...

They refused to let him die. General Liam Schaeffer was far too valuable an asset, a tactical genius with unparalleled knowledge of the merciless enemy. The human race could not afford to lose him, and so Alliance Command used every imaginable measure to keep him alive.

And each time he gave them flawless advice, each time Schaeffer proved the worth of his tactical knowledge, they were even more convinced of the need to keep using him....

Now, the eager young officer and the dour colonel leaned over his hospital bed, moving aside some of the tubes and respirator pumps so they could point out the projections. "Surveillance probes have tracked these large phalanx formations, General. Five thousand enemy ships heading into Sector 7 from various directions."

Now that the drugs made his brain alert and his thoughts sharp, Schaeffer flicked his gaze back and forth, studied the alien warships and the cluster configurations. Because his hands were weak and trembling, he asked the lieutenant to call up projected courses for the incursions, saw a time-lapse of their paths and stops, and watched the enemy phalanxes change course several times. The shipswarms moved in a random, unpredictable fashion.

Schaeffer stared until his eyes watered and his heart pounded, until he saw a faint echo of a pattern, which he recognized. All of the Alliance Command's genius tacticians had not seen it.

"Can you project their target destination, General?" asked Lieutenant Darvi. "We need to know where to mount our defenses. Where are the Agrec going to strike?"

Schaeffer stared at the ships, sank back into his sterile bed. Why couldn't they figure it out for themselves? "Let me die," he said.

"We need you, General," said Colonel Arlo. "Think of all the lives you could save."

Schaeffer did think about the lives he might save, and he thought of all those who had died under his command, too—young soldiers with far too much faith in him and not enough faith in themselves. Under any normal circumstances, numerous other experts would have emerged over the years. Alliance Command relied on him far too much.

"You're never wrong, General," said Darvi, as if Schaeffer needed encouragement. "Please help us. Look at these projections— you've got to have some insights."

Schaeffer sank into his pillow, feeling the vibrations of the equipment that kept him alive, the unwilling blood circulation, the stimulants, the medicines. Couldn't Colonel Arlo even *look* for himself? On the star charts, there were only six potential planetary targets that the alien invasion force might attack, and he saw the obvious track, but by now the hive mind had learned some modicum of deception. He was sure the shipswarms would divert and attack Khuldur, a small settlement of no more than five hundred people. He couldn't understand what the Agrec might want with the place, since it had few raw materials and no strategic value. Nevertheless, the aliens wanted it.

"Study the projections," he said weakly, knowing that they would keep coming to him every time he helped them, every time he gave them a correct answer. It had to stop. "They'll hit Santiago 3," he lied. "It's a prize. They'll try to take that."

The young officer was very excited. "Yes, Santiago 3! That's what I thought, but we needed verification from you, sir."

"Thank you, General," said Colonel Arlo, "and the human race thanks you for your service."

Schaeffer's heart felt heavy at what he had done, the five hundred colonists he had just doomed, but he also thought of all those young soldiers who would die if they engaged in a full battle over Khuldur. Probably far more than five hundred.

If he himself hadn't been lucky, if he had been killed as a young soldier in that first engagement on Farvin, what would have happened with the war? And what would have happened to the human race? No doubt they would have found some other hero, some other genius ... and they would have continued the fight, regardless. They saw him as a bastion, but they used him as a crutch.

But if Schaeffer let himself be wrong, if he proved that he was no longer perfect, maybe they would not bother to keep him alive and keep torturing him for answers. Then they would have to learn how to walk on their own two feet—and win their own damned war.

Schaeffer had already fought his.

As the two officers gathered equipment and notes, prepared to rush off and spread the news that General Schaeffer had spoken, he just wanted to fall back into darkness, warm sleep, and then oblivion.

But he opened his eyes again, needing to do one last thing. He couldn't just leave it that way. When he tried to call out, his voice was just a weak whisper, but the nurse heard him, and she called the officers back.

After watching the long-term and supposedly random course changes of the oncoming Agrec fleet, he had noticed something. Schaeffer didn't know how long it would take the others to see for themselves.

The colonel stepped to his bed, wrinkling his nose at the smell of chemicals, age, and death. "Yes, General, what is it?"

"The paths of those shipswarms ... not random. After this battle engagement, study the course changes carefully. You might see a pattern."

Colonel Arlo frowned. "After the engagement, what will it matter, sir?"

Schaeffer exhaled a long slow sigh. "Maybe nothing at all … or maybe it will lead you to the Agrec home world and the primary hive mind. Find that, and you can end this war once and for all."

The colonel nodded briskly. "Thank you, General. We'll look into it. But first we have to defend Santiago 3."

The two officers left as Schaeffer closed his eyes again, hoping the nurse would let the stimulants run out so that he could sleep, so that he could rest.

Surely that was enough? Surely enough at last.

Another military science fiction story, but this one is a little lighter. One day, the idea of "reserves" in the military struck me an odd way, and I thought of woefully inadequate recruits who were forced to sit in a room, only to be brought out in an absolute worst-case scenario.

Next, I wondered how battlefield commanders would act differently if they had a guaranteed rescue if a combat operation went south. How many more ridiculous risks would they take, leaving their cannon fodder behind?

The two ideas collided in this story, which I wrote in a one-week gap between finishing one novel and starting another.

ESCAPE HATCH

—I—

The mass of alien tentacles writhed over the side of the Earth Planetary Navy destroyer. When the *Far Horizon*'s Admiral Bruce Haldane saw the vicious things crash onto the deck and scatter in all directions, he knew the battle was lost. There was no stopping the swarm of Sluggos.

Rough seas rocked the destroyer, but the grim crew who manned the guns against the worm-things were not worried about getting seasick.

The enormous cluster of alien creatures also attacked from beneath the surface, hammering the *Far Horizon*'s armored hull. The thunderous clang was even louder than the explosive artillery. *How could something so soft and squishy sound so loud?* he wondered, then stalked along the deck, a weapon in each hand as he shot the swarming slugs. Each creature exploded with a disgusting splat of oozing protoplasm. The ship's crew were running up and down the open deck, wading through smashed Sluggos, but the things kept coming from below.

Unstoppable.

Each alien was the length and thickness of Haldane's forearm, looking like a beige banana slug with teeth. The Sluggos combined and moved in concert, wrapping their wormlike bodies together to form a larger organism. Thousands of Sluggos braided into a giant tentacle that rose up from the rough seas to wrap around the destroyer, and then dissolved into countless ravenous components again. The Sluggos squirmed forward, mouths chomping. They were blind, but they were hungry, and there were so many of them that the doomed crew had no place to hide.

Admiral Haldane was grim, but he drove back his panic. As their leader, he had to focus on the fight. His crew was yelling, some clearly fearful because they had just begun to realize they were all going to die. They didn't have an escape hatch. Knowing he could give his all and still live to fight another day let Haldane concentrate on the crisis and do what was necessary, without being crippled by fear of his own mortality.

"Keep shooting! By God, there's no shortage of targets!"

The lower decks had been infested, and evacuating sailors had come out into the open. One of the nearby seamen, his dungarees splotched with yellow-green ichor and bright red blood, fired his sidearm until it was empty, then snatched another still-hot weapon from the hands of a dying seaman on the deck. The wounded seaman's abdomen had been ripped open, and his guts spilled out like another swarm of Sluggos. Without pause, the desperate seaman continued firing, each bullet exploding one—or more—of the squirming aliens.

"Aye, sir. It's not a shortage of targets we're worried about, Admiral," he shouted over his shoulder. "It's running out of ammo."

Haldane kept firing his own sidearm, not even making a dent in the invasion. He shouted back, hoping he sounded encouraging, "According to the weapons locker manifest, we should have ten thousand rounds aboard the *Far Horizon*." The number sounded impressive, objectively, but not in comparison to the million hungry Sluggos swarming over the destroyer. He had opened the armory and distributed weapons as widely and as swiftly as possible, to the Marines as well as to any other sailor with fingers and thumbs.

Everyone aboard would be alien food before long. Haldane felt sorry for them, but he'd make sure they got a nice memorial ceremony back in La Diego.

After humanity had ventured away from Earth and set up fledgling colonies on the Moon, Mars, and the asteroid belt, nobody ever guessed that an alien invasion would target Earth's oceans. The invaders had landed in the Pacific, emerged from their interstellar spaceships, and began swarming through the seas.

The slimy creatures moved like a gigantic school of fish, thousands of separate pieces that formed a sentient community organism—an incomprehensible alien creature that managed to build starships, travel across space, to plunge into Earth's oceans, where they reproduced at a furious pace—whether by fission, or breeding, or eggs, no one knew—and swiftly became a terrible hazard.

They attacked ships, sinking commercial freighters, cruise liners, fishing vessels. The Earth Planetary Navy was little more than a token force, peacekeepers and emergency responders. It had been a long time since battle fleets went on a full-scale war footing. Now, the EPN went on the hunt, combing the waters in search of the enemy.

Sonar could detect the large clusters of Sluggos, which then vanished with each pulse and re-formed elsewhere. Admiral Haldane had already led two preliminary engagements, each one disastrous. He was about to make it three for three.

Reaching this point in the South Pacific, the suspected location of the original Sluggo starships, the *Far Horizon* had dropped dozens of depth pulsers hoping to destroy the underwater alien base. The explosions had been wonderful, creating rooster-tails of water like massive geysers. The shock waves should have ruined any Sluggo structures on the ocean floor.

The excitement was short-lived, though. The individual aliens had combined into a monstrous body, countless squirming components adding together like cells. Then the community organism rose up like the most twisted nightmare of any sailors' legend and attacked the *Far Horizon*.

The shapeless beast shifted and rearranged its bodily blueprint, first engulfing the destroyer with tentacles and then smashing onto the deck in a huge flat mass like a manta, which then dissolved into an overwhelming slimy army of individual Sluggos that could attack—and devour.

Constant gunfire continued to ring out, and even ten thousand rounds didn't last very long. When the crew ran out of ammo, they used metal pipes, tools, even small storage pods to smash the things. Someone had rigged a flamethrower and jetted fire that fried the wormlike aliens. When their protoplasm boiled, they exploded, but the Sluggos did not feel pain or fear, and more of them came forward. One young seaman thrashed as a dozen of the worm-things chewed into the meat of his thighs and calves, then tunneled through his chest. He kept screaming until one crawled down his throat.

Other seamen had better luck with fire extinguishers, driving the Sluggos away, briefly, but there was no place to hide. Each extinguisher ran out within minutes, and the crew used the empty tanks to smash more Sluggos.

"Turn the heavy-caliber guns down," Haldane yelled. "Fire into the water!"

"But, sir, that'll do nothing!"

"It'll make some big explosions," he shouted back. That was something at least.

At central fire control, weapons officers tilted the large-bore guns down, and the guns roared, but even the heavy shells did little more than stir up the Sluggos in the water. In response, a huge pseudopod composed of braided Sluggos lurched up, wavered in the air just long enough for Haldane to estimate the tens of thousands of hungry creatures that comprised it, then it dissociated in midair, creating a rain of hungry Sluggos that fell onto the *Far Horizon*.

Haldane had found shelter under the bridge wing, but he watched the crew get slaughtered. He had emptied both of his sidearms and he had no other defenses but his bare hands and his bootheels. The squirming aliens came at him like an unstoppable invertebrate tide....

No one in the EPN had had more direct experience with the Sluggos than Admiral Bruce Haldane. He had studied their movements firsthand in three engagements now, seen how they attacked. He made mental notes. Even though he didn't understand what he saw, his knowledge was irreplaceable. If Earth was going to win this war against the undersea invasion, *he* had to survive.

The overburdened destroyer was groaning, listing to starboard, clearly taking on water from belowdecks. The pounding Sluggos had chewed and torn through the lower hull and were even now swarming through the breach, infesting the ship even faster than seawater could fill it. Damage control crews had been devoured as they rushed to respond. The destroyer was going down.

As he backed against the bulkhead, he watched hundreds of Sluggos burst through the hatches, huge maggots writhing up the ladders and spilling onto the deck. Even with the din of gunfire, explosions, and shouts, Haldane could hear them moving around in the compartments below, feasting.

Then they came toward him.

Most of the *Far Horizon*'s crew had been slaughtered already, but Haldane stood straight and proud, facing the alien enemy. He owed it to the brave men and women who perished here. He would stay until the very last as the hordes of fleshy bodies and chewing mouths squirmed toward him. He kicked at the Sluggos, but more and more came.

The admiral raised his voice and announced to anyone left on deck who might be able to hear him, "I want to thank you all for your service. Your lives will not be lost in vain."

As the Sluggos swarmed over him, Haldane reached behind his head and hit the transfer pendant embedded at the base of his skull. His escape hatch.

He was going to miss this body, which had served him well for the past six weeks, but he gave little thought to the volunteer seaman who would transfer with him at the last moment. If Admiral Haldane timed it right, the volunteer would feel only a few seconds of pain as the Sluggos devoured him.

It was what the volunteer had signed up for. He was just cannon fodder, and he had played the odds. Haldane couldn't even remember his name. Now it was time for the man to do his duty so that the valuable, experienced naval admiral could live to fight another day.

Haldane felt the alien jaws rip into his flesh. The pain was horrific, and he was glad to be out of that body.

—II—

When Paulson Kenz picked up his mail, he expected to find bills, junk mailers, delinquent notices on his student loan, even another eviction threat because his low-paying job didn't earn him enough to pay the rent and eat both in the same week.

The urgent draft notice, however, was far worse than any stack of bills or legal notices.

Paulson stared at the official envelope for a long time. Some of his friends in equally dire financial straits had talked about joining the military, but in the same distant way that they might talk about travelling to the Moon or signing up for a stint at one of the asteroid colonies.

Paulson knew he wasn't military material by any stretch of the imagination. A recruitment officer should take one look at his scrawny figure and muscles that could at best be described as "bookish," and laugh out loud before telling him to find a job as an accountant or librarian.

But libraries weren't hiring these days, and Paulson had no aptitude for accounting. With the increasing attacks by the alien Sluggos, however, the Earth Planetary Navy wasn't so picky.

His dismissive parents always told Paulson he was going nowhere, and now he had arrived—at nowhere. But now, as he held the EPN summons in his hand, he felt a chill. He would much rather be going nowhere than into the planetary navy. Only the most desperate of military forces would take a bottom-of-the-barrel recruit like him, and if the EPN was that desperate then the human race was in dire straits indeed.

Retreating into his small apartment, he thought about calling his friends or his parents, but he didn't think his voice was stable enough for conversation. The draft notice allowed for no appeal. He needed to think about this, but the more Paulson considered his fate, the more terrified he became. He had been aware of the horrific alien invaders that attacked helpless vessels in the Pacific, but since he lived in a farming city in the Midwest, with little local industry, automated agriculture, nothing to attract tourists, and very few job prospects, Paulson hadn't paid much attention to the Sluggos.

The notice commanded him to report to the training facility at the La Diego Naval Yards within three days.

The draft summons was legally binding and intimidating. The fine print said that any prior employment or contractual obligations were henceforth superseded. Payments and debts would be put on hold until the end of his EPN service.

Paulson read pages of instructions, a list of what to pack, and a helpful pamphlet on ways to prepare for this "exciting new phase" of his life. He fixated on a paragraph that advised him in the strongest possible terms to prepare a detailed Last Will and Testament before departing for the training facility. "Don't leave your family and loved ones with estate entanglements. Do the last brave thing in the event that you are unable to return home. A sailor in the Earth Planetary Navy must be prepared."

"I'll be prepared to die at sea," Paulson muttered. He didn't even know how to swim, but he supposed that wouldn't matter. If he fell overboard into a sea roiling with voracious Sluggos, treading water wasn't going to be much help.

Sitting alone in his apartment, glad that he had managed to get the power turned back on, he activated his entertainment and information screens to watch the news, which suddenly seemed relevant to him. A terrible nautical engagement and complete defeat had just occurred five hundred miles off the coast of Hawaii. Paulson felt physically ill as he saw the frantic jittery footage of creatures that seemed to be equal parts teeth and slime. The Sluggos swarmed across the deck of the destroyer that had engaged the alien infestation. Crewmen snarling, yelling in pain, sprays of blood, a tentacle the size of a redwood tree crashing down onto the *Far Horizon*, collapsing the bridge deck and communication mast and cutting off the transmission.

On the report, a tall young man with haunted-looking eyes wore a pristine white officer's uniform, his chest bedecked with so many medals and decorations that he had trouble standing up straight. He stood at a podium addressing hundreds of uniformed sailors who stood at attention. Hundreds of media reporters directed their imagers in the officer's direction.

"I am Admiral Bruce Haldane," he said, "and I recently survived the *Far Horizon* engagement. I've faced the Sluggos three times now, and I've watched them destroy brave sailors, wreck civilian ships as well as military vessels. I am convinced there can be no negotiating with these creatures."

Paulson thought he seemed arrogant.

"With my experience and insights, I promise to do my best to develop an effective strategy to defeat these alien monsters. No more sailors need to shed blood into the sea. I am humbled by the sacrifice of all those who died on the *Far Horizon,* as well as the volunteer who formerly inhabited this body." Haldane touched his own shoulders and chest, as if to reassure himself of where and who he was. "That man gave his life so I could stand before you today and vow my revenge against the aliens. Thanks to him, I can lead the EPN's retaliatory strike and wipe out those squirming bastards once and for all!"

Admiral Haldane raised a fist, but his movements were jerky and uncertain, as if he hadn't quite adjusted to his new body. It seemed to fit him like a stiff pair of new boots.

The crowd cheered regardless, and the media imagers captured the drawn and determined expressions on the sailors' faces as they vowed to avenge their fallen comrades.

Looking at the crowd of EPN seamen, Paulson could not picture himself as one of them, no matter what the draft notice said. He felt as if he had swallowed a hand grenade, and it was still in his stomach, ticking down the last few seconds. He couldn't run, couldn't escape the summons. He was DNA imprinted, and he had been chosen by a flawed lottery system: no exceptions. And he certainly couldn't argue that he was too valuable in civilian life.

He liked to read and ponder but had never found the ambition to acquire a philosophy degree (which, in itself, would not have led to a lucrative career). He was healthy enough, but only due to biological good fortune; he wasn't overweight, thanks to a natural metabolism. But he was sweating now, as if he had just run a marathon. Paulson didn't have many loose ends to tie up in his life, because he didn't have much of a life.

He had to figure out some way to get to the La Diego base. Because budgets were tight, and all finances had to be devoted to constructing new Navy warships and weapons against the Sluggos, Paulson Kenz had to pay his own way to the last place on Earth he wanted to go.

The naval training center was aswarm with new recruits, herded about by junior officers as if they were a separated mass of Sluggos in human form. The chatter of conversation in the giant intake hangar was deafening; announcements over loudspeakers were garbled and incomprehensible. The background noise seemed to increase each time important instructions were given. Paulson expected this routine would have been more organized under normal times, but the EPN was undergoing quite an upheaval as they increased their ranks tenfold in response to the invasion.

Paulson stood among other recruits, some of them shiny-eyed and eager, jabbering with nervous enthusiasm. They pounded one another on the back, laughing and trying to outdo any braggadocio from their comrades. Paulson knew about such attitudes: patriotic young men and women ready to go off and kick some enemy butt. Most often that didn't turn out as planned. Some came home in body bags, others were lost forever. And the ones who did return were haunted for the rest of their lives.

Oddly, with so many disorganized people and so much chaos, the bureaucratic machinery hummed smoothly. Everyone flashed ID access cards and passed through human inventory kiosks into gigantic hangars where lines queued up, snaking around pedestals. Personnel Specialists studied each person that flowed into the larger base.

Paulson was confused and anxious, but he followed the person ahead of him, and he listened to instructions. When yeoman ran a quick gaze over him, studied his ID chip, then sent him into corpsman scan lines, he cooperated. He tried to keep his expression meek (which wasn't difficult at all). The intake officers studied the records displayed on their screens, narrowed their eyes, and frowned at him, then directed Paulson into a different line. Each time he met with more skepticism, was directed into a smaller line. He could tell he was being winnowed out.

They took blood samples and urine samples; they breathalyzed him; they performed a digital rectal examination, then a dental examination (mercifully changing gloves in between). They fitted a mesh hood around his scalp and took a brain scan. They gave him vision tests, and then they clucked at all the results.

One nurse who looked as if she had retired from a Valkyrie squad loomed over him, knitting her eyebrows together. She turned to the yeoman at her side and spoke loudly enough to be sure Paulson heard her, "I thought we hit the bottom of the barrel last week."

"Sorry," Paulson said. "If you'd like to excuse me from service, I'll understand."

The Valkyrie-nurse gave him such an intense glare that his

scrotal sac shriveled to the size of a prune, even though he had already been thoroughly checked for hernias.

"No one's excused," she said. "If nothing else, you'll do as cannon fodder."

—III—

Day by day, Admiral Bruce Haldane was growing accustomed to the new body, and he certainly had no time to waste. Fortunately, the volunteer had kept himself in good shape. The body was adequate, with a good frame, well-toned muscles. He was even handsome, in a way. Haldane was growing accustomed to what he saw in the mirror. Instead of being startled, he took the time to study his features, the dark hair, heavy eyebrows, the boyish expression of an innocent young recruit who had seen little horror in his life. But Haldane's eyes looked out from the face, and *he* had seen enough of war in the last few months.

Previously, his career had been soft and dull, but the Sluggos changed all that.

The volunteer's name had been Aaron Shelty, a seaman-apprentice who seemed a perfectly reasonable recruit for the Earth Planetary Navy, but he must have been a coward, because he refused to sign up for actual combat duty. *Too many people have grown as soft as the Sluggos*, Haldane thought.

After the mind transfer, Haldane had glanced through Shelty's dossier, looking at his grades, his performance in basic training. Everything seemed normal. Haldane couldn't understand why the man would sign up as cannon fodder. Shelty had left behind a fiancée, but she was young and pretty; she would find someone else before long. Shelty had parents and a sister, and they would all receive a compassionate and carefully-worded letter thanking them for Mr. Shelty's sacrifice aboard the *Far Horizon*. Haldane certainly appreciated the gesture, otherwise he would have died aboard the destroyer rather than his replacement.

It must have seemed like a good bargain when young Shelty had signed up for the program. The young man had gambled—whether through laziness or cowardice Haldane didn't know—that nothing would happen to Admiral Haldane. And the gamble had backfired on Shelty.

But Haldane benefited, and therefore the EPN benefited, and therefore the human race benefited. The admiral was alive, and he still had his expertise. The Earth Navy could count on him.

Yes, he was glad for Aaron Shelty's sacrifice, but was that sacrifice any more dramatic or extraordinary than that of all those seamen who had died, devoured or crushed under the onslaught of the alien slugs? Haldane didn't think so. Every person needed to do his or her duty, and Haldane needed to do his, even if it meant he had to swap bodies at the last minute and let the old body die on the battlefield. The war depended on him, and so it was worth the hassle.

Haldane looked in the mirror again, ran his fingers through the dark hair, made different expressions as he practiced the movement of his facial muscles. Yes, this body would do. Maybe he'd even pay a visit to Shelty's pretty fiancée. Now wouldn't *that* be a surprise!

But he didn't have time for that. There was a war on. After all the alien creatures were wiped out, however …

Unless something terrible happened again to him on the battlefield.

This time, the shock of the body transfer hadn't been as dramatic as when his original body was killed, when he'd been forced in that awful last second of indecision to push the transfer button on the implanted pendant, to give up his actual physical form, the one that had emerged from his mother's womb, the one he'd lived with all his life. But during the explosions, the firefight, and the horrific swarming Sluggos, after watching so many uniformed men and women torn to pieces around him, the decision hadn't been so difficult after all.

New body, same old job. He was back at EPN Headquarters in the La Diego main base, briefing world leaders, requesting new ships, more armaments, more depth pulsers, and an expanded fleet to attack the Sluggos.

As he drove in that morning, two Marines had tried to stop him at the outer gate. Though he had a new ID, the system had not updated his fingerprints, photographs, and DNA scans. Haldane made three increasingly angry calls until revised credentials were transmitted back to the guard shack.

After the *Far Horizon* tragedy, he had delivered his grand speech in this new body. Didn't they recognize him? Everyone on Earth should have seen the images of how the destroyer had been torn apart and sunk, all hands lost. How could these Marines not recognize Admiral Haldane's new body? He hated to be reminded that he wasn't as famous as he believed himself to be. Earth itself was under attack! Why wasn't every human being glued to their media and entertainment screens? Didn't they know that the fate of their planet was at stake?

After the fiasco at the guard shack, he finally made it to his office. As he entered, he still met the questioning stares, the double-takes from his staff as they tried to readjust to his new appearance. The admiral's uniform had been altered, but the rank insignia and nameplate were transferred over, same as before. Haldane was still himself, with his demeanor, his facial expressions. They would have to get used to it.

He sat behind his large desk and called up the day's intel reports of aerial flyovers and deep-water scans. His chief of staff, Ms. Tenn, entered the office and stood before his desk, running her eyes up and down his face and uniform. "I have your calendar, sir. If there's anything you need, please let me know."

"I need concentration time to reassess these images. Is there full documentation regarding new intel on the Sluggos? I need to plan our next strategy. There's some piece missing, and because I have the most experience, I'm the one to find it."

"It's all here, sir." Tenn leaned over the desk to activate Haldane's screen, calling up the messages he needed and spreading them out so he could sort and review them in whatever order he chose.

She brought him his usual bitter black coffee, but when he took a sip, it tasted strange. "Are you using a different blend, Lieutenant? Or does the brewer need cleaning?"

"No, Admiral. Same as always."

"Taste it."

He pushed the cup toward her, and she dutifully took a sip. "Tastes awful, sir, just like always."

Haldane shook his head. "Must be these new taste buds. Bring me a variety of coffees, lattes, cappuccinos, espressos. I need to sample them until I find one that tastes right on Aaron Shelty's tongue. Can't do my work without caffeine."

"Certainly, Admiral." She departed.

Haldane took another gulp of the bitter brew, struggled to swallow it, then pushed the cup away. That wouldn't do at all, and the inconvenience was troublesome. He'd have to compile a more detailed dossier about the next volunteer waiting in the wings. Shelty had passed all the required tests and his brain scan had been a match for Haldane's, but no one had thought to ask about his favorite foods or drinks. The admiral made a note of that.

On the screen, he called up the new messages. The Sluggos were damned difficult to locate under the water, but they were such a huge mass, millions of them writhing together, spreading out, moving like a gigantic school of fish. Each time sonar bursts tried to pinpoint the location of the main mass, the swarm faded away and reappeared elsewhere. As soon as the mass of Sluggos was spotted, attack aircraft would drop explosives, which would kill a lot of fish and individual Sluggos—thus the military scientists had plenty of specimens, but very few answers. Even after the most horrendous explosions, though, the main Sluggo body would reappear and continue to attack.

All the EPN efforts thus far had only pissed off the squirming invaders, but Haldane wasn't going to use that as an excuse to relent. Even ineffective explosions were far superior—from a PR standpoint if nothing else—to letting the Sluggos do whatever they liked. The aliens had not proven to be good neighbors.

As humans expanded into the solar system, no one found any evidence of ancient Martian races or prehistoric Venusians, no Selenites under the craters of the Moon, no civilizations under the ice sheets of Europa, no bizarre creatures drifting among the asteroids.

No one knew where the Sluggos came from. Their ships were detected at the edge of the solar system by bored teams of asteroid mappers, but no one noticed their speed or incoming trajectory until the invaders had almost reached Earth orbit. Though the human military scrambled, the metallic teardrop ships hammered into the atmosphere like shotgun pellets and plunged into the Pacific Ocean.

Ships were dispatched to the area to see if they could find wreckage of the alien vessels, while news pundits demanded rescue efforts. Subs and diving bells went down to the crashed ships to save the benevolent alien visitors before they drowned. (Even then,

Admiral Haldane knew it was a brash notion to assume that any alien visitor would breathe air instead of water.)

Considering the size of the alien ships, they should have been easy to find even in the deep water, but sonar detected nothing. The vessels seemed to have vaporized on impact.

The first attack struck a far-ranging Japanese whaler, the *Dragon Pearl*. The terrified crew transmitted images and distress signals, wailing for help as squirming conglomerate tentacles rose out of the water to smash the decks. After the initial horror subsided, Haldane thought that the scenes reminded him of a clip from a bad low-budget Japanese giant monster movie, some horrific rubber behemoth rising from the sea to toss about a toy model of a boat.

But the destruction of the *Dragon Pearl* was real, the Sluggos were real, and the alien mass had attacked other cargo ships, an oil tanker (causing great consternation among environmentalists who insisted that the resultant spill was a greater threat to Earth than the alien invasion), and even a large cruise ship—all passengers and crew slaughtered on formal night. Recovered surveillance cameras showed frantic, swanky passengers trying to flee in their fancy tuxedos or slinky cocktail gowns and high heels.

Admiral Haldane had led the first unsuccessful responses against the aliens, embarrassed because he couldn't even find the Sluggos. When he finally did locate the enemy, they had destroyed his ship, killed his crew, and forced him to evacuate into a different body.

But he was the first one to notice that the Sluggos were pulling some equipment down into the water after destroying the ships, as if they meant to use the components, metals, antennae, even some of the weapons pieces.

The *Far Horizon* had been the Earth Planetary Navy's most heavily armed destroyer, and that too had been utterly destroyed, but Haldane did not feel defeated. He was back again in a new body, and he would continue to fight—although if he continued to die during engagements against the enemy, it would look bad on his record.

Ms. Tenn returned carrying a tray with seven cups of various coffee drinks. "I brought you a variety of options, sir. One of these should do."

"Thank you, Lieutenant," he said, then had a horrible thought.

"God, I hope Shelty wasn't a tea drinker." He decided to be methodical about his testing. He closed all the records displayed on his screen. He would review them later.

Haldane fingered the implanted pendant at the base of his skull. Sooner or later he would go out on another brutal engagement. He couldn't put this off. "Ms. Tenn, I want you to go through recruiting records so we can prepare for the worst-case scenario. This body is certainly adequate, but there's no telling what might happen to me. Find me a new volunteer."

—IV—

Boot camp was hell—and Paulson meant that literally, as well as figuratively. (Yes, he did know the proper usage of the term.)

Throughout his life, Paulson was always the last person picked for any team sports activity. He played a good game of archaic chess, but no one considered that a "sport," despite his protestations. Any activity that required coordination, speed, strength, or other physical prowess was not his forte. He had done a good job as a statistician, however. When he suggested that he be considered for such a role in the EPN, the training officer simply scowled at Paulson as if he were a form of nematode even lower than the Sluggos.

Because the alien invasion was now of immediate relevance to him, Paulson wanted to spend every spare minute scouring information about the alien invaders infesting Earth's oceans, but that plan quickly went out the porthole. All day long, the training officer tortured the recruits, forced them to do appalling exercises, tested their endurance. He did his best to kill every single trainee through exhaustion, screaming muscles, and cardiac failure before they had a chance to confront their first Sluggo.

Paulson struggled to memorize the rank system of the Earth Planetary Navy—no, EPN called it a *rating* system, just to make it more confusing, he supposed. He struggled to understand who outranked (or was it outrated?) whom. As a practical matter, it made no difference, since as a seaman-recruit, Paulson Kenz was lower than absolutely everyone. Even among the trainees who had been inducted on the same day, Paulson's performance set him apart—and beneath them all.

Inside the gigantic hangars, the recruits marched in ranks, drilling like robots, following nonsensical orders—moving back and forth, side to side, and around in circles, as if that sort of regimented pageantry would impress the alien hordes.

Paulson was in the lowest pay grade, but had no opportunity to spend what he earned. He was too sore, too exhausted, and too miserable to read in the evenings. He felt nauseated, so he couldn't even eat the ill-seasoned chow they fed recruits. It seemed a sort of irony—perhaps intentional, perhaps a coincidence—that they had to eat seafood for every meal. Paulson plunged a fork into his fish sticks with a vengeance, as if attacking a surrogate Sluggo.

His fellow recruits sat together, growling as they watched footage of the carnivorous slug creatures massacring Earth Navy ships. Some of the pale recruits whimpered in terror and recorded desperate messages for their sweethearts, but Paulson was simply too weary, wrung-out, and broken. He didn't know how he would get through another day.

If he ever did face a mass of Sluggos, he would be too bruised, battered, and weary even to lift a sidearm.

The next day was worse, and so was the day after that. The training officer was trying to toughen them up. The recruits practiced in the shooting range, trying to bull's-eye holographic Sluggos and receiving points for each kill. Paulson proved to be a poor marksman in every respect, although his score improved when they gave him scattershot guns. Paulson fired so many pellets in so many directions that he couldn't help but hit some of the aliens.

"You're lucky," the training officer said. "If the Sluggos attack, there'll be so many of them even you'll be able to cause some damage."

Paulson shuddered. Yes, that made him feel very lucky indeed.

Some of the recruits called the storm tank *fun*—the psychopathic recruits, as far as Paulson was concerned. The training tank simulated a storm-swept sea, cold churning waves complete with whitecaps. The recruits were thrown into the tank and told to struggle their way to a rescue buoy. Once they reached the buoy, they had to key in a safety code and solve some sort of puzzle before they could be retrieved from the freezing water and blowing winds.

Paulson could barely keep himself above the surface, flailing his hands, going under, inhaling water and then coughing it up.

Simulated rain splashed his face so he couldn't see, but he felt stinging ice crystals. He shivered uncontrollably. He kicked his feet and tried to swim, but his sodden uniform was heavy and dragged him down. He could make out the other sailors reaching the rescue buoy, completing their tasks, and being yanked out by hover slings. Paulson couldn't do it, though. He went under, struggled back to the surface for a deep breath, and saw that he was drifting farther from the buoy. Even if he made it, he certainly couldn't remember the safety code. At the moment, he couldn't even remember his name.

He drowned during the exercise, one of three failures in the group.

But they revived him, and Paulson rolled over onto his hands and knees, retching onto the deck. He was still wet, freezing, miserable. All his muscles ached. His mouth tasted like vomit and seawater.

The training officer stood there, arms crossed over his chest, shaking his head. "Even a turd knows how to float. You're dumber than a turd. A complete and utter disgrace."

Paulson wasn't going to argue. He sucked a lungful of air and croaked, "I wouldn't want to do anything halfway, Sarge. Glad I'm not only a partial disgrace."

The training officer was not amused. On his pad he called up Paulson's records, then frowned to spot a fresh set of urgent high-priority orders.

"I'm just not cut out to be a seaman, sir," Paulson said.

The training officer roared, "Don't call me 'sir'! You don't deserve to call me 'sir,' turd!"

"Sorry," Paulson said. "It's all so confusing."

The training officer turned the pad around, showing Paulson's brain scan and a high-priority request from Admiral Bruce Haldane himself. "You see that, turd? You're a match—for better or worse, though I don't know why the admiral would accept someone like you. I can't force this decision on you, but I can offer to transfer you."

"I ... I don't know what you're talking about."

"Of course you don't, turd. You don't need to know. But here's something you actually *can* do—I suggest you take it."

When he met Admiral Haldane, Paulson recognized the man who had delivered the speech honoring the sacrifice of those who had lost their lives on the *Far Horizon*. In earlier media glimpses, Paulson had also seen images of Admiral Haldane's previous incarnation. This new version seemed younger, taller, less salty, but the hard expression was the same, as was the swagger of his movements ... and of course the nameplate on his chest beneath all the medals.

Haldane did not seem to be impressed. "You're the volunteer."

"Seaman-recruit Paulson Kenz, sir." He saluted, then hesitated, considered his words, and realized that 'sir' was indeed appropriate in this circumstance.

"You realize what you're being asked to do, seaman?"

"No, sir. No one's briefed me at all."

Haldane shot a glare at his chief of staff, a female officer who stood looking as prim as a mannequin in a department store window. "Sorry, Admiral, he must have slipped through the cracks. Seaman Kenz, you are being offered a chance to be Admiral Haldane's next alternate-in-waiting. We would like to install an interchange conduit at the base of your skull, which is linked to an identical one in the admiral's head."

Haldane turned, showed Paulson the implanted disc at the base of his skull.

"The admiral has a great deal of direct experience and innate knowledge about our enemy, about the tactics used by and against them. Such knowledge cannot be lost, nor can it be replaced. Therefore, the Earth Planetary Navy has developed extraordinary measures to preserve that brain trust—and you will help us do it."

"You mean, I'm going to become cannon fodder?" Paulson said.

"That is an inaccurate term," Haldane said. "The Sluggos don't use cannons."

"Why would I want to do that?" Paulson asked. "If you get in trouble, then I'll die, right?"

"That's a big 'if,' seaman. Until recently, I lived my entire life without dying, and I've learned a great deal with each successive engagement against the enemy. I believe we come closer to finding the key to their ultimate defeat with each encounter."

"In the meantime," Tenn interrupted, "you will be excused from any dangerous duty, any further training, any military drills. You'll have a comfortable existence. You'll be given quarters, food, and very few responsibilities. It's a cushy job, Seaman Kenz. You wait to be called up and hope you won't be. If you agree to be the admiral's alternate-in-waiting, then that will be your only duty for the duration of your contracted service."

Haldane seemed annoyed at the situation. "In other words, you just sit around and read or play games, although you're expected to keep yourself in shape." He raised his arms, flexed his muscles. "The previous owner of this body did a good job, and we'll count on the same from you. Are you willing to take the gamble? You're my escape hatch so I can live to fight another day." He paused, added a greater threat to his tone. "Your other alternative is to go back to boot camp and be put on the next ship, where you'll face an engagement of the Sluggos. In person."

Paulson swallowed hard. He'd seen the images of the *Far Horizon* massacre, listened to the howling crew, saw the chomping teeth of the Sluggos. He had watched how the aliens moved in eerie concert, forming a gigantic organism that was far more ferocious than the sum of its parts.

The decision wasn't hard for him.

"I accept, sir. It's a gamble, but it's really my only option. If I get out there facing those things as *me*, I know I won't survive." Paulson fingered the back of his head, felt the smooth hardness of his skull. He supposed the surgery was going to hurt. "I'll take my chances with you."

—V—

It came from beneath the sea.

The next time the mass of Sluggos appeared, they did not prey upon navy ships patrolling the open seas; rather, the new conglomerate monster rose up out of Pearl Harbor and attacked land for the first time.

Tour boats and naval patrol ships spotted the incoming surge, but no one understood what was happening at first. Hundreds of thousands of Sluggos swam in individually like the world's entire population of eels meeting in Hawaii for a convention. The arm-length creatures glided in under the surface, choking the channels, filling the harbor.

Tourist boats were buffeted by the swarms of soft shapes with sharp teeth. Naval destroyers, missile cruisers, fast frigates, and even a huge old battleship were brought to bear. General Quarters sounded and the crew raced to their stations. The dockyards were put on high alert.

The squirming wormlike things choked the harbor, but that was just a start. The Sluggo bodies coalesced, braiding together, building up like pieces in a gigantic wriggly mosaic sculpture—until a huge and hideous monster rose out of the sea.

Rushing down to the harbor from his satellite headquarters office, Admiral Haldane screamed for fishing boats and salvage cutters to string nets that would stop the numerous individual Sluggos from joining one another, but it was too late. The things became a gigantic mound of squirming flesh, as if a mad artist had made a nightmare sculpture out of living maggots. The Sluggo mass extruded pseudopods and began smashing any vessel in the harbor.

Admiral Haldane had been sent to Oahu, not for a tropical vacation but to organize the EPN Pacific Fleet's plan to dispatch numerous search-and-destroy subs that would find the Sluggos. Unfortunately, the alien monsters decided to be found right there on the Earth Navy's doorstep.

Pearl Harbor was full of navy ships, tourist boats, and cargo barges hauling goods in lightweight crates for launch at the Honolulu Spaceport. Like a child playing with toys in a bathtub, the conglomerate Sluggo monster crawled over vessels and pushed them under the water, crushing their hulls and sinking them. Other pseudopods snatched desirable equipment and whisked it away beneath the surface.

Admiral Haldane dispatched fighter jets loaded with missiles. As the giant monster hulked its way on top of the floating museum battleships and onto shore, the roaring jets launched missiles that blasted the huge monster, dispersing it into countless squirming Sluggos that sprayed in all directions. But the monstrous mass shuffled and reorganized itself somewhere else, heading toward the rocket launch area of the spaceport.

Haldane didn't like this one bit. "Let's try napalm. We must have some left over."

Tenn called up summaries on her datapad. "None of the new formula is weaponized yet, sir, but there may be some old leftovers in storage."

"Never let anything go to waste," Haldane said. "We might as well use it up."

"There's plenty of fuel spilled on the water from all those damaged ships, sir. Igniting that could be effective as well."

"Good idea. Let's do both."

The EPN battleships launched huge sprays of missiles, and the sky became a messy finger-painting of smoke, mostly from damaged structures, exploding naval ships, even one crashed jet when the Sluggo-beast had thrashed an unexpectedly whip-thin and long tentacle into the air to snatch and crush the plane, before hurling it onto the deck of a snorkeling cruise boat just being loaded with a senior citizens' tour group.

The Sluggos moved like an enormous blob, rising up to capsize cutters. Large-caliber artillery guns hammered away at the mass, destroying thousands of individual Sluggos, but the overall monster did not seem affected.

"Open the weapons lockers," Haldane yelled. "Distribute weapons to anyone who won't turn and run. Rifles, shrapnel pulsers, peashooters—I don't care."

"We may have a shortage of peashooters sir," Tenn said.

"That was a joke, Lieutenant."

"Very funny, sir."

Haldane thought this might be a war of attrition: humanity just needed to kill off enough of the individual Sluggos, which were easily destroyed. But the supply of squirming aliens seemed inexhaustible.

Out in the harbor, a group of sailors were making a last stand with rifles and hand grenades. No one could understand how all those little maggot things could work together to create a single massive and apparently intelligent organism. They kept tearing apart ships, stealing components. Haldane knew the aliens had built starships that had carried them to Earth from some other solar system.

But how did these silly little worms know what to do when they were linked together? A million humans certainly couldn't cooperate like that. Often it was hard to get three people to agree.

More light bombers roared overhead, dropping explosives, including cannisters of old napalm. The intensely hot flames from the jellied gasoline crisped the outer layers of squirming worms. They blackened and fell away, but new Sluggos boiled up to take their places. More and more Sluggos streamed into the harbor from the open sea, adding themselves to the monster's bulky conglomerate body. Even after so many individual aliens were destroyed, the overall bulk swelled.

The pseudopods extended outward, moving the mass away from the naval ships to the reserved spaceport area. The Sluggos snatched tall gantries and pulled rocket shuttles and girder structures down off the launch pads. The squirming creatures dragged those components into the water of the harbor.

Haldane shouted orders because he was expected to, but no one could hear him in the deafening noise. The oddest part was that the giant alien monster moved in silence. It simply created havoc without adding any extraterrestrial commentary.

Haldane considered calling in a nuclear strike. Oahu was beautiful, but there were other islands in the Pacific. And if it took such an extreme measure to get rid of the Sluggos once and for all, despite the loss of the entire population, including himself ...

He had grown fond of his new body from Aaron Shelty and didn't want to use the escape hatch too soon, especially now that he had seen the alternative-in-waiting, the scrawny slip of a man named Paulson Kenz. But Haldane couldn't think of himself at a time like this.

The tentacles broke the keel of an aircraft carrier that had entered the harbor, and that was enough to force Haldane's decision. He was really getting upset now. Yes, he had to call in a nuclear strike for the good of humanity.

Before he could issue the order, though, a slimy tentacle burst out of the water right at the shore's edge and swept all of them aside, including Admiral Haldane. He found himself flying through the air, flailing. Another series of explosions roared nearby.

He shouldn't have waited! He grabbed for the back of his head, trying to find the transfer pendant. Others were sailing through the air near him, screaming, bloody, broken.

There! He found the pendant. Emergency transfer with the volunteer—

But then Haldane slammed into the side of a boat house, splintering the shingles. The pain was brief, the unconsciousness swift.

This time, he doubted he would live to fight another day....

He awoke in the medevac hovercopter along with a dozen other broken and bleeding casualties. Haldane felt as if someone had made kindling of his ribs and spine. A corpsman hunched over him, poking and prodding until he got the proper response to his question of "Does that hurt?" Other doctors tended the wounded.

"I see by your insignia that you're an admiral," said the corpsman.

"I am, dammit!" As much blood came out as words. He could tell this was bad. He tried to lift his hands, but his arms were strapped down. "Help me. I'm Admiral Bruce Haldane. I need to activate my exchange pendant."

"Sorry, sir, I can't let you move. There could be internal damage."

Haldane was appalled. The corpsman didn't understand what was going on here. "I don't care about my injuries! Before I die, I need to transfer." He began coughing again and felt the warm blood on his lips.

"Good news for you, then, sir—you're not going to die. Just rest easy. You suffered some broken ribs, a shattered clavicle, probably a severe concussion. But our deep scans show no obvious internal bleeding. We just want to be careful."

"So I'm going to ... recover?" Haldane said. That shouldn't have been disappointing.

"Looks like it. We'll patch you up." The corpsman looked shell-shocked; his expression was gray. "You're one of the lucky ones. Over fifty percent fatality rate from the monster attack. They'll be a long time counting up the casualties. I think ..." He shook his head. "... I think Pearl Harbor is gone. Half of Honolulu is gone. Fires are raging. The Sluggos sank most of our fleet, destroyed the spaceport, then they withdrew."

"Is there any good news?" Haldane asked.

"I just told it to you. The Sluggos departed, slithering back into the ocean. That's the best news you'll hear."

"Oh."

"That, and the fact that you're going to live. Should be enough good news for the day, right, sir?"

The corpsman shot him full of sedative. As he sank down, Admiral Haldane knew he would be a long-time healing, which was upsetting. Thankfully he could keep this body, even though it was going to hurt like hell when he woke up. At least he wouldn't be a 90-pound weakling.

—VI—

Even with the tension that was always in the back of Paulson's mind, his daily duties here—as in, no useful duties whatsoever, only busy work so the EPN could feel confident in their investment— certainly beat basic training. Instead of being aboard a ship hunting for voracious alien monsters, his duty station was a giant rec room.

The surgery to install the transfer pendant was as unpleasant as he'd feared: having a hole drilled in the back of his head, a sensor plug and transmitter installed with a million self-seeking wires plunging into his brain, where it found the core of personality and memories. The exchange conduit would tear out, record, and transmit everything that was Paulson Kenz, then re-upload the very being of Admiral Bruce Haldane—in the event that circumstances warranted it. Paulson kept his fingers crossed and hoped.

Paulson had healed up after the quick coagulant slather, and the pain meds had been nice until they ran out (budget cuts, with all the best stuff reserved for any EPN soldiers wounded in combat).

There were fifteen other volunteers inside the guarded recreation hall. They were forced to remain in the La Diego base, but it wasn't so bad. All fifteen of them had the exchange conduit installed in their heads, tethered to other command officers or political leaders who were deemed too valuable to lose.

Two volunteers played ping-pong, but neither was very good at it. One man, who had already put on fifteen pounds, placed orders from the galley and ate all day long. Paulson knew the food was not at all tasty, but at least the quantity was comforting. Just this afternoon, though, a dietician had come in, to take control over the man's eating habits, and advise (as well as enforce) nutritious meals. "You are required to take care of your body," the dietician said in a decidedly threatening voice, "in case it should be needed."

The volunteers seemed to have a free ride, but they were obligated to take care of themselves. Although *they*, as individuals, weren't important, their bodies were considered vital to planetary defense, and the navy had made a considerable investment in them. Some volunteers took the task seriously and worked out in the fitness center, lifting weights, jogging on the treadmill. Paulson did the required calisthenics, but he had never seen the purpose in picking up heavy things and putting them back down again, or running on a piece of equipment that went nowhere.

He remembered how his parents had told him *he* was going nowhere, that he spent too much time reading, paying little attention to practical things. They had been right, according to their own definitions. Now, they were probably proud of him for being a part of the brave Earth Planetary Navy. If he were called upon to provide the mortal escape hatch for Admiral Haldane, they would be pleased as punch to tell their neighbors about how their good-for-nothing son had become a war hero.

Paulson didn't feel particularly brave. Any heroic end on his part would be completely out of his hands. Most of his fellow volunteers had resigned themselves to an imminent and unpleasant demise, grabbing as much life as they could in the meantime, playing games, horsing around, sleeping in. Several had written up a petition demanding access to a military-approved escort service, and that request was currently working its way up the chain of command.

Paulson was the only one who cared about the war against the Sluggos, and about increasing his chances for survival, as well as the rest of humanity's, in a worst-case scenario. Because he was cerebrally paired with Admiral Haldane, he requested access to the briefings on the invasion and records of prior Sluggo attacks, in hopes of teasing out any vulnerabilities. He studied news reports, although the most detailed, and most gruesome, footage was missing.

He requested additional intel, including the full classified reports, but since he was just a seaman-recruit, with the lowest possible security clearance, his request was summarily denied. So he submitted an appeal, documenting that he was the functional physical equivalent of Admiral Haldane, that his body—and therefore the structure of his brain—would be used by the leader of the Earth Planetary Navy. Therefore, any information might be beneficial, should the admiral be forced to swap bodies with him. Paulson also pointed out that if the admiral ever did activate the transfer protocol, Paulson himself would be rapidly devoured by aliens, and therefore all secrets would be safe.

The yeoman, who was harried and overworked, didn't entirely understand the nuances of the argument, but rather than risk annoying the real Admiral Haldane, he bumped the request up the chain. Somehow, it got approved. Accidentally, Paulson supposed.

In the rec hall/prison, he spent hours poring over the records, watching the movements of the Sluggos through the water during the rare times they were tracked. But whenever sonar rigs tried to track the large conglomeration, the entire mass vanished like a puff of smoke. Maybe they just dissociated into a million little worms again, invisible to sonar traces.

The EPN knew about where the alien invaders lived beneath the Pacific, a broad, general area where their starships must have landed. Supposedly, that was where their base might be.

He studied biological reports of the creatures. Many Sluggo specimens had been dissected, individual nematode-like things that had very little physical structure. Each Sluggo was just a sac with a few rudimentary organs, a digestive system, and a mouth with sharp teeth, but no eyes or other obvious sensory apparatus, not even a brain, just a small nerve cluster.

It made no sense that these things could combine into some gigantic entity that obviously had a structure and a purpose and was presumably intelligent. The Sluggos used tools, they built machinery, constructed spacecraft, and flew interstellar distances. Not bad for a bunch of hungry worms.

In the specimen tanks or dissection trays, they didn't look any more sophisticated than extraterrestrial leeches. When Sluggos moved en masse in the water, they looked like a gigantic school of fish, somehow moving with one mind. He shook his head.

Then the pendant at the base of his skull began to tingle.

The rec hall around him fuzzed. The ringing in his ears grew as loud as church bells, and he wavered. Other volunteers in the rec hall looked up, sensing something amiss.

"It's happening!"

This was too soon! He wasn't ready. No one had even told him Admiral Haldane was going out to fight with the Sluggos. It would have been nice to have a little more warning.

He felt as if his soul were rushing down a wind tunnel. He left his body, yelling—but without making any sound.

And when he woke up he was somewhere else, inside a different body. And he screamed in agony. He felt shattered bones, torn muscles, a bashed head, nerves that clamored about all the bodily damage. He tried to open his eyes, but he was surrounded by white blurs, moving faces. Doctors? If he was going to die, he wished he could at least stomp on one or two Sluggos first.

Then the pain was too much, and he faded into unconsciousness.

⚛

He awoke to find his own face staring down at him.

Paulson recognized himself, saw the body at the bedside—*am I really that scrawny?*—but realized that the eyes were different. Then the pain hit him again, so he wished he hadn't woken up. The agony was somewhat diminished from before, and he was a little foggier. He could feel painkillers like slimy, wet velvet working through his mind and body, but he could also feel the physical damage. He knew this body was mangled.

This wasn't his body in the first place ... so many things didn't feel right. Meanwhile, Paulson watched his own body pacing back and forth in the infirmary room, studying the medical equipment and monitors that provided a discordant symphony of bleeps. His own face turned toward him, and in all his life of looking at himself in a mirror, he had never seen his expression show such disapproval before.

And his reflected image had never talked back to him, either. "Good to see that you're awake. I need to explain the situation, and then be off to a briefing." His voice sounded funny.

Paulson croaked in a rough voice, "You're not dead." This had to be Admiral Haldane. The vocal cords weren't his own, and the tone sounded wrong in his head. His throat was sore—he must have been yelling or screaming before the swap.

"I was badly injured during the battle of Pearl Harbor. I thought I was a goner there for a while, and I almost used the transfer during the worst part, but I got walloped before I had the chance."

Paulson's body shrugged. Admiral Haldane touched his new shoulders, felt the bones there, encircled his wrist with thumb and forefinger. He clucked. "You really need to take better care of yourself, Kenz. Put on a few pounds, preferably muscle."

"I'll leave that up to you now, sir," Paulson said.

"This transfer is just temporary while that body heals," Haldane retorted. "The doctors said I was going to live, but the recovery would be hard and painful. I don't have time for that bullshit—there's a war on. And then I thought, what do I have *you* for? Now, you just lie there and heal. It's the least you can do in service to your country and your planet."

Haldane leaned over the infirmary bed and prodded the bandages in Paulson's side. Paulson gasped, nearly fainted from the rush of pain that exploded through him. Haldane continued. "A few broken ribs, lots of bruises, stitches in a half-dozen places. Oh, and they removed your spleen, but you can do without that. When was the last time you used your spleen?"

"Never noticed it before, sir," Paulson said, trying to be stoic.

"The medics are pumping you full of accelerated cell growth. Your body's got so many bruises all over that your skin has natural camouflage. But that'll heal. The bones will heal. The physical therapy is going to be rough, but you can handle it. I don't have time—I have meetings."

Paulson lay back and just felt the aches piled upon aches. He had dreaded being called upon to transfer with the admiral, but this, he supposed, was the best realistic scenario. He was still alive. He could lie here and recover in the admiral's place, as he asked.

And whenever the fuzzy painkillers wore off, maybe the EPN would even provide him with a reading library so he could catch up on some of the books he'd meant to read.

"Be quick about it healing," Admiral Haldane said, before turning around. "I'll want that body back again as soon as you've fixed it."

—VII—

Something about the scrawny body of Paulson Kenz inspired disrespect despite the medals and rank insignia on the uniform. Kenz was bookish, shy, the sort of person who simply begged to have beach sand kicked in his face by a bully of even modest proportions.

The more days Admiral Haldane lived inside the other body, the more he noticed the subtle attitude shifts toward him.

When the admiral entered the La Diego base headquarters, he carried his revised ID and temporary access cards, with Paulson's fingerprints and retina map transferred over to his diagnostics records. It was just a temporary situation, though, since he expected to swap back to his preferred body as soon as the damaged one was healed in sick bay.

Previously, Admiral Haldane's very presence had inspired instant deference, but in Paulson's body he had to work at it. As he marched down the passageway, a pair of junior officers strolled by, engrossed in conversation and paying little attention to him. Annoyed, Haldane placed himself directly in their path so that they were forced to look up and notice his insignia and name badge. They scrambled to give the proper salute accompanied by hasty apologies.

Haldane walked on, not entirely satisfied. War was all about sacrifices, he supposed. He could endure this one.

It wasn't just the fact that he felt physically weak, that he grew winded after climbing only five flights of stairs, that simple acts such as opening a pickle jar or carrying a box of classified printouts to the shredder were more difficult. He didn't like the way he looked when he took a shower, couldn't imagine suavely trying to pick up a woman in a bar or, even more embarrassing, taking her home where he would have to make bedroom excuses: "This isn't really my natural body. My normal endowment is much more impressive." He could already imagine the seen-it-all-before looks of skepticism....

He was still trying to get his office in order, breaking in a new chief of staff, since his adjutant Ms. Tenn had been inconveniently killed during the Sluggo attack on Pearl Harbor. Her death had caused innumerable problems.

In his office, the interim replacement had brought him the morning coffee, a cinnamon cappuccino which, after thorough testing, was what Haldane and Ms. Tenn had determined best suited his Aaron Shelty taste buds. He gave a grunt of thanks and sipped the coffee as he sat down—but it tasted awful. He had forgotten. Paulson Kenz's body preferred something else entirely. Haldane growled in his throat and drank the cinnamon cappuccino anyway, forcing it down because he simply didn't want to bother to get it done right.

He had work to do and a world to save.

The morning's reports made the day seem much brighter. He studied the new images and grinned, then he immediately called together his highest-level advisors.

The briefing room was full of high-ranking EPN officers, prominent politicians, and even businessmen in charge of massive amounts of funding—all the important people who could make the proper decisions without the delay of red tape. The secure conference room felt like a cave; the original design had been to evoke the comfortable camaraderie of an exclusive gentlemen's club.

"Gentlemen," Haldane said, before nodding toward the lone female in the room, "and ma'am. We have wonderful and fascinating intelligence—our reconnaissance has finally borne fruit!" In his ears, Kenz's voice sounded squeaky.

The lights in the briefing room dimmed further as he displayed images on the wall screens.

"With the attack on Pearl Harbor, the Sluggos showed their real intent. They are going to infest our oceans, then swallow up our islands, then devour our coastlines. Who knows, they may even chew canals wide enough to bring them all the way to Kansas. And as you well know"—he narrowed his eyes and swept his gaze across them—"we have no naval bases in Kansas."

He saw the determined faces around the room nodding gravely. An unnamed man in a business suit folded his hands and leaned forward. "You've already convinced us, Admiral. No one disputes the magnitude of the alien threat. Our shipyards and weapons factories, our naval construction operations have been blossoming like weeds. Just tell us what you *can* do, and we'll give you everything you need."

Haldane smiled. Throughout his EPN career, his ideas had been met with reluctance and resistance, thanks to narrow-minded individuals and the web of red tape they spun. Now, Admiral Haldane had everything he could possibly ask for. All he had to do was ask. Even in his scrawny body, these advisors looked to him, respected him, understood the weight of experience and wisdom he brought to these discussions.

Among the inner circle gathered here, he knew that at least six of them had transfer circuits implanted, because they were deemed to be powerful and influential enough to be classed as irreplaceable. They had their own escape hatch volunteers.

"I have faced the Sluggos several times in person, at the cost of two previous bodies and damage to a third. I've looked them in the eyes ... well, at least in the slimy membranes. I have watched men and women die all around me, and I've felt myself die. I know what it's like. I was aboard the *Far Horizon* until its last moments. I was there at Pearl Harbor. And I'll be there again at our final engagement."

He changed the images on the screens to show blurry sonar readings. "After the attack on Hawaii, the Sluggos withdrew with many vital spaceport components, dragging them beneath the sea. We've been trying to find their secret base. A fleet of fast mapping survey ships cruised over the surface, covering thousands of square miles of open sea. They were ready to map every inch of the damned Pacific if they needed to. And this is what they found."

He zoomed in. The sonar trace showed the gigantic mass of Sluggos that had formed the conglomerate monster. The echo was bigger than a hundred giant squids as it moved along the ocean floor. The first image of the huge alien mass was sharp, the second was fuzzed and blurry.

"With the third sonar ping," Haldane continued, "the Sluggo mass had vanished—as usual. But this time it's different, because we found where those creatures go to bed."

The sonar trace showed the ocean floor, a low-resolution image that nevertheless revealed a city of permanent undersea structures, a hodgepodge assembled from wreckage the creatures had stolen.

"Knowing where to look, we dropped off submersible

microcameras, self-guiding imagers that dove down to the coordinates. They were small enough to remain unnoticed—for a time."

Haldane displayed crisp video feeds as the submersible cameras dove to where the invaders had built their submerged fortress. At such a depth, the water was dark and murky; activating bright lights to penetrate the gloom, the microcameras revealed bizarre free-form sculptures, towers and domes that were welded together with mud and coral. The structures incorporated the wreckage of ship hulls, including the bridge tower of the *Far Horizon*, along with sunken wrecks dragged hundreds of miles from Oahu.

The buildings themselves, however, seemed to *squirm*. As the microcameras flitted closer, they revealed that the walls were also built out of Sluggos. The wormlike creatures piled up like soft flexible bricks, many of them dead, others dissolving and oozing into organic cement. Gantry structures stolen from the Honolulu spaceport served as frameworks, and individual Sluggos crawled up the girders, wrapping around them like putty.

"Unfortunately, the lights the cameras used to obtain these images attracted attention," Haldane said.

The images on the conference room screens switched to static one at a time. The last microcamera zoomed in on one of the eel-like creatures swimming toward it, its mouth gaping wide until it swallowed the camera, which valiantly transmitted a last few images of the alien digestive sac until the acid destroyed it.

Haldane crossed his arms over the many medals on his now-scrawny chest. "So there you have it, gentlemen." He nodded to the woman again, "And ma'am. We pinpointed their base. We know where they're lurking." It felt good to grin. "We have a large expeditionary sub being converted into a battle vessel. It was originally designed to complete a full sonar map of the ocean floor, but now we have more important work for it."

The man in the business suit nodded. "Ah, the *Prospector*. We funded that. One of our subsidiaries is developing domed underwater housing as condo time-shares, and we were going to lay claim to all that undeveloped real estate. We're having trouble selling shares, thanks to the Sluggo infestation."

Haldane nodded. "We know sonar does little good to track them, but we can arm the *Prospector* to the teeth. It's got a reinforced hull and expanded magazines to accommodate more than fifty torpedoes. I'll find a determined crew. We'll be ready to make our final assault within a week. I intend to lead the expedition myself and blow the living slime out of those Sluggos!" He smiled. "If I have your permission."

They gave him their exuberant approval, but the lone woman asked, "Why wait a week if we know where the Sluggos are now?"

"It'll take that long to get ready, ma'am. We have to give this our best shot."

Admiral Haldane had an ulterior motive. In a week, the infirmary would release his other body. Paulson Kenz had finished the basic healing process, and he was completing the final physical therapy schedules.

If he was going to defeat the alien invaders once and for all, Haldane certainly didn't want to be wearing this scrawny body for the history books.

—VIII—

After all the snide comments and complaints Admiral Haldane had made about Paulson's original weakling form, the young seaman-recruit wished the admiral had been more careful with this one. If Haldane hadn't let himself get so smashed up or killed— twice in fact—then Paulson wouldn't have to spend his days here in the infirmary being tortured by a Spanish Inquisition of physical therapists who used enhanced healing therapies and supercharged hormones that pummeled his muscles and bones until they knitted themselves together—or else.

The physical therapists had a bedside manner more appropriate for the Marquis de Sade than Florence Nightingale, and Paulson was very quickly convinced that he wanted to be released from their clutches as soon as possible. He longed to be back in the rec room hall again with nothing to do except study reports on the Sluggos.

Even here in sick bay, however, as soon as he grew strong enough, Paulson called up all available images of the Honolulu attack. Because so many vacationers spent time in Hawaii, most of the footage had been confiscated from homemade tourist videos. Paulson watched the rampaging conglomerate monster that had destroyed the ships in the harbor, the spaceport, the buildings on the shoreline.

He was more interested in poring over clips taken prior to the assembly of the Sluggo monster. He watched how the myriad organisms drew together like some kind of group mind, how the individual worm-things assembled into a much larger and adaptable body that reorganized itself according to circumstances. The Sluggo organism was clearly intelligent en masse, though the individual creatures showed only the most rudimentary brain activity. After the harbor attack and ransacking the ships and spaceport, some of the retreating Sluggos had maintained enough physical integrity to haul off the wreckage they desired, while the rest of the creatures dissolved like a mist of maggots.

Even if sonar couldn't track the massed alien organism underwater, fast ships could have followed the sunken ships and the spaceport gantries as the Sluggos hauled them away. But with Pearl Harbor, the EPN base, the waterfront, and the spaceport destroyed, no one managed to think that far ahead.

Paulson walked on a treadmill, limbering up his legs. He still felt lingering broken-glass pain in his ribs and shoulder. His numerous bruises had turned an alarming bouquet of colors, but the flesh tone was returning. The therapists often studied his body, finding patterns and designs in the discolorations. One even exclaimed that he saw the face of the Virgin Mary there. Paulson thought he was joking, but the man's voice held no sarcasm or humor whatsoever.

During the treadmill work, he sweated heavily and his pulse raced. He was ready to drop, but the therapists egged him on and threatened him. Paulson was surprised when they didn't enhance his sessions with a bullwhip just to keep him moving. After weeks of physical therapy, he began to long for the days of boot camp, which had been miserable enough, but at least he'd been able to sleep at night.

On the other hand, if he hadn't signed on to the escape hatch program, he would have been doomed to go out and fight the alien monsters. He probably would be a statistic from Pearl Harbor. In most ways, being dead was worse than physical therapy.

According to the doctors' estimates, given additional enhanced jolts of healing chemicals, in a few days he would swap back into his own body and return to the rec hall with all the other transfer volunteers. And wait.

Admiral Haldane appeared in the therapy center just as Paulson stumbled off the treadmill and the therapists yanked the monitor electrodes from his scalp and chest.

The admiral regarded him with obvious impatience.

"Hurry up and finish healing, Seaman Kenz. The clock is ticking, and I want that body back. I'm due to head into battle again, and I'd rather face the Sluggos wearing that"—he jabbed a finger toward Paulson's borrowed body—"than this."

"Healing as fast as I can, sir."

"He'll be ready on time, Admiral," said the physical therapist who had seen the Virgin Mary in his bruise patterns. "I'll give him a double maximum dose tonight."

Haldane seemed to consider Paulson as little more than a piece of equipment; he paid attention to the medical specialists instead. "And have you scheduled the cranial reset surgery yet?" He tapped the pendant on the back of his head—Paulson's own head—and glanced at Paulson, who stood panting and sweating beside the treadmill.

"Cranial surgery again, sir?" Paulson said. "I didn't agree to that."

"Yes, you did," Haldane said. "It's in the fine print. The transfer conduit is set for one-way transmission only, one-time use. It has to be that way, if you think about it. After I evacuate from a critical last-stand situation, I can't have my volunteer just hit the pendant again and reset."

Paulson ran his fingers along the small disc on the back of his head. "So now that we've transferred, we can't just switch back?"

"We'll just pop out the device and put in another one," said one of the medical techs. "Easy as replacing an eyeball. Piece of cake."

"You'll be happy to get your own body back, Seaman Kenz," said Haldane, "and I'll certainly be glad to have that one. We located the main undersea base where the Sluggos are building their fortress, and I'll be taking an expeditionary sub there rigged as a battleship with plenty of megatorpedoes and missiles. It'll be glorious!"

Paulson decided it was time to share what he had gleaned from his research on the aliens. "Sir, I've been studying the enemy behavior. The Sluggos seem to be a group organism, collectively intelligent but individually not much. The Sluggos are just like cells, bound together by some kind of telepathy. They cooperate, bond with synergy, and—"

"Yes, yes, very nice, Seaman Kenz," said Haldane. "With all the megatorps loaded aboard the *Prospector*, we'll blow the Sluggos to hell and level their undersea base. The ruins will be the next best tourist attraction since Atlantis."

<h3 style="text-align:center">—IX—</h3>

They didn't have time for a proper commissioning cruise aboard the *Prospector*. The crew would get accustomed to their battle sub, and he would get reacquainted with this body, by the time they reached the coordinates of the sunken alien base.

Admiral Haldane touched the sore spot in the back of his skull where the transfer conduit had been replaced. His freshly healed body still ached; he could feel the lingering remnants of bruises, and his bones twinged when he moved the wrong way. Nevertheless, it felt good to be out of that weakling form. These aches and pains were a good sort of hurt, like after a heavy workout. In the body of Paulson Kenz, his tired soreness just felt like hopeless surrender.

In the week since the discovery of the alien undersea base, the Sluggos had remained quiet, though aircraft and high-resolution satellites made several tentacle sightings.

Admiral Haldane was the EPN's highest-ranking officer and he insisted on commanding this mission, but he had never served aboard a sub before, so he let the actual captain, XO, navigator, and weapons officer do their jobs without interference. Normally, an admiral with Haldane's clout and experience would never have been risked on such a dangerous mission—and at least half the *Prospector*'s crew was convinced this would be a one-way trip. Admiral Haldane, though, intended to face the squirming enemy one last time. He wanted to see them all splattered into plankton-sized pieces.

The *Prospector* needed his background and experience during what was sure to be intense fighting. He knew the sub's crew might panic at the wrong moment, so he had to lead them with his proven abilities. Besides, he always had his escape hatch.

During the long and tedious voyage, Haldane spent much of his time on the bridge, watching the screens. The navigator sent sonar bursts, but the waters remained clear. He called for numerous drills and targeting simulations, loading and unloading torpedoes. The admiral also worked out in the sub's makeshift exercise area, limbering his restored body and working through the last aches and pains.

When the *Prospector* reached the coordinates of the Sluggo base, the sub, the crew, and Admiral Haldane's body were ready for action.

"We'll strike fast, and repeatedly," he said over the horn from the command deck, glancing over at the captain and XO. "Like ninjas. One megatorp after another after another. You all saw the size of that monster that attacked Pearl Harbor. I'd say twenty megatorps should be sufficient, and that leaves thirty more to obliterate the base." He waited for the resounding cheer, then glanced at the captain. "Captain, prepare your firing pattern."

The captain snapped, "Weps, Fire Control, you have your orders."

When they approached the target, the sonar technicians sent out pings to map the alien structures ahead. For an instant he saw a shadow of the monstrous conglomerate creature, but it disappeared by the time of the second burst.

In the blurred sonar images, he saw the huge alien structures, which seemed significantly larger than what the microcameras had recorded a week ago. Some of the towers appeared to be falling, the domes collapsing.

"That sonar resolution really sucks," he said.

"We're close enough that we can see with our own eyes, Admiral," said the XO. "Lighting it up now."

Haldane smiled with pride at the efficient crew. "Captain, I'll turn operations over to you. Handle all the details, please."

The sub's brilliant lights stabbed into the deep, dark water, illuminating the bizarre alien fortress. Around them, the water was aswarm with millions of the squirming eels, but the gigantic conglomerate monster was not in sight. The dismantled ship hulls and spaceport gantries stood on the sea floor—and they were slowly toppling down. The base seemed to be falling apart by itself.

Everyone stared at the startling images, momentarily frozen.

Haldane roared, "What are you waiting for? Fire control, launch megatorps!"

The crew had been tense and waiting, with hair-trigger fingers. The first megatorpedoes soared out like javelins on a tail of foam. The weapons crew was already loading the second volley even before the first had hit.

Haldane muttered to himself, "This is going to be good."

The torpedoes arrowed straight on target and struck the Sluggo base with glorious detonations. Haldane caught his breath as bright shock waves blossomed like an explosive cluster of flowers. The sonar techs switched off their ears before the close-range blasts rang out, and thunder reverberated through the *Prospector*'s hull. Haldane was caught off guard, but the rest of the crew hunkered down at their stations. Fire control shouted a succession of orders.

As admiral, he wanted to be in control and direct all activity, but the others reacted so quickly without him, like a well-oiled machine. Within seconds, another volley of megatorps was away. This would be a constant punishing brawl, and the squirming aliens didn't have a chance.

Explosions wrecked the undersea structures. The broken hulls and gantry frameworks were already toppling, but then he saw a flurry, as if the megatorps had startled a flock of carrion birds. Individual Sluggos boiled up from the patchwork structures by the thousands—tens of thousands.

Haldane realized that all those huddled invertebrates had been *holding the base together*, like living building blocks. Sluggos had covered the scrap components, but the explosions had stirred up all those creatures, which now abandoned the structures and swarmed toward the sub like angry hornets from hundreds of disturbed nests.

Contradictory orders echoed throughout the *Prospector*. Haldane intended to give some kind of brilliant insight that would allow the crew to make a wise and instantaneous response, but the best he could vocalize was, "Uh-oh. Keep firing megatorps."

The weapons officer yelled, and the crew aft in the torpedo room kept frantically loading volley after volley into the launch tubes like a fire brigade. Explosions hammered the crumbling alien base, but the uncertain and scattered cloud of free-swimming Sluggos simply swirled around. Then the swarm came toward the sub like an angry school of fish.

"Keep firing!" Haldane yelled, as if the crew needed any encouragement.

Countless writhing shapes formed a cloud that congealed around the *Prospector*. The squirming bodies in the swarm wove together, fastening one body to another, and another conglomerate alien creature formed itself like a giant fist around the battle sub.

The last three megatorps launched but became caught in the thick amorphous mass. The detonations were like sledge hammers, pounding the *Prospector*'s hull, throwing the crew to the deck. Haldane lost his balance and slammed into a control station, knocking the sonar tech aside. He climbed to his feet, shaking his head. On the main screens, they saw all the water go dark as the mass closed in.

"All megatorps gone, sir," said the captain. He looked sickened.

"Already? This is not possible!" Haldane said. "Fifty megatorps struck their targets! We destroyed the alien base!"

Nobody argued with him. The fire control and weapons officers knew the explosions had caused damage, but the huge squirming mass of Sluggos just reformed into a giant and powerful mass of angry flesh.

The *Prospector* groaned and shrieked as even the reinforced armor was bent beyond its tolerances. The intercom was filled with shouts.

"Watertight doors closing! Breach on Deck Five!" the XO yelled.

The battle sub lurched, and the deck tilted at an angle. The huge alien creature had grabbed the hull and was squeezing and shaking the *Prospector* as if it were nothing more than a toy.

"Another hull breach on Deck Three, Admiral," the XO yelled. "Water's coming in."

"And so are the Sluggos!"

The Prospector's captain gave him a beseeching look. "You've faced the Sluggos before, sir. In your experience, how should we fight off this thing? We need you to tell us."

Haldane didn't know, but he was aware that he had to escape. The sub would collapse any minute, and someone had to return with a full report to the main EPN base. Humanity would count on him to debrief his fellow admirals. With each engagement, Admiral Haldane learned more and more, and now he had to tell someone that even megatorps didn't work.

"Even failed missions can be instructive," he said, making sure he sounded brave. "But we have to keep fighting until the last possible second. Full ahead. Can we use our engines? Maybe we can break free of this slimy mass."

The captain gave the order while shaking his head. The engineer yelled through the horn. "The Sluggos are caught in the propellers. This vessel is frozen and shut down, and our reactor's at 110%. Any more of an overload and it's going to go critical—fifteen minutes, max."

Haldane thought fifteen minutes sounded highly optimistic. "If the reactor goes critical, maybe that'll take out these things. We all have to be brave right now." Their bravery, of course, would manifest differently from his own.

"Sluggos inside the sub!" yelled someone from the torpedo room. "They broke the hatches, pushed their way through the tubes! We're taking on water—water and Sluggos. Compartment's filling up!"

Haldane wanted more details, but the torpedo officer spent too much time screaming and so wasn't very helpful. More damage reports came from other decks. "Thousands of Sluggos are aboard!"

Haldane thought of the wriggling forms, slithering along the decks like carnivorous maggots, attacking anything that moved. The *Prospector*'s hull groaned and lurched again. The captain and XO looked at each other, expressions white.

Haldane was amazed at how swiftly the invading Sluggos reached the command deck. He had faced these awful things before, had seen the horde wipe out Pearl Harbor, and seen them take down the *Far Horizon*, had felt them squirming over his body and sinking fangs into his flesh in the seconds before he activated the escape hatch transfer.

Knowing there was nothing to do and no point in delaying, Haldane faced the bridge crew. This was their last stand. They were out of weapons; alien invaders had breached the hull. Without question, the *Prospector* was doomed.

Haldane accepted the inevitable. Although he wasn't looking forward to escaping into the scrawny body of seaman-recruit Paulson Kenz, he knew that even a weakling form was better than a dead one.

"Thank you for your service and bravery, crewmen. Your deaths will not be in vain. I shall deliver the story of your brave final battle, your last stand for humanity."

The weapons officer gaped at him. "You're just bugging out!"

The XO glowered. "He's saving his own skin."

Haldane lifted his chin. "I'm living to fight another day. It's the only way Earth will defeat these monsters."

Twenty of the squirming, sharp-fanged Sluggos lurched onto the bridge, and several crewmen yelled in terror. Haldane touched the transfer pendant in the base of his skull.

As reality faded around him, he was indeed proud of the *Prospector*'s crew. He saw their faces ... but for some reason, they didn't seem particularly glad to know that he, at least, would survive.

When Paulson Kenz felt the wrenching inside his head and found himself whisked back into Admiral Haldane's surrogate body, he knew the poop had hit the fan—industrial-sized cargo load of poop.

Struggling with disorientation, he found himself on the command deck of the battle sub that had gone to attack the Sluggo undersea base. It was a shocking transition from his comfortable padded chair in the rec hall, where he'd been studying reports of the mission, looking at the parameters of the *Prospector*.

He had gone over the list of added weapons, the reinforced hull, the fifty megatorpedoes loaded aboard. From what he suspected about the alien biology, Paulson was skeptical that explosive kinetic weapons would solve the problem at all. But Admiral Haldane had not demonstrated much ability to think outside the box.

He would assume he had enough firepower to level the alien base, then return to cheers and parades. The problem was, blasting the Sluggo monster to pieces wouldn't help, because it was already in pieces. The alien swarm was fundamentally composed of countless individual units bound together by some kind of common telepathy.

Admiral Haldane had not been interested in hearing any suggestions from a scrawny piece of cannon fodder, though.

Knowing the sub intended to engage the invaders' base, Paulson had watched the meager intel as it came in, preparing himself for the worst, since the admiral's previous engagements had not turned out well—especially not for the "escape hatch" volunteers. The waiting was maddening.

The other volunteers in the rec room amused themselves by playing ping-pong or engaging in interactive games. None of them bothered to become friends, sure that any one of them could be called to duty and dispatched at any time.

Paulson could feel them looking at him with pity. Admiral Haldane's track record, and his recklessness (which Haldane tried to characterize as bravery), was no secret. Right now, he was leading his battle sub to the monstrous horde. Paulson hoped for the best, but he didn't get his wish.

This time, when the conduit in his head activated, he knew exactly what was going on—and he was ready.

He braced himself during the transition, and when he gazed out through a different set of eyes, this time he wasn't in a safe sick bay, nor was he being evac'd from a battlefield.

Instead, he saw several slithering, eel-like creatures with round hungry-mouths and white diamond-like teeth. They squirmed forward along the deck, bursting onto the bridge, or command deck, or whatever it was called on a submarine. The alarms were deafening, as were the shouts of the *Prospector*'s crew. Uniformed men and women made their last stand and fought the Sluggos, stomping and hammering, using any possible weapon. The sub's captain had a handgun and shot into the soft masses, and they exploded like snot-filled water balloons. Some bullets whanged and ricocheted off the bulkheads, making the other crewmen duck.

Through the main port, Paulson saw only a solid writhing mass of interlinked Sluggo bodies, as if someone had placed the worm aliens into a trash compactor and smashed them up against the *Prospector*.

Paulson only had a second to assess the situation. More Sluggos slid through the hatch onto the bridge; twenty were already making their way to the controls. Two bloodied seamen threw themselves against the bulkhead door, ramming their shoulders and pushing the heavy metal hatch into its jamb, slicing two Sluggos in half.

The captain, the XO, the weapons officer, the fire-control officer, the sonar tech—all of them were completely disregarding Paulson.

He had an idea, but he needed their help, and their attention. "Captain, give me a situation report," he barked, surprised at the sound of his own voice.

The startled captain turned to look at him. "You're not the admiral—you're just cannon fodder."

"We're all cannon fodder, but I'm wearing the uniform. I've got the rank, I have the authority … and I have an idea. What's our weapons situation? Tell me what's happened and where we are."

"We're up a creek without a paddle," the XO cried. "Megatorps gone, and our hull is completely engulfed by Sluggos. At least four hull breaches, and the aliens are swarming through all the decks."

The engineering officer wiped sweat from her forehead. "Structural failure imminent, sir. Catastrophic hull collapse in three minutes." Her voice was hoarse. "Or less."

"I predicted the megatorpedoes would be ineffective," he said.

"I wish you'd been in the admiral's body before we got in this mess, then," the captain said.

Paulson didn't want to argue. "Do we still have sonar?"

The sonar tech climbed back to his feet, held onto the anchored chair. "Sonar didn't do any good, sir."

Paulson believed they'd been misinterpreting the results. The Sluggo monster didn't know how to become invisible to the sonar pings; rather, the massive organism had actually *broken apart* and then recoalesced.

"I want a sonar burst, the loudest boom you can make, Mr. Lieutenant—Ensign … sorry, I don't know your rank."

"My rate," said the sonar tech.

"Does the sonar work or not?" Paulson snapped. From the design specs, he knew the *Prospector* had been built as a survey vessel, with a full complement of sonar mapping gear.

"We can send out a ping as loud as bad rap music coming from a car stereo."

"Then let's hope it sounds as annoying as that."

As the sonar tech scrambled with his controls, Paulson yelled to the communications officer, "Send a message throughout the ship … the sub, or whatever. Close all compartment doors, seal off the bulkheads. We need to separate the clusters of Sluggos." He had noticed that after the crew sealed the door to the bridge deck, the individual worm creatures were less lively, more disoriented, and without a driving goal. "We need to divide and conquer. The Sluggos are a conglomerate organism. If you separate the pieces, the pieces are no longer intelligent."

The sonar tech removed his ears. "Here we go." He activated a loud pulse that thrummed out. The response was immediate and startling.

The Sluggo mass surrounding the *Prospector* shivered and broke apart like flies taking flight from a pile of manure. At the main port, Paulson saw hundreds of the things peel off from where they'd been compacted against the view port, and they scattered away from the sub. Even the Sluggos inside the command deck were dazed from the sonar blast, which gave other crew enough time to stomp on them and pop their body sacs.

"Another ping! Keep it up!" Paulson shouted.

The tech stared wide-eyed at the controls. "Did you see that?"

Paulson ran over and grabbed him. "Keep pinging! The sonar disrupts whatever binds them together into a collective organism. It may be our only chance!"

The tech launched another loud boom, and most of the remaining Sluggos drifted away from the sub's hull like flakes of dandruff.

"I can keep pinging all day!" the tech yelled excitedly.

"You may have to do that. Call the engine room—see if that freed our propellers so we can get the heck out of here."

"They're called screws, sir," said the engineer.

The reactor room called up to the bridge. "We're free—and the reactor's running at peak. I'm going to burn off some of our excess by setting off at top speed."

While studying so many reports, Paulson had tried to determine what held the Sluggos together like a million brain cells in a single coordinated organism. Now he was grinning. "Keep hitting them with sonar blasts, and they won't give us any more trouble. Our pulses are scrambling the single intelligent creature into countless unintelligent cells. They won't be able to reassemble into anything big enough to threaten us."

Now that the main port was clear, Paulson could see the ocean around him. He saw the wreckage strewn on the sea floor, the components and debris the Sluggos had used as a structural framework. The megatorps had indeed destroyed the base at least, but if the big structures were held together by conglomerated Sluggos, the aliens could just rebuild as soon as the individual worm-things settled down. By then, though, the *Prospector* would be far away. So long as the sonar pulses kept scrambling the Sluggo mass, the sub could move unimpeded.

Another sonar boom resounded through the water. The sea around them was a boiling swarm, but the scrambled creatures didn't attack the sub. Inside, the crew were rapidly dispatching the Sluggos one at a time.

"Blow all ballast," Paulson ordered in his loudest command voice, then turned to the captain and whispered, "That's the best way to get us to the surface, isn't it?"

The sub's captain turned to look at him with a dawning respect. "Indeed, Admiral. I'll take it from here, sir. You've already saved the day."

"You may have saved the human race," the XO added.

The captain ordered, "Put us on the ceiling!" He nodded at Paulson. "You might want to hold onto something."

Soon, the *Prospector* breached the surface like a humpback whale. It was a short but exciting ride, and for the first time Paulson felt excited about being part of the Earth Planetary Navy. On the scope, the seas were peaceful and Sluggo-free.

"Our comm systems are damaged," the XO said. "Can't send anybody the good news until we make repairs."

"Then we have to get back to port and report," Paulson said, glad to be getting out of this with his skin intact. "We're going to live to fight another day."

—XI—

From the main press podium at the La Diego Earth Navy base, Admiral Bruce Haldane wore his formal uniform again, the one that had been re-re-tailored to fit Paulson Kenz's scrawny body. It was his body now, a permanent swap now that the *Prospector* had been lost. But he could always upgrade. He had already sent out a call to the recruitment offices and among the current sailors. Thanks to the Sluggo threat, new recruits were being drafted by the tens of thousands, processed as quickly as was bureaucratically possible. Certainly, with so many choices available, there must be someone better qualified than this wet-noodle bookworm.

Still, the escape hatch had worked, and Haldane was relieved to be safe again. He vowed to carry on the fight for Earth....

As soon as he had transferred out of his body aboard the battle sub, he found himself in the recreation hall along with the other lazy slobs who took the easy way out, all those young men who were too afraid to face down the voracious Sluggos as Haldane had done—several times.

Settling into the bookworm's body, he brushed himself off, glared at the rest of the volunteers, and marched to the guarded door, demanding to be taken to base headquarters. Medical monitors would have picked up the transfer signal, so they would come to investigate before long, but he needed to meet with the advisory board, issue his report, and add his new information to the growing backlog of data. Someday, his experiences might allow teams of human geniuses to discover some small weakness in the aliens.

And he also had to make his announcement, putting forth a brave face for the people of Earth.

At first, the guards didn't want to let him out of the rec hall/prison. They looked at Paulson's scrawny body and regarded him with skepticism.

"I am Admiral Haldane, I tell you! Let me loose, I have to make my report."

The guards raised their eyebrows. "Sure, you are. And you expect us to just release you without confirmation?"

"I'm *me*, dammit! That's all the confirmation you should need." Haldane realized that he would have to correct this flaw in the system.

One of the other volunteers looked up from a suspended game of ping-pong. "That one's been acting awfully strange. Could be an adverse reaction to the conduit surgery."

The others nodded. "I wouldn't believe him."

These cowardly slackers didn't respect him! "This is nonsense!" Haldane shouted at the guard. "I outrank you. I'm your admiral!"

"I heard him talking," said another volunteer. "He said he was going to escape and find a black-market surgeon who would pop out a plug for a fee."

The lazy bastards were setting him up! Haldane was furious.

Finally, a signal from medical command informed the guards that Haldane's transfer protocol had been activated, and that the escape hatch swap had been successful. He gave an annoyed huff toward the slovenly volunteers who thought it was all a joke, then he stormed out. This was an emergency, not a minute to lose!

Ever since the *Prospector*'s launch, all of Earth was waiting to hear the news. They expected to learn that the invaders had been annihilated, their base destroyed, and any other Sluggos from the Sluggo planet would see that the Earth Planetary Navy was nothing to mess around with.

When he delivered his speech in his weakling body, though—not the one that had departed aboard the battle sub—he could see dismay ripple through the crowd. They'd already figured out that the mission had failed, that the Sluggos were still a threat … and they assumed that the *Prospector* had been lost with all hands. That much was obvious, because otherwise the admiral would never have used his last-ditch escape plan.

The captain of the submarine would have gone down with his ship, as expected, but a war hero like Bruce Haldane had survived to rouse the troops, to inspire the populace and honor the sacrifices of those who had fallen in battle, as well as to advise the EPN's tactical experts.

Standing at the podium, he activated the loudspeaker systems. His words pounded out across the gathered crowd. "You may not recognize me, but I am Admiral Bruce Haldane. And I have just come from the embattled submarine *Prospector*. With fifty megatorpedoes, we wrought terrible damage to the alien base, but the Sluggo retaliation was swift and overwhelming. They engulfed the sub, and I … I regret the loss of all hands."

He cleared his throat. "A list of all names will be made available to you in subsequent press packets." He lifted his chin and kept his tone stoic. "However, even failures are instructive. We believed that a megatorp bombardment was our best possible hope, but now we'll just have to try something else. Maybe undersea nuclear saturation. It's worth a try."

He drew a breath. "Let us pause for a moment of silence to honor all those who sacrificed themselves aboard the *Prospector*." He closed his eyes, bowed his head—and then an actual signal from the *Prospector* spoiled the moment.

The excited announcement broke through on the loudspeakers. The media reporters were abuzz. The battle sub had survived after all, had surfaced intact and was now making its way at best speed back to land!

Admiral Haldane straightened his cap, squared his shoulders, and forced a smile. "Oh … well, then. This is wonderful news."

—XII—

An escort of EPN destroyers met the *Prospector* as it approached the La Diego harbor. People gathered on public docks to welcome the victorious vessel with remarkable fanfare. The cheers from the crowd were deafening.

When Admiral Haldane went to greet them as part of a formal reception party, he was all smiles and pride.

In the days it had taken the battle sub to return, the *Prospector*'s crew had become heroes. No further Sluggo attacks or even sightings had been reported. The sub's captain had transmitted that they had only escaped by using the "sonar defense suggestion" of "Admiral Kenz" to great success, and they believed they had found a way to eliminate the alien invaders once and for all.

"Admiral Kenz" indeed! Haldane fumed inwardly.

As the *Prospector* docked and Admiral Haldane stepped out to greet them, the captain and the XO disembarked with an altogether too smug looking seaman-recruit Paulson Kenz. The sailors looked battered and bruised, their uniforms tattered. Haldane thought their disheveled appearance was strictly for dramatic effect, because even after the Sluggos had swarmed through the decks, the officers and crew must have had a clean change of clothes aboard.

Haldane said, "I'm so pleased you all made it." He waited for the sub's captain to salute, and the man did so, but reluctantly, keeping his eyes fixated on the admiral's insignia rather than his face. "We welcome your return home, and we look forward to your report about the end of the engagement."

The XO blurted out, "Our report will include how you abandoned us, Admiral Haldane—how you took us into danger with reckless disregard for the lives of the *Prospector*'s officers and crew."

Haldane was shocked. "I led an attack that had a reasonable probability of success, but it didn't work. Such are the fortunes of war."

"Excuse me," said the sub's captain, "but Admiral Kenz said he advised against your method from the outset, but you refused to listen to his advice."

"His *advice*?" Haldane spluttered. "*Admiral* Kenz? He's just a recruit, cannon fodder! I'm the real admiral!"

"As far as I'm concerned, you relinquished that title when you abandoned the ship and crew." The captain cleared his throat. "Sir."

"I was required to survive," Haldane said. "I waited until the last possible moment, when there was no hope for survival. I saw no other way."

"And yet ..." The XO nodded at Paulson Kenz. "After you fled for your life, this untried seaman-recruit assessed the situation, solved the problem, saved all our lives, and defeated the Sluggos—in about two minutes. I believe that's called a battlefield promotion, sir."

With a sinking sensation in his gut, Haldane realized that all of this was being recorded and transmitted live.

In the familiar strong and handsome body, Paulson Kenz said, "I've even worked out a way that we can use continuous sonar for complete victory. You see, each pulse scrambles the Sluggo hive mind, breaks it apart. If we bring in numerous subs and keep hammering them with sonar so that the individual creatures cannot recoalesce, then we can use nets or tanks as a harvesting system. If we winnow down the individual Sluggos so that no more than a hundred or so can gather in any single place, the group intelligence won't come back. Divide and conquer. It may take time, but we can simply whittle them away until there are no more Sluggos left."

"Thank you for that interesting suggestion, recruit." Haldane put all the scorn he could possibly muster into his voice. "We'll have our experts take it under advisement. For now, it's best if we initiate the transfer protocol again, swap back so you can have your original body, and I'll make my announcements and appearances in—"

Paulson raised his head. "Sorry, sir, but as you informed me, it's a one-way transfer protocol. We'll have to reinstall and surgically reset the conduits, but there's no time to go through that now. I need to present my findings to the command advisory board. There's a war on, you know."

The captain and the XO ignored Haldane and looked at Kenz. "What are your orders, Admiral?"

Paulson looked flustered. "Well, we need the submarine fixed up and cleaned, for one thing. Then we have to discuss how to implement my sonar strategy so we get rid of the Sluggos."

"I demand my body back!" Haldane said.

Paulson plucked at his sleeve. "I don't believe this is your original body any more than that one is. Meanwhile, you can spend time in the recreation hall with the other cannon fodder volunteers. You should have plenty of time to write a personal letter of sympathy to the families of each of those *seamen* who died during the attack on the *Prospector* ... and on the *Far Horizon* ... for starters."

"But you're just a ... a nobody!" cried Haldane.

The sub's captain said, "We believe Admiral Kenz has valuable insights and irreplaceable knowledge and experience. The EPN could not afford to lose him, so he must be preserved at all costs."

"Yes," the XO added, "it would be a grave threat to the human race if Admiral Kenz were to be lost in combat. I'm sure the escape hatch conduits can be adjusted. You can wait with the other volunteers." He narrowed his eyes and gave Haldane a withering look. "Don't worry, you'll be called to do your duty, if needed."

I like to go camping—to get away from it all, to unplug and just enjoy a few rugged days of eating at a picnic table, bedding down in a sleeping bag, and roughing it.

My wife does not. She never wants to be separated from her technology, her conveniences, and her comforts.

I've watched the younger generation grow extraordinarily stressed when they're forced to take even a day away from their phones or social media. They're also incapable of performing simple and obvious tasks that were vital to survival in the good old days, like building a fire or filtering water. (I watched one of my nephews struggle to figure out how to use a can opener, because he had only known pop-top cans!)

For the anthology The Future We Wish We Had, *we all told stories about the shiny future predicted by the Jetsons or Disney's Tomorrowland.*

I imagined how people, even in that perfect shiny future, might still have trouble roughing it.

GOOD OLD DAYS

When the signal rang, George told the door to answer itself, but the mailbot insisted on a thumbprint signature for the delivery. With a sigh, he was forced to make the extra effort of doing it in person.

"Hello, Mr. J.!" said the cheery, buzzing voice of the mailbot. In his metal arms he carried a large crate. "Special delivery for you. Boy, I wonder what it is."

George pressed his thumb against the scanning plate on the mailbot's smooth forehead. "Jane!" he called over his shoulder. "What have you been ordering now?"

Jane, his wife, walked up with a bounce in her step. "George, dear, you know I don't order anything anymore. The catalogs make the purchases all by themselves."

He frowned. "Well, I certainly didn't order this." He stepped aside to make room for the mailbot. "You don't expect me to carry that heavy thing?"

"Of course not, Mr. J. You can expect *service* from your postal service." The mailbot strutted inside and set the crate in the middle of the floor.

Creaking along, Rosie the maidbot wheeled forward, tsking at the condition of the box. "Just look at those smudges and the dust. Very unsanitary." She bustled about, tidying up the package's exterior.

George waited for the big crate to open automatically, then realized he would have to do it manually since the package had no standard automation. He struggled with the flaps and seals. "Whatever it is, we're not ordering from this company again."

Inside, he found a sealed envelope (which, again, he had to open by hand) and a sheet of actual paper. Not quite sure what to do, George slipped the paper into a reader and the words spilled out, announcing his name and address and ID number in a very official-sounding voice.

"We regret to inform you that your Uncle Asimov has died. These are his personal effects, and you are his only known heir. He has also bequeathed you his property and his home. By accepting his package and reading this letter, you have agreed to the terms of his estate."

George started to grin at their windfall, but then the letter-reader continued, "Mr. Asimov owed a substantial amount of back taxes and assessments. Your account has been debited to pay off these debts, as well as the delivery fee."

"Your Uncle Asimov?" Jane asked. "George, dear, isn't he that crazy old hermit out in the desert?"

"Yes, it was the last place in the country where he could live off the grid. He actually liked that sort of thing." He looked down to scrutinize the contents of the box, hoping that the value of the items inside would at least pay for the delivery charge. He sneezed.

Rosie wheeled forward like a steel filing drawn to a magnet. "Dust! Real dust! Let me take care of that before you catch some sort of disease." The maidbot sprayed disinfectant all around the area.

When she was finished, George rummaged around inside the crate. Jane peered over his shoulder. "It's like a museum in there."

"Or a junkyard." George picked up round, cylindrical metal containers, each with a faded label. He realized they were cans of food, preserved chili and soup. He sniffed one of the cans, smelling nothing but old metal. The picture on the label certainly looked unappetizing.

"Why would anybody want this stuff?" Jane asked. "Do you suppose that means Uncle Asimov didn't even have a food replicator out in the desert?"

"I don't think he even had electricity, Jane. Maybe not running water, maybe not even a self-cleaning hygiene station."

The maidbot buzzed her disapproval while Jane shuddered in horror.

Next he found actual hard copies of books and magazines so old that the paper was brown and crumbly. Underneath those was a stack of yellowed newspapers, wasteful old-fashioned informational devices that were published only once daily, regardless of how often the actual news changed.

George was still digging items out of the crate when his blonde teenage daughter, Judy, and his boy, Elroy, arrived home from the preprogrammed school simulations. Seeing the crate and instantly assuming they had received gifts from someone, Judy let out a delighted shriek, then frowned in disappointment.

George had picked up a pack of a powdery brown substance that smelled vaguely like a cup of coffee from the food replicator, though he couldn't see how the ground substance could turn itself into coffee. Next to it there was a strange contraption, like a pitcher made of metal. He took the pieces apart but couldn't understand their function.

Boisterous Elroy piped up, "That's a coffee percolator, Pop! We studied that in ancient history class."

"A coffee percolator? You mean Uncle Asimov had a special machine just to make coffee?" George held up the filter basket, peering through the tiny holes. "Can it be reprogrammed to do other things?"

"No, Pop. You add the water yourself and then ..." he hesitated. "Well, then you do something to it. I wasn't exactly paying attention in class."

"Tell you what, Elroy—if you figure out how this percolator works, I'll consider it your ancient history homework. Afterward, what do you say we spend some quality time together? We can watch those holos of people throwing a baseball back and forth."

"Gee, Pop, I'll do it!" The boy spent two whole minutes digging through one informational archive after another until he found a set of rigorously detailed instructions. After all that effort, George certainly considered that the boy had earned his reward....

Much later, exhausted from watching the holos of people engaged in strenuous exercise, George tucked Elroy into bed, patted the kid on the head, then went about his evening routine. He went back to look at the coffee percolator, perplexed. He thought of his mysterious and eccentric uncle, unable to understand what could have driven the old man to shun everyday modern conveniences. Why would Uncle Asimov intentionally make his life more difficult than it needed to be? As George read through the complicated instructions, on a whim, he decided to go through the process.

He opened the package of ground beans, assembled the gadget's components, then asked the household computer to find an adapter so that he could plug the machine into the power grid. The coffee-making steps were quite intricate, and George had never done anything so convoluted before. It took him three separate tries before he finally figured it out. "People used to go through a great many tribulations just to make a simple cup of coffee," he said to himself. Uncle Asimov had presumably gone through the grueling process every single day!

When George was done, however, listening to the gurgle of water pumping through the filter basket and grounds, it all made a certain amount of sense to him. When the smell of coffee rose into the air, it seemed delicious, fresh.

Jane came out, ready for bed. Sniffing the air, she looked at him and the coffee percolator. "George, dear, what are you doing?"

Triumphantly, he said, "I'm making coffee."

"If you want coffee, just tell the replicator to make you a cup."

"It's an experiment, dear. Let's try some." He burned his fingers as he lifted the percolator from the wrong end, then poured two cups of the steaming black liquid.

Jane came forward skeptically. "It smells like any other cup of coffee."

He drew in a deep breath, then took a sip. "Delicious! I think it's better than what the replicator makes."

Jane took a drink with great trepidation, as if afraid the old hermit's supplies might be laced with some unusual toxin. "It tastes exactly the same as the coffee we usually drink, George."

But he insisted that wasn't so. Perhaps the very effort he had expended in making the hot beverage increased his own satisfaction. Jane was not sure what to make of this change in her husband's behavior. He gave her a peck on the cheek. "You can go to bed without me, dear. I think I'll stay up a while longer."

She went to bed, leaving him to his unusual preoccupation. George drank the cup of coffee, then poured a second one.

He picked the faded old magazines from the crate and gingerly began thumbing through the pages. Uncle Asimov had kept these publications for so many years. How many times had he read them? George considered feeding the pages into the automatic reader so he could enjoy the articles. Then, drawing a deep breath and setting his jaw with determination, he sat back with his hand-made cup of coffee and read the words for himself. He found it quite an unusual experience. Though he hadn't intended to, George stayed up long into the night.

⚛

The next day at his job in the factory, George looked down at the industrial line, the clanking conveyor belts, the whirring robot arms busily producing the best sprockets money could buy, the mechanical inspectors that monitored all the steps in the operation. Wearing his supervisor's cap and uniform, George stood at his post and watched the robots, just as he had done every day in his career.

Though he was a supervisor, George didn't exactly know what he was doing. The more he thought about it, he realized that he had never really known what he was doing.

He saw his boss in the glassed-in office, lording over the assembly line. He was a short, balding man with dark hair and a large mustache. George had always thought of him as a good boss, though the man's temper was often on a short fuse. George had never really thought about it before, but he didn't quite understand what his boss did either. His job seemed to entail looking down at George and his fellow supervisors, as they in turn looked down at the robotic assembly line. The robots automatically did everything on their own.

George left his station, his brow furrowed with questions. He took the whirring lift platform that raised him up to the boss's office. The balding man was quite surprised to see him. "Why have you left your post? That simply isn't done!"

"But why not, Mr. S.?" He fumbled to articulate his question. "What am I actually *doing* down there?"

"The assembly line can't be run without you. A supervisor at every station, and a station for every supervisor. How do you expect sprockets to be made and for us to meet our inventory goals if you shirk your duties? The whole company depends on you, um—" He looked at the name patch on George's shirt. "George."

"But, sir, what is my job? I don't even know what a sprocket is."

The boss scratched his mustache and sat down at his desk. "George, don't ask me such complicated questions. Sprockets are vitally important items, and you've got a job to do."

"Actually, sir, the robots are doing it. They run everything on the assembly line. In all my years of working here at the sprocket factory I haven't had to push a single button."

"Then that proves you're doing a good job. No breakdowns, no emergencies. Keep up the good work, George."

"Mr. S., does anybody really know how anything works in this factory?"

"That's in the hands of the general manager." With a jerk of his head, Mr. S. nodded toward the ceiling, indicating other floors in the skyscraper overhead.

George went back to his station and watched the robots continue to work for the rest of the day.

That night he came home from work with a brilliant idea. The rest of the family considered it a disaster.

While Judy and Elroy sat at the table and Jane pondered the evening meal in front of the food replicator, George sauntered into the kitchen holding a can of chili and a can of soup. "Let's try these. It'll be like nothing we've ever had before."

Judy seemed horrified. "The pictures on the label look gross."

"Where's your sense of adventure? We'll heat up our own food … as soon as I figure out how to do it."

Elroy got into the spirit of the challenge. "Don't we have to rub sticks together or something, Pop?"

"Of course not. Maybe we can use a heating plate. I wonder how long it takes."

The first experiment turned into an unpleasant experience. The instructions printed on the label—which George was proud to read by himself—didn't say anything about having to open the can first before exposing it to high heat. The soup exploded into a dripping, hot mess.

Rosie the maidbot complained as she wheeled back and forth to clean up every drop.

George did better with the can of chili, and soon each of them had a small bowl of a lumpy red-brown mixture that didn't look even as appetizing as the faded illustration on the label. Elroy, sitting beside his father, good-naturedly took several bites. Jane was stoic as she tasted the meal. Judy refused and slipped over to the replicator to make herself a different snack, much to George's disappointment.

He expected that most of them would prepare a different meal for themselves later on, but he insisted that this was quite tasty. The fact of making it for himself added a sense of accomplishment that increased the flavor of the meal (though his stomach gurgled unpleasantly and his mouth tasted strange for hours afterward).

In the evening, when it was time for them to plan their upcoming family vacation, Judy was the first to pipe up, bubbling with excitement at her own suggestion. "I've always wanted to go to CentroMetropolis. We can see the shows and the museums."

"And the boys," Elroy added sarcastically.

"And the *shows*," Judy insisted.

"Sounds boring," Elroy said. "I want to go on a virtual immersion vacation! Every kind of game simulation! We've got a dome right here in the city, and Pop can get discount tickets from the factory."

"We're not all going to play virtual games." Judy rolled her eyes. "That's for kids."

Jane sighed. "Wouldn't a few days at a spa be nice? Temperature-controlled water jets, zero-gravity relaxation chambers, massagebots that can work your sore muscles for hours? It's not easy being a homemaker these days, you know. You kids just wait until you grow up and have families of your own."

George, however, cut off all further argument. He had already made his decision, and he was sure his family would enjoy it. It would be quite an exciting experience, if only they kept open minds.

"This year we'll do something we've never done before. We're going out to visit where my Uncle Asimov lived."

George flew the family bubblecar out past the city and into the next city (which looked exactly the same as the last), then to the next city, and the next. He remained cheerful, anticipating what they would find out in the rugged swatch of uncivilized land in the middle of the barren, reddish desert.

The bubblecar whistled and hummed as it cruised along under its computerized guidance. Though George sat in the driver's seat, he didn't actually fly the craft. The guidance systems took care of everything for him, but he had always felt in control. He ignored the two kids picking on each other in the back seat as the bubblecar streaked onward. Beside him in the front, Jane seemed quite uneasy about where they were going.

"Are we there yet?" Elroy said. "It's been an hour."

"It's been fifty minutes," George said.

"Seems like forever," Judy complained. "When are we going to stop? Shouldn't we take a rest break?"

Eventually, the neatly organized buildings dropped away, the traffic thinned, and soon the landscape was like something George had seen on a Martian pioneer adventure video. The ground was rocky and barren, dotted with sagebrush and cactus, broken by huge outcrops of rock that didn't look at all like real skyscrapers.

Judy squealed when she saw dark, four-legged creatures munching on the unappetizing foliage. "Look, wild animals! We're not actually going down there, are we?"

"Those are cattle, I think, Judy. Real cattle." He searched his memory. "They were the inspiration for many of the meat products our food replicator makes." Gazing down at the clumsy creatures, though, George didn't think they looked at all like any of the steaks, burgers, or sausages he happily received on a plate that came out of the delivery chute.

"Do they attack people, Pop? Are they dangerous?"

"Of course not, son. We won't be going anywhere close to them."

The bubblecar's metallic voice said, "Reaching end of automatic guidance network. Air travel no longer safe or recommended. It is advised that you turn around and go back."

"See, Daddy? We shouldn't have come here. Let's go to CentroMetropolis."

"Aww, that's two hours from here," Elroy complained.

George's voice was firm. "We're almost there. Uncle Asimov's trailer is just up ahead."

The bubblecar said, "Without grid guidance, it is suggested that you land and proceed on foot from this point."

"On foot!" Judy cried. "Does that mean … *walk*?"

"Yes, I think it's only a mile."

"What's a mile, Pop?" Elroy asked.

"A long, long way," Jane said. "George, are you sure this is a good idea?"

He landed the bubblecar in the middle of the desert. They seemed to be far from anywhere. Had anyone ever been so alone, so isolated? As the transparent dome lifted and they climbed out into the hot sun, George took a deep breath, noting the strange smells, the dust in the air, the spice of sage.

"What if one of those … cattle comes after us?" Judy asked.

"Uncle Asimov was fine. He lived out here by himself most of his life."

"Yes, Daddy, and he died."

George strode forward, leaving footprints on the ground in the real dirt. He pointed to a white structure on a rise in the distance. "There's his trailer." Even Jane was uncertain about how far away it looked, and she was concerned they might get lost, though the bubblecar was perfectly visible and so was the trailer.

Elroy bounded ahead, and Jane warned him to watch out for rattlesnakes, scorpions, tarantulas, jaguars, and any other terrible creature she could think of. After five minutes, the boy lost his steam and began complaining. Judy whined about how dirty she was getting. Tight-lipped, Jane followed with obvious disapproval.

The trailer turned out to be a ramshackle affair made of patched metal siding, solar-power panels on the roof, a water pump in the back. George tried to imagine being out here all by himself day after day without any instant news updates or real-time transmissions of the latest robotic baseball games.

"He really was a caveman!" Elroy looked around with eyes as wide as saucers.

When George pulled open the door, it creaked unnervingly. Jane stepped inside and shuddered. "Rosie would blow an entire circuit bank if she looked at this. There's dirt everywhere!"

They poked around, looking at the kitchen cabinets and a

countertop that contained an actual stove and actual sink, though no one wanted to trust the water that came gurgling out of the tap. Elroy found the bathroom and the shower and called out for them to look at the exotic, primitive fixtures.

"That was called a toilet," George said. He had looked up historical background before they'd begun their vacation.

He paced through the cramped rooms of the trailer, wondering about what his Uncle Asimov must have done all day long. When they found the small rickety bed with its spring mattress, Jane frowned in a combination of disgust and dismay. "Unsanitary conditions and ... no conveniences. Your Uncle Asimov was crazy, George. It's so sad. Just think of what kind of life he could have had if he'd gone into the city. He could have been a productive member of society."

George faltered at the thought. Now that he had begun to pay attention to his job and home life, he wasn't sure what he himself was doing to be "productive."

Jane stood with her hands on her narrow hips, shaking her head. "I guess we'll never know why he did this to himself. It's like he was being punished."

"Uncle Asimov knew how to take care of himself. He was self-sufficient. I bet he built most of this trailer with his own hands."

"Do you think he used a spear to hunt for his food?" Elroy asked. "Maybe he killed some of those cattle, or jackrabbits, or prairie dogs."

"Whatever he did, he did it his own way. He must have felt a sense of accomplishment in just getting through each day." George recalled how good he'd felt with the single task of making a pot of coffee with the old-fashioned percolator.

"How inconvenient," Jane insisted. "It must have been impossible for him! I'll bet he was very miserable."

George wasn't so sure. "I bet he was happy."

Judy laughed in disbelief. "Nobody could be happy out here. Just think of everything he was missing."

"But he had things most of us don't even remember."

Jane remained unconvinced. "What does that have to do with anything? So much unnecessary work. It's such a shame."

"And now this place is all ours, for what it's worth," George said, grinning. "Uncle Asimov willed it to me."

"But what do we *do* with this place?" Jane said with growing horror in her voice.

"We'll keep it. I just might come back, spend a whole two hours next time."

"If you do that, George, you're doing it alone." Jane was completely no-nonsense. Under the sunshine and with her own perspiration, her always-perfect hairdo had begun to come undone.

He just smiled mysteriously at her. "That's the idea."

Elroy pushed the creaking door and went back out into the bright sunlight, where he saw a lizard scuttle across the sand. "Can we go, Pop? Please?" The boy's normally cheerful voice carried a whining tone. "We could get back home in time to play a game or two in the virtual immersion dome. Wouldn't that be neat, Pop?"

He saw that Jane had been ready to go from the moment they set down in the desert. Before the situation could grow entirely unpleasant, George agreed. Ironically, both of the kids had plenty of energy as they hurried back toward the waiting bubblecar.

George had seen what he needed to see, and he would remember this for a long time. His family grumbled and complained, but their words washed off of him as he felt a strange sense of possibilities. He had a spring in his step.

Elroy and Judy scrambled into the bubblecar, gasping and panting and moaning with the effort. Jane settled into her usual position beside him in the front of the craft. He sealed the dome over them, raised the vehicle in the air, and whirred away.

"It'll be good to get home and back to normal, now that you've had your little adventure, George." Jane had the patient tolerance of a woman who had been married a long time.

"Yes, dear."

The bubblecar picked up speed, and they flew back toward the city. When no one was looking, though, George surreptitiously switched off the auto-pilot, took the controls, and piloted the bubblecar by himself all the way home.

Another early story of mine, "Carrier" fits right into the adventure science fiction genre, like Star Trek *or* Star Wars. *A lone woman space pilot in a scavenger ship searches for remnants of alien civilizations or derelict ships, and she encounters more than she bargained for.*

This story has many seeds of later stories and novels I would write. The main character's interaction with her clever and amusing computer assistant formed the model for many of my other stories. I liked the derelict alien spaceship and the deadly discovery she makes inside so much that I incorporated that plotline into my Saga of Shadows trilogy.

In this short story, though, you get the tale in its distilled state.

CARRIER

I n the dark shadows of the long-dead bridge, she found the captain's last log entry. Hesitantly, her fingers trembling with excitement, she punched the few buttons she had deciphered on the dusty control panel, feeding the log tape into her portable JR computer extension.

"Would you translate that for me please, Junior?"

"I will try, Mary Coven," answered the computer via the linkup with the main JR on Coven's ship.

"If you can do it, I'll let you call me just Mary."

"Thank you, Mary."

"Translate it *first*, Junior," she snapped, turning to look around the stiflingly small bridge of the derelict vessel, feeling the shadows push against her spacesuit.

On his first attempt to navigate the *Proud Mary*, Coven's ship, Junior had almost run them into the ancient craft. The derelict was a series of cylinders strung together like a long train, each marked with a bold, glowing red triangle. An intact starship of the Population I race—the find of the millennium!

Coven had hastily suited up and boarded the other ship, moving from compartment to compartment in awe, trying to figure out who would build a starship that seemed to be half sickbay, half morgue. Time had changed anything organic into a thin coating of dust; but the beautiful, desperate paintings that covered the walls stood undisturbed by the time that had passed since the artist had added his atoms to the dusty floor.

Magnificent alien landscapes swept across the ship's walls, somehow conveying that the artist knew he would never see home again. Coven blinked. She had murals like that on the walls of the *Proud Mary*—but this artist had stopped suddenly, in the middle of a painting. She briefly wondered why, but then she found the bridge, and excitement made her forget her concern.

A Population I ship. She grinned in amazement even though the craft was not as remarkable as imagination and rumor had made them out to be. The ancient race, built almost into demigods by wild stories and fantastic speculation, had completely vanished, leaving behind only tantalizing scraps of their dead civilization.

Earth, in its undying quest to gather knowledge, created what it called the Astro-Archaeology Foundation to assimilate those tiny fragments of Population I scattered so thinly about the explored portion of the galaxy. When the artifacts came in too slowly to keep the Foundation busy, the "Star Search" was instigated, offering large sums of money to those people who might not otherwise look hard enough, if the only incentive was doing one's duty for all humanity.

Now, as she took in this ancient ship, Mary Coven could call herself the most successful of all the scavengers who had scoured space for any scrap connected with Population I. She wondered how many people would kill to be where she was now.

"Hurry up, Junior!"

Coven had found a different artifact once before, a small Plasticine scrap of an art object, half buried in the wastes of a backwater planet. The Plasticine had been painted with the tantalizing picture of a human-looking arm decorated with fine red lines.

With the generous reward she had received from the "Star Search" fund, Coven had bought herself a new JR computer, choosing one with a personality rather than the more efficient standard model. Hell, she could *fly* the ship herself; what she really needed was someone to talk to. It got lonely on some of those long flights. She just wished Junior wasn't so naive at times.

"All finished, Mary."

"Well, play it then!"

A viewscreen on Junior's console lit up as an image of the

Population I captain formed. He looked vaguely human, with grayish skin and a turned-up nose, but his face and arms were covered with livid red lines, searing into his body, eating him away. He trembled and spoke in a shaky tone. Junior's calm, artificial voice filled in the English equivalents, drowning out the captain's alien character.

"If you listen to this recording, I shed grief that you have ignored our clear warnings of the red three-corners. We are a plague ship! And if you have intruded into our environment, you too have the disease. Do not return to your origin!"

"Sorry buddy, some of us are bright enough not to take off our spacesuits," Coven commented under her breath.

"We, the first victims, isolated ourselves at the outbreak of the plague, hoping to save our race—but we were too late. We are quarantined, and the pestilence burns through all worlds, killing off my people. They are all dying ... dying ..."

The screen flickered, then turned gray. "I have another very short clip tagged onto the end of this tape, Mary. Would you like to hear it?"

"Go ahead."

The captain's image appeared again, and this time the disease had ravaged him so that he could barely remain seated in his chair. "I have worked much thought into the possibility that a survivor might find our plague ship and rebirth the disease. I have made it so that this ship will self-destruct when the last of us dies. Oh— untranslatable, Mary, but I believe it is an alien expletive—why am I even recording this?"

The screen winked out. Coven looked around the haunting ship, admiring a few of the shadowy paintings in the pools of light spattered down the corridor. The thin, filmy dust, all that remained of the quarantined victims, showed her footprints clearly.

Junior spoke, breaking the silence. "I have found a small malfunction in the self-destruct sequence—but I have corrected it."

Coven froze. "What?"

"My programming specifically instructs that I correct malfunctions as I find them, Mary. You know that. I did not do anything wrong, did I?"

"Oh, Junior! How much time is left?"

"Thirty-two alien time units."

"Well, how long is an 'alien time unit'?"

"I will check through the main library. One moment, Mary ..."

"*No!*" She grabbed the portable console and sprinted toward the airlock that connected to her ship. Her finger punched the hatch release, but it would not open.

The tinny voice of JR came through a speaker in the wall. "I can't let you through until you have been properly decontaminated, Mary."

"Junior! Let me in."

"It is standard procedure, Mary."

"Then get us out of here!"

"Mary, I cannot fly the ship all by myself. I was just installed, and you haven't taught me everything yet."

"Then let me in, dammit."

"But, Mary_"

"If you don't open this stupid hatch we'll both be ... terminated!"

"Well ... all right, Mary."

Then JR grudgingly slid the airlock hatch into its recess, and Coven raced to the cockpit, leaping into her seat. Rapid acceleration slammed her back against the chair as *Proud Mary* lurched away from the doomed craft.

The Population I plague ship turned into a sun behind them, casting weird shadows through the viewscreens.

"All that knowledge ..." Junior sighed.

"All that money," Coven moaned.

Mary Coven didn't look in mirrors much. Not that she was displeased with what she saw there—silver-brown hair, faint lines beginning to etch themselves around steely eyes—but she had no use for them. It wasn't until several days later that she noticed the red spiderweb of ruptured blood vessels beginning to trace its way along her cheeks, just like the captain of the Population I ship.

Her initial feeling of stricken helplessness lasted only a moment, as she stared at her reflection with a despairing outcry poised on her lips. Coven forced down the frantic thoughts blasting through her mind. Plague! She had the plague! She needed help, couldn't figure out the disease's cycle herself. She had to get back to Earth!

A cold chill crept through her as her composure returned. She didn't dare return to Earth. This disease had wiped out the entire Population I race. She just couldn't take the risk, vainly hoping that a cure could be found.

Coven made up her mind. She would go only within transmitting distance of Earth to tell them what had happened—she couldn't think of having *Proud Mary* placed on the list of missing ships—and to give them all the information she had taken from the Population I plague ship. Junior had at least gotten pictures of the ship, the log recordings, and a superficial gleaning from the library computer. She had contracted a deadly disease just to get that knowledge; someone may as well benefit from it.

Coven looked wistfully at the murals covering her own walls, great vistas of the Alps, the Grand Canyon, Mount Rushmore, the Black Forest, a South American jungle ... which made her think of similar paintings on the Population I ship. She never thought they looked so beautiful.

"Junior," Coven spoke quietly to the ship, leaning back in her chair with a sigh, "did I ever tell you why I left Earth?"

"No, Mary."

"I grew up in a dirty, ugly city filled with dirty, ugly people. And when I had fought my way out of the slums to see the real world, I found that the rest wasn't so pretty either, not what I thought it would be at all. So I left." Coven looked again at the old vistas of Earth. Things might have been different if her expectations hadn't been so high.

Over the next few days, Coven watched the red intaglio of plague creeping down her cheeks and neck, beginning to lace her arms. Her hands had developed a bothersome trembling which she could not control, and at times she found it increasingly difficult to breathe.

The Earth fell away from *Proud Mary* like a shed tear. Coven had stopped only long enough to tell the authorities that she wouldn't be coming back, and to transmit the data Junior had obtained on the Population I ship.

The Astro-Archaeology Foundation immediately named her the recipient of their most generous reward. Coven snapped into the transmitter, asking what in the world she was supposed to do with it.

"Shall we give it to your next of kin?" they had asked.

"If I had any next of kin, would I spend all my time out here alone?"

She listened to the confused pause. There had been someone once, but he had meant nothing to her. When he fell ill from some strange virus with a Latin name, she dragged him to the hospital, when everyone else would have left him to die in the alley, to rot and become compost for a new crop of garbage. Perhaps she should have left him; it would have saved the doctors the trouble of killing him. It was an accident, they said, we injected him with the wrong vaccine. It happened from time to time. They treated a lot of people, and they couldn't be right every time. It was a good thing he had meant nothing to her. Coven was glad she could forget all about it.

The voice interrupted her thoughts, "Um … what shall we do with your monetary compensation then?"

Coven thought of several things the stuffy bureaucrat could do with it, but answered, "Why don't you use it to make me a martyr? Build a statue and put it next to my memorial."

Where do you go to die?

A star named Meyer: a blood-red dwarf surrounded by a tight halo of rubble, scattered asteroids in nothing resembling an ecliptic. The faint star grew larger day by day, slowly becoming prominent across the rich field of stars ahead of the *Proud Mary*.

"Do you want to play another game of chess, Mary?"

"No, Junior."

"I promise I will not try so hard this time."

"I said *no*."

"But I'm bored, Mary."

"You can't be bored. You're a computer."

"Oh, well, *you* are bored, then."

Mary didn't answer.

The JR was silent for a few moments, then continued, "Do you know there is another ship following us, Mary?"

She snapped up, looking out the viewport, but could see nothing in the dizzying infinity of stars. "What?"

"It started to follow about a day after we left Earth, when you delivered your message."

Coven scowled. "Tell it to go away."

"It refuses to acknowledge."

"What kind of a ship is it?"

"Similar to ours, only slightly more efficient. We cannot outrun it —and it is slowly gaining on us."

"The pilot sure doesn't want to go to Meyer. I've been there and, believe me, it's not the party spot of the galaxy. It's got some broken asteroids around it, and I'm hoping to find a comfortable one. But what does that idiot want?"

Silence fell on the ship as Junior paused, trying to communicate with the other ship. "He says he wants to dock."

Coven almost jumped, her arms shaking as the red lines burned their way down into her marrow. "Is he *crazy*? Tell him to kiss off, Junior."

Junior paused, as if uncomfortable. "But then he will be mad at me, Mary."

Coven pursed her lips, thinking. "All right, Junior. Check your charts and see if you can plot a roundabout route to Meyer. Now let me talk to that Burnhead following us, and when I signal, hit the brakes and change course. That should throw him off."

"Hit the brakes, Mary?"

"Decelerate rapidly. At the speed we're going, his ship will be out of range before he realizes we've made a complete fool out of him."

Coven frowned smugly as the JR opened a direct commlink to the other ship. She refused to allow a visual linkup, waiting until Junior said the man on the other end was listening.

"Look, Space Cadet, I've got the *plague*! You don't want to see me. Everything I got from Population I has been sent to Earth. You're wasting your time. Now *leave me alone*!"

Coven signaled to one of Junior's optical sensors, then braced herself as *Proud Mary* lurched onto a new course. She watched as the following ship blazed past like a bullet to vanish instantly in the distance.

"Bye, bye, sucker."

Meyer loomed ahead of them like a drop of clotting blood. Junior analyzed the scattered clumps of asteroids, checking out some of the major ones, searching for a place for Coven to stay.

They entered the outer fringes of the distorted belt, passing into the thin forest of rocks. Junior's voice sounded anxious as he broke Coven's bleary silence in the cockpit.

"It is not my fault, Mary."

Coven looked up and tried to focus her eyes behind the pounding in her head. "What isn't your fault, Junior?"

"Our friend is back."

She stiffened, her fingers clenching convulsively in the grip of the advancing plague. "*How?*"

"He had a fairly good idea of where we were going, Mary."

"How close is he?"

"Still far from visual range, but he has definitely found us."

"Well, lose him again!"

"How, Mary?"

She drew in a deep breath. A muscle on her neck twitched violently. "All right, Junior, pay attention. I'm going to give you a lesson on how to get rid of a pain in the ass!"

"I have no bodily parts, Mary."

"Shut up and listen. Find a dense concentration of asteroids and shoot through them, placing them between us and his line of sight. Then alter course to find another tight cloud of rocks and do the same thing a couple of times until he has no way of knowing where we are."

Coven slumped in her chair, fighting to keep her vision straight. Over the days it had taken to finally reach Meyer, her arms had developed a perpetual trembling that occasionally turned into a seizure. Deep-seated headaches dug into her mind, and her vision blurred often. She had given up looking in the mirror, and tried not to notice the livid red tracery engraved into her arms. Junior now had almost complete control over the *Proud Mary*, and Coven's conscience nagged at her for trusting the inexperienced JR to do stunt-flying in the asteroid field. But she certainly could not have done any better herself.

"Now what, Mary?" Junior repeated, and Coven realized that

she had passed out briefly. Junior had taken them through several passages of asteroids.

Coven's mind spun as she tried to remember what she had planned. "Okay, Junior. Now plot a typical orbit around one of those asteroids and inject us into it. Kill all the engines, and we'll drift in the arms of the Holy Laws of Physics for a while. He has no way of seeing that we're not just another rock, unless he comes into visual range of us. And the chances of that are ..."

"Would you like me to calculate them, Mary?"

"No! Just get him off my back!"

Proud Mary drifted in an elliptical orbit for a day and a half, undisturbed, slowly wheeling around the red star Meyer. Mary Coven passed through fits of violent trembling, throbbing headaches. And the broken scarlet lines seemed to sear deeper into her skin. She alternated periods of tranquilizers and stimulants, trying to decide which worked better.

Junior's insistent voice brought her out of a half-conscious state, slumped in the cockpit. Coven opened bleary eyes and fixed her gaze on the mural of the Badlands for a long moment before acknowledging.

"I think I have found a suitable asteroid for you, Mary."

"Give me some statistics."

"It is a sun-grazer of greater-than-average mass. It has a temporary atmosphere like a comet now that it's near the star, mostly nitrogen and some oxygen. Mean surface temperature is thirteen degrees centigrade."

Coven nodded, focusing her attention. "A little chilly, but what can I expect?"

"It will be able to support you for a few months before it gets too close to the star. During perihelion, the entire surface will be molten."

Coven smiled grimly. "That's what I wanted. I don't want anybody else to come here and catch my little cold. Besides, it looks like I won't be needing a place for more than ... a short while."

"Shall I take you there, Mary?"

"What are you waiting for?"

Dust settled around the *Proud Mary*, slowly clearing around the viewports, and Coven looked out at the asteroid she had chosen. She took the last four of her stimulants, found an oxygen mask, and told Junior she wanted to go outside.

"I must warn you, Mary, to take the proper precautions. You may become exposed to contaminated air."

Coven huffed. "Junior, haven't you been *listening*? I've already got the damned plague!"

The JR didn't answer, but instead slid open the first airlock hatch. Coven stepped inside the chamber and waited to be cycled through. The second hatch opened, and she stepped onto new soil.

Coven smiled ironically and spoke. "I hereby name you asteroid Quarantine."

The blood-red sheen of Meyer thickened the sky to a viscous purple, staining the lifeless scattered rocks in an eerie forest of shadows. The landscape was woven and broken, much like her, and she shivered in the chilly air. Then she decided to build a campfire as she had seen in some of the old pictures, and smiled in a burst of unwelcome nostalgia.

After convincing Junior to leave the double hatch of *Proud Mary* open, Coven collected a pile of combustibles and cleared a campsite within a cluster of rock pinnacles near the ship. Gritting her teeth to help control her trembling hands, she tried to light the pile of charts, cushions, and scrap paper, finally succeeding.

Coven leaned back against a cold rock, staring deep into the fire that was struggling to stay lit in the small oxygen content of the air. Brilliant points of light sparkled above her, other asteroids moving with Quarantine around the red dwarf. The dead asteroid was deeply silent. She couldn't even hear her own breathing.

A muffled sound came from inside the ship, as if Junior was calling to her, but Coven ignored it, trying to resist the clutches of unconsciousness that tugged at her. The stimulants weren't working.

A noise appeared off to her side, clear and unexpected in the thin air. She roused herself, then turned to look with reluctant, unfocusing eyes on a man, sealed completely behind the black visor of a full spacesuit. He stepped out of the shadows and walked toward her. Even here he had followed.

"Mary Coven."

Shock paralyzed her for an instant as she gagged on a quick gasp of air. Her limbs shuddered violently, but somehow she found the strength to lurch to her feet and run. Her breath was almost gone and the cold, filtered air of Quarantine stabbed at her deteriorating lungs.

She danced across the broken, low-gravity surface, winding her way through mazes of fallen rocks. The man followed, but his bulky spacesuit slowed his pursuit. Coven pulled ahead, hoping she would lose him in the jumbled labyrinth of broken rock, wondering how he could possibly have found her, but then she realized how few asteroids around Meyer were capable of supporting life.

Coven quickly became exhausted. Her body shuddered, finding it almost impossible to breathe in the grip of the disease. She stumbled, falling to the rocky dust as both knees gave out simultaneously.

In the distance behind her she could hear the clank of the man's heavy boots as he crunched across the surface, following her. Desperately, she crawled into a shallow cave, hoping to hide in the shadows. Trembling, she fell against the far wall, shuddering with another seizure, her very marrow trying to crawl out of her bones.

He stood silhouetted in the cave opening, a bulky figure against the bloody sky. "You can't run away anymore, Mary."

She picked up a rock from the ground and threw it, trying to smash his black faceplate. But her trembling arm sent the stone flying off to the man's side.

"No violence now!" he snapped.

"Who are you? What do you want?"

"You have something from Population I. As a fellow scavenger, I want it."

"I told you, Burnhead, I gave everything to Earth! I have nothing left!"

"You have the *plague*," he answered quietly and moved toward her.

In Coven's shocked silence, he removed a medical kit from his suit and fumbled with a syringe in thickly gloved hands. He grabbed her red-laced arm and jabbed the needle into her skin, beginning to draw blood.

"The 'Star Search' charter specifically states that they will pay substantially for *any* remnant of the Population I race. And this is the virus that destroyed them. What could be more important than that?"

He paused, looking into her wide, steely eyes from behind his opaque mask. "Think of how much we can learn about their physiology just by studying the disease that killed them off. Since you have declined your reward, I'm sure the Foundation will be much more generous with my own compensation."

Coven found her outrage was enough to let her shout at him. "You're crazy! What if the plague gets loose? It'll destroy the human race just like it wiped out Population I!"

The man filled a second vial of blood, poking her other arm when one artery seemed to run dry. "They'll take the proper precautions. Don't be such a pessimist."

"I grew up in the slums, Buddy-boy. I am, by definition, a pessimist."

The man didn't listen. He clipped the two vials of blood into his medical kit and carefully sterilized his equipment. "Thank you, Mary Coven."

She cried out after him. "You're botching up my entire sacrifice! I might as well have gone back to Earth and died in a comfortable hospital bed."

He turned his faceless helmet at her. "We all make bad judgments." And then he was gone.

Coven stayed in the cave a long time before she slowly got up on unsteady legs and began to stumble back to the *Proud Mary*. The doors were still wide open, and Junior's voice was incessantly calling for her.

"Mary! Mary!"

She went haltingly inside, and blood rushed painfully to her head. She stopped the JR's excited chatter, "1 know, Junior. He's already gone."

The computer paused as if waiting to spring a surprise. "But he'll be back."

She lifted her eyes to one of the speakers, frowning, then she winced as pain shot through her body. "What?"

"I thought you might like some company, rather than being alone on this asteroid. So, after he had left his ship, I contacted his computer—a primitive thing: no personality, able to do only its main functions, unable to stand up to even the weakest argument—and I reprogrammed it. Shortly after takeoff, his computer will direct the thermal energy from his engines into the cockpit, quickly raising the temperature to about three hundred degrees centigrade."

Junior's voice seemed to hint that he took pride in his new understanding of human nature. "So, the pilot will decide he was much more comfortable here on Quarantine and he will come back to you, Mary."

Coven stared at the JR console, eyes wide. "Three *hundred* centigrade! Junior! He is a biological organism. At that temperature we ... combust!"

A flicker of light caught her eye, and she looked up into the purplish sky to see a brilliant shooting star falling back to the asteroid.

"I am sorry, Mary." Junior sounded crushed. "Did I do something wrong again?"

Coven absently rubbed her arm where the man had drawn blood from her. Then she slowly forced a smile, wondering if Junior was truly as naive as be seemed to be or—?

"No, Junior. You did just fine."

When I worked at the Lawrence Livermore National Laboratory as a technical writer by day and struggling science fiction writer by night, I met visiting researcher Doug Beason. Doug was a high-energy physicist and an officer in the Air Force, and also an aspiring writer who had published a few stories in the same small press magazines as I had. Naturally, we gravitated toward each other and decided to write a story together.

This was our second effort. We developed a unique idea for organic solar sails grown for use in the inner solar system among space stations filled with different cultures.

In his youth, Doug had spent time in the Philippines at the Subic Bay Naval Base, and he drew upon those experiences to add a unique flavor to the story.

"If I Fell, Would I Fall" was published in Amazing Stories Magazine, one of our first professional publications, and later reprinted in a solar sail anthology edited by David Brin.

Not satisfied with just that, Doug and I expanded this idea into our full novel Lifeline, which we sold to Bantam Books as part of a three-book contract. So that was an auspicious first meeting for the two of us.

You can read the full story in Lifeline.

IF I FELL, WOULD I FALL

(with Doug Beason)

Encased in the vast organic solar sail creature, Ramis watched through the monitors, studying his course. The Earth seemed like an oil painting below him, reaching out to swallow him in its oceans.

But the sail-creature's orbit approached no closer than two Earth radii at its nearest point, then swooped back out again toward L-5. Leaving the planet behind, they climbed toward the Orbitech 1 colony.

Ramis shifted his position in the cramped cyst as the sail-creature tacked the solar wind. He had no room to move, no place to stretch. After sitting for a week, it began to frustrate him to tears. He took paranoid care not to bump or damage the seven sail-creature embryos at his feet.

The boy snapped open the faceplate of his spacesuit and filled his lungs with humid air. Ramis didn't want to leave the helmet open long; hard radiation still penetrated even the sail-creature's tough exoskeleton—but the fresh oxygen in the cavity drove back the claustrophobic dankness for a while. The air smelled wet from the thick wall-kelp growing unchecked inside the cyst. On the rescue mission he brought several kelp nodules, enough to start a forest growing along the walls of Orbitech 1, and it gave him food to eat for the journey.

Ramis groped around the spongy cyst until he found the joystick controls for the external video camera. Swiveling the camera, he focused on the bright pinpoint of the L-5 colony waxing closer and closer. A week ago the starving colony had been invisible against the stars. Now, under high magnification he could just make out the two counter-rotating wheels of Orbitech 1. Also at L-5, the Soviet station revolved slowly into view on the fringe of the gravity well.

After the war, time was growing short for them—for him, for everybody.

"Calling Orbitech 1!" Ramis squinted at the screen in front of him. Why weren't they answering? "Orbitech 1 come in please."

Ramis muttered under his breath. He had been talking to himself too much in the past few days. "How am I supposed to rescue you if you won't answer?" He snapped the helmet shut.

Maybe his radio's gain was too weak. Maybe he had used the batteries too much over the past few days, discussing his orbit with people on the Filipino colony, the Aguinaldo—his home—just to quell his loneliness and isolation. As he'd swung close to Earth, he had scanned the radio bands. Briefly he caught a burst of political rhetoric, but it faded into static before he could make sense of it.

To keep himself occupied, he squinted at the crosshairs on the video screen. The camera angle constantly changed to account for the Orbitech colony's motion. By centering the image in the crosshairs, the sail-creature would tack ahead and arrive at the right position to intercept the colony in its orbit. He was off course by only a fraction of a radian, but with thousands of kilometers left to travel, he would miss Orbitech 1 with room to spare.

Time to steer again. Ramis withdrew a small knife then looked at the crosshairs, judging the angle from inside the cyst. With the point of the blade he poked the creature's sensitive internal membrane.

The cyst tightened. Ramis felt a tension, a ripple, as the sail's reflexes turned it away from the knife's prick. The lumbering movement seemed to take years, but the L-5 colony finally drifted to the center of the crosshairs again.

Once more, he tried counting stars, then making up rhymes, reciting the biblical passages he had had to memorize during catechism years before. Anything to make him forget about the boredom for a while, or to forget about his incredibly slim chances for ever returning to the Aguinaldo. If he could only stretch his legs.

Ramis remembered coming by accident upon the Aguinaldo's

president, Yoli Magsaysay, four months before. The leader stood staring out a greenhouse window, mesmerized by the image of Earth—from here the planet shone blue and beautiful, looking unscarred from its last war. In the harsh shadows, Magsaysay appeared thin, with mottled brown skin and flecks of gray and white peppering his bushy hair. He moved painfully on joints calcified from years in low gravity.

Unaware of Ramis, Magsaysay muttered to himself. "We've always been able to find plenty of reasons for war, no matter how many problems we eliminate. A terrorist explodes an atomic weapon, and the fingerpointing escalates—"

Ramis startled the leader. "But they just can't leave us here to starve! How are we supposed to survive without the supply ships?"

Magsaysay turned back to Earth. "They have no choice. The war did not destroy them, but it caused enough damage that they cannot possibly send any more ships up here. It will be ten or more years before they can rebuild ... they must conquer their own problems before they can come back for us.

"We people on the Lagrange colonies are just more casualties in another war. Our numbers are already written in their books. We are on our own."

Ramis had a frightening, claustrophobic realization of just how isolated they were on the colonies, stranded with no ships even to get to each other or back to Earth. The last shuttle-transport had been hijacked by a gang of desperate people from Orbitech 1 and crash landed near Clavius Base on the Moon. The Lagrange colonies' few feeble attempts at self-sustenance—their symbolic but tiny hydroponic fields of wheat, corn, and rice—would not be enough to last them very long.

But the Filipino bioengineering mavericks kept the people on the Aguinaldo alive, just barely, with a strain of experimental wall-kelp and the sail-creatures developed years before.

The wall-kelp tasted bland, but it was better than no food. Ramis and all the others had been eating nothing else for four months now, ever since the supplies from Earth had dwindled away. Cut off and isolated at L-4, the Aguinaldo had listened to the transmissions from Orbitech 1. The pitiful pleas for help growing gradually more desperate; the grim news of starvation, rioting, and even hints of cannibalism. The Soviets in their colony had fallen silent soon after the war. The Filipino colonists could do nothing but listen—they had no ship to send, no help to offer.

Until now.

Inside the sail-creature, looking at Orbitech 1, Ramis felt like he was falling, falling down toward the station. Space gave him no reference, no horizon, no gravity. The direction "down" was where things fell when you dropped them ... but out in space, everywhere was "down."

Ramis groped out to touch the walls of the cyst, searching for stability, trying to fight off the sickening vertigo. He would be falling forever, because there was no place to land.

He squeezed shut his eyes. Sleep came, and with it, tumultuous memories....

Being at Jumpoff, at one end-cap of the Aguinaldo's cylinder, was like standing at the bottom of a gargantuan well. The lightaxis stretched above as Ramis floated at one end of the zero-G core. He squinted to see the other end, ten kilometers away. The column of fiberoptic threads making up the lightaxis glowed with raw sunlight. Clusters of children played in the core, punctuated by sail-creatures darting in and out, keeping the youngsters away from the lightaxis. Adults circumnavigated the rim, leaping from bouncer to bouncer in an ever-accelerating race around the circumpond.

Living areas curled up around the cylindrical colony's side, snaking across the fields, the rice paddies, stadiums, streams, and the circumferential Sibyuan Sea. Fields of taro and abaca dotted the living areas. Experimental sectors of wall-kelp covered the remainder of the Aguinaldo, allowing little of the colony's metallic structure to show.

Revolving around the long lightaxis, Ramis's whole world seemed as though it might collapse and fall to the center. The sight always made him dizzy.

Pushing off, Ramis closed his eyes. As a child, he could always escape here, be alone. His thoughts drifted to the Council of Twenty. After all the talk, all the rhetoric, they finally had decided to try and help the L-5 colonies.

Dr. Sandovaal had bullied them to try a desperate attempt,

exploiting the sail-creatures. The creatures had both mitochondria and chloroplasts within their cell walls: They were both plant and animal, a one-in-a-million accidental success from the bioengineering labs. Somehow everything had worked exactly right; everything fit together, everything functioned as it should.

And when exposed to vacuum, Sandovaal argued that the creatures would still metabolize, using the hard solar radiation for direct photosynthesis. It would be the sail-creature's last gasp for survival … its fins would elongate in a feeble attempt to maximize its light-collecting area for photosynthesis. The sail-creatures would metamorphose and take on their plant attributes, becoming a largely immobile receptor of solar radiation.

Working in vacuum, the bioengineers had attempted to accelerate the growth of three of the creatures. As the Aguinaldo's Chief Scientist, Dr. Sandovaal directed the ejection of the first anesthetized creature. It had exploded from its own internal pressure, unable to compensate for the vacuum fast enough.

On the next attempt, they did not drug the second creature into complete dormancy—and it successfully expanded in the cold vacuum. But its metamorphosis had been too fast, too violent for the restraining hooks connecting it to the Aguinaldo. The sail-creature had torn free and drifted away.

Ramis was there, peering out the windowplates as two engineers wearing manned-maneuvering units jetted after the still-growing sail, but they could not recapture the creature and turn it around without damaging the thin membrane. The two engineers looked like tiny dolls as they floated back to the docking bay, side by side.

But the third creature had survived the accelerated metamorphosis. The bioengineers oriented the sail-creature's proto-sails edge-on to the Sun to prevent the solar photons from accelerating the sail before the process was complete. Day by day the creature's fins spread out, becoming vast cell-thin sails, immense and opaque, hundreds of kilometers to a side, as the creature desperately tried to soak up light. The main bodily core became rigid and exceedingly tough, like an organic "hull."

Ramis would have to ride inside, go to the L-5 colony.

President Magsaysay, Ramis's mentor, had gone out of his way to be with the boy, trying to talk to him, spend time together. But

Ramis wanted to be alone, to think. After all, Ramis had been picked for the mission—he deserved some time alone.

Now he ached for any company at all.

***

"What we want to do is this, so pay attention, boy." Dr. Sandovaal rapped on the surface of the stereotank with his old-fashioned pointer stick. The image in the tank jiggled, then focused again into a diagram of the Earth-Moon system.

"When we release you from the Aguinaldo, you will turn the sail so that it faces the Sun, taking the full momentum of the solar photons. You will then be moving 'backward' in orbit, relative to L-4. In about three hours, this will provide enough braking to slow you from our normal orbital velocity down to three kilometers per second. You must then turn your sail edgewise—you will drop like a stone toward Earth, skim past it at a distance of about an extra Earth radius, and then head back up to where you started."

On the stereotank a blue dashed line appeared, tracing Ramis's planned trajectory. "But while you've been going down and coming back up, the Moon, L-4, and L-5 have been continuing their own orbits. By the time you return to the starting point, L-5 will be there instead of L-4."

Ramis studied the diagram. "So I am just killing time by going down to Earth? Waiting for the other points to change position?"

President Magsaysay watched Ramis, looking troubled, but Ramis ignored him, keeping a brave, calm expression on his face. Sandovaal rapped his fingers on the polished tabletop. "Correct! Think of it as being on a merry-go-round. You are on one horse, which is the Aguinaldo. You hop off the merry-go-round, wait for the next horse to pass by—which is the Moon—and then hop back on when the third horse comes into position. That is Orbitech 1."

"But how long is this going to take?" Magsaysay stared at the dashed blue line, as if counting time.

"Nine or ten days, depending on how large we can grow the sail and how accurately the boy can maneuver with it. We cannot leave him out there any longer than absolutely necessary—his suit and the sail-creature's exoskeleton will provide little protection from the cosmic radiation … and we want to reach Orbitech as soon as possible."

Ramis remained silent for a moment, looking around the empty chamber. The room was large, dominated by a long meeting table surrounded by unoccupied chairs. Overhead, shadows of passing pedal-kites and playing children crossed over the skylights of the chamber. Ramis set his mouth. "The sail-creature—it will die, now that the metamorphosis has taken place?"

"Eventually." Sandovaal blinked his eyes at Ramis, as if wondering at the relevance of the boy's comment.

Ramis swallowed. "How long do I have?"

"We cannot implant you too soon—the creature's physical structure is still hardening, you see. Still forming a rigid sheath to keep the new sails in place. But the timing will be close—after we encyst you, the trip should take ten days."

"You told me that. I want to know how long the sail-creature will live."

Sandovaal switched off the stereotank, letting the images fade back into the murk. As the lights came up, Ramis watched Magsaysay nod to Sandovaal. Sandovaal pursed his lips. "It will die within two weeks, or possibly less. We have too little data to be confident. However, we will provide you with hormone injections to induce nerve reactions—you should still be able to move its sails. If the sail-creature ceases to respond before you reach Orbitech 1, you will not be able to steer. And then you will be trapped."

Magsaysay's shoulders sagged and he started to speak up, but Sandovaal cut him off. "But it is still possible. I am confident."

The President did not look greatly consoled. He turned again to Ramis, as if pleading with him to change his mind. Ramis stood, his face expressionless as he pushed away from the meeting table. "Thank you, Dr. Sandovaal." He strode from the room and headed for Jumpoff to drift alone in the core.

⚛

Ramis was cramped, hot. The air in the cyst stifled him. The pain in his joints ached without relief. He felt dizzy most of the time now, sick to his stomach. Dr. Sandovaal had warned him that the suit might not protect him enough from the hard radiation—and

164

he would have no chance if a large solar flare occurred. He envisioned a long time recovering from this journey ... if he survived at all.

The sail-creature hardly responded to Ramis's course-adjusting maneuvers anymore. Reluctant, Ramis had to resort to deep, vicious jabs with the knife to get the creature to turn even a little.

But the L-5 colony filled up most of the viewscreen, like a rotating dumbbell with two wheels spinning on a central axle.

Ramis reached out and stroked the cyst's inner membrane through the thick jungle of wall-kelp growing unchecked inside the cavity. He didn't know if the creature could feel him, or respond, but he continued to caress. It kept his hands occupied.

Ramis conserved the batteries in his transceiver, using it only occasionally to send a signal to the L-5 colony; he had long ago passed out of range of the Aguinaldo. Magsaysay had promised that they would continue to transmit to Orbitech 1, telling them what to expect, how they could receive the life-saving supplies Ramis was bringing them. But the boy had no way of knowing if those messages had been acknowledged, or even received. Was anybody alive on the Orbitech colony?

The wheels' metallic surfaces glinted in the sunlight, causing bright flares and smears on the video screen. The colony's observation windows glimmered with light from the inside, naked and devoid of wall-kelp. It looked strange to Ramis, but he could not focus the video camera enough to see inside.

What if he found no one at all? How would he ever get back? He would never even get inside the colony unless someone opened the airlock and took him in. And the sail-creature was almost dead— that left Ramis with no way back home.

"Orbitech 1, I am almost to you."

A loud meaningless crackle returned, but Ramis kept trying. They had to know he was coming. No one could mistake the sight of the vast organic solar sail drifting closer every day. He almost missed it when a weak voice came from the speaker. He knew his transceiver battery was almost dead.

"###tech here### Ready###receive you."

As Ramis caressed the inner membrane of the sail-creature, he silently willed the behemoth to remain alive just a short while longer.

They rapidly closed on the L-5 colony. To slow him down enough so that impact with the colony would not kill him, Ramis had to collapse the sail-creature's broad and beautiful sails, draw them in to cushion him from the crash.

Orbitech 1 gleamed on the monitor. He knew which end would have the docking bay, where the people would be waiting for him. He watched the wheels turning, one clockwise, the other counterclockwise. With each rotation of the colony, the creature drifted nearer. Ramis swallowed. The picture on the monitor screen blurred from his tears.

Moving slowly, Ramis withdrew the pressurized vial from its cellophane pack, along with the tiny explosive-driven carrier pellets.

He had to judge when the time was right. He had to know, and he could not hesitate. If he botched this up, then he would have done all this for nothing, and made a martyr of himself as well.

And more importantly, he would have extinguished the last hope of survival for those inside the L-5 colony.

He could see the details of the airlock now, the Orbitechnologies corporate logo, the viewing windows on either side of it. The colony swelled to fill the entire video screen.

Ramis felt the sweat of his fingers inside the gloves, holding the vial of pressurized trigger-hormone, slick against the mylar of his suit. He rammed the hypodermic cartridge inside the sail-creature's membrane and ejected its contents.

Reacting with incredible slowness, the sails collapsed. They drew in toward the cyst, lumbering together as a butterfly might bring in its wings. The cell-thin sails stretched scores of kilometers out in front of the cyst. With the sudden movement wispy fragments tore away, rippling like the shrouds of a ghost.

The sail-creature's crumpled body struck the L-5 colony, pushing against the tattered ends of its sails. Ramis felt the impact ripple through the creature's flesh, but the boy was padded by the curtains of wall-kelp and kilometers of sail. The minute-long collision dragged on; it seemed to take hours.

He felt himself drifting back again, rebounding. Suddenly, panic burned through him. If he drifted out of the colony's grasp, then he would be stranded again, without even the sails for maneuvering.

The video monitor was dark; outside, the cameras had been covered up by folds of the collapsed sails. Ramis sealed his helmet, made certain that the sail-creature embryos were protected in their airtight canisters, then he took out his knife.

He had to get out; he had to do something before it was too late. Ramis shouted again into the transmitter. Nothing. He saw that he had left it on—the battery was dead.

He hesitated only a moment, then plunged the knife into the tough membrane, trying to cut his way out of the cyst. When the blade broke through to the outside, decompression almost ripped the knife out of his hand. The out-rushing air tore the gash open wider, but acting as a jet to push him back toward the colony. Ramis continued to saw with the knife edge. Crystals sparkled as the humidity inside the cyst flash-froze, layering everything with a thin coating of ice. One of the wall-kelp bladders burst and froze in the same second.

Ramis could see partly through the opening in the cyst, and then he felt a tug on the carcass of the sail-creature. He peered out and saw several figures in spacesuits near him, attaching a tether to keep him from drifting with the recoil from impact.

The boy felt drained with relief, but he could not yet relax. He kept hacking with his knife, trying to make the opening wide enough for him to emerge. One of the suited figures swam up in front of him, face to face, nodding.

Ramis was startled to see behind the faceplate a thin, fearful expression, but the face bore a look of hope and wonderment that cut through weeks of despair.

The boy emerged from the hulk of the dead sail-creature, feeling like a newborn coming out of a womb. He turned back to see the creature's shriveled remains. The once-magnificent sails now looked as if someone had crumpled up a gigantic wad of paper and tossed it aside.

Sharp needles of pain struck him in his joints, and uneasy tremors raced through his muscles. But it felt wonderful just to move again, to stretch, to be free. He stared down and saw only an infinity of stars, not the curved wall of the Aguinaldo as he was accustomed to seeing. If he started to fall, he would keep falling forever and ever....

Dizzy, he looked up at the large observation windows on either side of the airlock. Pressed against them he saw scattered faces with large gaps between them—pitifully few faces. They looked as gaunt and anxious as the one he had seen inside the suit.

One of the men wrestled the knife from his hand. Ramis was too weary to struggle, so he released it and kicked toward the airlock. He tried to make motions to show them what they needed to get from the cyst. He saw them taking out the sail-creature embryos; they also needed to remove the wall-kelp nodules. The wall-kelp would survive for some time in the vacuum, but they needed to bring it inside as soon as possible.

As he drifted through the maw of the towering docking bay doors, another spacesuited figure took his arm and directed him to one of the doors at the wall. He supposed it was an elevator shaft. His legs continued to tremble, and he felt ready to dissolve inside his suit.

Behind him, he saw the suited figures cutting at the dead creature's crumpled sails, getting at its body core. The severed tissue-thin sails drifted away as the L-5 colony continued in its orbit.

Though he felt incredibly weary and dizzy from his journey, Ramis waited by the elevator shaft and watched the other colonists bring in the wall-kelp and embryos. The frozen kelp strands were still edible, and the central nodules would survive. His escort seemed impatient and urged him to enter the elevator.

As the spokeshaft elevator descended, the chamber filled with air. Ramis could feel his weight increase as they traveled out to the rim of the wheel where the artificial gravity was strongest.

His escort cracked open his helmet and indicated for Ramis to do the same. Ramis took a deep breath of the warm, stale air of the industrial colony. A potpourri of odors wafted past, very different from the humid stifling air of the cramped cyst. The smell was metallic, scrubbed clean—more artificial than the Aguinaldo's.

A buzz of people surrounded the elevator. Arms reached out to embrace him, and he almost collapsed in their grasp. He looked frantically around. The men with the embryos must have gone into one of the other elevators into another part of the wheel. Ramis stood on his tip-toes and called out, wondering what he should do. "Wait—the sail-creatures! They are my only way back! I need to tell you about the wall-kelp—"

One man stepped up to him, pushing his way through the

crowd. "—Curtis Brahms, Acting Director of Orbitech 1." He seemed to be out of breath. He shook Ramis's gloved hand. "Welcome to our colony. I hope you brought a miracle with you. We had only … unpleasant options left."

Ramis studied the man, trying to quell the urgency he felt. "The wall-kelp is a chance for you to survive."

"It's been taken to a safe place. You can speak to our scientists after we've shown you your quarters. You're in the same boat with the rest of us, I'm afraid. You'll be here a while."

The boy tried not to think of the Aguinaldo, of the many years he would have to live here before the other sail-creature embryos reached maturity.

But a ripple of optimism ran through the crowd. Though he knew the bad times weren't over, somehow he felt the birth of a new spirit of hope.

In my mid-fifties, I went back to college to get my MFA, taking various interesting-sounding classes in order to collect enough credits for my degree. One of those classes was on Romance Writing, and the instructor gave us brief exercises to explore different techniques popular in the genre.

For this flash-fiction erotica assignment, we were supposed to write a striptease scene. Fortunately for me, the instructor didn't specify that it had to be about a human....

SHOW ME SOME SKIN

Veils! Why are there so many veils covering every scrap of my skin, when I know from the outset that the lusty, leering, unshaven men in this mining colony only want to see *skin*? That's what I'm here for, though I don't understand it.

I step out on stage to the hoots and whistles and catcalls, but most important to me, I can feel the blazing light shining down, hungry lights, delicious lights. The lasers flicker around in tempo with the exotic synthesizer music that doesn't sound like music at all to me. I would much prefer the cold and dusty wind outside on the planetoid's surface.

I am a native lifeform here, and a human form is not natural to me, but it's what is required … desired.

I begin to peel off the gauzy veils from my head, trying to match the rhythm of the incomprehensible music, and as the cloth slides away from my green skin, I can feel the light, tingling, nourishing.

The whistles from the audience build to a frenzy, as if the men have never seen a forehead before, or a delicate nose, or cheeks. Yes, it is green skin, but these men are covered with so much dust and alkali that they don't care; they just want the sight of clean, feminine skin.

I know this form is beautiful to them, and I pucker my lips, let out a long sigh even though I don't need to breathe. I keep unwinding the veils, showing a smooth green shoulder, just enough skin that the grain patterns are discernible, whorls and ripples as the lines of sap travel through my body.

The light shining down is like a feast to me, previously blocked by the cloth, and I have to control myself to keep from simply flinging away all the garments, to expose all of my thirsty and hungry skin to the nourishing light. But the miners don't want that. They want to be teased.

I have to do as I am told, or I and all of my compatriots will not be allowed to stand alone, simply turning our naked and receptive bodies up to the harsh sun. This world has minerals in the soil and water, and plenty of sunshine, but not much else. We have what we need, but these miners have come to scrape away the minerals, the crystals they call gems. I dance to keep them happy, so that my people can be left alone.

I unwrap more of my garments, exposing both arms, my shoulders, slipping down to the curve of my firm breasts with brown nipples that someone compared to beautiful round knots in pine wood.

The music keeps throbbing, and I begin to sway as if there is sunlight and wind. All of my people sway in the wind. We are flexible, and I am flexible now.

I keep pulling off the garments down to my hips. I raise one of my legs, showing a bare, perfectly formed foot. They are cheering now, maddened with desire. I am the idealized form for I have shaped my body like this, and I enjoy the attention. I thrive on the last few moments.

My people survive by photosynthesizing the sunlight. My green skin drinks in the nourishment we need, and when we reproduce, we do so with pollen and seeds. We find it very gratifying.

But this is not what the humans want. They call for me to "Take it all off!" And I oblige, pulling away the cloth skirt, exposing the rest of my body to the bright and hungry lights. I turn the curve of my hips, and then the moment is gone and I hear their groans of disappointment, their mutters.

Even though I have laid myself bare and removed all my garments, stood there in my naked glory with my hips thrust forward and my legs spread, a plant-based alien has nothing more of interest for even the lustiest of these invading miners.

I'm not always grim and serious. This is a humorous twist of some classic science fiction tropes.

Time travel and its associated paradoxes have created numerous headaches (and generated numerous story ideas) for generations of SF writers. Just imagine the legal troubles all of those paradoxes might cause!

I always intended to write more stories in this series. You may eventually see additional cases from the law offices of Paradox & Greenblatt.

PARADOX & GREENBLATT, ATTORNEYS AT LAW

You might say our little firm specializes in contradictions. In a few years Aaron Greenblatt and I are sure to be millionaire visionaries overloaded with cases, but right now our field of law is still in its infancy. We've carved out a new niche, and people are already starting to find us.

Since we can't afford a receptionist (not yet) Aaron took the call. But because he was up to his nostrils in a corporate lawsuit—a client suing Time Travel Expeditions for refusing to let him go to the late Cretaceous on a dinosaur hunt—he passed the case to me.

"Line one for you, Marty," he said as I came out of the lav, wiping my hands. "New case on the hook. Simple attempted murder, I think. Guy sounds frantic."

"They all sound frantic." I pursed my lips. "Is time travel involved?"

He nodded, and I knew there would be nothing "simple" about the case. Fortunately, temporal complications are right up our firm's alley. We're forward-thinkers, my partner and I—*and* backward-thinkers, when it's effective. That's why people call us when nobody else knows what the hell to do.

I picked up the phone and punched the solitary blinking light. "Marty Paramus here. How can I help you?"

The man talked a mile a minute in a thin, squeaky voice; even if he hadn't been panicked, it probably would have sounded unpleasant. "All I did was try to stop him from buying her some deep-fried artichoke hearts. How could that be construed as attempted murder? They can't pin anything on me, can they? Why would they think I was trying to kill anybody?"

"Maybe you'd better tell me, Mr. ... uh?"

"Hendergast. Lionel Hendergast. And I read the terms of the contract very carefully before we went back in time. It didn't say anything about deep-fried artichoke hearts."

I sighed. "What was your location, Mr. Hendergast?"

"Santa Cruz Boardwalk. The place with all the rides and the arcade games. They have concession stands and—"

"Sure, but *when* was this?"

"Umm, two days ago."

I hate having to pry all the obvious information out of a client. "Not in your time. I mean in *real* time."

"Oh, um, fifty-two years ago."

"Ah." I made a noise that hinted at a deeper understanding than I really had, yet. "One of those nostalgic life-was-better-back-then tours."

Now he sounded defensive. "Nothing illegal about them, Mr. Paramus. They're perfectly legitimate."

"So you said. But someone must think you broke the rules, or you wouldn't have been arrested. Was this person allergic to artichoke hearts or something?"

"No, not at all. And it wasn't the artichoke hearts. I was just trying to prevent him from buying them for her. I didn't want the two of them to meet."

A light bulb winked on inside my head. "Oh, one of those."

"Altering history" cases were my bread and butter.

The jail's attorney-client meeting room wasn't much better than a cell. The cinderblock walls were covered with a hardened slime of seafoam-green paint. The chairs around the table creaked, and veritable stalactites of petrified chewing gum adorned the table's underside. Since prisoners weren't allowed to chew gum, their lawyers must have been responsible for this mess. Some attorneys give the whole field a bad name.

Lionel Hendergast was in his mid-twenties but looked at least a decade older than that. His too-round face, set atop a long and skinny neck, reminded me of a smiling jack-o'-lantern balanced on a stalk. His long-fingered hands fidgeted. He looked toward me as if I were a superhero swooping in to the rescue.

"I need to understand exactly what you've done, Mr. Hendergast. Tell me the truth, and don't hold back anything. No bullshit. We have attorney-client privilege here, and I need to know what I'm working with."

"I'm innocent."

I rolled my eyes. "Listen, Mr. Hendergast—Lionel—my job is to get you off the hook for the crime of which you're accused. Let's save the declarations of innocence for the judge, okay? Now, start from the beginning."

He swallowed, took a deep breath, then said, "I took a trip back in time to the Santa Cruz Beach Boardwalk to 1973, as I said. You can get the brochure from the time travel company I used. There's nothing wrong with it, absolutely not."

"And why did you want to go to Santa Cruz?"

He shrugged unconvincingly. "The old carousel, the carnival rides, the games where you throw a ball and knock down bottles. And then there's the beach, cotton candy, churros, hot dogs, giant pretzels."

"And artichoke hearts," I prodded.

Lionel swiveled nervously in his chair, which made a protesting creak. "Deep-fried artichoke hearts are sort of a specialty there. A woman nearing the front of the line had dropped her wallet on the ground not ten feet away, but she didn't know it yet. In a few minutes, she was going to order deep-fried artichoke hearts—and when she discovered she had no money to pay, the man behind her in line would step up like a knight in shining armor, pay for her artichoke hearts, and help her search for her wallet. They'd find it, and then go out to dinner. The rest is history."

"And you seem to know the details of this history quite well. What exactly were you going to do?"

"Well, I found the woman's wallet, on purpose, so I could give it back to her. Nothing illegal in that, is there?"

I nodded, already frowning. "Thereby preventing the man

behind her from doing a good deed, stopping them from going to dinner, and"—I held my hands out—"accomplishing what?"

"If they didn't meet, then they wouldn't get married. And if they didn't get married, then they wouldn't have a son who is the true spawn of all evil."

"The Damien defense doesn't hold up in court, you know. I can cite several precedents."

"But if I had succeeded, who would have known? There would've been no crime because nothing would have happened. How can they accuse me of anything?"

"Because recorded history is admissible in a court of law," I said. "So by attempting to keep these two people from meeting, you were effectively trying to commit a murder by preventing someone from being born."

"If, if, if!" Hendergast looked much more agitated now. "But I didn't do it, so how can they hold me?"

The legal system has never been good at adapting to rapid change. Law tends to be reactive instead of proactive. When new technology changes the face of the world, the last people to deal with it—right behind senior citizens and vested union workers—are judges and the law. Remember copyright suits in the early days of the internet, when the uses and abuses of intellectual property zoomed ahead of the lawmakers like an Indy 500 race car passing an Amish horse cart?

Now, in an era of time travel tourism, with the often-contradictory restrictions the companies impose upon themselves, legal problems have been springing up like wildflowers in a manure field. Aaron Greenblatt and I formed our partnership to go after these cases. We are, in effect, creating major precedents with every case we take, win or lose.

Where was a person like Lionel Hendergast to turn? Everyone is entitled to legal representation. He didn't entirely understand the charges against him, and I was fairly certain that the judge wouldn't know what to do either. Judges dislike being forced to make up their minds from scratch, instead of finding a sufficiently similar case from which they can copy what their predecessors have done.

"Do you ever sit back and play the 'What if?' game, Mr. Paramus?" Lionel asked, startling me. "If a certain event had changed, how would your life be different? If your parents hadn't gotten divorced, your dad might not have killed himself, your mom might not have married some abusive truck driver and moved off to Nevada where she won't return your calls or even give you her correct street address? That sort of thing?"

I looked at him. Now we might finally be getting somewhere. "I've seen *It's a Wonderful Life*. Four times, in fact, including the alternate-ending version. I'm very familiar with 'What if?' Who were you trying to kill and what was the result you hoped to achieve?"

"I wasn't trying to *kill* anyone," he insisted.

From the frightened little-boy expression on Lionel's round face, I could see he wasn't a violent man. He could never have taken a gun to someone or cut the brake cables on his victim's car. He wouldn't even have had the stomach to pay a professional hit man. No, he had wanted to achieve his goal in a way that would let him sleep at night.

"The man was Delano R. Franklin," he said. "You won't find a more vile and despicable man on the face of this Earth."

I didn't want to argue with my client, though I could have pointed out some pretty likely candidates for the vile-and-despicable championship. "Much as it may pain me to say this, Lionel, being unpleasant isn't against the law."

"My parents were happily married, a long time ago. My dad had a good job. He owned a furniture store. And my mom was a receptionist in a car dealership—a dealership owned by Mr. Franklin. We had a nice home in the suburbs. I was supposed to get a puppy that Christmas."

"How old were you?"

"Four."

"And you remember all these details?"

He wouldn't look at me. "Not really, but I've heard about it a thousand times. My parents couldn't stop arguing about that day my dad took time off in the afternoon. He decided to surprise my mother over at the car dealership by bringing her a dozen long-stemmed roses."

"How romantic," I said.

"At the car dealership they take a late lunch hour so they can take care of the customer rush between noon and one. When my dad couldn't find anyone at the reception counter, he went to the back room and opened the door—only to find my mom flat on the desk with her skirt hiked up to her hips, legs wrapped around Franklin's neck, and him pumping away into her."

It wasn't the first time I had heard this sort of story. "I can see how that would ruin a marriage."

"My dad went nuts. He tried to attack Franklin and as a result, ended up in jail with charges of assault. Franklin had most of our local officials in his pocket—small town. At first my mom insisted that Franklin threatened to fire her if she didn't have sex with him. In the resulting scandal, she changed her story, saying that the affair had gone on for a while, that Franklin wanted to marry her. My parents split up, but as soon as the divorce was final, the creep wanted nothing to do with her. He kicked my mom out. She had no job, and by that time my dad had lost his furniture store."

"Sounds like a mess. So what happened to little Lionel?"

"We lived in Seaside, California—that's not far from Santa Cruz and Monterey. My dad got drunk one day and drove too fast along Highway 1."

I'd been there. "Some spectacular cliffs and tight curves on that stretch of highway."

Miserably, Lionel nodded. "The road curved, and my dad went straight. Suicide was suspected, but nobody ever proved it. Then, one day my mom just packed up, dropped me off at foster care, and left. Said she hated me because I was just like my father. I lived in six different homes until I was sixteen and old enough to emancipate myself."

I tried to sound sympathetic. "Not a very happy childhood."

"Meanwhile, Delano R. Franklin did quite well with his car dealership. In fact, he opened three more. He married some bimbo, divorced her when she got wrinkles, then married another one. Never had kids, but I think his wives were young enough to be his daughters."

I wanted to cut the rant short. "All right, but what does this have to do with deep-fried artichoke hearts?"

Tears started running down his cheeks. "I remembered my mother yelling at Franklin once. He had wooed her by telling romantic stories, describing how his own parents met. The man who would be Franklin's father came to the rescue, helped find a lady's wallet at the artichoke stand, took her out to eat ... and eventually spawned this inkblot on the human race, a uniting of sperm and egg that any compassionate God would have prevented!"

I paced around the table, locking my hands behind my back. "So you figured that if you kept Franklin's biological mother and father from meeting, he would never have been born, your parents' marriage would have remained happy, and your life would have been wonderful."

"That's about it, Mr. Paramus. But Franklin had someone watching me, so I got caught."

"Watching you? How could he possibly have suspected such an absurd thing?"

"Because I, uh ..." Lionel blushed. "I told him. I couldn't help myself. I wanted the scumbag to know he was about to be removed from existence."

I groaned. In this business, the only thing worse than a hardened criminal is an unconscionably stupid client.

"You have to get me out of here, Mr. Paramus!" Given the circumstances, an unreasonable demand. "That holding cell is a nightmare. It smells. There's no privacy even for the toilet, and they took blood samples to test me for HIV and other diseases. They drew my blood! That means other people in the cell must have those terrible diseases. What if I—"

"It's just standard procedure, Lionel." I snapped my briefcase shut. "Let me work on this and see what I can come up with. I'll try to get you bail. I'll talk to Mr. Franklin and his attorney on the off chance I can get them to drop the charges."

It was certainly a long shot, but I wanted to give poor Lionel something to cling to.

I set up a meeting in the "boardroom" of the dumpy offices Aaron and I shared. I doubted I could impress Delano Franklin, but maybe I could convince him it wasn't worth the trouble to press charges. Lionel Hendergast had almost no money, and when I learned who Franklin had hired for his own counsel to go after civil damages, I knew that money—or at least showmanship—would be a primary factor in this case.

If you look in the dictionary next to the definition of the word "shyster," you'll find a picture of Kosimo Arkulian. He was overweight, with thinning steel-gray hair in a greasy comb-over that fooled nobody. He wore too many rings, too many gold chains, and a too-large gold watch, and he spoke too loudly. You've seen Arkulian on television with his boisterous ads, flashing his jewelry and his smile, treating everyone with a hangnail of a complaint as the next big millionaire in the lawsuit sweepstakes.

When Arkulian sat down beside his client, I could tell it was going to be a testosterone war between those two men. Both were accustomed to being in charge.

I gave my most pleasant smile. "Can I offer you coffee or a soda?"

"No, thank you," Franklin said.

"This isn't a social call," Arkulian answered in a brusque tone.

"There's always time for good manners." I looked at the clock on the wall. It was 1:00. "How about Scotch, then?" I had to get Franklin to take something. "Or a bourbon? I have a very good bourbon, Booker's." From my research, I knew Franklin was quite fond of both.

"If your bourbon's expensive, I'll have one of those," he said.

Arkulian shot him a glance. "I wouldn't advise it—"

"I'm not going to get sloshed," Franklin said. "Besides, I see a genuine irony in soaking this guy for a good expensive drink."

Arkulian grinned. "Then I'll have one, too."

I had been careful to wash everything in our kitchenette before the meeting started. I quickly poured three glasses of fine bourbon, neat, and handed one to Franklin and one to Arkulian. The third I placed in front of me in a comradely gesture, though I barely sipped from it. I had a feeling I'd need to keep my wits sharp.

Franklin looked like a distinguished late-middle-aged businessman gone bad. If groomed well, he could have fit comfortably into any high-society function, but he had let himself grow a beer gut. His clothes were garish, something he no doubt thought younger women found attractive. The ladies probably laughed at him until they found out how much money he had, then they played along but still laughed at him behind his back.

I tried my best gambit, pumping up the sob story, practicing how it would sound before a jury, although it was unlikely this case would ever go to trial. The law was too uncertain, the convolutions and intangibilities of time paradox too difficult for the average person to grasp.

"None of this has any bearing on what your client tried to do to my client," Arkulian said. "Sure, the poor kid had a troubled life. His mother had an affair with my client some twenty-six years ago, which led to the breakup of his parents' marriage. Boo-hoo. As if that story doesn't reflect half of the American public."

Maybe your half, I thought, but kept a tight smile on my face.

"Mr. Hendergast attempted to murder my client. It's as simple as—"

Impatient with letting his lawyer do all the talking, Franklin interrupted. "Wait a minute. This is far worse than just attempted murder." As if he needed the fortification of liquid courage to face what had almost happened, Franklin grabbed his tumbler of bourbon, and took a long drink. He set the glass down, and I could see the smear his lips had made on the edge. "If Lionel Hendergast had gunned me down in the parking lot of one of my car dealerships, he might have killed me, yes, but my legacy would have been left behind—my car dealerships, my friends ..."

"Your ex-wives," I pointed out.

"Some of them remember me fondly." He didn't even blush.

Arkulian picked up the story. "You see, what Mr. Hendergast was attempting to do would have erased my client entirely from existence. He would have obliterated the man named Delano R. Franklin from the universe, leaving no memory of him. Nothing he ever accomplished in this life would have remained. Complete annihilation. An unspeakably heinous crime! And if Mr. Hendergast had succeeded, it would have been the perfect crime, too. No one would ever have known what he did, since there would have been no evidence, no body, no victim."

I had heard my share of "perfect crime" stories, and I had to admit, this ranked right up there with the best. I didn't offer them another drink. "What exactly is it you want from my client?"

"I want him to go to jail," Franklin said. "I want him to be locked up so that I don't have to worry every morning that he's going to sneak back on another time travel expedition and try again to erase my existence."

Arkulian smiled and folded his fingers. I couldn't imagine how he could fit them together with all those rings on his knuckles. "I'm guessing the publicity on this case will give a remarkable boost to my business—and don't expect me to believe you haven't thought of the same thing, Mr. Paramus."

He was right, of course. I shrugged. "Publicity is free, after all, and TV ads are a bit out of my price range." Ambulance-chasing seemed to be paying off quite well for Arkulian. I couldn't resist taking a small jab at him. "How much *do* ten of those rings cost?"

Miffed, Arkulian stood up. "If there's nothing else, Paramus? We'll see you in court."

I let the two men show themselves out, staying behind in the boardroom. When they were gone, I took a clean handkerchief, carefully lifted the near-empty bourbon glass Franklin had used, and made sure there were sufficient saliva traces on the rim. This was all I'd need.

Predictably, a media frenzy surrounded the case. Arkulian held a large press conference in which he grandstanded, accusing me of leaking the story in order to get publicity. Within an hour I had a press conference of my own, accusing him of the same. Both of us received plenty of coverage, and neither of us ever admitted to making a few discreet phone calls and tipping reporters off.

Lionel put his complete trust in me, which always sparks that uncomfortable paternal feeling. But I hadn't been kidding when I told him the law is still murky in these sorts of cases. Nobody had any idea which way it would go, and even my "ace in the hole" was a long shot. I still hadn't got the lab results back.

For the preliminary hearing, we were assigned an ancient female judge, the Honorable Bernadette Maddox. I was uneasy about her age. In my experience, elderly judges don't deal well with the second- and third-order implications of rapidly changing technologies. I'd rather have had the youngest, most computer-savvy person on the bench.

I still held out some hope that Bernadette Maddox was a sweet old lady, and the sob-story aspect would work on her. Not a chance.

"Mr. Arkulian!" she roared from the bench in a battle-axe voice before he had even finished his pompous remark. "You will sit down, shut up, and let me run this show." I looked over at my rival with a twinge of sympathy. So much for the nice old lady bit. "And you will remove that disgusting cheap jewelry in my courtroom unless you have an appointment with Time Travel Expeditions to go back to the days of disco."

"Your Honor, my personal appearance has no bearing on—"

"You will remove the jewelry because it hurts my eyes. I can't even see your client through the glare from all those rings."

Cowed, Arkulian left the room. A nervous Lionel sat at the bench next to me, whispering, "Was that a good sign?"

"It wasn't so much a sign—more like a demonstration. The judge is only showing him who's boss. And let me warn you ahead of time, she's going to feel she needs to even the score and scold me as well at some point. Expect it and try not to get too upset."

"What are we going to do, Mr. Paramus?" He sounded so miserable. I felt sorry for this kid who had lost his parents, his Norman Rockwell childhood, and a lifetime of happiness, all because of Delano R. Franklin.

I had dug into Franklin's background, perhaps even more than Lionel had. There was no question in my mind that the world would be a better place if Franklin had never been born. He had left a decades-long trail of ex-wives and shady business dealings behind him. His primary legacy was a handful of auto dealerships, but since he had no heirs and couldn't keep employees around long enough to put them in positions of authority and responsibility, no one would take over the car lots upon his death, and they'd probably be liquidated. Even without Lionel's time travel help, Franklin would vanish.

Since we were the defendants, we sat back and listened as a now-unadorned Arkulian outlined the civil part of the case, explaining time travel paradoxes in painstaking detail, using examples culled not from any law library but from classic science fiction stories. He was long-winded and explained too much to the judge, treating her as if she were incapable of grasping the classic grandfather paradox.

I kept checking my watch as I mentally rehearsed my opening statement. The courier should have been here by now. I would have preferred hard facts to fast-talking, but I could proceed either way. As Arkulian rambled on and on, even Franklin looked bored.

Finally, it was my turn. I hoped the judge would stall just to give me a few more minutes, but she puckered her wrinkled lips and leaned over like a hawk from the bench. "Now then, Mr. Paramus, let's hear what you have to say. I trust you can be more succinct—or at least more interesting—than Mr. Arkulian."

I stood up and cleared my throat. Still no sign of my delivery person, and I really wanted to know which direction to go. Either my ace in the hole was a high trump or a discard. With a sigh, I reached into my briefcase and pulled out a carefully prepared document. "Your Honor, I wish I did not have to do this, but would it be possible to request a brief continuance? I have not yet received an important piece of evidence that has a strong bearing on this case."

Lionel looked over at me, surprised. "What evidence?"

"A continuance?" the judge said with a snort. "I've been sitting here all morning, Mr. Paramus! You could have said this at the very beginning. How long are you asking for?" I was about to get my scolding, and Judge Maddox was clearly primed to let loose with even more venom than she had inflicted on Arkulian.

Suddenly the large doors were flung open at the back of the courtroom. The bailiff tried to stop a man from entering, but my partner Aaron Greenblatt sidestepped him. He marched in, waving a document in his left hand. "Excuse me, your Honor. Please pardon the interruption."

I stifled a laugh. It was a real Perry Mason moment. I suspected Aaron had always wanted to do that.

My partner's face was stoic; I hated the way he covered his emotions. He could have at least grinned or frowned to give me an inkling of what he held in his hands.

Judge Maddox lifted her gavel, looking more inclined to hit Aaron in the head with it than to rap her bench.

I blurted, "Your Honor, I withdraw my request for a continuance —so long as my associate can hand me that paper." I turned, not waiting for her answer as Aaron handed the lab results to me. He finally broke into a grin as I scanned the numbers and the comparison charts.

With a huge sigh of relief, I turned back to the bench. "Your Honor, in light of recent developments I request that the attempted murder charges against my client be dropped."

Arkulian growled, "What are you playing at, Paramus?"

"I'll ask the questions here, Mr. Arkulian," the judge said, rapping her gavel for good measure. "Well then—what *are* you playing at, Mr. Paramus?"

Bernadette Maddox already knew the sordid Peyton Place story of the ruined marriage, the broken family, the miserable life Lionel Hendergast had lived because of Franklin's actions.

"Your Honor, the prosecution's client was not entirely forthcoming about how long his affair with my client's mother lasted. If I might recap: when Lionel Hendergast was four years old, his father discovered Mr. Franklin and my client's mother *in flagrante delicto*, which triggered the chain of events leading to the crime of which my client is accused."

"And?" Judge Maddox said, drawing out the word.

"In fact, the affair had gone on for at least five years previous." I fluttered the sheet of lab data. "I have here the results of DNA tests comparing the blood sample my client gave to the county jail with samples I obtained from Mr. Franklin."

I smiled sweetly at them. Franklin appeared confused. Arkulian was outraged, realizing I had probably tested the saliva left behind on his drinking glass—an old trick.

"These results prove conclusively that the father of Lionel Hendergast is not the man he always believed, but rather Mr. Delano R. Franklin."

Lionel's eyes fairly popped out of their sockets. The judge sat up, suddenly much more interested. Both Arkulian and Franklin bellowed angrily as if in competition with each other until finally Arkulian stood up in a huff, reacting in the way he had seen too many lawyers react on TV shows. "I object! This has no bearing—"

"This has total bearing," I said.

Lionel looked as if he might faint, slide off the chair, and land on the courtroom floor. I put a steadying hand on his shoulder. He looked over at the prosecutor's table, and his two words came out in a squeak. "My father?"

I forged ahead. "The prosecution has interpreted this crime entirely wrong, your Honor. My client is accused of going back in time with the intent of preventing Mr. Franklin from ever being born. But if he had done that, then Lionel Hendergast would've erased *himself* from existence as well. He would have wiped out his own father, thereby ensuring that he himself could never be born."

I smiled. The judge seemed to be considering my line of reasoning. After all, Arkulian had prepped her in excruciating detail about grandfather paradoxes and the like.

"Therefore, instead of attempted murder, my client is guilty, at best, of attempted *suicide*—for which I recommend he be remanded for therapy and treatment, not incarceration."

"This is preposterous!" Arkulian yelled. "Even if Mr. Hendergast *had* accidentally erased himself, his original intention was to do the same to my client. His own death would merely have been incidental to his stated objective. The primary target of his malicious actions was still Delano Franklin."

With a sigh of infinite patience, I looked witheringly at Arkulian, then turned back to the judge. "Again, my esteemed colleague is mistaken."

The judge was actually listening now, fascinated by the implications. I had mapped out the strategy until it made my own head spin.

"My client is accused of *attempted* murder. However, based on these lab results, such an action would be temporally impossible." I waited a beat. "If Mr. Hendergast had actually succeeded in what the prosecution alleges was his intent, then he himself would never have been born. In which case, he could never have gone back in time to prevent Mr. Franklin's parents from meeting. How can my client be charged with attempting a crime that is fundamentally impossible to commit?"

"This is outrageous! Why not debate how many angels can dance on a pinhead?" Arkulian said.

I shrugged in the prosecutor's direction. "It's a standard time travel paradox, your Honor. As Mr. Arkulian explained to the court so exhaustively."

Lionel was still staring in wonder over at the prosecutor's table. "Daddy?"

The judge rapped her gavel loudly. "I'm announcing a recess for at least two hours—so I can take some aspirin and give it time to work."

When the judge finally dismissed all charges against Lionel, I was relatively sure Arkulian wouldn't take it to appeal. The hardest part was explaining the convoluted matter to journalists afterward, so they could report it accurately; in the end, it proved too intricate for most of the wire services.

Aaron and I celebrated by going out for a fine dinner. We compared notes on cases, and he got me up to speed on his time-travel dinosaur-hunting lawsuit. I came back to the office late at night by myself—after all, that's where I kept the best bourbon—and saw the light blinking on the answering machine. Multiple messages. Four more cases waiting, none of them simple. Some actually sounded like they would be fun. Certainly precedent-setting.

Oddly, after the fallout, Lionel actually reconciled with his biological father. Months later, when I drove past one of Franklin's car dealerships, I saw a crew replacing the big sign with a new one: FRANKLIN & SON.

Funny how things turn out. Sometimes people just need a second chance, even when they aren't looking for it.

The US Air Force unofficially claims that the best fighter pilots have balls the size of grapefruits and brains the size of a pea. Some might say that the same qualities would be required to walk in the legendary Harlan Ellison's footsteps. Harlan was always a hard act to follow, and it was daunting even to try.

This is a sequel to Harlan's classic Outer Limits teleplay, "Soldier." When I first asked if he would let me play in his world and create a new tale, he was skeptical. Very skeptical. He growled at me, "I've never done a sequel to a single one of my stories. I never felt the need. If I got it right the first time, I've said all I needed to say."

Over the course of my writing career I have gathered a lot of rejection slips, and I never gave up even when common sense dictated that I should. So, I stood my ground with Harlan and challenged him. "Look, you've developed this sprawling scenario of a devastating future war, where soldiers are bred and trained to do nothing but fight from birth to death. Are you telling me that there's only ONE story to be told in that whole world?"

He thought a bit, and then he changed his mind. "All right. Just make sure it's good."

So, I got to play with Harlan Ellison's toys.

"Prisoner of War" is my tap-dance on Harlan's stage, set in the devastating world of "Soldier," which was a huge influence on me from the first time I saw it on TV. This is a story about another set of warriors in a never-ending war, men bred for nothing but the battleground—and how they cope with the horrors of … peace.

As a final note, this story was written on the road during the most grueling book-signing tour I ever hope to do—a nationwide blitz of twenty-seven cities in twenty-eight days (during which, in the event in Hollywood, I set the Guinness World Record for "Largest Single-Author

Book Signing"). I dictated "Prisoner of War" in an unknown number of hotel rooms, wandering down city sidewalks, or at whatever park happened to be closest, before I had to begin the day's work of interviews and autograph sessions. The chance to do something creative and emotionally engaging gave me something to look forward to during the long, long month.

PRISONER OF WAR

The first Enemy laser-lances blazed across the battlefield at an unknown time of day. No one paid attention to the hour during a firefight anyway. Neither Barto nor any of his squad-mates could see the sun or moon overhead: too much smoke and haze and blast debris filled the air, along with the smell of blood and burning.

A soldier had to be ready at any time or place. A soldier would fight until the fight was over. An endless Now filled their existence, a razor-edged flow of life-for-the-moment, and the slightest distraction or daydream could end the Now ... forever.

With a clatter of dusty armor and a hum of returned weapons-fire, the defenders charged forward, Barto among them. They had no terrain maps or battle plans, only unseen commanders bellowing instructions into their helmet earpieces.

Greasy fires guttered and smoked from explosions, but as long as a soldier could draw breath, the air always smelled sweet enough. Somehow, the flames still found organic material to burn, though only a few skeletal trees remained standing. The horizon was like broken, jagged teeth. No discernible structures remained, only blistered destruction and the endless bedlam of combat.

To a man who had known no other life, Barto found the landscape familiar and comforting.

"Down!" his point man Arviq screamed loudly enough so that Barto could hear it through the armored helmet. A bolt of white-hot energy seared the ground in front of them, turning the blasted soil into glass. The ricochet stitched a broken-windshield pattern of lethal cuts across the armored chest of one comrade five meters away.

The victim was in a different part of the squad; Barto knew him only by serial number instead of a more personal, chosen name. Now the man was a casualty of war; his serial number would be displayed in fine print on the memorial lists back at the crèche—for two days. And then it would be erased forever.

Barto and Arviq both dove to the bottom of the trench as more well-aimed laser-lances embroidered the ground and the slumping walls of the ditch. As he hunched over to shield himself, the helmet's speakers continued to pound commands: "KILL … KILL … KILL …"

The Enemy assault ended with a brief hesitation, like an indrawn breath. The soldiers around Barto paused, regrouped, then scrambled to their feet, leaving the fallen comrade behind. Later, regardless of the battle's outcome, trained bloodhounds would retrieve the body parts and drag them back to HQ in their jaws. After the proper casualty statistics had been recorded, the KIA corpses would be efficiently incinerated.

In the middle of a firefight, Barto and Arviq could not be bothered by such things. They had been trained never to think of fallen comrades; it was beyond the purview of their mission. The voice in the helmet speakers changed, took on a different note: "RETALIATE … RETALIATE … RETALIATE …"

With a howl and a roar enhanced by adrenaline injections from inside the armor suits, Barto and his squad moved as a unit. Programmed endorphins poured into their bloodstreams at the moment of battle frenzy, and they surged out of the trench. The Enemy encampment could not be far, and they silently swore to unleash a slaughter that would outmatch anything their opponents had ever done … though this most recent attack was assuredly a response to their own previous day's offensive.

Moving as a unit, the squad clambered over debris, around craters, and out into the open. They ran beyond monofilament barricades that would slice the limb off an unwary soldier, then into a sonic minefield whose layout shone on the eye-visor screen inside each helmet.

With a self-assured gait across the no-man's-land, the soldiers moved like a pack of killer rats, laser-lances slung in their arms. They bellowed and snarled, pumping each other up. As he ran, Barto studied the sonic minefield grid in his visor, sidestepping instinctively.

From their embankment, the Enemy began to fire again. The smoky air became a lattice of deadly lines in all directions. Barto continued running. Beside him, Arviq pressed the stock of his weapon against his armored breastplate, pumping blast after blast toward the unseen Enemy.

Then a laser-lance seared close to Barto's helmet, blistering the top layer of semi-reflective silver. Static blasted across his eye visor, and he couldn't see. He made one false sidestep and yelled. He could no longer find the grid display, could no longer even see the actual ground.

Just as his foot came down in the wrong place, Arviq grabbed his arm and yanked him aside, using their combined momentum. The sonic mine exploded, vomiting debris and shrapnel with pounding sound waves that fractured the plates of Barto's armor, pulverizing the bones in his leg. But he fell out of the mine's focused kill radius and lay biting back the pain.

He propped himself up and ripped off his slagged helmet, blinking with naked eyes at the real sky. Arviq had saved his life— just as Barto would have done for his squad-mate had their situations been reversed.

Always trust your comrades. Your life is theirs. That was how it had always been.

And even if he did fall to Enemy attack, the bloodhounds would haul his body to HQ, and he would receive an appropriate military farewell before he returned to the earth—mission accomplished. A soldier's duty was to fight, and Barto had been performing that duty for all of his conscious life.

As he activated his rescue transmitter and fumbled for the medpak, the rest of the soldiers charged forward, leaving him behind. Arviq didn't even spare him a backward glance.

⚛

Some said the war had gone on forever—and since no one kept track of history anymore, the statement could not be proved false.

Barto knew only the military life. He had emerged from a tank in the soldiers' crèche with the programming wired into his brain, fully aware, fully grown, and knowing his assignment. If ever he had any questions or doubts, the command voices in his helmet would answer them.

Barto knew primarily that he had to kill the Enemy. He knew that he had to protect his comrades, that the squad was the sum of his existence. No good soldier could rest until every last Enemy had been eradicated, down to their feline spies, down to the bloodhounds that dragged away Enemy KIAs.

Winning this war might well take an eternity, but Barto was willing to fight for that long. Every moment of his life had encompassed either fighting, or learning new techniques to kill and to survive, or resting so that he could fight again the next day.

There was no time for anything else. There was no need for anything else.

Barto remembered when he'd been younger, not long out of the tank. His muscles were wiry, his body flexible without the stiffness of constant abuse. His skin had been smooth, free of the intaglio of scars from a thousand close dances with death. Barto and his squad-mates—apprentices all—had fought hand-to-hand in the crèche gymnasium, occasionally breaking each other's bones or knocking each other unconscious. None of them had yet earned their armor, their protection, or their weapons. They couldn't even call themselves soldiers....

Now consigned to the HQ infirmary and repair shop, as he drifted in a soup of pain and unconsciousness, Barto revisited the long-ago moment he had first grasped a specialized piece of equipment designed to maim and kill. The soldier trainees had learned early on in their drill that any object was a potential weapon —but this was a spear, a long rough bar of old steel with a sharpened point that gleamed white and silver in the unforgiving lights. A weapon, his own weapon.

He spun it around in his hand, feeling its weight—a deadly impaling device that could be used against the oncoming Enemy.

Later, his advanced training would of course include hand-to-hand combat against other soldiers, human opponents ... but not at first. All trainees were expendable, but if the young men could be salvaged, then the military programming services would turn them into killers.

For months, Barto received somatic instruction and physical drilling by one of the rare old veterans who had survived years of combat. The veteran had a wealth of experience and survival instincts that could not be matched even by the most sophisticated computers. He made sure that Barto fought to the limit of his abilities.

Swinging the spear against nothing, feeling his body move, Barto reacted to the barked commands of the veteran instructor. Response without thought. He learned how to make the weapon into a part of him, an extension of his reflexes. He was the weapon; the spear was just an augmentation.

Then they gave him a taste of blood, real blood. They wanted him to get in the habit of killing.

The small metal-walled arena was like an echo chamber, a large underground room with simulated rock outcroppings, a fallen tree, and other sharp obstacles. Barto didn't question the reality of the scenario. The environment itself was a tool to be used.

During that exercise, the veteran instructor let him wear his helmet ... but nothing else. Stripped naked, he gripped the spear in his hand and glared through the visor. The helmet earphones gave him reassuring commands in his ears, directions, suggestions. Otherwise, Barto felt helpless—but no soldier was ever helpless, because a helpless man could not become a soldier.

Underground, the arena door groaned open, and barricade bars moved away. Barto tensed. He gripped the metal shaft of the spear despite the sweat on his palms.

Suddenly, a whirlwind of bristles and scales, sharp hooves and long tusks launched itself like a projectile. An enhanced boar with scarlet eyes snarled and plowed forward, searching for a target, something against which to vent its anger.

And Barto was the only other creature in the room.

On high pedestals in the gallery above, three enhanced cats watched, blinking their gold-green eyes. The feline spy commanders observed for the invisible overlords who wanted to see how the freshly detanked soldiers reacted in their first real life-or-death test.

The boar charged. Barto jabbed with the spear, but he was too tentative. Before, he had only thrust at imaginary opponents and an occasional hologram projected inside his visor. Now, though, the boar came on like a locomotive. The spear glanced off, opening a mere stinging scratch in the creature's skin. Barto had not imagined its hide could be so tough, its bones so hard. He had made the first, terrible mistake in this duel.

The trivial wound enraged the beast.

Barto dove to one side over a synthetic rock, and the boar rammed into the artificial tree trunk. It spun around, shaking its head, tusks gleaming. The ivory spears in its mouth looked much more deadly than Barto's primitive weapon. The boar attacked again.

A moment of panic rose up like an illusion, but he pounded it back, and the fear evaporated, bringing a rush of adrenaline. The chemical and electronic components in his body released the substance, making Barto see red rage of his own.

The enhanced boar recovered itself and snorted. Barto knew he had a better chance of striking the target in motion if he didn't use a tiny pinpoint thrust; instead, he swung the heavy metal bar sideways like a cudgel. The sturdy steel bashed the creature's thick skull. The sound of the impact rang out in the hollow room.

The cats watched from their pedestals.

The boar squealed and thrashed. Barto saw that its eyes held an increased intelligence, like that found in the feline spies and in the daredevil bloodhounds that retrieved bodies from the battlefield. The boar responded with a calculated counterattack, trying to outthink this naked human opponent, this would-be soldier. Barto smiled; the boar was the Enemy.

In the frenzy of battle, Barto no longer thought like an intelligent human being. Instead, he relied only on instinct and unbearable bloodlust. He rushed in without forethought, without care, without any sense of self-preservation. After all … he had a spear.

The boar tried to feint, to react, but Barto gave the Enemy no chance. He swung again with the staff, drawing a bright red line of blood and putting out one of the beast's eyes. Crimson and yellow body fluids oozed through smashed skin on the boar's snout. It leapt forward, driven by insanity and pain.

Now, Barto used the spear with finesse.

A great calm flowed through him, as if the rest of the world had slowed down, and he saw exactly what to do, exactly where to hold the spear. The sharpened point neatly plunged through the ribcage of the beast and skewered its lungs and heart. Showering a wet-iron smell in the air, the creature lay quivering, trembling ... dying.

When Barto came back to his senses, he saw that his legs had been slashed open by the boar's tusks. The deep gouges left him bleeding, but oddly without any sense of pain or injury. He looked down and studied the corpse of his opponent, the Enemy. Now he had killed. Barto had fresh blood on his hands, real blood from a vanquished opponent.

He liked the sensation.

He knew that this had been no simple exercise. He knew the boar could well have killed him, and that other trainees who had vanished from the barracks must have failed this part of their instruction.

But Barto had succeeded. He was a killer now, and he was one step closer to becoming a soldier.

Time didn't matter. For a soldier, time never mattered. He awoke hours, or days, later back in the HQ infirmary and repair shop— patched up, drugged, but fully aware. A hairless chimpanzee tended him, leaning over in a cloud of disinfectant scents and bad breath. The chimp medical techs knew how to bandage and fix battlefield wounds. They could do no surgery that required finesse, but the soldiers required nothing that needed delicacy for cosmetic effect.

Once injured, if a soldier could be fixed, he would be sent back to the battlefield. If his wounds caused the chimp med-techs too much trouble, he would be eliminated. Every surviving member of the squad bore his share of scars, burns, scabs, and callouses. No one paid attention to these trophies of war; they were part of a soldier's life, not a badge of honor or bravery.

Since Barto hadn't been eliminated, he assumed he must have been fixed.

He sat up on the infirmary cot, and the hairless chimpanzees hurried over, uttering quiet reassurances, a few English words, a few soothing grunts. Triggered by his awakening, a signal was automatically sent back to his squad commander.

Barto listened to an assessment of his repaired leg, his stitched muscles and skin, and his bruises and contusions. Not too bad, he thought. He'd suffered worse, sometimes even in training with other soldiers (especially during the initial few months, when they'd first been given their own sets of armor).

He remembered that back then his comrade Arviq in particular had thought himself invincible....

During downtime before the soldiers crawled into their assigned sleeping bins, the other squad members were required to file through the infirmary to see their injured comrades. Some came only because of orders to do so; most of them would rather have been sleeping.

But the invisible commanders planted instructions to go to the infirmary simply so that other soldiers could see the wounded, could see what could happen to them if they weren't careful ... but also so they could see that they just might survive.

Recovering, Barto sat up in the uncomfortable infirmary bed and watched the other soldiers come in. His pain went away with another automatic rush of endorphins to deaden his unpleasant sensations ... or perhaps his own determination was enough to quell the nerve-fire of agony.

The fighters filed by. He recognized few of them, all strangers without armor and helmets, though he could have identified each one by the serial numbers displayed on their fatigues. These were soldiers, cogs in a fighting machine. They didn't have time to be individuals.

When Arviq came up at the end of the line, he stood brusque, nodding gruffly. "You'll mend," he said.

"Thank you for saving me," Barto answered. It was the closest thing they'd had to a conversation in a long time.

"It's my duty. I await the day when you can fight with us again." He marched out, and the others followed him. Barto lay back and attempted to sleep, to regain his strength. Through sheer force of will, he growled at his cells and tissues to work harder, to knit the injuries and restore him to full health....

Day after day, lying in the infirmary and waiting proved far more difficult than any combat situation Barto had ever encountered. Finally, after a maddening week of intensive recuperation, directed therapy aided by medical technology and powerful drugs, he was released from his hospital prison and sent back to the front.

Where he belonged.

The battlefield screamed with pain and destruction, explosions, fire, and death—but to Barto, after being so long in the sheltered quiet of the infirmary, the tumult was a shout of exuberance. He was glad to be here.

The soldiers raced across the ground, each in his own squad position, weapons drawn. They had already driven back the Enemy, and now the fire of laser-lances grew even thicker around them as the others became desperate. They pressed ahead, deeper into enemy territory than they had ever gone before.

Their helmet locators for sonic mines and shrapnel grenades buzzed constantly, but the reptilian part of Barto's brain reacted without volition, hardwired into fighting and killing. He dodged and weaved, keeping himself alive.

His point-man, Arviq, jogged close beside him, and Barto extended his peripheral vision behind the dark visor to enfold his comrade into an invisible protective sphere. He would assist his partner if he got into trouble—not out of any sense of payback or obligation, but because it was an automatic response, his own assignment. He would have done the same for any other soldier, any member of his squad—anyone but the Enemy.

Precision-guided mortars scribed parabolas through the air and exploded close to any concentration of soldiers who did not display the proper transponders. Amidst screams and thunder, a massive triple detonation wiped out over half of Barto's squad, but the others did not fall back, did not even pause. They drove onward, continued the push. The fallen comrades would be taken care of somehow, though no one knew how the bloodhounds would ever make it this deep into Enemy-held territory.

This far behind the main battle lines, the Enemy numbers themselves were dwindling, and Barto fired and fired again. The laser-lance thrummed in his gauntleted hands, skewering a distant man's chest plate and leaving a smoking hole.

But it wasn't really a man, after all. It was the Enemy.

The chase continued, and the survivors of Barto's squad ran in the direction of what must have been Enemy HQ. In his dry, dusty mouth he could taste the sweet honey of victory.

But suddenly, unexpectedly, they triggered a row of booby traps that did not appear on their helmet sensors. Camouflaged catapults popped up, spraying near-invisible clouds of netting, monofilament webs as insubstantial as smoke but sharper than the most deadly razor.

The flying webwork engulfed four soldiers near him, and they fell into neatly butchered pieces. But oddly enough, so did three of the Enemy men rushing in retreat, as if they themselves hadn't known of these defenses. But their own visor sensors must have been keyed to booby traps they themselves had planted....

Though the questions astonished him, Barto did not pause. His job was not to analyze. Paraplegic computer tacticians and the invisible battlefield commanders did all that work. The voices in his helmet told him to push forward, and so he pushed forward.

Arviq ran beside him, still firing his laser-lance—and numbly Barto realized that most of the other soldiers were dead. His squad had been decimated ... but the Enemy was nearly eradicated as well.

War often required sacrifices, and many soldiers died. But a victory would pay the bloody cost ten times over. They had never gone so far.

The thrill of seeing the Enemy nearly exterminated gave Barto all the enthusiasm he needed, even without an adrenaline rush augmented by injectors in his armor. With a shared glance behind opaque visors, he and Arviq both had the same thought, and ran forward with their four remaining companions. They couldn't stop now.

Then large gun emplacements popped out of the ground, more massive than anything he had ever seen before. Barto reeled in unaccustomed confusion—the Enemy had never exhibited technology like this! Automated fire rained down on them, super powerful laser-lances far more devastating than any of the handheld rifles.

Soldiers screamed. The blasts were like belts of incinerating flame, vaporizing armor and leaving not even bones for the bloodhounds to retrieve. The firepower pummeled anyone who came close, whether friend or Enemy. They had no chance, no chance at all.

An explosion ripped out a deep crater ten meters from them. Someone screamed, but Barto had no voice. The automated superlasers continued to track across the ground, pinpointing armor, crushing any movement. Barto watched the beams sweep closer, vaporizing everything in the vicinity. His four remaining squad members died in a puff of blood-smoke and molten armor plate.

On impulse he grabbed Arviq and shoved him hard toward the fresh crater. Together, the two dove into the raw trench just as the splash of disintegration passed over them. The voices in his helmet turned to a rainstorm of incomprehensible static.

Within moments the battle stopped. Everyone else was dead.

All of the laser fire and explosions ceased. All the Enemy, all of the squad, every living thing had been annihilated.

Without saying a word, Arviq hauled himself to his hands and knees and reached over to shake Barto, who also recovered his balance. The two of them sat panting for a moment, stunned but still determined. Neither of them—in fact, no one they knew—had ever been so far behind Enemy lines.

They rose up slowly and carefully into the crackling silence, afraid of other targeted automated systems. Clods of dry dirt fell from their armor. Dust and crackling ash roiled through the air ... but nothing else moved.

"We won?" Barto asked. "Is the war over?"

"I hope not." Arviq turned to him, his mouth a grim line beneath the opaque visor of the helmet. "The war will never be over. But we may have won this battle."

Barto raised his helmet over the rim of the blasted crater. No weapons responded to the motion. The battlefield remained eerily quiet with only the faint sound of coughing fires and settling dust.

"Must be the Enemy encampment," Arviq said with a grunt. "Increased defenses—maybe even HQ." He grinned. "Success!"

But Barto wasn't so sure. Moving with tense caution, he climbed away from the crater. "No, not HQ. The defenses killed as many of them as us. ID transponders were useless."

Arviq joined him, sole survivors on the sprawling battlefield. Barto could see where the huge gun emplacements had raised up. Adjusting his visor filters, he spotted different infrared signatures, metallic traces, solid structures and hollow passages beneath the scarred ground.

Amazed, Barto crept forward. "We've discovered something. We're required to investigate."

"No, back to HQ," Arviq said. "We must report. Our squad was wiped out."

But Barto shook him off. He stood determined, looking ahead across the scabbed landscape. "Not until we have hard reconnaissance. This could be important."

Arviq hesitated only a moment. Neither outranked the other, and they had no time for argument, but the other soldier quickly came to his own decision. "Yes. Reconnaissance is part of our mission."

Most of the time, sly intelligent cats would creep through the darkness, observing Enemy strongholds and reporting back to HQ. But the squad had gone farther into Enemy territory than any known advance, and they might have new information. That was the most important thing. They weren't doing it for the glory or for a possible promotion, or for any sort of reward. Barto and Arviq would take the risk because it was their duty.

"My head, my thoughts ... are empty," Arviq said, tapping his helmet.

Barto adjusted his earphones, but still received no transmission and no commands. An uneasy silence echoed in his head. The speakers growled no more repetitive commands to attack and kill.

"How can you stand it?" Arviq looked at him.

Barto took a deep breath. "No choice. Tolerate it."

Crouched low, they trudged toward the automated gun emplacements, but the motion sensors did not reactivate. The weapons had gone through their program and wiped out the threat. Somehow, the two comrades had slipped through the cracks. They could move forward.

Barto and Arviq found a metal hatchplate in the half-hidden superstructure of the enormous laser-lances. Barto sat down and pressed his helmet against the hatch, carefully listening for any vibration, fully tense. Any moment now he expected the destructive fire to rain out again.

He tugged on the hatch, looking for access controls. "We can infiltrate," he said. "It's an underground bunker. Maybe weapons storage. We can bring supplies or power packs back to HQ."

Together they wiped off dust and blasted dirt from the plate, used tools at their armor belts to crack open the seals, and finally they lifted the heavy hatch.

Still no voices came to their heads, no instructions. The two soldiers were on their own. Barto didn't like it one bit.

They dropped down into the opening, where a steel ladder led into a maw of shadows. They descended, gripping rung after rung with gauntleted hands. If this was Enemy HQ, Barto thought, it was a much larger complex than anything he and his squad had ever lived in.

Finally, the ladder ended in an underground tunnel with the hatch cover high above them. Barto paused for a moment to scan the surroundings, then they walked forward into dim silence. The tunnels seemed empty, barely used, abandoned for a long time. Barto realized the Enemy soldiers could not have emerged from this place. No one had walked down these access tunnels in a long, long time.

As point man, Arviq led the way. He strode forward, hands on his weapons, ready for anything. A soldier had to be flexible and determined. The small tunnel lights gave little illumination, but their helmet visors augmented the ambient photons.

Cameras in their helmets recorded everything as reconnaissance files to be downloaded back in HQ. They continued for what seemed like miles, trudging deeper and deeper into the earth. This place was an important facility, possibly a central complex ... but Barto couldn't begin to understand it.

From up ahead came a faint throbbing from generators and heavy machinery. Finally, they saw brighter light, thick windows, rectangular plates that shone through to another world, a subterranean complex that seemed like a mythical land. Inside huge grottoes, pale ethereal people moved about wearing bright colors. Plants of a shockingly lush green, garish hues that Barto had never seen before, drew the two of them forward like magnets.

"What is this?" Arviq asked. "Some kind of trick?"

"Paradise."

As the soldiers approached, unable to believe what they were seeing, they crossed an unseen threshold, a booby trap. They heard a brief hum, a crackle of power surge. Barto reacted just in time to feel a sinking despair—but not fast enough to get out of the way.

A pressing white light engulfed both of them, swallowing them up. In an instant, Barto's visor turned black, then so did his eyes.

When he awoke, the assault on his senses nearly knocked him back into protective unconsciousness. Sounds, smells, colors bombarded him like weapons fire. His armor and helmet had been stripped away, leaving him vulnerable; without it, he felt helpless, soft-skinned, like a worm.

The bed beneath him was warm and soft, disorienting. A gentle and cozy light surrounded him instead of the familiar garish white to which he was accustomed back in his own barracks. Each breath of the humid air was perfumed with a sweet, flowery scent that nauseated him.

Was this an infirmary? Barto turned his head gently, and a raging pain clamored inside his skull. The place reminded him oddly of the time he had been helpless and healing from his previous injury … but he saw no hairless chimpanzees, no robotic medical attendants. The sheets were soft and slick, vastly different from the other rough, sterile coverings.

Grogginess smothered his mind and body. Barto tried to return to full awareness … but something was wrong. His body remained sluggish and unresponsive, as if the accustomed chemical stimulants were not being released according to program. He needed adrenalin; he needed endorphins.

Arviq lay on another bed beside him, similarly prone, similarly stripped of his armor. When Barto turned his head and directed his gaze in the opposite direction, he was astonished to find another person by his shoulder. Not one of the enhanced animals bred to attend the regiment … but a woman, a lovely creature with short, honey-brown hair and a shimmering purple garment so brilliant and dazzling that it made his eyes ache.

Responding with combat readiness, he sat up with a lurch—but the woman rushed over and shushed him with a gentle touch. "Quiet now. Everything's all right. You are safe here." Her voice sounded like sweet syrup. Alien.

Arviq stirred beside him, groaning in confusion and growing rage.

Then Barto remembered a legend, a story told on the field during the quiet times between battles when some soldiers were more frightened than others. It was a hopeful myth of what happened to brave and dedicated fighters after a death in battle. Was this ... Valhalla?

He glanced over at Arviq, his face contorted with confusion. His eyes glimmered with dark fires. "Are we dead?"

The woman laughed like tinkling crystal. "No, soldier. We are people like yourselves, human beings."

She didn't look like him, though, or any other person he had ever seen. Barto shook his head, refusing to acknowledge the pain left over inside. He'd had enough experience with pain. "You're not ... soldiers."

The woman smiled and leaned closer to him. A warmth radiated from her scrubbed and lotioned skin. He had never noticed a person's physical features before, never paid attention ... and he'd never seen anything so beautiful in his life.

"Everyone is a soldier," he said, "either for our side, or the Enemy."

The woman continued to give him a slightly superior smile. "You are soldiers, my friends ... but we are not. Not here." She gave a gesture to indicate her entire underground world. "After all, it's a war. You're fighting and dying." Her thin, dark eyebrows rose up in graceful arches on her forehead. "Did it never occur to you to ask exactly what you're fighting ... for?"

With a sudden burst of energy and an outcry of rage, Arviq lunged up from his bed, reaching out with clawlike hands, his face full of fury. Even without armor or weapons, any soldier knew how to kill with his bare hands. Somehow he found the energy to lash out, to propel himself into a combat frame of mind.

The woman staggered back from the infirmary beds, startled. Barto saw shadows, more people moving behind observation windows, automatic devices activating. There was another flash of white light, and again he lost consciousness.

When Barto awoke once more, he was alone in a room, clad in soft pajamas with more slick sheets wrapped around him. He found his bed too pliant, too yielding, as if it meant to be comfortable with a vengeance.

The gentle sound of running water trickled from speakers embedded in the wall. The white noise had a soothing effect, the opposite of the perpetual, pressuring commands that had droned into his ears from helmet speakers. Now, the image of a soporific, bubbling brook made him want to lie motionless in a stupor.

He no longer even seemed alive.

This room was smaller, the walls painted pastel colors instead of clean white. The illumination was muted and warm, like sunlight through amber. It made his head fuzzy.

Stiffly, Barto rolled over and found that Arviq wasn't with him this time. His comrade had been taken elsewhere. Was this some sort of insidious Enemy plan? Divide and conquer, separate the squad members.

Had he fallen into some new kind of warfare that went beyond violence and destruction to this personality-destroying brainwashing technique? Barto snarled and tried to find a way to escape—a captured soldier's duty was to escape at all costs.

He didn't hear a door open, felt no movement of the air—but suddenly the beautiful woman stood there with him, setting a platter down on a ledge formed out of the substance of the wall. She leaned over his bed, her entire body smelling of gentle flowers and perfumes. She smiled down at him, parting soft lips to reveal even white teeth. Barto started, ready to fight with hand-to-hand techniques even without his armor or his weapons—but she made no threatening move.

"My name is Juliette," she said, then waited as if he was supposed to recognize some significance to the name.

He answered as he had been drilled. "Barto. Corporal. E21TFDN." He rolled off the serial number in a singsong chant, "Eetoowun teeyeff deeyenn." He had spoken it more than any other word in his lifetime. Then he formed his mouth into a grim line. That was all he had been trained to say. The Enemy rarely, if ever, took prisoners. Everyone died on the battlefield.

"I brought food for you … Barto." Juliette picked up a steaming, spicy-smelling bowl from the tray on the ledge. It contained some kind of broth laced with vegetables, even a little meat.

Though he could withstand long periods of fasting, Barto realized how hungry he was. He'd been trained to shut off the hunger pangs and nerve twinges in his digestive system. But he also knew to take nourishment whenever possible, to maintain his strength.

She extended a spoon, and Barto raised his head to accept a mouthful. The spoon was metal with rounded edges. Even such a crude and innocuous weapon could be used in many different ways as a killing instrument. He could have snatched it from her—but he did not, taking the mouthful instead.

The flavors exploded around his tongue, and Barto nearly choked. It was too intense, too spiced, too fresh—experiences his mouth had never had. Back in the barracks all soldiers ate a common meal, a protein-rich gruel that served as sustenance and nothing else. He'd never before dined on a preparation in which someone had cared about its flavors. He didn't find it at all pleasant.

Juliette gave him another mouthful, and he forced himself to eat it. But he did not let down his guard for an instant.

"The stun-field should have no residual effect on you, Barto," she said. "You'll regain your strength in no time." Her voice sounded odd in his ears, pitched with a higher timbre, musical rather than the implacable instructions that had poured into his ears from the helmet's speakers.

"I'm strong enough," Barto said. "Where is my comrade?"

"He's safe and being tended—but we thought it best to separate you." She took the bowl away, then stood back to appraise him. "I'm curious about you, Barto, Corporal, E21TFDN. I want to be your friend—so let's just use our first names, all right?" She brushed her hand along his arm, and he recoiled at her touch; it felt like warm feathers tickling across the skin. "Can you stand up? I'd like to take you for a walk to show you where you are."

Barto did not argue with her. Regardless of her intentions, Juliette's offer would allow him to continue his reconnaissance. She could show him whatever she wished, and he would gather information. Without the helmet visor and its implanted cameras, he would have to observe with his own eyes, and remember details. But it could be done.

As he swung off the bed, the loose-fitting pajamas felt strange on him, not hard enough, not safe. He walked on the balls of his bare feet, every muscle tense, searching for mysterious threats as Juliette led him out of the room. She took him down underground corridors into even richer light. They passed beautiful images of scenery, forgotten forests and lost mountains ... waterfalls and lakes unlike anything he had ever seen on the battle-scarred combat fields.

"Who are you people?" Barto said. "What is this place?"

"We're civilians. We went underground centuries ago to escape the fighting, while our armies defended us against the invasion."

Barto tried to assess the information, to fit it like puzzle pieces into the sparse information in his mind. "My squad is ... part of the defenders? We fight against the invaders?"

She looked at him with a curious, placid expression. Her pale skin, delicate bone structure, and pointed chin gave her an ethereal, elfin appearance. "No one knows which side is which anymore."

Other people, similarly pale-skinned and soft-looking, observed the pair as they walked by. Some smiled, some drew back in fear. Many regarded him with cold, fish-like interest. Juliette seemed to enjoy the attention she received just by being with him.

Barto scanned his surroundings for a way to escape and return to his squad. But then he remembered that, except for Arviq, all of his comrades were dead, annihilated by the immense gun emplacements that protected this underground shelter. Back at his own HQ, the databases must have already recorded him and his point man as casualties of war.

Juliette talked as they continued, her voice a pleasant mélange of words. She told him of their days of peace and shelter down below, how the survivors had made an entire world down here by excavating tunnel after tunnel. There, the civilians did what she called "the great work of humanity"—composing music, dabbling in art, writing poetry and literature ... though, if they remained isolated down here without experiencing the hard edge of life, Barto didn't know how they found any material to incorporate into their creations.

Though she turned at intersections, descended to different levels, walked in circles, Barto never lost his bearings. He imprinted a map of everything they encountered, knowing he might need to use it later. On his own.

Juliette took him to a greenhouse where the smells nearly stifled him: humid air, the odors of vegetation and mulch, flowers bursting forth like explosions from mortar fire. Pollinating insects flitted from blossom to blossom, and brilliantly ripe vegetables and fruits made his eyes hurt.

He heard the drip of irrigation systems, saw colorful birds hopping from plant to plant, and a shiver went up his spine. Everything was so quiet here, so gentle. It made him feel too full of energy, too restless.

Barto remembered when he'd been forced to recuperate in the HQ infirmary as the hairless chimpanzees tended to him. He had been bored and frustrated ... but with a goal—to heal, so he could go back and fight. He had managed to wait until his body returned to its optimal condition, when he could go out and serve his purpose in life.

Here, though, these people had a quiet calmness about them, an air of superiority ... with nothing else to do. Juliette seemed to enjoy it, seemed proud of being a civilian.

Barto had never experienced such vibrant beauty, the smells, the music

... the sense of peace. His body rebelled at the thought, but as the hours went by in the beautiful woman's company he began to feel his resistance crumbling. This was all new to him.

As she showed him their underground "paradise," Barto followed her and listened. Finally, in exasperation, he turned to Juliette and asked, "So there's no war here?" He couldn't believe it. Such a concept had never occurred to him. "No battles?"

"Oh, we have a little." Juliette smiled, then gestured him forward. "Here, let me show you. Maybe you'll find it comforting."

She led him down smooth passages where the temperature grew cooler, the smell more metallic. They walked down glass-walled hallways until they reached a control center.

Battle plans. Tactical maps. Troop movement displays.

"This is how we maintain our edge, Barto, and our window on the outside world." Juliette's people sat at stations in front of the shifting screens, their fingers raised across control panels. Terrain grids spread out in front of them in bristling colors.

High-resolution panels showed other soldiers, people in familiar armor and helmets, jittery point-of-view images transmitted from visor cameras. Civilian men and women leaned over, punching in commands and speaking into microphones.

"Move left. Open fire."

Another man with a deep voice droned, "Kill the Enemy. Kill the Enemy. Kill the Enemy." He sounded bored. The others looked very relaxed in their positions.

Barto stared with shock as he realized that these were the voices he'd heard in his helmet all his life: directing him, helping him plan his attack. These were his ultimate commanders in the war.

Astonished, Barto looked over to see Arviq also standing inside the control room, chaperoned by a civilian man, also dressed in a loose jumpsuit. His point man's chaperone demonstrated the workings of the controls. Arviq's eyes were wide as he watched the battle.

Sensing the new arrivals, Arviq looked up to see Barto. Their eyes met, and hot understanding flashed between them. This was the ultimate headquarters of their army. Arviq reeled from the revelation, but Barto felt a nagging question in the back of his mind. He wondered if other civilians in this control room might be directing the Enemy troops in a similar fashion.

Safe in their protected bunkers, these isolated civilians played the deadly war like a game, an exercise. They'd lived here for so long, so comfortably, they seemed uninterested in winning the conflict or ending the crisis ... merely in maintaining what they already had.

"So you see, Barto," Juliette said, touching his arm again—this time he did not withdraw so quickly—"we understand what you go through. We're familiar with the war, we're there with you inside your head during even the most terrible missions. We know how difficult it is for the soldiers." She smiled. "That's why I'm very glad to offer you asylum here. Stay with us." Now she sounded coy. "I'd be ... very interested in getting to know you better."

Arviq glowered, out of his element. The chaperone next to him nodded toward Juliette, and she said, "You see, Gunnar is also taking good care of your comrade. Stay here. Consider it well-deserved R&R."

Barto looked around, saw the controllers, heard the familiar command voices. He answered gruffly, "I'm a soldier. I follow orders." Even if it meant he must stop fighting for a while.

Once the two prisoners had resigned themselves to their situation, they were allowed to speak with each other, though neither Barto nor Arviq had ever had much use for conversation. For a week they had made no violent gestures and learned to "behave themselves"—as Juliette described it. As a reward, Barto and Arviq were allowed to sit next to each other in the dining hall.

The room was a large chamber with plush seats and long tables. Lights sparkled from prisms overhead, and the air was redolent with the rich smells of exotic dishes. Various salads and broiled fishes and interesting soups were spread before them. The hall echoed with a murmur of voices.

In his training sessions, Barto learned about the horrors of being a POW, should such a fate ever befall him. But he was now confused, not sure which orders to follow, what was the proper course of action. Juliette had insisted he was their honored guest, not a prisoner. Should he still try to escape? These civilians had given him food and shelter, and a soft bed, though he desperately wanted his narrow basket-bunk back. He longed for the decisive voice in his ears that commanded him to do his duty—but Barto no longer knew exactly what his duty was.

Arviq looked at his plate and poked at the gaudy, frilly dishes that had been served to him. Other soft-skinned civilians walked by, staring at them, whispering to each other. One reached out to touch Arviq on the shoulder, as if on a dare; the soldier lashed out like a python, and the two observers scampered away giggling, as if titillated by the thrill they'd just received.

Barto felt as if he and his point man were on display, specimens for a zoo ... or humiliated members of a captured Enemy force, dragged before the public as trophies. Shrouded in silence, Arviq seemed to be doing a slow burn as he sat staring at his food, glaring at the other people.

Barto tried to calm himself. His own emotions seemed so much flatter since he'd been brought underground, his mind dulled—as if the adrenaline pump, endorphin enhancers, even his root survival instincts had been neutralized. Listening to the muted drone of conversation and music around them, he thought back longingly to the cacophony in the mess hall at his old barracks.

He remembered the clatter of metal trays, the crash of armor plates as soldiers jostled each other. With wordless camaraderie, the squad members sat on hard benches, grabbed their utensils, and gobbled their tasteless food. Together, they recharged their batteries and stoked the fires that they would need for combat in their next mission.

While none of the soldiers knew each other very well, each knew his place in life, his purpose ... and his Enemy. These underground civilians had nothing to compare with that.

Juliette sauntered up to them, her elfin features positively glowing, as if Barto's presence had increased her own standing among her people. She walked with her tall friend, Gunnar, who had spent days escorting Arviq. She looked down at the food on Barto's plate and clucked in a mock scolding tone that he should eat more.

Barto felt a strange sensation in his stomach and heart, as if he were basking in the sunlight of her presence. How could Juliette make him feel proud that she had chosen him for her special attentions? He had never been singled out for anything before.

On the days when Juliette brought him to the breakfast hall, Barto was glad to see her, eager to hear her voice, just to look upon her face. As his senses had become accustomed to his environment, his tongue relished the taste of fresh fruits and breads. The flower scents in the air smelled sweet, and he didn't flinch when Juliette touched him this time, taking him by the elbow. He liked the softness of her fingertips, the way they moved up and down his arm. He felt that he wanted to be even closer to her, to allow her into the walled fortress of himself.

"Do you like it with us here?" Juliette said with a hopeful, even plaintive, lilt to her voice. Ignoring Arviq, she touched the lumpy intaglio of scars on his forearm, tracing patterns and imagining his terrible wounds, as if she had never seen such marks before. "I'd like for you to stay with us, Barto ... with me." She reached across the table to clasp his hand, and he felt the urge to withdraw. What was she doing?

Gunnar's narrow face seemed drawn and concerned. He shook his head gravely. "You know how he's been trained. You know what this man has been through. He's not a toy for you, Juliette."

"I know exactly what he is," she answered. They both talked as if Barto wasn't even there. "And that doesn't change my wishes one bit."

With intent, flicking eyes, Barto followed the conversation, the conflict. If Juliette wanted him to stay here—and he vehemently wished that she did—then he would stay.

He'd seen the control chambers, the computer screens. He knew that these were the ultimate commanders of the war, the people who issued the instructions through his helmet speakers. His job had been to defend these civilians, to protect them ... and if Juliette should happen to give him leave to stop the fighting and stay here, with her, then he would follow orders.

Moving around behind him at the dining table, Juliette held out a large purple flower, its petals like a soft starburst. With particular care, she slid it into the close-cropped dark hair behind his right ear. Then she clapped at her audacity and at the spectacle she had made. He flushed.

Barto did not remove the flower, knowing it was somehow special to Juliette. The other civilians in the dining hall spoke to each other, pleased and entertained. Then Juliette danced away with tall Gunnar beside her, leaving the two soldiers to continue eating under the scrutiny of the curious observers.

Arviq looked across the table at him, scowling at his comrade's behavior. He narrowed his flinty eyes at the flower in Barto's hair. "You look like a fool," he growled, and snatched it away.

Back in his too-peaceful quarters with the door sealed and locked from the outside, he lay on his too-comfortable bed and then finally curled up on the hard floor. He would sleep better that way....

He dreamed of other times, when there hadn't been so much peace, when he had felt alive and useful and necessary. Where he had known his place in the world.

After one particularly furious foray, he, Arviq, and five other squad members crept ahead, continuing to approach the blasted Enemy territory even after the main conflict was over. They followed trails of blood and footprints, drag marks left by the bloodhounds that had come to retrieve the bodies of Enemy soldiers.

In the dream Barto increased his visor's sensitivity to search for infrared traces of organic waste or warm blood droplets. The enhanced bloodhounds were not trained to cover their trails, and with their heavy, mangled burdens, they left a path that was easy to follow, even across the blistered landscape.

The squad followed the trail back to a shielded Enemy encampment. Barto and his comrades prided themselves in their bravery (or foolhardiness), and they charged into the bunkers with their weapons drawn, their adrenaline packs tuned to full output. Their laser-lances blasted the hinges off the doors and made short work of the plasrock bricks that shored up the damaged buildings.

Within moments, Barto's squad had breached the outer defenses and came in firing. No mercy. Many Enemy soldiers were still in their armor, but their weapons were locked in recharging racks. Others fought hand-to-hand, never giving up.

Barto's team suffered heavy losses, but during the fight he was dizzy with exhilaration. By himself, he vanquished fifteen of the Enemy soldiers; altogether, his squad destroyed the entire outpost. Total victory.

Throughout the combat exercise, during the screams and explosions, the violence and death, Barto had felt a sure camaraderie between his fellow soldiers. He never let doubt enter his mind, never a question. He knew exactly what he was doing here.

The Enemy bloodhounds, locked in their small home-kennels, bayed until Arviq cut them all down. The dogs seemed to know they had been responsible for betraying their masters' location.

With a resounding cheer of triumph, the survivors of Barto's team gave a shout to celebrate the defeat of the Enemy. Then, as part of a ritual for such infrequent but absolute victories, the men reached down to tear the helmets off the Enemy corpses, taking them for souvenirs.

Barto removed the helmet from the soldier he had just killed, then looked down to see the visage of the Enemy.

In his dream, the face belonged to Juliette.

As days of contained rage and frustration built within him, Arviq found that he didn't even need the supplemental adrenaline pump from his dismantled armor. This was all wrong! His blood boiled, his anger rose into a thunderstorm of fury—and he unleashed it upon the walls, the bed, anything in his room. His cell.

Arviq didn't want to be a prisoner of war. He wanted to fight, to kill the Enemy. He had been bred and trained for nothing else.

The quiet stillness of this underground civilian world, the soft fabrics, the perfumes, and the too-tasteful food … all pushed him into a frenzy. He tore the coverings off his bed and thrashed about, ripping the sheets to shreds. He howled and screamed without words, a bestial cry of damnation. He pounded on the door, but it only rattled in its grooves. Then he threw himself upon the bedframe itself, yanking and pulling, until finally he uprooted it from the walls.

He didn't know if anyone was watching him, nor did he care.

Arviq hurled himself against the metal wall, battering his shoulders, bruising his muscles, but feeling no pain. His body was accustomed to running on the ragged edge of energy, and he had been resting here for days, storing up power in his muscles. Now he released it all in his frenzy.

His attack made marks on the wall, left some smears of his own blood. His fists caused dents. The sealed door rattled again in its tracks; it seemed looser now. He pounded and pounded, receiving no answer.

Finally, Arviq returned to the ruined bedframe, wrenching free a strip of metal that he could use as a crowbar. He had to escape. He had to get back. He didn't belong here.

He wedged the ragged end of torn metal into the door track and pushed, prying … bending. The door began to buckle, and Arviq worked even harder.

After his nightmares had left him like exorcised demons, Barto fell into a deep slumber and awoke incredibly refreshed. Sometime in the middle of the night he had crawled back into his bed and rested peacefully.

A soldier had to be flexible, had to adapt to new circumstances. At last, he had begun to do just that.

When Gunnar and Juliette came to fetch him, he sensed their tension. The other civilians continued to stare at him, as they had done for days, but now they held a greater glint of fear in their eyes, a more uncertain look on their faces. Barto couldn't understand it, because for the first time since he'd come to this place of sanctuary, he felt more relaxed, more at ease, as if his life had indeed changed.

Seeing how the underground people had changed, how their attitude toward him had shifted, Barto knew something must have occurred. He could sense it. "What has happened?" he said.

Gunnar looked at him and answered crisply, "Your friend Arviq has gone on a rampage. He broke out of his room, and he's escaped."

Barto bolted to his feet. He understood Arviq's impulses. He had felt them himself, and now alarm bells rang out in his head. "What has he done?"

Juliette took a deep breath and blinked her deep brown eyes, as if the subject itself made her uncomfortable. "He broke his way out of the room. He smashed some windows in the corridors, destroyed one of our greenhouses. That was an hour or so ago. No one has seen him since."

Barto pushed his half-finished breakfast away and stood tall and strong. Called back to active duty. He didn't need any more sustenance, no more food to distract him. His mind became focused again, delving into the old hunter/survival mentality.

"I know how he thinks, and I know what he's doing," Barto said. "You cannot let him get away."

"We can't stop him," Gunnar said. "He'd kill all of us if we tried."

Barto shook his head. "You don't understand what Arviq can do, or what will happen if he gets away from this place. You can't just ignore him." Then he looked over at Juliette again. He finally admitted to himself that she was beautiful.

"Can you stop him?" Juliette said. "It would be to protect us."

"I will need my armor and my helmet if I'm going to do this right."

At first the armor felt rough and strange, but rapidly Barto adopted it as a second skin. The protective covering belonged, as much a part of him as his bones and muscles.

Looking at her soldier, Juliette wore a concerned expression, as if he had too easily stepped over the brink. Barto saw something unreadable deep within her brown eyes, a flush on her elfin face, as he picked up the helmet. He looked at her uncertainly one last time, then seated it firmly on his head. He pressed the side speakers against his ears, lowering the visor in place so that he looked at her through filters and scanning devices instead of his own eyes.

Barto drew a deep breath, stretching his chest against the breastplate armor plate. He flexed his arms against the hard bicep plates, the forearm protections, the gauntlets. His torso was solid and impenetrable. His legs and back, shoulders, hips, everything could withstand the worst that Arviq threw against him.

Barto was invincible.

"I must stop him before he leaves," he said. "He'll report the location of this place to HQ."

Juliette hesitated, moved forward and then stopped, as if she wanted to embrace him but was afraid to. Barto was glad she didn't. He didn't want to get close to her, like this.

The tall chaperone, Gunnar, stood beside her, his face grim, and he drew her back. "Let him go now, Juliette. He has a mission."

Barto turned and marched out of the room, summoning up his mental map of the underground civilian sanctuary. He would begin in Arviq's quarters, where the point man had smashed his own room and broken loose. It would not be too difficult to pick up his former comrade's trail. Barto knew how to track down a quarry.

Leaving the other inhabitants behind, he followed the tunnels. Most of the civilians reacted with fear when they saw him now. They hid within their own quarters or clustered together in the communal halls, though only one unarmed soldier had gone on a rampage. It was all beyond their experience.

All of these people cowered down here, helpless. And Barto was the only one who could protect them.

Though Arviq had not been able to retrieve his armor or his weapons, Barto did not underestimate him. A properly trained soldier could fashion defensive materials out of just about anything.

At the pried-open door, he stood motionless, assessing Arviq's damaged room, saw how his comrade had wrenched open the barricade using a piece of the bedframe as a lever, how he had battered the walls with his bare hands. Barto saw blood but knew that Arviq would pay no attention to such minor cuts and bruises. Not Arviq.

Barto had seen him through much worse.

One time on a reconnaissance and destruction mission, Barto and his point man had ventured into the crumbling ruins of what must have been an impossibly large building, now scarred, empty, and blasted. The structure had fallen into rubble with haphazard girders and broken glass protruding from poured stone walls.

They had chased several Enemies into the wreckage. Their senses screamed that it was probably an ambush, but still the two soldiers had followed, weapons drawn, confident that they could defeat their opponents. He and Arviq separated and traveled along different passageways, using their scanners to pick up infrared footprint traces.

Barto had proceeded cautiously, but Arviq, incensed and determined, charged through the darkened halls, knocking wreckage aside. Finally, he had crashed down a rickety iron staircase that shattered into rust as he stepped on it. And he dropped through to the underlevels....

When Barto had found him later, he saw that Arviq had broken his left leg in two places and had sprained his right ankle. His helmet visor was cracked and damaged—yet still Arviq had pulled himself along to find the Enemy. He certainly had.

Though severely injured and at an extreme disadvantage, Arviq had slaughtered both of the Enemy soldiers....

From their missions together, Barto knew that his comrade was utterly relentless, feeling no pain and no fatigue. Nothing would stop him from escaping the underground enclave. He would never give up.

And neither would Barto give up. He was the only thing that could keep this civilian paradise protected and intact.

He strode out and moved briskly along the corridors. His bootsteps ricocheted off the metal walls. Arviq had smashed windows and thrown loose objects from side to side, leaving a painfully clear trail—until he had learned better and sensibly stopped his rampage.

Then tracking him became more of a challenge. Barto called up a detailed implanted map of all the underground corridors, which Juliette had added to the information systems in his helmet.

Arviq was running blind, by instinct, just trying to escape, but his movements displayed a pattern. On the map gleaming inside his visor, Barto could see the best paths, learn where to go ... where to intercede.

Arviq didn't have a chance against a fully armed, fully outfitted soldier, like Barto.

He marched along, his senses tuned to a high pitch. He moved carefully in case the other soldier had set up some kind of booby trap or ambush. That was to be expected. Arviq must know Barto would come after him.

Because the other soldier was without his armor, his bare feet left a trail of infrared images on the clean floorplates. The marks were old and fading, but still identifiable with Arviq's genetic signature: droplets of sweat, skin particles, even stride length gave evidence of his passage. The other man was still bleeding from one of the cuts he'd inflicted upon himself in escaping from the room; occasionally a telltale crimson droplet reinforced Barto's tracking.

The control voice returned, insistent and self-confident. It comforted Barto, who had lived his conscious life hearing the words: "KILL THE ENEMY! KILL THE ENEMY! KILL THE ENEMY!" He no longer felt so alone.

According to the map display, Arviq had made it to within several hundred meters of the long access ladder that led up a shaft to the outside—the battleground where their squad had been killed.

But Barto also knew he had cornered his quarry.

At an intersection of the dimly lit corridors, a framework of girders and support beams held up the ceiling. The place had been long-abandoned by the underground civilians.

Barto's visor-sensors detected a large smear of blood at floor level in a corner, as if Arviq had rested there … or as if he had encountered an Enemy, and they had struggled, hand-to-hand. The blood was fresh, wet, warm in IR—like a sign emblazoned there to draw his attention.

Too late, he realized the ambush. From the shadowed support girders above, Arviq let out a loud cry and dropped on top of him. Though he had no armor and no weapons, the other soldier crashed down upon him with brute force. Barto might have found the conflict absurd if Arviq hadn't been so determined, so passionate— if the other man hadn't been his own comrade for so long.

Arviq wrapped his left arm in a vice-lock around Barto's neck, trying to wrench the helmet off his head. With his other hand he tried to grab one of the ID-locked weapons sealed in armored holsters on Barto's hips.

Barto rose up like a tank, as if his armor gave him stimulus and energy, though Juliette had told him his artificial adrenaline pumps were disconnected from the suit.

Inside his ears, the helmet commanders shouted, "KILL THE ENEMY! KILL THE ENEMY! DON'T LET HIM ESCAPE!" With a weird disorientation, Barto thought the voice sounded like Gunnar's.

Without letting go, Arviq fought like a wild thing, clamping his knees on either side of Barto's armored chest, trying to tear the helmet off. When Barto staggered backward, slamming his comrade against the metal wall, Arviq let out an explosive exhale of pain and surprise. Barto recovered his balance and slammed him against the wall a second time.

Arviq struggled but would not let go. He continued pounding with naked fists against the impenetrable armor.

"Come with me!" Arviq shouted loudly enough to penetrate the heavy ear coverings, to break through the harsh command voice. "Let's go back to HQ. Back to our lives, Barto! We don't belong here."

Barto bent over and butted him against the wall, hearing ribs crack this time. Arviq's grip finally loosened. He wheezed in pain, coughed blood. "Let me go then. Just let me run from here. I'll leave." Arviq slumped to one side and scrambled to his feet. Blood from his raw wounds smeared Barto's scuffed armor.

"Can't let you do that," Barto answered. "You must stay here.

The commanders gave their orders. Defy them, and you're a traitor."

Arviq stood up, glaring at him. His face was uncovered, his emotions unmasked. "This isn't what we were made for. We are soldiers. War is our life. Not this ... where we're pets on display." Barto had never really studied his comrade's face before. "What happens when they get bored with us?"

Barto pressed his gloved palm against the hilt of his ID-coded blaster weapon. The device detected its proper owner and released its grip in the holster. Barto yanked the weapon free, held it in his hand.

Not far down the corridor, he could see the tarnished rungs that rose up the dark shaft. It would take so little for Arviq to scramble up the ladder, pop the heavy hatch—and be out, all alone on the blasted battlefield. Without armor or weapons, he didn't have much chance of survival—but Arviq seemed desperate enough to take that option.

Arviq gathered himself up, glared at his former comrade and stepped away. "I know what I am, and what to do." With the back of his hand, he wiped a smear of blood from his mouth. "Which one of us is the traitor, truly?" He turned and, moving slowly, not threateningly, took a step toward the ladder, the escape.

Barto raised the weapon. "Halt."

Arviq turned to look at him with flinty, determined eyes. "I'm dead down here anyway. If I can't get back onto the battlefield, then you may as well blast me now."

Barto powered up his weapon.

The other soldier took two more steps down the corridor.

Inside the helmet, Gunnar's voice shouted, "KILL THE ENEMY! DON'T LET HIM ESCAPE. YOU MUST PROTECT US. KILL HIM!" Barto leveled the blaster at the target.

Then he heard another voice—Juliette's—muffled and distant, but coming closer. She cried out, running down the long-abandoned corridors toward him. "Don't shoot, Barto. You must learn not to kill if you're going to stay here."

"Kill! Kill!" Gunnar's voice bellowed.

Arviq turned as Juliette appeared, all alone, her elfin face distraught. Then he used the moment of distraction to dash toward the rungs.

"KILL!" shouted the voice in Barto's ears again. And he did.

Depressing the firing stud, he blasted his former comrade in the back as he ran. Arviq had no armor, no protection whatsoever. The bolt flared out and incinerated him, turning the other man into a smoking pile of burned bones and cooked flesh that fell in a heap on the floor, as if still trying to run.

"No!" Juliette cried out, but it sounded like a pout. Barto turned to see her standing there. Her expression was stricken, and then even more terrified as he faced her, the charged weapon still in his hand. "I wanted you to stay here with me," she said. "It's a better life, but you've got to learn not to kill. Stay away from violence. You've earned it. You could live here with me in peace and enjoy your life, escape the horrors of war."

"They're not horrors," Barto said in a flat voice. He refused to take off his helmet. He was a soldier now, fully armed, ready to fight. "It's the only thing I know." He holstered the warm blaster. "I can't stay here as a prisoner of war."

"But you're a free man among us," Juliette pleaded, refusing to come closer. She seemed as much confused as saddened. She couldn't understand why he would make this choice.

"I am still a prisoner," he said. "War holds me prisoner." He stood at attention, as if the feline spies were watching him from the shadows. "I must live by fighting, and I must die by fighting. I have no way to escape that."

He understood now that this place, despite its comforts and its new experiences, could not possibly be for him. Not for a soldier.

He didn't begrudge Juliette her civilian life, her pampered existence—and if these people were indeed the commanders in the war, if he was a soldier charged with protecting them, then he must go back and do his duty until death inevitably claimed him on the battlefield. And if he should happen to survive, then he would grow old and train other soldiers until the war was won and the Enemy completely vanquished.

There was nothing else for him to do.

Juliette watched him with despair, then a flash of anger in her brown eyes. Finally, her slender shoulders drooped in defeat. She said nothing else, just watched him with a flush in her cheeks.

Barto didn't know what he had really meant to her ... if he had merely been a trophy from the battlefield, something that increased her prestige among her people—or if she had really cared for him, in a way.

At the moment it didn't matter. It was irrelevant information.

Leaving his dead comrade behind, sad that the bloodhounds could never retrieve Arviq and take him back to where he could be buried with full military honors, Barto climbed the rungs of the ladder.

It was a long way to the surface, but when he released the hatch and climbed out under the open, bruised sky, he stared for a long moment. He breathed the burnt air, studied the roiling dust from distant explosions.

He lifted his visor to stare out across the stricken field with his own eyes, then he shut the hatch behind him, sealing Juliette and her world underground, keeping her secret safe. And then he strode off, heading in the direction of his HQ.

It would feel good to get back to the business of fighting once again.

When my friend Janet Berliner teamed with famous illusionist David Copperfield to put together an anthology of magic-themed stories, I thought of Arthur C. Clarke's famous quote. "Any sufficiently advanced technology is indistinguishable from magic."

How else can you do a science fiction story about magic?

On one of our trips to Las Vegas, Janet arranged for Rebecca and me to see Copperfield's show at Caesar's Palace and to meet him backstage afterward. When the anthology was published, I went to New York for a gala book signing, which Copperfield also attended along with his then-girlfriend Claudia Schiffer. (How much attention do you think us mere authors received at the event?)

Janet passed away in 2012. I've met David Copperfield several times since then, and we even developed a collaborative thriller project that, unfortunately, never got off the ground. But he did give me a private tour of his workshop and amazing magic museum, and he had me (and my parents) as his guests at his show at the MGM ... so it was a pretty good score, nevertheless!

TECHNOMAGIC

"Any sufficiently advanced technology is indistinguishable from magic."

— ARTHUR C. CLARKE

"Twenty-seven years for a rescue ship? You've got to be kidding! What am I supposed to do on this planet in the meantime? How am I—"

— TAURINDO ALPHA PRIME, LAST TRANSMISSION
FROM SCOUT VESSEL BEFORE CRASHING IN THE
NEVADA DESERT (LOOSELY TRANSLATED)

The first garish posters had said *The Great Taurindo!*—some over-enthusiastic publicist's idea, not mine—but my fame grew so rapidly that within a few years the marquees in the Las Vegas amphitheaters shouted my name in letters even taller than I was. (And I am slightly greater in height than the average Earthling, though I look just like one of them.)

The evening's crowd was sprawled out at various tables, more than could comfortably fit in the room, thanks to the outrageous ticket prices people were willing to pay to see me perform. The rich ones sat in the best seats, drinking expensive cocktails, while busloads of budget tour groups crammed together at the long tables, jabbering their schemes for how to win at the nickel slots.

Everyone fell silent as the show began. I cracked my knuckles in the shadows at the edge of the stage, waiting, making sure my smile looked right. Many species in the Galaxy believe the flashing of one's teeth to be a threatening gesture, but on Earth it's considered friendly. Just another of the odd details about them.

The master of ceremonies announced me as the "World's! Greatest! Magician!" Sometimes I'm called a magician, other times an "illusionist"—neither of which is truly accurate, since what I do is not magic nor illusion, but the real thing ... courtesy of my planet's highly advanced technology. None of the spectators knew that, though.

The broad stage reminded me of when I had taken my oral exam before the xeno-sociology degree committee back on the homeworld. I strode out and took my bow as I introduced the evening's first spectacle.

"Remember the old saw about the woman being cut in half in a box?" I said. The audience chuckles. No one from my planet would have understood the reference, but this was a hoary old trick performed *ad nauseam* by Earth magicians. Simple enough to master, but I had added a new twist. "Tonight I'll show you a *new saw*, a very large saw in fact." I smiled again.

The lights flashed. Hot white beams reflected from the highly polished, stainless-steel teeth of the giant chainsaw blade that would slice me in two before their very eyes.

The audience loved the show so far—my lovely assistants were wearing even skimpier outfits than usual.

"I won't hide in a box, I won't use mirrors or distractions. I will lie on this table in plain sight, and this chainsaw will cut me in half —*as you watch!* You'll see it all, every second of it."

The music built. The lights dimmed.

I stepped back into the artificially deep shadows at the back of the stage, and then I sent my perfect clone forward out into the brilliant light. He was an identical match for my body, cell for cell, although his brain was completely blank. It was all the vapid simulacrum could do to stagger across the stage and lie down on the table under the motionless chainsaw.

The beautiful assistants strapped him down, and he didn't resist, instinctively smiling out at the audience like an idiot. All clones smile. It's a secret they seem to share in their brainlessness.

The eyes of all the men in the audience were trying to catch a glimpse of just a bit more through my assistants' scanty uniforms and paid little attention to the mechanics of the actual trick. Others were trying to figure out what the gimmick was—while some few, the blessed ones, remained happy enough just to be entertained.

The music swelled loud and dramatic. The chainsaw blade spun up with a loud roar that built to a threatening whine, like a dentist's drill for King Kong.

The lighting technicians slipped a thick red gel over the spotlights, bathing the stage in an ominous crimson glow, as the deadly blade began to descend, rattling as the chain teeth whipped around and around in a circle. The clone lay twitching on the table, bound by the restraints and staring with uncomprehending eyes up at the sharp spinning blade about to rip him to shreds.

That's show biz, as they say.

Timing was everything now, and I had to depend on my crew. They knew what they were supposed to do.

The chainsaw slammed down, ripping through the clone's ribcage and sparking on the steel tabletop. Blood flew in a bright arc —one of the more picturesque ones, I thought. The clone let out a shriek of instinctive pain that was abruptly cut off ... then all the lights went out for an instant to be replaced by only a single faint spotlight on the retracting chainsaw blade still slowly spinning, dripping blood.

The audience swelled with thin screams. I wondered how many of them would faint this time, though I had done this trick many times and they must have *known* there would be no accident. Not this time. Not any time.

I could have kept the lights up, of course, since this was all real. I could have shown the audience the gory, anatomically correct mess on the table. But that would have gone beyond the bounds of good clean entertainment. Instead, the glimpse of the bloodied saw and the clone's genuine scream was all they needed to know.

As the lights dropped to black, the automatic nanocritters— microscopic destructive robots—began the busy-work of taking my clone apart cell by cell, dissolving him into a simple protein mass in the space of less than a minute. And when the entire body was denatured, the liquid obediently seeped into drains in the table (placed there ostensibly for spilled blood). I would use the protein mass to grow a clone for another performance.

The lights came up again with enough flash and dazzle to temporarily blind the audience, and there I stood in the middle of the stage, intact and smiling, taking my bow to thunderous applause—as always.

Outside the bright lights of the casino, I melted into the crowd, where I could study the way humans interact. I've never gotten tired of it, even after so many years.

On the sidewalk at a street corner, where impatient pedestrians waited for DON'T WALK to change to WALK, I saw an aspiring magician walking among the people, pestering them, showing off to the best of his ability. Doing card tricks, pulling colored scarves from his sleeves—amateurish stuff, but I stopped in mid-stride with a warm glow of nostalgia. Perhaps he hoped for some sort of special attention as he stood overshadowed by the huge marquee for *The Great Taurindo!*

I watched him for a while. This struggling magician with stars in his eyes and the reckless hope for fame reminded me of one of the first Earthlings I had ever met....

Just before my burned-out scout ship crashed out on this planet's desert wastelands, I was able to salvage only a few things from the hulk. After transmitting my distress call and pinpointing my position for the eventual rescue ship, I hurried away from the ship as the self-destruct nanocritters began to turn the hull and engines to indefinable dust.

Swallowing hard, I hiked across the rocky scrub in the general direction of the large city I had spotted just before impact.

Because of my profession studying alien cultures, I had been through the "first contact" routine numerous times before, and this one went off without a hitch. But as I ambled through the streets of Las Vegas, trying to fit in while staring wide-eyed around me, I came upon a street magician. He had a battered cardboard box open on the sidewalk, in which had been scattered bits of paper and round metal (obviously the monetary currency in use).

The magician extended a deck of playing cards to passers-by, asking them to select a card, whose identity he would then guess. In another trick he hid a bright red ball under one of three bowls, rapidly shuffled them around, then asked someone to find it—and invariably they guessed wrong.

At first, I suspected these humans had telepathic powers, but as I watched I soon realized this was not the case. The magician was merely fooling his audience with sleight of hand. And people were tossing him money for it.

I watched him for some time, but since I had no local currency to give for the performance, I wandered away.

I began to think that I could do such stunts, only better—given my superior technology. Among the few items I had snagged from the ship before its quiet self-destruct was the wonderful Central Autonomic Molecular Device—a complex whirlwind computer, synthesizer, and nanotechnology processor. I called it the "gizmo," ignoring the pretentious technical terminology that I didn't understand anyway. The machine was far beyond my level of education and training—I was a xeno-sociologist and observer, not an engineer. The palm-sized gizmo *worked*, and that was all I needed to know during my exile here.

I was stuck on Earth for twenty-seven years, and I would have to make something of myself in the meantime. And magic fascinated these people.

As I assimilated into this culture, I came upon an interesting observation called Clarke's Law. It said that "Any sufficiently advanced technology is indistinguishable from magic." The postulate had been derived by a visionary who also developed the concept for this planet's geosynchronous communication satellites, had popularized the idea for the space elevator as an alternative to expendable launch vehicles, and had also written the story for an amusing film called *2001: A Space Odyssey*, which I enjoyed very much. (I wonder if Mr. Clarke's awe of alien intelligences might have been so great if he'd had the pleasure of meeting the bovine slugs of Merricus or endured the screeching carrion ballets of Vulpine Five, however.)

Clarke's postulate about technology and magic gave me an idea. With the gizmo to serve me, I simply had to learn what sort of magic the Earthlings wanted to see and how to make a good show out of it.

Showmanship proved to be the hardest part. Simply displaying an endless string of miracles would not be enough. (Besides, Central Authority back home would have been very annoyed if I accidentally started a new religion on Earth.)

I watched Earth's best performers, astonishing magicians and illusionists, trying to learn the secret to a good show. At times I was confounded, wondering if these showmen somehow had access to contraband extraterrestrial technology themselves. It didn't matter —I knew my gizmo was superior to anything they might have. I could do better.

It took me a long time to understand their attitude toward entertainment—but once I did, it became a key to grasping the human psyche. While Earthlings are endlessly curious and easily perplexed, these people honestly didn't want to know *how* a magic trick was performed. They might claim so, and half mean it, but they would rather be intrigued and amazed. They'd be outraged if every magician went on their endless talk shows and explained all the secrets.

That would squash the thrill for them, the *magic*.

One of my simplest tricks (and therefore one of my favorites) was transporting myself instantaneously from one part of the arena to another. It was a trivial teleportation gimmick—but with the appropriate buildup, the music, the lights, the smoke and mirrors, the gorgeous assistants, and pounding drums, it became an amazing feat. Other Earth magicians had done similar acts, some with people, some with animals—but no one did it with my method (so far as I know).

After selecting a volunteer from the audience—a fidgety young man with too-short pants and a sweat-stained polyester shirt—I climbed into a vertical metal box at the back of my stage, holding the lid open. An identical box stood at the far end of the seats, a good distance away, containing my unwitting volunteer. The young man stood inside the box as if it were a coffin, looking out and wanting to shrink away from the sudden attention.

The assistants sealed the door of his box. The young man's eyes were bugging out and his throat bobbed as he gulped.

Waving from the stage, I closed the door on my box, activating the instantaneous teleportation circuit in the gizmo strapped to my waist.

Less than a second later, I emerged intact in the opposite booth, while assistants opened the box on the stage, allowing the wide-eyed volunteer to stumble out, gawking in amazement and completely at a loss as to how he had traveled a hundred meters in an instant. He rubbed his still-tingling skin and blinked into the bright lights and the applause. He grinned like a clone.

⚛

My promoters and agents (*these* people are true aliens, even among Earthlings) kept insisting that I do bigger and more daring stunts—and I obliged, attempting to surpass even the greatest illusions ever performed by master magicians. Though some of the spectacles required more power, my precious gizmo had a century-and-a-half useful lifespan, according to its warranty. I trusted the engineers from my planet. They knew what they were doing.

Most outrageous trick: I made the Empire State Building vanish at midnight, right under floodlights and helicopters and in front of the slack-jawed faces of the gathered crowd.

In the blind instant when the spotlights shut off, I touched the gizmo at my waist to *disintegrate* the entire skyscraper, all 102 stories (plus television tower). When the lights came back up again, only shaven foundations remained of one of the tallest buildings on this planet. A few disconcerting sparks flickered up from severed electrical cables, nothing more.

I sincerely hoped the publicists had evacuated the building as they'd promised.

Once the cheers and applause began to subside, we dropped the lights again and I re-integrated the building, according to its molecular pattern stored in the gizmo's computer. Simple enough, when you think about it, given a little bit of engineering know-how … or at least a machine that can do it all for you.

⚛

Then I made my big mistake.

It was a trick I had done dozens of times, and it had never proved difficult before. Overconfident, I let my guard down, forgetting how truly alien these Earthlings are, how they panic when there isn't the least bit of danger. I "screwed up," to use their own quaint phrase.

For the finale of my act I had taken to *flying*—my trademark performance, as it were. I strapped an auxiliary anti-gravity pack to my chest just below the gizmo itself, using it to levitate and flit about the stage.

As always, it gave the Earthlings an added thrill to see a randomly chosen audience member fly along with me. (Showmanship, showmanship!) This evening I had picked out a pretty young blonde with a good figure, gleaming smile, and giggly personality—audiences responded best to sexy volunteers, though the anti-grav belt could have lifted even one of the hefty matriarchs who sat sipping wine coolers and killing time before they got back to the slot machines.

"Are you ready to fly?" I asked the young lady, raising my rich voice for the audience. Her eyes were as large as those of the mantis people that had nearly devoured me on Karnak Delta. Her name was Tiffany, naturally.

I held her trembling hand as the assistants came out with hoops, swooping them around me to prove that I had no wires attached to my body, no flying harness (just the gizmo and a small anti-grav generator). Tiffany saw the tests and she saw my face and then looked around. Standing right beside me, she knew better than anyone else that this was no trick.

I held her snugly around the waist like Superman and Lois Lane, and we lifted off, drifting above the stage. I should have noticed her growing uneasiness. We were skewered by the blazing spotlights that tracked our every movement, drifting back and forth. Tiffany was stunned—but her amazement lasted only a moment.

When I soared out over the audience and the tables, alas, it proved too much for her. She became hysterical to get down, struggling in my grasp so that I had to clutch her just to keep her from plummeting to the stage.

"Stop it!" I whispered, but she didn't hear me. The audience was too busy shouting their *ooohs!* and *aaaahs!* I whisked us back over the stage. The flying routine was the climactic end to my show, and I wanted to milk it for as long as possible—but I couldn't swoop around and do my typical stunts with a writhing, panic-stricken human in my arms!

Tiffany clutched my shirt, her long fingernails scratching my chest, grabbing for anything to hold on to. Her hands snatched the thin strap that bound the gizmo to my waist. The strap snapped.

The gizmo fell thirty feet down to the hard stage.

I heard a *clunk*, then a broken *tinkle*. The audience muttered, wondering if they had caught me at something. The spotlights weren't on the stage floor where my woefully damaged device lay, so I covered the gaffe quickly by shouting, "Tiffany, calm down! I think your teeth just fell out."

This brought a chuckle as I lowered us to the far end of the stage with the last trickle of reserve power in the anti-grav belt. I felt sick inside, but "the show must go on," so I took my bows and said my goodnights, letting Tiffany return to her giggling friends. She would probably tell them how much fun it had been.

When the lights went down, I dashed across the stage to retrieve the debris and hurried back to my dressing room, where I refused all visitors for the rest of the night....

I stared down in dismay at the broken innards of the gizmo, the convoluted circuits, the delicately imprinted control paths and microchips far beyond any technology Earth has ever created. The warranty wouldn't do me any good now.

As I said before, I am a xeno-sociologist, not an engineer. I stared down at my ruined miracle-working machine and thought again of Clarke's Law. The electronic paths and schematics meant absolutely nothing to me. The high-tech gizmo might as well have been magic.

I knew this would be my last night of performing. Without the gizmo the Great Taurindo was nothing, unless I learned how to do magic the hard way....

So the years passed. I had amassed a considerable fortune during my years as a star, and I was able to continue living comfortably, though I never set foot on the stage again. I became something of a legend, the reclusive master illusionist who had suddenly quit performing and would tell no one why. I gave no interviews. Numerous books were written about me and my reasons, offering wild speculations, though none so preposterous as the truth.

In the privacy of my home, I continued to practice a few tricks for my own entertainment. I became quite proficient, actually, but nothing good enough to meet the expectations of those who had seen me perform before.

When at last the twenty-seven years had passed, and I received the signal from the rescue ship, I felt an overwhelming joy ... as well as a not-inconsiderable sadness at leaving this interesting backwater planet.

I rushed into the desert to the pickup point, abandoning my home and all my possessions at the darkest hour of night—my sudden disappearance would only increase the mystique about me —and ran to meet the ship.

The pilot and crew were in a great hurry. A Cultural Inspector from Central Authority hustled me off to my seat in the passenger compartment, and we roared back out through Earth's atmosphere. Finally, when we had reached our hypercruise speed, the Cultural Inspector came to debrief me—and I had been waiting for her.

"So, Taurindo Alpha Prime," she said, "you have spent many years on this planet. Tell me what you have learned of their culture."

I smiled. "I can do better than that—I can show you."

From a pocket in my jumpsuit I withdrew a standard deck, shuffled with a dazzling flourish and a snapping blur of sound, then fanned and extended them toward her.

"Pick a card," I said, "any card."

Ah, true romance!

I've mentioned in other introductions that I had a rather unsuccessful and frustrating dating life during my college years, which is reflected in some of my stories. (Don't worry, I write much rosier romantic stories now that I've been happily married to Rebecca for more than three decades.)

In "Mating Ritual," I took the writing challenge of understanding a genuinely alien mindset, set on a world that is decidedly unlike Earth. How does romance work for a species more like black widow spiders than humans? What sort of pickup lines would a black widow alien use? "Come on, big boy, let me show you a good time ... even if it's brief."

"Mating Ritual" is another story that I found in the vault while gathering the materials for this set of collections, and I think it has great ideas and a good twist.

But it's probably not one to read on date night.

MATING RITUAL

His nest is complete, and the moons are full. He feels the hormones singing through his body. Now he must wait for a female to come, a mate.

He has chosen the place well—just below the rim of the crater, but deep enough that the sand-winds can cause no damage. Here, the heat from the rocks will convince his mate that this nest will be an adequate place for their—for *her*—hatchlings. With the excitement building within him, he has arranged the long and beautiful shards of pink crystal in the corner, the floor. He has spun a fine web for their wedding bed.

At last ready, he steps to the edge of the cave and lifts his glossy wing coverings, exposing the orifices up and down his segmented abdomen. He carefully releases a modulated burst of pheromones into the air. By now he has become skilled at attracting the most beautiful and receptive females; it is an art he has mastered better than any other male of his race. He named himself Survivor. Even after so many times, he still savors the growing anticipation, the danger, the promise of unspeakable pleasure.

Survivor looks out into the deep purple sky. The green tendrils of the aurora flutter in a magnetic wind, almost touching the jagged rocky landscape. Overhead, the meteors have started to fall again, slashing white lines across the night. Some of them are so close he can hear the whistle as they burn up in the thin air. He wonders if the meteoroids have existed all their centuries only for this final flash of glory, or if they are driven by forces beyond their comprehension or control.

Below him, at the bottom of the steep-walled crater, he knows the *leems* are gathering under the rocks in glittering, ropy bundles. They have long ago devoured the carcasses of all his previous mates....

To augment the message of the pheromones, Survivor briskly rubs his wing coverings together, sending a powerful mating *trrrrilll* to echo in the cold air. He steps back into the cave, to wait. The waiting is the hardest part.

With the comb on his foreleg, he again preens the tuft beneath his mandibles. He has crushed some of the sharp cave crystal into a powder, mixing it with saliva to scour and polish his chitin to a gleaming luster. He is ready. He knows what to expect. His brother has showed him the full mating ritual long ago, and even now Survivor wishes the brother were still here.

He and his brother had been joined together at hatching. Through a genetic mishap, one of their forelegs and part of their carapace had fused, making them physically inseparable. Their mother had left the hatching pile long before, when she had seen the fertilized eggs close to fruition. The other hatchlings, mostly males, saw the deformity of the two joined brothers and attacked them, trying to destroy what they saw as an unacceptable anomaly. But the two brothers, linked by their physical bond, fought together and drove off the haphazard attacks of the other hatchlings. They forced the others out of the cave and, after they had vanished from sight, Survivor and his brother took flight themselves.

The species is solitary, and the brothers had no elders to pass on knowledge from the previous generations; they had no one to ask— only the ever-present voice of Instinct, which screamed *Do This Now* whenever it chose. Always at the back of their minds, this inner voice clamored, crying out that the species is meant to be alone, apart, with no contact save for that one time in their lives, to mate. In the beginning, the brother listened to his Instinct and tried to kill the parasitic sibling, to cast off Survivor's too-close carcass—the brother was always the stronger and larger of the two. But finally, both brothers fought and defeated their *Instinct* instead, learning how to cope with companionship.

As they matured together, all of life was a mystery to them. As two, they could fend off predators that no single one of them could hope to resist. They burrowed a fine cave, and they hunted successfully.

Then came the terrible time when their minds could no longer tell them what to do. Their bodies, their hormones turned traitor and drove them nearly to a frenzy they could not control or understand—the mating drive.

It struck Survivor's brother first. Barely able to communicate, he told his sibling how he must build a nest, and Survivor helped him, uncomprehending. They worked to carve a place from the rocks, to prepare for the eggs, to spin his web. Though they were joined by one foreleg and part of the carapace, they had learned to move well together, as one. The job was finished quickly, as the moons waxed toward full in the sky.

Survivor stood by his brother as the other sent his pheromones into the air, as he sounded his mating *trrrilll*. He waited by his brother's side for a roving, hunting female to come, but not knowing what else to expect.

When she arrived, both brothers were amazed. They had not seen another of their kind since the hatching; now as the hunting female entered the cave, they both saw how strange and exotic she was. Survivor found her intriguing, even though his own hormones had not yet begun to flow. Her wing casings looked somewhat battered, and their polish had dulled—she had already borne several sets of eggs, and Survivor marveled at how powerful and wise she must have been to survive so long in their world. Her hunting pincers seemed strong enough to crush rock.

The female gave Survivor only a sidelong glance and turned instead to his brother. He had begun to exude a different pheromone, one that seemed to excite her receptors. Though joined to his brother's body, Survivor was effectively a nonentity for them —he did not give off the proper scent, and the driving force of Instinct told them that only a single male and female should be present at the mating.

The female went to the web hammock and slowly climbed upon it, letting the strands support her abdomen as her many legs dangled below. She released a pheromone of her own, and the brother immediately clambered upon her back, sliding his underbody on her smooth wing casings. He used the middle set of legs to engage the mating hooks, locking the two of them together. Survivor was pulled along, curious and trying to be unobtrusive; they ignored him entirely. He watched, studying, knowing this same thing would be happening to him soon.

After the larger brother had mounted his mate, he began to move slowly forward and backward while the female remained incredibly still. A moment later Survivor felt his brother's entire body convulse, and the brother emitted a hum that frightened Survivor with its intensity.

Through the backs of her faceted eyes, the female seemed to be watching him coldly. The larger brother collapsed upon her in total exhaustion, an uncanny lethargy that made it almost impossible for him to move. The female disengaged the mating hooks and pulled herself out from under him, letting the spent male rest upon the web bed. Survivor watched her. She turned back to the brother, who seemed too exhausted to even glance at her....

Survivor's thoughts of the past are interrupted by the sound of wings in the air and an answering, higher-pitched *trrrilll*. A female has come. Knowing this, his body reaches an even greater peak of anticipation. The enormous *wanting* is like a vast hole within his exoskeleton. He turns away from the cave opening, self-consciously hiding the stump of his foreleg and the jagged, broken edge of his carapace.

He must be careful. He must be completely aware, completely in control.

The female appears, landing at the edge of the cave. Survivor watches breathlessly as she enters, questing, hesitant, attracted by his pheromones. She is beautiful—young, with lustrous and glowing chitin; she is curious, driven by her own hormones. This is her first time, and she doesn't know what to do. A part of him wants to relax slightly in relief, but his mind will not allow it—the mating ritual is too dangerous.

He leads her to the nest, rubbing her carapace, preening her feelers. She grows more excited as he releases the second pheromone. She sees the web he has woven and delights in the long shards of pink crystal he has placed around it. The female unleashes her reciprocal pheromone and almost immediately moves onto the mating bed, rocking slowly as the web cushions her smooth abdomen. Her legs hang leisurely, with the two hunting pincers nearly touching the floor.

Survivor almost loses himself to blind physical action as her hypnotic scents strike his receptors. He screams silently inside to restore a portion of his control, but not so much that he is unable to enjoy himself.

The female is ready for mating, very ready. As he mounts her from the back he can feel the heat of her excitement penetrating her exoskeleton. His soft abdomen brushes against her liquid-smooth chitin. With slow movements, savoring each gesture, Survivor locks their mating hooks. Fastened to him, she opens her mating canal, and he allows the gonad-bridge to merge from his lower abdomen, pushing inside her warm, wet interior.

They are joined. This is almost like being joined to his brother, but Survivor has no *feeling* for this female. He is still alone.

But then, as he moves more rapidly within her, his own senses begin to overshadow his thoughts. The female seems puzzled, yet not uncomfortable. Her ruthless Instinct tells her what to do, but only one step at a time.

Then he can feel the oncoming climax of their mating. He wants to savor the moment, but he cannot restrain himself. His nerves begin to send ecstatic messages to his brain, first only from the lower abdomen and then, like a chain reaction, the fire spreads through his body, through his limbs and mind. This is the pinnacle of his life, the most intense pleasure in the universe. As he explosively releases his fertilization into the female's egg cavity, Survivor shrieks a joyous hum of ecstasy so intense it borders on pain. The female squirms.

He is spent. The fire of pleasure raging through him has left his muscles like lifeless ash. He cannot think—the lethargy and the exhaustion cripples him. Dimly, he becomes aware of the female disengaging the mating hooks. Survivor can feel her wing coverings —cool now—slide from beneath him. He sinks to the yielding web, swaying slightly. He is alone on their wedding bed.

A dim part of his mind screams with distant urgency, easily ignored. Then another part of his mind shouts the same warning, and another—links are forged and soon his thoughts emerge from the murk.

His traitorous Instinct insists that he sleep, relax, cease to resist....

But Survivor grasps another Instinct, the survival Instinct, and pulls his awareness out of the lethargy. Use of his body returns to him at the last possible moment, and he is able to snatch one of the long shards of pink crystal from the floor.

He reaches up with all his might and plunges the sharp crystal deep into the female's thorax as she lunges at him with both razor-sharp hunting pincers.

The pink crystal severs the ganglia to her brain, and he leaves it embedded there as she collapses to the floor of the cave. She looks shocked and betrayed, but her expressions fade as she dies. In a moment, he knows it will seem odd that *she* should feel betrayed.

The female's gaping thorax leaks blackish-green ichor onto Survivor's beautiful crystals. Her blood is the same color as his brother's.

He remembers watching, long ago, as the old female slew his brother after they had completed their mating. Exhausted, not knowing what to expect and with only his Instinct for guidance, his brother could not defend himself when the mated female reached forward with arrogant confidence to neatly snip off his head with her hunting pincers.

His dead weight dragged Survivor to the floor of the cave. Survivor was pinned beneath the brother's carcass, horrified, as the female carefully cleaned her claws. Luckily, since he was unaroused, he gave off no odor, and it did not occur to the female to kill him. Instinct hadn't prepared her for any unexpected contingencies, any other witnesses of the mating ritual. Only one male and female are supposed to be present at a mating—and the male always dies. No one escapes to warn others, and the females will not tell.

Survivor was trapped in his brother's nest, numb with shock and confusion. Soon, though, the reason became clear—the female, while gestating the eggs, cannot roam hunting food to satisfy her voracious appetite. Instead, she feeds on her murdered mate.

He could not move his brother's larger bulk, which kept him trapped in the nest. If he had tried to drag the other's carcass away, he suspected the female would stop him. Finally, when his fear and revulsion had hardened him enough, Survivor was able to break a sliver of sharp pink crystal from the cave wall. Working with a desperate patience, he used the crystal to saw his forelimb from his junction with his brother's. He used the blunted end of a rock to chop at the fused carapace, freeing him at last.

The pain was incredible, but the enormous *loneliness* hurt even more. His brother was dead, butchered, and Survivor was left alone in the world, like the rest of his kind. He managed to stumble away from the body, shedding droplets of ichor from the stump of his foreleg.

The female looked at him apathetically with her glittering black eyes. Survivor could already see the eggs growing within her.

Now, having seen and felt the nearness of death, he wanted to live, to *survive*, more than ever before. The deformity that had chained Survivor and his brother together had now let him witness the true end of the mating ritual. Though he was shaking with an almost paralyzing intensity, he flew away from the cave, fleeing into the dark purple sky as the female turned again to the brother's carcass and began to feed.

Much later, when the hormones finally drove him into his own mating frenzy, Survivor was prepared. He defied Instinct. He survived the mating ritual. Since then, he had mated many times....

Now, he takes the dead body of the murderous female from his nest, dragging her across the floor of the cave and scattering the broken crystals. In anger and disgust, he heaves her out into the crater where she falls slowly in the low gravity, shattering into bits of flesh and broken chitin as she strikes the crater wall and slides down into the pit. Soon, he can see the *leems* grow brighter; they will devour her carcass in minutes.

Survivor is elated and refreshed, vibrantly alive. His entire lower abdomen feels warm and tingling from the surges of ecstasy. Though it is dangerous, the mating is intensely pleasurable—at least for the male of the species. This feeling is far too desirable for one to be satisfied with having it only *once* in a brief lifespan.

The moons will begin to wane in a few days. He must rest, and prepare for the next time. The lust, the hunger for the ecstasy will return soon. And he must find another mate.

This story is the culmination of the possibilities inherent in my Alternitech multiverse series. How much can you do with timeline prospectors hunting through alternate realities for unique differences?

What would happen if one of these timeline prospectors met an alternate version of her own life—or many of them—so they could discuss their choices, their personal disasters, their triumphs? Would they use their own experiences to help other versions of themselves become better people? What a conversation that would be!

In this story, I use the same character from "An Innocent Presumption" earlier in this volume.

Have you ever asked yourself, "What would you have done differently?" In this story, a person can see all the possibilities.

THE BISTRO OF ALTERNATE REALITIES

The problem with closely parallel universes is that they all look the same. Sometimes, it takes an expert to notice the subtle differences, and only a professional timeline hunter can find variations for profitable exploitation by Alternitech Corp.

Heather Rheims arrived through the portal and took a deep, sweet breath to adjust herself to seemingly familiar surroundings. Among the myriad possible realities, the technology of Alternitech could fling her into nearby universes, worlds where decisions and alternatives had just slightly frayed the course of history. Thus, the city looked the same, the people were the same, most of the daily newspapers ran similar headlines … but some things were different. She just had to make her assessment.

Heather was the first one to reach the coffee shop. After wavering between possibilities, she chose a large table with eight chairs, which had always been sufficient for the doppelgangers who would show up. She picked a seat, then moved her pack to a different one, where she could see the door.

Leaving her equipment and her detailed archaeological notes on the table, she went to the coffee bar where the gaunt-looking young man with a wispy goatee—it was always a young man with a wispy goatee, no matter what universe she was in—and stared at the variety of hot and cold drinks, caffeinated and decaffeinated, sweet and bitter. Too many choices.

Though she came to the bistro on almost every journey through Alternitech's portals, she still had trouble making up her mind. Some people ordered the same hot beverage day after day, but Heather had never settled into a comfortable routine.

Unfortunately, that led to a crisis of decision every time she was faced with ordering coffee. After vacillating, she finally asked for a cappuccino with an extra shot of espresso, since she'd been feeling run-down. She took her wide cup back to the table and opened her thinscreen laptop so she could call up the esoteric archaeological details she was supposed to know by heart.

As a timeline hunter, Heather had been sent off into parallel universes in search of everything from medical breakthroughs to new music by the Beatles to conspiracy evidence in the JFK assassination. This time, she was a proxy archaeologist. She sipped her cappuccino and wiped foam off her lips before perusing the lengthy summaries of recent findings of ancient Greece and the Peloponnesian Wars.

Archaeology was not a rigorous science of trial and error and analysis: Finding artifacts that had been buried for untold centuries in uninhabited areas was primarily a matter of serendipity and luck. Some Turkish shepherd might go looking for part of his flock and discover a pile of ancient armor, the ruins of a fallen city, or documents sealed inside airtight containers. A single accidental find, like the Dead Sea Scrolls, might change the field forever—at least that was what the passionate young researcher Bruce Wanderlos had told Heather when he'd first hired her.

"Just because someone stumbled upon the ruins of ancient Troy in our timeline, doesn't mean the same accident happened in others." His eyes were bright, his pale brown hair curly and unkempt, but with a natural looseness that made the mess appear intentional and attractive. "And thus, the converse must also be true."

After receiving a large university grant Bruce had taken the controversial step of contracting Alternitech rather than going himself out into the field. Heather was assigned to go through the portal and look over current archaeology journals. "It's desk research, I know, and not terribly exciting—but if you copy the records of other digs, other discoveries that haven't been made yet in our universe, then I'll know exactly where to look here."

"Isn't that cheating?" Heather had asked.

He seemed so taken aback by her suggestion that she found him endearing. "This is acquiring information for science and history and the enrichment of mankind. It's not a game."

Now, in the coffee shop, she scrolled through items Bruce might be particularly interested in. The sophisticated software on her thinscreen allowed her to upload online records of any number of timeline-specific archaeological journals and scan for differences. The hardest part was deciding which place to go first. On one of her initial searches for Bruce, she had stopped at Mrs. Coffee Belgian Café and Bistro, intending just to have a cappuccino or a mocha while she planned her strategy—and then she'd discovered something incredibly alarming.

The door opened, and the tinkling silver bell announced the arrival of a new customer. She looked up to see, as expected, another Heather. She wondered which one this was and how many would be arriving for today's kaffeeklatsch. The other Heather, nearly identical except for her blouse, came over to drop her backpack in the chair beside Heather.

The barista blinked in surprise, as he always did, but by now most of the employees of Mrs. Coffee were used to the unusual event, convinced by the absurd explanation that all the Heathers were part of a Lookalike Club.

The new Heather went to the counter, swept her long cinnamon-brown hair out of her eyes and tucked it behind her shoulders. She decisively ordered a cappuccino, but without a shot of espresso. Heather wondered if maybe she should have done the same; did she really need the extra caffeine? She looked up to see another identical person step through the door. They would all be arriving soon.

Since, in her own world, Alternitech sent timeline hunters to parallel universes seeking to exploit differences, it only made sense that in many of those similar realities, other Alternitechs would send other timeline hunters, many of whom would be Heather's counterparts. The first time they'd stumbled upon each other was quite a shock, then a delight. Eventually Heather and her counterparts discovered that they could pool their resources.

Two more Heathers entered the coffee shop and bistro, standing in line to order their drinks, many of which were the same, though others had subtle variations, as was to be expected. Heather sat back and watched them all.

In the mix of universes, the people weren't always the same, but by now some of her doppelgangers were familiar to her. Most obvious was the Heather with a thin childhood scar on her cheek, a mark from when an abrupt gust of wind had blown a screen door into her face. Heather remembered that incident when she was a girl, but she had ducked aside and not been cut, as had most of her counterparts.

The first alternate Heather brought her cappuccino back to the table and sat down. Her opening question immediately identified her as Gloomy Heather. They all had quick nicknames, like the Seven Dwarves. "So are you dating anyone yet? I'm not. How's life in your timeline?"

Heather took another sip from her large cup to hide her embarrassment. "Not dating anyone at the moment, but it hasn't been that long."

"That archaeology guy's awfully cute," said another Heather, the one who had earned the nickname of Intense. "If my Sasha wasn't so damned good in bed, I'd ask Bruce out in a minute."

Intense Heather had hooked up with a fiery-eyed young rock musician, and the two had gone supernova with their initial romance. Intense rarely talked about anything else, and she had shown Sasha's picture to them all, in case they had a chance to bump into him in their own parallel universes. "Don't miss your chance. I almost did. Luckiest drink I ever spilled."

Intense had accidentally stumbled in a crowded bar on her way to a table of her own, spilling a glass of red wine on Sasha as he'd been heading for the door. He had responded with a flash of anger, and Intense Heather offered such abject apologies that the young musician burst into laughter and invited her to dinner. That had been the start.

So far, though, in every other parallel universe the Heathers had missed their chance, stumbling but catching the wine before it spilled, or losing Sasha before he walked out the door and never encountering him again. Heather had botched the opportunity entirely; when she mentally backtracked to the night in question, she realized that she had stayed home, unable to decide where to go.

Scar Heather sat down, picking up the conversation. "I'm flirting with Bruce, but I think he's just shy."

"Maybe I'll ask him out," said Gloomy, "but he'll probably say no."

"So what if he says no?" Intense responded. "You're not any worse off than if you don't ask at all. It's a no-brainer."

Heather found herself nodding. She had sensed the shy archaeologist's attraction for her, which he masked as appreciation for the successful work she'd done so far. Maybe she would push a little harder so that at least she'd have something to talk about with her counterparts the next time Intense bragged about her wild escapades with Sasha.

The smiling one who sat down was obviously Happily-Ever-After Heather, the one incarnation of all her parallel lives where circumstances had turned out perfect in every way. Two years before, most of the Heathers had been in a steady relationship with a computer programmer and part-time graphic designer named Perry. They'd fit together fairly well, but then Heather's sister Jamie had been killed, and the tragedy had torn her apart. Withdrawing, she'd taken out her resentment on Perry, and the two of them had parted.

But circumstances were slightly different in the universe of Happily-Ever-After Heather. Jamie had accidentally avoided becoming a random victim, and Happily-Ever-After had never faced the insurmountable stress in her relationship with Perry. Though they'd reached a crisis of personal goals and feelings, they had decided to work out their differences, investing in their bond instead of drawing apart. Perry and Happily-Ever-After had gotten married a year later, and now they had a fine home, both had good careers, and everything was perfect. The other Heathers halfway resented their counterpart, but most of all they envied her....

When finally all of the alternate Heathers had their coffees and sat down at the table, Intense Heather unzipped her pack and withdrew her thinscreen. "Time to get down to business. The portals will be back before you know it." All eight of them looked at their watches with comical simultaneity.

Each Heather took out her carefully culled and organized database of archaeological information from her own universe. Instead of spending hours sifting through library records or digging out obscure references in journals, all the Heathers sat down for coffee and conversation. That way they could simply exchange all the files they had collated from their homes. In an hour of swapping and comparing records, the eight Heathers could achieve as many discoveries as if they had gone on eight separate timeline hunts.

This cooperative efficiency had made her quite a success in all her incarnations—at least all of the ones who showed up at the coffee shop. Heather's counterparts and their identical goals yielded a synergy that allowed each of them to deliver clue after clue to the endearingly appreciative Bruce Wanderlos. Most of the differences turned out to be of no interest to anyone, but occasionally they hit the jackpot.

And while their thinscreens were humming and exchanging, compiling and rejecting, Heather had a chance to listen to advice from her alternate selves. It was like having a sounding board better than a best friend, drawing upon common experience and shared hearts. The Heathers who had made bad decisions did their best to help those who had not yet encountered the risky situation.

At first, Heather had been somewhat hurt to discover that they'd labeled her Indecisive Heather, but the reasons were obvious even to herself, and she couldn't fault them for it. She had come to depend on these conversations and personal strategy sessions. She rarely made up her own mind anymore, but hesitated too often, losing opportunities.

"I've got an idea," said Intense, slurping her double espresso. She targeted Gloomy. "You always say you missed your chance, that by sheer bad luck you're never in the right place at the right time. Believe me, half of it's your own problem because you don't take any chances—but here I'm offering you one. Switch with me. Go home to my universe and spend a day or two with Sasha."

Gloomy's eyes widened. "I couldn't do that. He's your—"

"And you think he'd be cheating on me if he slept with you? You are me. God, if I was the one who hadn't been laid in two years, I'd sure hope one of you might take pity on me."

"But … but how will I ever fool him? We don't have the same history. We look the same, but your personality's entirely—"

"You wouldn't have to fool him, Heather dear. He knows what I do for a living. In fact, he'd get a kick out of it, and you'd give me a rest. Frankly, I'm a bit sore, and I could do with a day or two of just sitting at home and reading a book. You've probably got the same unread novels on your shelf that I do."

The other Heathers immediately went into a detailed discussion about the morality and wisdom of this plan. Heather suspected many of them were secretly hoping for their own chance with Sasha.

Happily-Ever-After looked deeply uncomfortable. "Your lives are what you made them, every mistake, every decision. Why can't you be satisfied with the way things are? It's nice to compare notes with each other, but this is drastic."

"Sure," said Scar. "Listen to advice from the one who has a perfect life." Happily-Ever-After blushed as if ashamed of her own good fortune.

When all their databases had been exchanged, they finished their coffees and picked up the dishes. Heather was glad she didn't have to make the choice that Gloomy Heather faced. It would have taken her a month to make up her mind.

"All right," said Gloomy, "if I don't do this, you'll never let me complain again." She forced a wan smile. "I'll go back through your portal, you go back through mine." Gloomy and Intense shook hands like businessmen, then realized how absurd they looked and gave each other a simultaneous hug.

"Be careful, Sasha just might burn you out," Intense said.

"That'll be ... quite a new experience for me," Gloomy answered.

They all split up. Heather shouldered her backpack and went to her own rendezvous point, where the discreet portal would shimmer through the air.

They would all meet again at another bistro in another parallel universe.

When she delivered her results to the technicians at Alternitech, Bruce Wanderlos was there waiting with a shy smile. While he skimmed the results, she went to the locker room to shower and change, getting back into decent clothes instead of the plain "don't notice me" outfit Alternitech asked its timeline hunters to wear.

Before she left for the day, though, the archaeologist met her outside the dressing room door. His eyes were shining, his face flushed, and he took a quick step toward her as if he wanted to give her a happy kiss. "You don't realize what you found there! There's a fleet of Greek warships sunk in a bay off the Anatolian Peninsula. They've been preserved in the deep, cold water. According to these papers, one of the archaeologists believes it was Agamemnon's fleet in the Trojan War!"

Heather recognized that such a discovery would make a name for Bruce. "Sounds like you've got your work cut out for you."

Bruce shook his head and drew a deep breath. "I don't know how I can ever thank you. I just wish—"

Impulsively, remembering her Intense and Happily-Ever-After counterparts, she said quickly before she could think about it too much, "Well, you could ask me out for a drink—or dinner, if you feel really grateful."

He seemed taken aback. "I didn't know that—I didn't think ... are you sure it's all right if we mix business and socialization?"

Heather raised her eyebrows. "Bruce, if this is as big a discovery as you say, you won't need to hire my services anymore."

"All right." He was delighted at his doubly unexpected good fortune.

She gave him her number and address, and they arranged a time. "Oh, and Bruce?" Heather called, giddy at her own good luck. "If this discovery is so significant, you better find someplace that doesn't just serve hamburgers."

"I ... I'll make reservations."

"Just because a seafood chain has the word 'lobster' in its name doesn't mean it's a fancy restaurant," said Scar, but she looked more amused than disappointed.

Heather sat back and drank from her double mocha. "Well, I don't care. It was the nicest evening I've had in a long time."

"He took me to an Italian restaurant," said Silly Heather, who always had trouble opening up her real feelings and covered it all with a joke, even among her identical counterparts.

Happily-Ever-After just grinned. "I'm so pleased you finally made the decision to do it. Part of me wishes you'd try to patch things up with Perry, though, because we're so happy together."

"We know," groaned Intense.

"Perry's married again in my universe," said Heather. "I took too long—"

"He's only engaged in mine," said Scar.

Quiet Heather watched them all; she was one of the few who hadn't gotten up the nerve to nudge Bruce into a date, but she looked as if she might change her mind.

Intense seemed inordinately edgy and disturbed. All the doppelgangers were curious to hear the story of Gloomy's "perfectly licit" affair with the passionate Sasha ... but Gloomy hadn't joined them today, or the previous two meetings.

"I'm sure it turned out all right," Heather said, sensing how deeply disturbed her normally gruff counterpart was.

"She probably just wants him for a few more days to get her fill," Scar suggested.

"Sasha can sometimes be a little ... intense."

"You're a perfect match for him then," Silly said. Some of the other Heathers chuckled, but the Intense one did not.

"Bruce asked me out again," Heather announced, "on his own initiative this time."

"How long do you think I should wait until I sleep with him?" said another one.

"Are you kidding? He could barely manage a goodnight kiss."

"He's shy, not celibate," said Scar.

"Did you ask about his family?"

"Did you tell him about Jamie?"

"He seemed very sad to hear it when I did."

"How serious is he about all this?"

"How serious am I about this? It's too soon to ask those questions."

"He's never been married, has he?"

"No. I asked him point blank."

"I wish he wouldn't hold his fork like that. Nobody ever taught him table manners."

"We had pizza, so I didn't get a chance to notice."

"Who cares about his table manners? It's his personality that counts, and Bruce is very nice."

Heather listened to the rapid-fire exchange of alternative dates that she could have had. It seemed as if she got to know Bruce

Wanderlos better by hearing all the comparisons … but it was unfair. Did she really need all of these surrogate Heathers to live her life for her?

"You're all pathetic," said Intense. "Just listen to yourselves! I was always fairly strong and independent—and so are all of you. But now you sound like a bunch of airhead cheerleaders in a locker room."

"Excuse me," said Happily-Ever-After, "but you were insufferable yourself when you started seeing Sasha. I don't think I'm the only one who was tired of hearing about all your sex."

"Maybe you're just upset to be away from him," said Quiet Heather.

"Or maybe you're jealous because another one of us is with him," said Scar, "despite all of your assertions to the contrary."

Someone else came into the bistro, and Intense looked up quickly, hoping that she would see her Gloomy counterpart return, but it was just a middle-aged man looking for a sandwich. Angry and frustrated, Intense grabbed her pack and took her thinscreen, though she hadn't finished exchanging files with all of her doppelgangers. She stormed out of the coffee shop while the other Heathers looked after her.

"Something's worse than she's admitting," said Heather. "Most of us would be worried in that situation, but not go ballistic."

Scar finished her coffee while Happily-Ever-After gathered their cups. "We still haven't settled how fast should we push this with Bruce. How far do we go?"

"We'll each have to decide that for ourselves," said Heather.

All of the others looked at her in surprise as if she had just told a joke.

⚛

On their second date Heather and Bruce went out to a foreign film with subtitles that Heather thought was supposed to impress her, though neither of them much enjoyed—or understood—the movie. Following the lead of what some of her counterparts had done, she decided to tell him about her sister Jamie, showed him pictures. As she expected, Bruce was very understanding and compassionate without being maudlin.

Still, she felt odd every moment, a strange sense of déjà vu—as if she were stuck in an old rerun of *It's a Wonderful Life*. Some people would have considered it an advantage to test out choices and decisions, then rewind and try again if they didn't work. Would Bruce himself think it was cheating, in a completely different sense from how he used someone else's archaeology work?

In an awkward yet sweet way, he asked her to come to his apartment for coffee—she was getting tired of coffee, but she listened to his words, which he had obviously rehearsed in front of a mirror. She ended up staying for three hours, but the whole time they just sat on the sofa and talked. He didn't even try to kiss her until she was about to leave. Heather supposed that the next time she met her counterparts in the coffee shop, her doppelgangers would be full of alternate endings for this evening, some of them lurid, some of them embarrassing. But she liked the way her own had turned out, with or without coaching from her other selves....

Thanks to Heather's results, Bruce now had more archaeological work than he could handle for years. Alternitech timeline hunters were expensive, and his grant money had nearly run out, so he finished his request for Heather's services, though he intended to keep seeing her on a more personal level.

On her last outing for the project, Heather went tentatively back to Mrs. Coffee, not sure if she even wanted to keep discussing their budding relationship with the other Heathers. Part of the excitement of romance was the spontaneity, the unpredictability, and she had an unfair advantage if she already knew a dozen possible ways that any evening might turn out.

Intense Heather's boyfriend Sasha seemed too unpredictable, a loose cannon with mood swings and fiery passion, while her own former relationship with Perry had been too sedate and comfortable. She didn't know how it was going to turn out with Bruce ... and she wasn't sure she wanted to know. This wasn't being indecisive, as was her too-common flaw—it was being accepting.

Though the archaeology project was over, the Heathers would continue to meet in the coffee shop, discussing ways to increase their discoveries in alternate timelines. But Heather wasn't sure she was interested in talking about her personal life. Maybe she wanted to make her own choices for a change.

Today she was one of the last to arrive. Inside, it looked as if

Intense was having a nervous breakdown. She shouted, "You don't understand! I'm terrified for her. I got her into this! I egged her into making her decision—and what if Sasha's hurt her?"

"He wouldn't hurt her," said one of the other Heathers, trying to be soothing.

"Oh, and you're the expert on his unstable personality? He's got problems. He flies into rages. He's supposed to take medication, but all the time the asshole convinces himself he doesn't need it."

"That doesn't sound like the man you've been talking about all along," said Scar.

Intense wrung her hands. "He's not like that usually. He can be sweet and romantic and passionate—but other times he just flies off the handle. I could sense he was getting impatient with me, said I was too domineering, that I was like a bulldozer. I thought maybe he'd want someone a bit more passive. I thought he'd like her. But sometimes being passive just provokes the abusive streak in him. What if he's killed her? My God!"

"You're overreacting, Heather."

"Am I? It's been five times, and she hasn't come back. And you know that I can't return to my own universe unless she comes through and opens the portal. There has to be an exchange. I can't just go get her."

"It was a decision that she made," Heather said, standing beside the crowded table.

Looking alarmed at the discord among the identical women, the goateed barista stood close to the phone as if contemplating a call to 9-1-1.

Heather continued, looking at her counterparts. "You made up your mind. She made up her mind. We've all made up our minds—but we spend endless hours in here talking and discussing and gossiping. Dammit, my whole life has become a committee!"

"But what am I supposed to do about ... her?" Intense said. She seemed to know something much more dangerous about Sasha than she had ever revealed to them, especially Gloomy.

"Do whatever you decide, and then you'll have to live with it."

Seeing the group of Heathers in the coffee shop, she wondered how many other counterparts had already left the kaffeeklatsch, not wanting to hear about other lives or experience regrets for incorrect decisions. Of all the infinite universes, maybe only this handful of

Heathers felt the need to commiserate with each other, share secrets and depend upon someone else.

She didn't even bother to remove her backpack. "I'd better be off doing my work. This isn't … what I want anymore. It's my life, after all, and I feel like I'm in a room full of dress rehearsals."

"Don't you want to wait and find out if the other Heather comes back?" said Intense. "Maybe she's all right, or maybe Sasha just kept her for an extra while."

"You know, I've decided it isn't relevant to me," she answered. "Because there are probably timelines where it happens every possible way. I need to focus on my life as a participant, not a spectator."

"Wait, you'll want to hear about what happened with Bruce last night," said Scar, raising her eyebrows. Several of the others leaned forward, eager as predators.

"What happened on your own date?" someone asked her before she could leave. "Weren't you supposed to go out with him again, too?"

But Heather turned away. "I'll just keep it to myself, for good or bad. Why should I live vicariously through all of you, when I can do it myself first-hand?"

From the set of troubled looks on their faces, Heather realized she had struck a nerve, that the thoughts had crossed most of their minds already. "Good luck," she said to herself and to all of them, then left the coffee shop behind.

What is the next step in the evolution of humanity? Or is there more than one branch?

That was the question posed by editors Les Johnson and Robert E. Hampson in their anthology Stellaris: People of the Stars. *They wanted authors to posit an upgrade, a mutation, or other development in the human species.*

Having taken many long road trips in my life, and imagining the crew aboard long interstellar voyages, I thought of how useful it might be to speed up or slow down time from your own frame of reference.

There's a classic Star Trek episode called "Wink of an Eye," where a group of people can speed up their metabolism so fast that they move in a blur, while the normal crew around them stand motionless like statues. Or imagine the other way around: wouldn't it be great to slow down your metabolism, so that a years-long interstellar voyage seems to pass in an instant? Think of all the food and life support that would save.

All those possibilities made for a great science fiction story.

TIME FLIES

A life is measured in seconds, days, years—even centuries, now that we have genetic modifications. When all is said and done, each life has a set number of minutes, but no one knows that number, which is set only by God and by destiny. Those minutes wind down to zero, *tick tock*, over the course of a life, and ultimately, we can't change the number that has been ordained for us. But if we can speed up or slow down our frame of reference, we can make the outside *objective* time last for as long as we like.

That's why starship fliers seem to be immortal from an outsider's point of view. We have the same number of minutes as anyone else, but thanks to our special metabolic modifications, we know how to shut down our internal clocks for the centuries, or millennia, that we drift between the stars. From our point of view, it's just a regular lifespan, but stretched out like a thin membrane across infinity. We can control our own perception of time, and the ship is like its own separate continuum moving endlessly throughout the galaxy.

As engineer, I was the first member of the crew to speed back up to realtime as the *Time's Arrow* approached the new star system. It's my job to run a check on all systems, though the old starship had been so modified and reinforced that nothing sort of a cosmic disaster would have caused so much as a hiccup. But I don't like to think I'm obsolete.

According to the flight plan, we had just spent two hundred years en route to this average star system with its one cataloged colony planet, called Irrac if the old records were still accurate. Captain Dorothea had chosen it as the next stop on our ever-wandering trade route. No one among the small crew had disagreed with her, not that we ever did. We didn't have anyplace else to go. *Time's Arrow* was our own little traveling universe, and everything else was just a side trip.

Moving through the silent ship with the other nine crewmembers still in slowtime, I checked the engine systems, the fuel and water levels, which were supplemented by interstellar gases we had scooped up over the past couple of centuries. Planetfall was still a month away, but we had preparations to make. I saw the others like statues lounging about wherever they had decided to crank down their metabolism to near-zero entropy, like the cozy heater in our rec room turned down to the tiniest pilot light.

I warmed up the rec room, getting it ready for our crew meeting as soon as the others returned to the normal flow of time. Next, I went to the command module, the bridge portion of the ship, which was nearly always empty except for when we reached a planet and the interesting activity started.

In the cold of the command module, I wore a warm sweater. Since I would only be there for a few moments, I saw no need to waste the time and energy to warm up this section of the ship ... not yet. While everyone else still blissfully and invisibly passed the time without wasting minutes of their lifespan, I transmitted our prerecorded welcome message to the system ahead, announcing to Irrac that the *Time's Arrow* was a private commercial vessel filled with exotic cargo that we wished to trade. Our last stop, two centuries ago in subjective time, was the inhabited moon Jherilla, circling a gas giant. The people on the planet ahead probably knew little of their neighbors anyway, and we didn't want to scare the locals by telling them just how long we'd really been on our voyage.

After sending my introductions, I asked Irrac to send a transmission burst with samplers of their language and dialect, information on their culture and customs so the *Time's Arrow* could more easily interact when we arrived. Since all planets were so isolated and scattered, no one could guess what sort of welcome we might receive, and it was good to be prepared. We had defensive weapons, but rarely needed to use them. No one on Irrac was expecting us, and we hoped for a nice, profitable landing.

I decided to allow a week before checking again to see their response.

Still moving at normal speed, I rejoined the crew where they all sat motionless in the galley. Everyone wore comfortable uniforms, no need to be formal after all this time. Captain Dorothea rested in her favorite chair, beautiful, in her midforties, with smooth features, a pointed chin, a sharp gaze when she was displeased and a sparkle when she was happy. Right now, her eyes just looked like glass. With her near-zero metabolism, Dorothea couldn't see anything moving at my speed. I gave her a quick peck on the cheek, which was much less interesting than when she actually participated in a kiss. I chose an empty chair next to her at the small dining table, and dropped back down into slowtime.

Long ago when the *Time's Arrow* first set off on its endless voyage, the crew would all go to quarters or settle in special travel beds for the long journey ahead, knowing we wouldn't move an inch for centuries at a time. Eventually we realized that we noticed nothing in slowtime anyway, so we no longer bothered with the formalities.

Time's Arrow was a privately owned, self-sufficient commercial ship, and we had all joined aboard for the adventure, a life of trading among the colonies scattered across the galaxy, and that's exactly what we had done. When we departed from Earth ten thousand years ago, objective time, none of us really grasped the time scales involved....

After waiting a week, which passed faster than the blink of an eye from my point of view, I sped up to realtime again and returned to the command module to check for a response from Irrac. Now that the ship was closer, scans showed a viable planet ahead. I was glad to see that the colonists had responded with friendly surprise, transmitting complete files about their environment, culture, history, as well as their eagerness to welcome us. If the signs didn't look right, we could have opted to bypass the system and head off to the next destination, but Irrac seemed fine, so I allowed the ship to continue on its three-week journey to the planet.

Dorothea sped up first, then our eight other crewmembers who served as scouts, botanists, manual labor, and "other duties as assigned." Other than Doctor Max, their roles were ambiguous, not that it mattered. Everyone did his or her own chores aboard ship, and the ship did most everything else.

Delman accepted the duty as chef and prepared our wakeup meal, a stew of preserved meats and vegetables we had picked up at one of our other stops, I couldn't remember which. Most of us weren't even hungry, because in our timeframe it hadn't been very long since we'd eaten our traditional bon voyage meal after leaving Jherilla. Delman was a good cook, though, and he made excellent use of the various flavorings and spices available. I filled my plate and sat next to Captain Dorothea, presenting my report as we all ate. No need to waste minutes on a boring formal meeting when we could take care of the details at dinner conversation.

"The people on Irrac seem friendly, thrilled to receive out-of-town visitors." I played some of the recordings from the colony leader. The evolution of dialect and language over the centuries made him difficult to understand, but thanks to the records transmitted by the colonists, we were easily able to update our language chips. I displayed images of Irrac's grassy hills, sweeping green fields, exotic animals, thick forests, pleasant-looking cities and villages.

"Beautiful place," said Amos, one of our scouts. "A lot better than most of the hardscrabble outposts we see."

"Looks like they hit the jackpot in the colony roulette," Dorothea said. "Are they covering anything up, Garrett?"

"Nothing major," I said. I had only scanned through the records once, but the signs would be obvious. We'd encountered nightmare settlements before.

After humanity spread across thousands of colony worlds, societies changed and evolved in unpredictable ways over centuries of isolation. We'd gotten good at detecting the signs of horrific dictatorships or repressive religious societies. Here, though, the bright colors and casual nature of the Irrac garments, the openness of their architecture, how freely the people moved about their streets, their free conversation and interactions all implied a normal healthy society.

"I sent them our detailed manifest from the cargo hold," I said. "They probably don't understand what half of the stuff is, but we'll show it off anyway. Right now, they're scrambling to find goods or raw materials that we'll accept in trade. It looks like a good place to stop, Captain."

Doctor Max agreed with his characteristic chuckle, and the others looked forward to another shore leave, even though they had barely noticed the two centuries of passage since the last one on Jherilla. Aboard the *Time's Arrow*, it was just one planet after another with a fast-forward journey in between.

But Amos was surly. He had grown clearly impatient at the previous three or four stops. "I'm sick of this routine. I really can't stand the shit anymore."

"Then stay awake in realtime and redecorate your quarters," Dorothea said. "Take up a hobby." Over the past couple awakenings she'd grown impatient with his attitude.

"It just feels pointless." Amos rested his elbows on the table, looking down at his barely eaten food. "We had a great haul at Jherilla. We're all rich, but what do we do with it?"

"We're going to trade it for other things on Irrac, and then we'll do it again. And again and again," said Elber, one of the other scouts. "It's what you signed up for."

"Ten thousand years ago." He picked at his vegetables and meat.

"I thought you wanted to see the galaxy," Dorothea said.

"I've seen it." Amos glanced at the images of Irrac, and his face took on a wistful look. "Maybe I just want to settle down."

"Go right ahead," said Delman. "Plant your roots in the dirt. More shares for the rest of us."

Frustrated, Amos scowled at him. "Shares for what? What is it for?"

I scooped the last few bites off my plate and stood. I'd never been much interested in conversation, and especially not arguments. "I've got to prep for orbit and landing. When I get the engines reset and the orbital curves plotted, I'm dropping back down to slowtime. You all can debate the meaning of life for the next three weeks if you like. I don't want to waste my time on something I can't answer."

I left the galley and returned to the command module and transmitted a positive response to the colony, this time using perfect Irrac dialect. And since I'd have to be here when we reached the planet so I could guide the ship in, I didn't even bother to leave the bridge deck. I took a seat in the padded chair and dropped down to zero.

$\mathcal{X}$

When I sped back up to realtime three weeks later, the planet filled my view as if a huge world had popped out right in front of me. Irrac had all the right colors: blue, green, and brown with swirls of white clouds, breathable atmosphere, temperate climate. The scan showed more than a hundred cities scattered across several continents. The *Time's Arrow* comm log showed countless unanswered messages and reports the colonists had transmitted to us as they grew excited at our approach, although I had made it abundantly clear in the last transmission that the crew would be in slowtime and no one could respond.

The starship had automatically gone into orbit. Dorothea came to the bridge and placed a hand on my shoulder as we both observed the planet. "It all looks good," I said. "No military buildup, no panic or unrest."

"Then take us down. No need to be skittish. We spent two centuries getting here, and you and I only woke once at the same time for a little exercise." She smiled.

I put my hand on top of hers. "That was a couple of hours well spent." Yes, even after thousands of years she was still a damn fine woman.

We were surprised to discover that Amos had returned to realtime a full day before the rest of us so he could review the Irrac transmissions in private. He'd even used the comm to speak to people down in the main city, even though such an unauthorized transmission was technically forbidden.

The other seven crewmembers sped up on their own schedule, and everyone was fully awake and alert as *Time's Arrow* descended to a large open area outside the main city. It wasn't an actual spaceport, but our ship easily made do.

A large welcoming committee had gathered for us, cheering crowds waving colorful banners to welcome the exotic visitors from so far away. I thought of parades and marching bands on Earth, but I wondered if anyone other than the *Time's Arrow* crew even remembered such things from more than ten thousand years in the past.

Though I'd been the one to make initial contact with the colony leader, Dorothea was the face of our expedition. I prefer to stay in the background, not needing the applause or the attention; in fact, I don't like it. As we emerged, I stood with my companions in formal uniforms, just another part of the crew. Captain Dorothea gave an engaging and inspirational speech about our journey, told of the wonders *Time's Arrow* had seen and the exotic goods we brought. She explained how much she appreciated such a warm welcome from the people of Irrac.

I had heard the speech close to thirty times before, and so, without anyone noticing, I slowed down my internal clock so that the boring part sped by in just a few subjective seconds.

Oddly enough, Amos was singled out and welcomed by the people. All of Irrac knew who he was because of the direct conversations he'd sent from the ship while the rest of us were in slowtime. Families came to meet Amos, starry eyed, giving him warm embraces. He surprised us further when he informed the captain he'd been specially invited to join a large clan grouping for feasts and parties. Normally, the crew kept close to one another, but shore leave was shore leave. When the opportunity arose, we all caroused and sampled the local pleasures. This wasn't overly unusual.

For the next several days we unloaded the extensive goods we had carried from planet to planet. The exotic items, the metals and materials, strange artwork, music recordings, jewelry, incredible food samples from other worlds—to the humble people of Irrac it was all breathtakingly priceless. The town leaders despaired that they had nothing we would find of value in trade.

What they didn't understand was that a normal, pleasant colony was a rare thing, and their forested hills provided a wealth of beautiful lumber. The wood seemed all too common and of little value to Irrac, but Dorothea insisted it was worth its weight in gold, a cliché that the dialect chips translated into the appropriate local phrasing. Gold, in fact, was easily obtained on any number of rocky asteroids, but tall trees were extremely valuable, and the captain knew she could sell the lumber at a premium on some other austere colony where real wood was a rarity. Dorothea and the colony leader were both satisfied with their bargain, and our mission to this world was a complete success.

Except when Amos came up to us on the day before our departure. I had just emerged from the cargo hold, wiping my hands on a towel after storing more than five metric tons of fresh wood, and saw the crewman nervously reporting to the captain. "I've made up my mind, Dorothea. I'm staying here."

A pretty young woman stood next to Amos, a little blander than his usual type. She had a little girl at her side no more than three years old, clutching her mother's hand. They both stared in awe at our landed starship.

Dorothea's brow drew together, and her eyes didn't have much of a sparkle at the moment. "You're staying behind ... how?"

"I'm opting out of my contract. I'd like a reasonable share of profits so I can set up a stake and make a good home for myself here. I'd like to live the rest of my life on Irrac. It's the best place we've seen in a long time." He reached out to take the young woman's hand, and she gave him an adoring look. "Alila's family has offered her to me in marriage. She lost her husband last year, and her beautiful little daughter here has no father." He swallowed and said, "I've always wanted a family. Now I can have everything I want. If I stay here."

I stepped forward, still rubbing my hands on the towel. "If you do that, there's no turning back, Amos. You want to spend the rest of your life in realtime?"

"I can always drop down if I need to, turn into Rip Van Winkle." He chuckled at the joke, which he knew that no one understood but us. "Why would I want to? I'll have a home, a wife, a daughter to adopt, maybe other children someday. I'll be comfortable and happy for my lifespan, however long that might be. Isn't that what we all want? I can finally have it."

"Your life will be over in the blink of an eye," Dorothea said. "On the *Time's Arrow*, you'll keep traveling for centuries and centuries."

Amos shook his head. "If I choose to live out my time here with Alila, what's wrong with that?"

"Nothing at all," Dorothea said with a resigned sigh. "Nothing at all. Go with my blessing. I know you've been dissatisfied for a long time. We'll figure out how to pay you in some currency that's valuable to these people. The ship will just get by with one less crew member from now on."

I refrained from pointing out that *Time's Arrow* could get by with almost no crew at all, but the ten of us had been together for so long, this was like losing a family member.

Over the following day, we all said our farewells. Every hour, the condensers had filtered and stored air, so our reserves were at capacity. I loaded up our reservoirs with water from a local body of water. We were ready to go.

I kept expecting Amos to lose his nerve and change his mind, but he didn't. The clan units welcomed him, and he seemed anxious to begin his life with his new wife and daughter. As *Time's Arrow* departed, leaving Irrac, I zoomed in on the image of the crowds waving goodbye. I saw Amos staring at us with a triumphant and satisfied expression.

He would be dust by the next time I had a chance to think about him.

Six more centuries passed en route to our next destination, a planet called Riece on the old charts. It was a long trip, but the point of our constant nomadic mission was not to reach any particular place. The journey itself was its own goal, one world after another. The expansive galaxy, all the places we could go and see, and all the history we were unrolling behind us—*that* was what mattered to me.

Time's Arrow was hardened and self-sufficient, with low-level AI monitoring systems to take care of any routine maintenance, so the ship could effectively fly through empty space forever. Even so, I still made it a habit to return to realtime once every year or two, just to have a look around. Yes, I was burning minutes of my lifespan, but I enjoyed the solitude, slowly wandering through the ship, looking at the motionless slowtime figures of my eight remaining fellow crewmembers. Sometimes a person just likes to have time to think.

I would sit alone in the command module and stare out at the empty sea of stars and imagine the distances, how many uncounted years that starlight had been shining, the same way that *Time's*

Arrow had been flying through the void. From my perspective, we had left Irrac only a few days ago, but I knew that by now Amos was long dead, as was his young wife. The pretty little daughter would have grown up, started her own family, grown old, and died, along with the next generation and the next.

But we were still here, still flying.

Amos could have still been alive, but he'd chosen to stay behind. I hoped he didn't regret his decision after we left. I tried to imagine myself doing that, but couldn't. Life wasn't a race or an endurance test, and the universe didn't hand out a prize for the person who managed to stick around longest. As I looked out at the stars, I imagined an ancient sea captain gazing across the uncharted ocean and hoping there must be some new land beyond the horizon.

What I wanted was to see the universe, but also to see the universe *change*. With my own eyes, I was watching the cosmos evolve, stars form, nebulas coalesce. It was like observing the universe on fast-forward.

The *Time's Arrow* crew was my family, and Captain Dorothea was my lover. Often on my brief maintenance walks, when I was the only one in realtime, I would look at her calm and beautiful face, the frozen expression reflecting whatever thoughts had been in her mind when she'd dropped down to slowtime.

The captain and I had our arrangement. We would agree on a schedule and both speed up simultaneously so we'd have the silent ship to ourselves, privacy for our lovemaking. I would often accelerate a few minutes before Dorothea awoke so I could be standing there with a smile. When she became animated and looked at me with that sparkle of anticipation in her eyes, I'd fold my arms around her and pull her close. With the rest of the crew unaware, she didn't have to be the captain and I didn't have to be the engineer. We became just two human bodies touching. Captain Dorothea was independent and firm, I liked my alone time, but we both needed a certain amount of companionship. I'm not sure any of the crew even knew about our relationship.

Dorothea and I would sometimes take an hour or more to make love, in no hurry. Afterward, we would just lie together in her captain's bunk, feeling the warmth of skin and sweat. This time, we talked about Amos, because I couldn't stop thinking of him on Irrac, his home, and his family. He had a bed, a kitchen, chores to do, bills to pay, mundane concerns that none of us aboard *Time's Arrow* had thought about in millennia. And he was long gone, though I remembered seeing him only a few hours ago.

"You think he was happy?" Dorothea asked.

"I think he's dead now. Was the happiness worth burning all of his years so fast?"

She mused for a long moment before finally answering, "The measure of a life is what you do with it, not how long it lasts."

"I liked Amos, so I'll be optimistic," I said, stroking her hair. "But I'm not going to turn the ship around and fly back to Irrac to see if his name is still listed in their history books."

She chuckled and kissed me. "We don't look at history books, Garrett. They're not relevant. We're just moving forward, always forward."

We stayed awake long enough to make love again, and then we both dropped to slowtime while still lying in her bunk. I would speed up in a year or two anyway for my maintenance round, and I could get dressed then.

⚛

Toward the end of the six-century run to Riece, I grew bored and only sped up every fifteen years or so. Constantly outbound for millennia, by now *Time's Arrow* had reached the far fringe and some of the most isolated colonies in the expansion of the human race. Any colonists who had traveled this far either had truly grandiose dreams or they were running from something.

Over the past several decades on our journey, I had picked up a few scattered broadcast transmissions from Riece, so I knew the colony was still there. When we were a year out from the system, I returned to realtime, intending to do a little preliminary snooping—and I immediately smelled smoke, an old, bitter tang of wrongness that hadn't been fully scrubbed by the near-dormant life-support systems.

Feeling sudden urgency, I accelerated, moving even faster than realtime. In a blur I raced to the monitoring systems, found that there had indeed been a serious fire in the rec room—three years ago, by ship's time. After so long, there was no need to hurry, but I still ran.

The rec room was a scorched mess, smoky, still sealed. The basic fire-suppression systems must have failed. *Time's Arrow* was ten thousand years old, after all. I ran a diagnostic every century, but maybe I had grown complacent. The heater unit, which Captain Dorothea considered a homey touch, had malfunctioned, starting a fire.

Three crew members had burned to death, unrecognizable at first glance. Their bodies were charred, one had collapsed on the floor, and I soon identified them as Delman, Thea, and Olivia. They had been sitting around the table, and I saw playing cards. A poker game. Apparently, they had arranged to speed up to realtime to enjoy a card game while the rest of us were dormant. Neither I nor Captain Dorothea had been invited. I wondered how long that had been going on.

For some reason, the three had dropped into slowtime after finishing a round, maybe taking a break, and they had burned to death before even realizing what was going on. Olivia, the one collapsed on the floor, had apparently sped up to normal ... but too late. She had dropped from the flames or smoke inhalation. All three were truly dead, not just slowed down to zero.

Worse, although the main fire in the rec room had been suppressed by the automated systems, an electrical fire had raced through the conduits, causing more severe damage to other parts of the ship.

I ran up to the bridge to scan the monitors and see how bad the situation was. The command module was intact—it was the most secure bastion on the vessel and could fly as its own self-contained starship—but one of the stern engines and some systems in the cargo bay were severely damaged.

I checked the log and navigation systems, verifying that we were still a year out from Riece. Even if I spent weeks, or even months, of my own time, alone, I couldn't complete the repairs here. I could patch up some of the basic systems but I needed a place to land, a technological society, or at least the raw materials for the fabricators. I transmitted a distress signal to the distant colony planet, letting them know we were coming. This would give them months more notice than we usually did, but *Time's Arrow* needed their help.

I scanned for more transmissions from Riece, but the people were quiet, either shy, reclusive, or they had fallen back to more primitive technology, which might make full repairs more challenging for me.

Keeping the news to myself for now—what could the captain or anyone else do at this point?—I stayed in realtime for a week inspecting ship systems, doing the grim work myself. I took the three bodies to the infirmary and packaged them up. Doctor Max might want to have a look, but I doubted he'd have the ambition to perform an autopsy. There was nothing he could do for Delman, Thea, and Olivia.

I fixed the systems I could, but the burn was especially extensive in the cargo bay controls. Finally, I roused Captain Dorothea from slowtime so I could give my full report. When I told her, I watched the hard beauty of her face melt into grief. She realized the loss of our friends, our family, how greatly our crew was diminished, not only after Amos left us at Irrac, but now three dead in the fire. We only had six crewmembers remaining.

Since the two of us were still alone in our own time continuum, I held her, sharing strength. When she composed herself, she asked, "We're still on course to Riece? You're confident we can make repairs there?"

I shrugged. "Reasonably confident. I can't get a good read on their tech level, but I can make do with whatever they've got."

"Let's wait until we're a month out. We can tell the others when they awaken. We'll all go down to Riece and make everything right."

More sluggish than usual due to the damage in the cargo module's stern engine, *Time's Arrow* headed down toward the surface of Riece. I still didn't know what to expect.

We had entered into orbit, identified the largest cities, verified that Riece was a technological civilization, although one with minimal radiofrequency chatter. I had contacted them from the command module, describing our situation and listing the cargo we had to trade. Riece sent only intermittent acknowledgments from a bland-looking shorthaired woman, Renna Qo, who claimed to speak for the people. She gave coordinates for us to land, showing neither threat nor exuberance. In order to repair the lower cargo modules and the engine, we didn't have much choice.

"You'd think they'd be a little more excited to receive out-of-town visitors," Dorothea muttered.

The four other crewmembers were still dealing with the loss of Delman, Thea, and Olivia in the rec room fire. As engineer, I explained that the damage was mostly confined to the lower module of the ship and that *Time's Arrow* could fly just fine for now even with the reduced crew.

"The main thing is to make repairs," I said. "I've already taken care of the electronics and life support. The command module and the living quarters are fine. Our fabricators can make the necessary components from basic planetary materials even if Riece doesn't have the manufacturing capability. Given a stable work environment, I'll fix the cargo module and the supplementary stern engine in a few days."

"Sounds like a week of vacation on Riece. Let's hope it's a nice place," said Dr. Max.

"With pretty girls at least," said Elber. "Or pretty guys." The other two remaining scouts, Henrik and Anya, agreed.

I set us down where Renna Qo had directed in a textbook maneuver, despite the sluggish response from the lower half of the ship. Only about fifty people had gathered on the fringe of the landing area, though I had expected a much larger crowd. The Riece natives were gaunt, pale skinned, and wore drab clothes. They had an odd sameness about them, and they didn't even seem to talk with one another. We had scanned for weapons and found none. The people weren't a threat, just uninterested.

I remembered the banners and the cheering reception on Irrac. This was quiet and subdued.

While Captain Dorothea, Dr. Max, and the three scouts emerged for the traditional raised hand and "I come in peace" greeting, I went to the cargo vault to prepare our wares for display. Even after all this time, the air inside the cargo hold still held the sweet resinous scent of the sealed and preserved lumber. Other crates of goods were stacked up and neatly inventoried after our numerous stops along the way.

Now that I was down in the cargo bay myself, I looked around. I hadn't been fully candid with the crew about just how damaged the lower-level systems were. And after ten thousand years of voyaging, every system could use an overhaul. I hoped Riece had the right facilities to let me accomplish my work.

I thought enviously of Amos staying behind on Irrac. That pleasant world would have been a much nicer place to work, while Riece seemed flat and exhausted, compatible with human life but not an Eden by any means.

I opened the cargo bay doors so the gathered natives could see our warehouse. At the nearby disembarkation ramp, the captain, Doctor Max, Elber, Anya, and Henrik came forward to greet the people. The Riece reception committee stood eerily silent without cheers or whistles, not even background conversation. I spotted Renna Qo, the inflectionless woman who had served as their spokesperson. She stepped forward.

Dorothea acknowledged her. "Thank you for receiving the *Time's Arrow*. Our journey from planet to planet has lasted thousands of years, and now we need your help. We bring many goods to trade, along with the full database of our travels so you can learn what humanity has been doing over the millennia since you left home."

She paused, waiting for a response. The people of Riece stepped forward as if to greet them. Renna Qo's expression remained flat.

Dorothea continued, "Your planet is very isolated, and I know you haven't received many offworld visitors. We look forward to learning more about you." She extended a hand as Renna came close. "We'll also need a place to make repairs to our ship. We'll be self-sufficient, though we'd like your support."

"We cannot allow the contamination," said Renna Qo. "The mind of Riece has decided. You will be purged."

Immediately wary, Elber, Henrik, and Anya drew their weapons. Dr. Max raised his hands. "Now, now! There's no reason to—"

The crowd of fifty fell silent, moving in an eerie unison. They concentrated, then hummed.

Dorothea's head exploded.

Even sheltered inside the cargo bay, I felt a pounding roar in my head, destructive thoughts like a telepathic battering ram. We had run scans and verified that the people were unarmed, but these people had developed some kind of mental powers, a group mind that could attack us with their thoughts.

Elber screamed and dropped to his knees, clutching his head as if to hold his skull together. Dr. Max yelled, and blood leaked out of his eyes and ears, then his brains boiled out of his eyes. Henrik and Anya turned to run, eyes squeezed shut, screaming as they ran back up the ramp, but they managed only three steps before both fell flat as if someone had struck them on the head with a heavy club.

Even shielded inside the cargo hold, I felt the throbbing through the hull. The natives pressed closer as if to storm the ship.

Barely able to see, I staggered to the cargo bay controls and sealed the door. The heavily reinforced slab slammed shut. The people pressed around the ship, and waves of their deadly thoughts vibrated through the hull. I didn't know how long I could last against that onslaught.

The lower cargo module with its damaged systems and the malfunctioning stern engine would be dead weight in the planet's gravity well. I knew what I had to do. Sooner or later their telepathic battering ram would kill me. I couldn't stick around to find out.

Sweating, seeing red static in my vision, I reached the command module and threw myself into the bridge seat. The pounding in my brain was so great I couldn't think of grief or shock, couldn't react to seeing Dorothea's head split open, to the loss of my remaining comrades. The people of Riece pressed forward against the ship.

The upper section of *Time's Arrow*, the command module and living quarters, had everything I needed. The cargo half of the ship was a hindrance, and I couldn't take off with it. I blasted the explosive bolts and separated the command and habitation module from the bottom section, burning more fuel than was wise, but I had to tear away from the leftover carcass of the ship. I left my dead captain, my crewmates, and all of our cargo surrounded by murderous natives.

As the command module rose higher and higher, roaring away from the colony, I felt my thoughts grow still. The aggressive mental attack faded with distance. I touched my face and found blood coming out of my nose.

As soon as I reached orbit, I set course at random, a straight line out of the Riece system. I just needed to get far away, find a place where I could recover.

As soon as the ship was flying, I fled into slowtime so I could escape, all by myself.

When I was a year away from Riece, I returned to realtime in order to assess where I was, what had happened, and what my options were. I had no captain, no doctor, no scouts, no crewmates ... no family or friends. *Time's Arrow* was so far out on the rim, I would have to change course and follow along the spiral for centuries before I reached the next known colony. Even so, it was only a name on an old star map that was impossibly out of date. If the people of Riece had evolved into telekinetic, xenophobic murderers, how could I know what the next planet might hold?

And what would I do there when I arrived? I had only the command and habitation module, and no cargo to trade. Yes, I had information and the ship's records of our journey, and many colony worlds would be happy to receive an exotic traveler such as myself. But I still had reservations.

Time's Arrow could travel forever, for all intents and purposes, but entering into orbit, dropping down to a planet's surface, and then climbing back up out of the gravity well burned a lot of fuel and added the most wear-and-tear to the ship.

I thought again of how I hoped Amos had lived a long and happy life on Irrac. I had criticized his decision at the time, but maybe Amos had been right. He was long, long dead, but here I was alone on a ship on the far rim, where colonies were breathtakingly far apart. I could turn around and head back into the more densely populated star systems ... or I could keep going outward.

I took stock. Since it was only me aboard, and since the ship's systems were highly efficient, I had enough food, water, and air to supply myself for centuries even in my subjective frame of reference, and that was more than enough. After all my life, after ten thousand objective years flying across the galaxy in *Time's Arrow*, I didn't like the idea of going backward.

In fact, as I sat in the command module and looked at the sparse star field before me, I realized that if I dropped down to my slowest possible subjective speed after accelerating the ship, I could keep cruising practically until the end of time. I would drop back into realtime once every thousand years or so and have a look around.

It seemed as good as my other options.

There's something unique and egotistical about knowing you're the last human—at least this version of human—in all of existence, in all of the universe. Given the length of our journey, maybe I already was.

If I kept flying, I'd have a front-row seat to watch the evolution and maybe even the end of the universe. I had my lifespan, my allotted number of minutes, whatever it was—and I also had the ability to stretch out that lifespan as long as I could.

I had forever, and forever seemed a worthy goal.

I set the course of the *Time's Arrow* out of the galaxy and flew into the great unknown. I triggered myself to awaken once a century, once a millennium, once every ten thousand years.

The ship drifted on, and my minutes ticked away. I wondered how far I would get.

But every time I awakened I saw the same thing. Blackness and stars.

Blackness and stars.

Blackness and stars.

Something no one else had ever seen.

Blackness and stars.

Blackness and stars.

Forever.

"Attention all planets of the Solar Federation: We have assumed control."

When I was in high school, I discovered Rush through their album 2112, which was one of twelve albums I received after joining the Columbia Record Club. It was a dystopian science fiction concept album set in a repressive future, in which the harsh priests from the Temples of Syrinx crack down on all artistic expression. A young man finds a mysterious guitar in the ruins and learns how to play it.

That album was like an atomic bomb in my imagination, and Geddy Lee's high, shrieking voice, along with the pounding guitars of Alex Lifeson and the drums of Neil Peart were tailor-made to annoy my parents. I loved it. I even had the poster of the three guys in their corny white kimonos on my bedroom wall. I played that album over and over again, along with every other Rush album.

Fast forward many years later, I was good friends with Neil Peart, and we had collaborated on "Drumbeats" (included in another volume of this set) and the first two novels in our steampunk Clockwork trilogy. I suggested doing a novel version of 2112, but Neil wasn't interested. That was too far in his creative rear-view mirror, decades in the past, and he was focused on entirely different things.

However, the wheels kept turning, and I decided to do something different than just a novelization of 2112. I wanted to do a sequel, to pick up where that ominous and intriguing final line left us: "Attention all planets of the Solar Federation: We have assumed control."

Because we were deep into writing the Clockwork universe, I found a way to layer that multiverse into a story that would really interest Neil.

Even if you're not a Rush fan, "2113" is still a great dystopian story. Besides, it already has a soundtrack.

2113

—I—

High above Earth, a portal tore open from a parallel universe. The moonstone gate spread wider, shimmering with both possibilities and threat—the largest gateway the Elder Race had ever created.

Coming home.

Similar doorways opened above the domed lunar base, the sprawling Mars outpost, the mining stations on the moons of Jupiter, the outposts in the rings of Saturn, even the artificial habitats drifting above the hostile clouds of Venus.

An armada of dreamships crossed over, passing through the gates: titanic vessels made of ethereal arcs and lines that fit no standard design. An overwhelming force, one ship after another—the Oracles knew they would not get a second chance.

On the bridge of the lead dreamship, the pearlescent viewing wall cleared to show a magnified view of the crowded cities of Earth below. Seated in white robes on his command dais, Oracle Fulcrum studied the rigid metropolis with disappointment. "We heard the call, but I only hope that the spark hasn't already been snuffed out."

Beside him, Oracle Anchor said, "We thought this branch of humanity had withered and died. I had surrendered all hope for Earth."

Fulcrum stroked his silky beard. "We must never surrender hope, for then we surrender everything." He gazed at the landscape as the dreamships cruised over North America. The identical blockish buildings and the precise geometrical layout sparked a deep, sharp sadness in him. This Earth, one of the original birthplaces of mankind, was now just a dry, brittle remnant of the human spirit. "Our ancestors abandoned them, but maybe there is something worth saving down there."

Looming tall in every city on the continent, like threats erected in perfectly cut stone, were the implacable Temples of Syrinx, each mammoth structure crowned by a glowing Red Star—the only splash of color in a gray and ordered world.

The metropolis was a hive of identical gray buildings constructed according to an uncompromising master plan. Fulcrum saw no sign of the grace or imagination of the human heart. That alone angered him. Human beings were not drones to live in a beehive.

As the dreamships descended through the atmosphere and awakened the stifled cities, the optical lenses flexed to expand the image. The view rocketed downward through the clouds so the Oracles could see swarms of people in the streets, all of them wearing specific uniforms to denote their classes, their professions. In wonder and fear, they looked up as gigantic dreamships filled the skies, dwarfing even the enormous temples.

"Somewhere among those great masses there was a spark," Fulcrum said. "We have to find it and nurture it."

"Or create other sparks," said Oracle Axis, who was always the most optimistic of the group. She did not seem so disappointed to see the stagnation. "Those people can be rescued—and it's long-past time."

History had become myth, simplified and clarified by many retellings. Centuries ago when a dark starvation settled over the Earth, when rigid rules and intolerance began to strangle freedom of expression, all the dreamers—musicians, artists, writers, poets, architects, engineers, theoreticians ... anyone who represented the great sweep of civilization—had become targets. They were rounded up, locked away, and punished for their questions and their creativity. Harsh leaders tried to stamp out any spark of imagination, convinced that rule-followers were easier to control.

There could have been a long and bloody purge—but the dreamers fought back in a different way. By creating the moonstone gates, they could slip away to a parallel but different universe, and they all simply ... *left*. The imaginers, the creatives, and the rule-breakers had flooded away by the millions, taking with them their vibrant songs, poems, and ideas—the very heart and soul of the human race. They left the rest behind, like a snake shedding a useless old skin.

Those days had been lost in the mists of legend and the exaggeration of centuries. In their new home, the refugees built a stunning and glorious civilization, everything a person could aspire to, guided and encouraged by the Oracles. Some debated among themselves whether the castoff remnants of humanity would ever emerge from their self-inflicted dark ages, but after the silent passage of so many years even the debates had faded into esoterica ...

Now, though, millions of people stared up at the dreamships with wide eyes. They were like sheep. They had forgotten how to understand the extraordinary.

Oracle Anchor whispered, "A seed can lie dormant for years before it germinates. We know the seed is still down there, if we can find it."

Fulcrum received a transmission from the rest of his armada throughout the solar system. All dreamships were in position. He rose to his feet from the dais, and when he activated the communication crystal, his voice boomed across all the frequencies controlled by the Temples of Syrinx.

Fulcrum wore a grim expression. "Attention all planets of the Solar Federation—we have assumed control."

—II—

As the other Priests of Syrinx responded with panic, Father Brown just shook his head. "We never should have excavated Red Sector A." The weight of dismay felt as heavy as the cyclopean temple walls around him. "The workers found something there. We knew it was a dangerous area."

A frantic Brother Theo stared at the wall imagers that showed gigantic dreamships closing in. "Red Sector A? That was just a routine expansion for a new Temple District. How does it concern us now? We have to fight these invaders!"

Brother Adam could not believe what he was seeing on the screens. "What is this enemy? Who are they?"

For some time, Father Brown had dreaded that his earlier actions would trigger a dangerous retaliation. He had asked the computers to run probability calculations, and he had expressed his concerns in private with the Great Face. Ever since that naïve young man had appeared before them with the ancient guitar he had found in the rubble …

"It's the Elder Race," he said. "They've come home at last."

Brother Simon let out a hysterical laugh. "That's just a myth whispered by weak-minded fools!"

"Do those ships look like myths?"

Father Brown had known that forbidden remnants of the past were buried beneath Red Sector A, but the Temple computers had chosen that area for the next expansion. One of the excavation workers had indeed found a very dangerous artifact, showing it off to the Priests, proud of the music he had taught himself to play. Father Brown had put a stop to that as soon as he saw the risk, but such things were like noxious weeds and not easily eradicated.

Now, the Elder Race had returned.

The synergy screens in the main hall projected panicked reports from the Priests on the lunar colony and on Mars. Within hours, due to the signal lag, he would likely receive similar alarmed calls from the rings of Saturn, the moons of Jupiter. The Solar Federation was overwhelmed.

Father Brown's priority, though, was to save Earth—and save himself.

First order of business, he evacuated the sycophants from the Temple and closed the thick vault doors, turning the main Temple into a fortress. Or a prison.

He activated Earth's planetary defenses, which were too small and too late. He launched squadron after squadron of defensive Nforcer gunships, which launched from their fenced hangars like a flurry of angry wasps. They soared skyward with conventional weapons blazing against the incomprehensible dreamships, but the Nforcers were trained to quash civil unrest, hold the Red Star high, and keep the populace content. They were not meant to fight a full-scale military action.

Outside, the milling mob beseeched the Priests for protection and guidance. Inside the Temple, though, the rest of the Priests looked to Father Brown to save them—but *he* always looked to the computers, the Halls of Wisdom and Calculation that guided every aspect of daily life.

"With me!" he said. "We need to consult the Great Face."

Hurrying through a labyrinth of thick-walled catacombs, Father Brown descended into the heart of the enormous structure until they reached the sacred computer core. Inside the holy vault, the walls gleamed with hypnotic and arcane patterns, circuits etched with hieroglyphic engrams.

A crackling ball of energy in the chamber coalesced in the air to form a benevolent human face, an old man with a paternal, yet also terrible, expression. It hung suspended there, staring at the visitors.

Brothers Theo, Simon, and Adam fell to their knees, beseeching the cybernetic god, but Father Brown stood straight and faced the computer deity. "We are under attack. Tell us what to do."

After he'd been ordained as High Priest, Father Brown was granted access to the most secret records of ancient humanity, a hidden vault of treasures and mysteries beneath the computer core. There, he had seen the relics left behind by the Elder Race, as well as even more ancient libraries. He knew this projected image of the Great Face was taken from an ancient film called *The Wizard of Oz*.

The paternal image brightened. "My sensors detected these enemy ships, but I cannot analyze their capabilities. Their technology is far superior to our own."

"Our citizens will look to the Priests to save them," said Father Brown. "We must tell them something. We must *do* something."

The Great Face said, "The people look to us for every decision, every action. This does not fit the plan."

Brother Theo cried, "How do we defeat them? We must drive away the invaders."

"I have run projections, followed many paths of probabilities. All conclusions are the same." The kindly holographic face frowned. "There is no probability of our victory."

Father Brown felt as if a brick had fallen on his heart. He thought again about the discoveries in Red Sector A, a haunted place that had been left abandoned since the Elder Race departed. Too many memories were there, too many relics ... too much danger.

He did not dare cast blame on the computers, though, as he faced the benevolent image. Again, he remembered the young man expecting to be rewarded for his forbidden music. That incident, Father Brown knew, was merely the tip of the iceberg. He wondered what else the young man had found down there ...

—III—

From a journal found in Red Sector A:

I'm writing this because I need to document what I found and what happened afterward, and I don't know how else to do it. This isn't a report I can file with my supervisor, not something I can share with my fellow excavators. I don't understand it myself.

It delights me. It fascinates me. It terrifies me.

A job like any other job, on a day like any other day. I woke to the approved morning fanfare. My small apartment contained everything I could want—and how could I possibly want much of anything? Everyone had the same apartment based on the same design; my living arrangements as a single man wouldn't change until a marriage approval came from the Temples, and then my wife and I—whoever she might be—would move into a new apartment, identical to what all married couples had, until we started a family, and then we would move into the approved couple-with-family apartment design.

At my bedside was that month's approved novel. Everyone was reading it, and I dutifully went through a chapter a night. The story resembled the previous month's novel, but the character names were different; therefore, it was an entirely new story.

I put on my standard uniform as a mid-level excavator; I was pleased to display the Red Star on my right breast. My crew cleared away old debris to make room for immense new temples and countless living structures. It was a job to take pride in ... just like everyone 's job.

Heading toward work, I followed the flow of people along arrow-straight boulevards. A peppy morning march played on speakers mounted on the buildings so that everyone walked with the same rhythm, the same smiles. Cruising the skies overhead but low to the buildings, armored Nforcer patrol cars made us all feel safe.

Arriving for work, I joined my crew, which had been assigned to a new expansion project in Red Sector A. We would open up an old section of ruins to be paved over as the foundation for another gigantic temple. I liked seeing progress. What a nice contented world.

As we rolled out to the work site, I sat in peaceful silence next to my co-workers. I knew them well enough, but we were not encouraged to form friendships. We did our jobs like busy little honeybees.

The tallest ruins in the sector had already been leveled by large destructor equipment, broken shards and girders hauled away to be recycled into new construction material. My crew of excavators was trained to explore beneath the surface; we mapped the voids, followed the intact passageways, and found unstable chambers left behind by the Elder Race, who had departed centuries before and left the rest of our race to clean up their messes.

Excavators wore helmets and tough clothing; we carried lights, tools, and logbooks to keep a careful record of our explorations. Each excavator was assigned a territory and range, given a generalized map. After checking in with our prime supervisor, we split up and headed into the ruins. No one questioned the assignment. The Priests would not have sent us here if it was unsafe.

As I descended into the initial shaft, I hummed to myself the tune of that week's featured song. I was clear-eyed and devoted to my task. I had done this work many times, but never in a place so full of dust and buried memories.

For the first three hours I made my way through typical shafts, following basement vaults, documenting underground structures, and measuring the stability of the walls. My helmet light pierced the air, creating a cone of suspended dust motes. The thick concrete walls were sturdy, the ceilings stable, and I laid down a detailed map of my solitary explorations.

No one had been down here in centuries. When I saw a handprint on the wall I wondered if it had been made by a wild-eyed barbarian of the Elder Race. I placed my hand on top of it, curious, and found that the outline matched mine; when I took my palm away, the edges were smudged, and I could no longer tell what was my print and what belonged to that long-forgotten person.

I opened doorways that shrieked on rusty and corroded hinges; I descended unstable metal stairs to even deeper levels where I could feel the oppressive weight of years above me. I finally reached a dead end where the ceiling and walls had collapsed in a pile of debris. I marked the location on my log, and I was about to turn back when I heard a trickling noise—running water. When I moved some of the fallen slabs of artificial rock, the sound grew louder, coming from the darkness behind the cave-in, and when I inhaled, the air was a rush of pure moisture, like a fresh breeze after a spring rainstorm.

With my curiosity piqued, I had to see for myself. I cleared more rubble, shone my helmet light inside, and discovered a large chamber, like a cave full of shadows and treasures. A ribbon of water streamed through a ragged hole in the ceiling, a waterfall that filled the mysterious place with a flowing peace. Either I had gone so deep beneath the surface that this was a natural underground stream, or more likely a water conduit had broken above, spilling through the tunnels until the water found its way here, where it drained through the floor of the chamber.

Intrigued, I wormed my way through the rubble until I emerged into the chamber. It was like a museum. I found incomprehensible machinery, unusual objects that looked like framed mirrors, lenses connected with wires and long-dormant generators ... sculptures, tapestries, and fabrics nearly disintegrated with age.

Paintings leaned against the walls, portraits of long-vanished people in ancient costumes, brooding expressions, and a regal bearing. One painting looked like an old king—but it was entirely different from the benevolent grandfatherly Great Face of the computers that watched over the Solar Federation. I stared at the portraits, and they seemed to stare back at me.

My first instinct was to rush back to report to the prime supervisor, but some indefinable caution struck me. What if the Priests destroyed all such objects? I wanted to cling to these things, to explore and experience them. I could always report them later.

I came upon a clutter of books, volumes filled with stories, essays, poetry—titles I had never seen on the approved list. And I found one bound volume that was empty, blank pages and no title. Why would anyone publish a book with no words? It seemed to be waiting for someone else to write a story.

That is what I am doing now.

—IV—

The dreamships from the Elder Race engulfed the cities of Earth in a show of color and force. At the helm, Oracle Fulcrum studied the gray-clad stick figures that stood confused, afraid, and waiting for guidance. The citizens looked meek, without ambition. That drive had been bred out of them long ago, and their creativity had atrophied. As Fulcrum viewed the ominous temples and the blazing Red Star, he vowed to reawaken these shadowy scarecrows and restore the human spirit.

Following commands issued from the Priests, squadrons of overconfident Nforcer airships roared out to face the strange vessels. The security troops were incapable of imagining the weapons and exotic defenses that had been developed by the Elder Race throughout centuries of creative freedom and exuberant experimentation.

Before traveling through the moonstone gates, the Oracles had agreed there would be no senseless killing. However misguided and grim these people were, they were still humanity's long-lost stepchildren. The signal they had received from the awakened dream amplifier showed that at least someone here still had a spark of creativity.

As the Nforcer gunships opened fire with weapons that merely skated across the slick pearlescent surfaces of the dreamships, Fulcrum directed his crew. "Deploy shrouds. Remove those ships from the conflict before they cause any more harm."

The dreamships launched glowing soap bubbles that struck and surrounded the Nforcer craft, bottling them up. The shroudfields rendered the security troops impotent, but did not physically harm the soldiers inside. Engulfed by the soap-bubble shrouds, the Nforcer gunships dropped to the ground, where they lay like pearls.

Oracle Axis suggested an important symbolic gesture, and the dreamships flew toward the main Temple of Syrinx, where they unleashed one of their rare destructive weapons and blasted down the glowing Red Star. Fulcrum took immense satisfaction from the act.

Even as more bristling Nforcer gunships closed in, Fulcrum knew the rest of his armada could easily take care of the resistance. In the meantime, he had a more important goal. "We need to find the one who sent us the signal. He may need help."

Leaving the rest of the dreamships to close around the Great Temple, Fulcrum guided his own vessel to track down the triggered dream resonator, a relic left behind the great exodus, perhaps in hopes that worthy dreamers might someday awaken.

After his dreamship landed in the barren flats where destructor machinery had leveled the old ruins, Fulcrum, Anchor, and Axis emerged with a crew of acolytes. Fulcrum pointed at an access passage leading underground. "A vault is down there. We need to find it."

Working together, they picked their way into the cleared catacombs, exploring deeper until they came upon a pile of rubble that blocked a much larger chamber. Oracle Fulcrum helped the acolytes clear the obstruction, and they climbed through into a vault that was filled with ghosts of disappointment and the smell of death. To illuminate the room, they dispatched a swarm of lightspheres that darted around the relics, which included an antique but still functional dream resonator.

A dead body lay sprawled on the floor. He had been there for some time.

"Too late," said Oracle Anchor.

Fulcrum felt the heat of anger in his blood. He knelt beside the body. "Despair can be as powerful as a dream. If you are the only one in an entire world who hears the dream, that makes the despair even more powerful."

A book—a journal—lay beside the body, as if the young man had placed it reverently there before the end. As his anger toward the Priests of Syrinx grew, Fulcrum picked up the diary.

—V—

From a journal found in Red Sector A:

I don't know exactly why, but I made no notation of the vault in my official report for that day. As far as the prime supervisor knew, the catacombs dead-ended in the rockfall and there was nothing beyond. Such a report would call no attention to the place and give me time to investigate further.

A chime in my helmet informed me that my shift was about to end and that the rest of the excavation crew was to report back to the rendezvous point. I was disappointed because there seemed so much to learn from the items in the grotto.

The next day I reported for work with a greater anticipation than I had ever experienced. While the rest of the excavators worked through other tunnels beneath the ruins, I came back to my secret chamber. Something changed inside me as I saw all the ancient miracles. I didn't understand what was happening to me.

In a corner, I discovered a strange device covered with dust. It had a long neck and a large resonating box that was strung with wires. When I picked it up, unable to imagine what it was for, the strings startled me with a tone that was instantly pleasing. I touched the other strings, then plucked them, realizing that each string made a different note. Was that what this artifact had been designed for? For communication? When I plucked the strings in sequence, I suddenly realized—music! This device created music.

It was called a guitar, I learned later, and I began to experiment. If I plucked the strings simultaneously, I could make combined tones; or I could strum them all with a different rhythm. If I moved my grip and shortened the strings, that also changed the sound. It was amazing how many pleasing tones could come from only six strings.

Excited about my discovery and wanting to tell someone, but not knowing who might appreciate it, I chose to write down my activities in the empty book. The journal seemed to have been left there for just this purpose ...

On my way to the work site the next day, the transport vehicle played a familiar background melody that was always there but rarely listened to. I thought of the stringed musical instrument and wondered if I could play those notes myself.

Once I returned to the marvelous vault with the waterfall, I picked up the instrument and brushed it off, removing the dust, thinking that a little bit of care might make the sounds brighter or fresher.

As I plucked out melodies on the guitar, each tune was a new discovery. At first I fumbled clumsily, but soon I learned how to play, and the music gave me great joy. I created, which was such a satisfactory experience that I wanted to share with my crewmates and my prime supervisor. This was something so precious, so unexpected, it could change the world! Had the Elder Race stolen real music from us when they left Earth? Had the Priests forgotten how to make new music?

This was far too important to show my comrades in the workplace. No, this was something vital. As a good citizen, I had to present my marvelous discovery to Father Brown himself in the Great Temple. I would show all the Priests of Syrinx and give them the joy that this guitar gave me. Yes, I was galvanized now. I knew what to do.

I practiced until my fingers were sore. I developed complex and joyful tunes, and then with a spring in my step, I left my secret cave carrying the guitar. I had a mission.

—VI—

Surrounded by the shimmering circuit-board walls inside the computer vault, Brothers Theo, Simon, and Adam begged the Great Face that hovered in the air. "Please tell us how we can drive away these invaders."

"We have nothing that can fight against them!"

On the synergy screens, they had watched the full squadrons of gunships so easily neutralized, and the giant invading vessels simply landed wherever they liked. The Priests did not have a gigantic military force, since the days of large-scale battle had faded long ago with the perfect consolidation of the Solar Federation. The Nforcers were in no way equipped to defend against a massive external armada, their weapons designed instead to monitor the citizenry and snuff out any signs of unrest.

The paternal image of the Great Face blinked as if giving the matter some thought. "I have recalculated, added further data. The situation is even worse than previous projections. Given the technologies the invaders have already demonstrated, no favorable outcome is possible for the Temples of Syrinx."

Father Brown had expected nothing else. The Priests and their computers had made a fatal oversight in assuming that the Elder Race would never return. "This could end in surrender, or in violence," he said. "But it will end."

Unlike his fellow Priests, Father Brown had seen the true threat posed by the young man with his shining eyes when he came to play his beautiful, dangerous music, expecting to be *rewarded* ...

Nothing in the young man's prior service record showed him to be unduly imaginative, nor offered any indication that he was dissatisfied with his contented world. He had given the Priests no cause for concern—until he appeared before them, bold, energized, and showing off what he called an "ancient miracle" that he had discovered in the ruins beneath Red Sector A. "I know it's most unusual ..." He held up a musical instrument from ages past and began to play the strings with intense concentration. He plucked out tones, found a melody, and grinned as he played it again.

The other Priests listened, at first more confused than horrified, and, when he was finished, the young man grinned stupidly. After the silence fell, without music, without comment, the young man struck up another song, as if that might help his case rather than increase his own danger.

The poor naïve fool!

"What is the purpose of this?" asked Brother Theo, finally. "We already have music. Why do you need more?"

"But this is *my* music."

Father Brown rose, pulling his powerful presence around him. "What use would the average citizen have for such things? Should they all start to make their own music?"

"But ... listen," the young man pleaded, then started to play again.

"Stop! Those relics were buried deep in the tunnels—where they belong. *Buried!* The Elder Race abandoned us, and they took their sickness with them. After centuries of united effort, we created the stable Solar Federation. We made the Red Star a symbol of consistent happiness. We do not need these frivolous distractions. We have our work to do—and so do you."

The other Priests took their cue from Father Brown, glowering at the young man, but the fool didn't know when to give up. Although his face fell and his eyes stung with tears, he refused to turn away. "But there's something here, Father. Let me play another. I know it will reach you." He began to strum again, but Father Brown strode forward, furious, terrible, and knowing he had to crack down on this crisis. He hoped and prayed to the computer god that he had acted in time, before this insanity infected others.

He ripped the guitar from the young man's trembling hands. "Don't annoy us further. Your purpose is to serve the Solar Federation. Your masters are the Priests of Syrinx. This ... noise is a waste of your time. And ours."

Knowing that it would devastate the young man—but better one citizen than all of civilization—Father Brown smashed the guitar across his knee, snapping the stem, jangling the wires. He tore it apart, dropped the resonating box on the stone floor, and stomped the rest into splinters.

The young man stared in horror, as if the Priest had broken him in half and likewise ground him under his heel. Father Brown summoned uniformed Nforcers to escort the man away. Their heavy boots thundered across the floor of the Great Hall, whisking the man out but leaving the destroyed shards of the guitar.

The other Priests were confused by Father Brown's extreme reaction, but he kept his face a stony mask, secretly terrified that this young man's discovery would still cause a great deal of trouble ...

And his worst fears had come to pass.

A report came in from one of the besieged Venus habitats, and the walls of the computer vault resolved into images. Sparks flew behind a panicked High Priest in the control chamber of the sealed orbiting habitat. "We are overwhelmed! Enemy ships brushed aside all our weapons, and they are swarming our habitat with small ships. They've attached to our hull!" The distraught Priest drew a deep breath and found the steel of resolve. "We cannot let our citizens be corrupted. This is our final play."

The High Priest of the Venus habitat set his station reactors on a slow buildup and overload—and within ten minutes the entire habitat exploded, terminating the transmission. Inside the computer vault, the screen reverted to the Red Star logo, while the Great Face hovered in the air, expressionless.

Commandeering the communication systems inside the vault, Father Brown sent out a broadcast to any remaining defenders of Earth. He understood that this Temple would be their last stand. In order to let his cadre of Priests survive just a little longer, he recalled all operational Nforcer armored ships, all ground fighters, all uniformed soldiers and ordered them to form a cordon around the Great Temple.

"Yes, that will be enough!" said Brother Theo. "It has to be enough. We can hold them off."

"We 'll be safe in here," Brother Adam echoed, as if to reassure himself. "We 'll withstand the invaders. No one can break into this fortress and harm us."

In the center of the vault, the benevolent visage of the old man closed his eyes, then winked out as all the great computers shut down.

—VII—

From a journal found in Red Sector A:

After the Priests of Syrinx crushed my dreams, I was shaking so badly I could barely walk. My heart felt cold and empty. I should have returned home, but my assigned apartment was not home to me. The reminder of my colorless existence would only emphasize how bleak this world was, and how silent it was without the joy of the music I had discovered.

Now that Father Brown had destroyed my precious guitar, I didn't even have music of my own. Why couldn't the Priests hear what I heard? How could they not feel the wonderful energy evoked by those bright silvery notes? How could Father Brown dismiss that ancient miracle as a mere toy?

And how could music have destroyed the Elder Race? It didn't make sense to me, but questions were not encouraged in our contented world.

The city streets were empty, unwelcoming. I rode the automated transport lines and then walked for hours through the dark until I made my way out to Red Sector A. I had the haunted treasure-filled place all to myself.

When I reached my beautiful serene cave, the trickling sound of the waterfall tried to comfort me, as did the memory of my music. I stared at the ancient portraits of anonymous people, but they were strangers offering no sympathy and no support.

My heart had been broken. I was lost, exhausted. My mind seemed to shut down, as if Father Brown had smashed a bridge of hope just as he had smashed my guitar.

Unable to face even my own company, I lay down on the hard stone floor next to the waterfall and retreated into sleep. As I drifted off, the strange connected mirrors and lenses from the ancient devices nearby began to hum and glow. But rather than waking me, the thrumming light enfolded me and dragged me deeper into sleep ...

That night I experienced a dream unlike any other. At first I heard guitar strings playing music my music—then the murky dream images turned into a vivid landscape, a wondrous vision of paradise with colorful towers, majestic architecture. I had never seen or even imagined a place like this, so how could I be envisioning it?

I found myself transported—there was no other word for it—to a spiral staircase that seemed to overlook infinite possibilities. Atop that staircase a wise bearded man in a gleaming white robe stood before me. He spread his hands wide to encompass all that he and his people had accomplished. "The dream has awakened at last," said the Oracle. "And the dream is you."

"Yes ..." I replied. "I am dreaming."

"More than dreaming. This is real, but a different reality." The Oracle swept his hands aside and showed me the panorama of a vibrant world that made my very existence ache with color, music, scents, blossoms, and fireworks of the imagination.

"We departed from the original Earth long ago, and we have thrived," the Oracle explained. "Look at all we have done ... and the human spirit is just beginning. You are part of it. This is what your life might be. This is what your world could be, if only you all would open your eyes and your hearts again."

My heart swelled with the impossible possibilities, surging so bright in my mind that I was thrust back into wakefulness—and I sat up blinking in the cave.

I know the Oracle was trying to give me hope, but when I emerged from my fitful sleep, the dream and the Oracle had done me no service. Before, I had not known such a place could ever exist ... but now I had touched it, tasted it, experienced it.

And it was gone.

My world was gray and monotonous. The music was all the same. The Priests of Syrinx mistook a numb and soulless world for a contented world.

And I knew I could never have what I had seen in that dream ... I huddled in my secret chamber for days. I had brought some food and my excavator's toolkit with me, but nothing else. I drank from the waterfall, but it had a metallic bitter taste. I wasn't hungry. Nourishment didn't interest me, when I knew I was starving for other things. I grew weaker day by day, and my broken heart was even heavier in my chest.

After Father Brown had cast me out of the Great Temple, I had not returned home, had not reported to work. I would face severe punishment if I decided to go back and pretend that nothing had happened ... but how could I return there? Under the Red Star, there was no life, no existence that I wanted to have. The wonderful cruel dream had shown me everything I was missing, and those hours of sleep were the only time I had ever felt truly alive.

In the depths of my despair, the only spark I clung to was that I could somehow return to that world in my dreams. Permanently. I know I can never get there in this life; perhaps the path to that wondrous place lies through another doorway entirely. A sleep from which I cannot awaken.

I have a sharp cutter in my toolkit, and I'm sure it will be swift. This will be the last entry in my journal.

—VIII—

As Oracle Fulcrum finished reading the poor man's last words, the simmering uneasiness and disappointment inside him became a bright fury. With reddened eyes, he turned to the others. "So much lost here. So much potential. Just think of what these people could have created if they hadn't been smothered by the Priests of Syrinx."

Anchor was openly weeping, and Axis comforted him. "We don't even know his name," she said, taking the journal and rereading some of the pages.

"He is all of us, and every person here—or who they might have been." Fulcrum felt heartsick that this victim would never again hear music, nor experience the wonders that the Elder Race were bringing back to this Earth, or the *new* things this prodigal arm of humanity could create once they were liberated.

Fulcrum's anger became a white hot determination. He gestured for the others to join him. "We will build a memorial for this young man, and he will become a symbol for the new world. But first ..." He narrowed his eyes and saw the steel in their eyes as well. "Before the forest can thrive, we have to clear out the deadwood."

As their dreamships converged above the Great Temple, Fulcrum received reports from the other dreamships across the Solar Federation. He was saddened to learn that one of the orbiting Venus habitats had chosen to self-destruct rather than surrender. The other two habitats were now under the control of the Elder Race; the frightened inhabitants were disoriented, not sure what these new masters would bring.

A dreamship signal from stations in the rings of Saturn pronounced victory, as well as outposts on the moons of Jupiter. Fulcrum was surprised to hear from the sprawling colonies on Mars, where previously unexpected resistance groups seized the opportunity to overthrow the Priests themselves in spontaneous internal uprisings.

But Oracle Fulcrum needed to see the Great Temple fall. He would be among the conquerors as they surged into the hall. After reading the young man's journal, he would confront Father Brown in person.

As armored Nforcers converged around the Temple in a last defense, Fulcrum and his comrades moved through the streets. He looked at the citizens, sure that some of them at least must have hungry minds.

Axis and Anchor directed the acolyte soldiers to tear down the Red Star banners and replace them with bright makeshift pennants —the design didn't matter, so long as it was an outpouring of colors and imagination. Celebratory fireworks exploded and sparkled like chrysanthemums in the sky.

Every citizen of the Solar Federation had followed instructions for so long, facing no choices or concerns, that they didn't know what to do with freedom. How many of them had dormant dreams like that young guitar player? How many of them secretly wrote poems, or drew sketches, but were afraid to show them to anyone? Now, they no longer needed to be afraid. They could achieve anything they liked, create anything they might imagine. They just needed to be shown how. They needed to be granted *permission* to unlock their imaginations.

As the returning members of the Elder Race marched through the city, they were all smiles and exuberance. Next to him, as they closed on the Great Temple, Oracle Axis hesitated. She lowered her voice as she stared at the uniformly clad men and women, their averted gazes. "It's a barren creative desert instead of a lush rainforest of ideas. I never imagined it would be so … desolate."

"Even a desert bursts into bloom after the rain," Fulcrum pointed out. "And we bring the rain."

"But they're so … meek," said Anchor, keeping his voice low.

Fulcrum did not agree. "Dreamers have a hidden strength that is often mistaken for meekness by those who have power."

The landed dreamships opened and played music. Representatives and counselors emerged, talking to the citizens, reassuring them. It was just a start.

When the armies finally arrived at the Great Temple, a wall of armored Nforcers blocked them, but Fulcrum did not have the patience to use a gentle hand. "We won't caress the boot heel that crushed the life out of these people. This has been much too long in coming."

From forward weapons ports, the dreamships emanated a rippling rainbow wedge that pushed through the cordon of armored vehicles and defensive barricades. The clustered Nforcers fired their weapons ineffectually against the shimmering shield, but the colorful wedge split them apart like a divided sea, clearing the way for the Elder Race to enter the mammoth Temple.

"Bring it down," Fulcrum said.

Over the centuries, the Elder Race had invented matter-manipulation devices that allowed sculptors to work on the scale of mountains, to build and assemble anything they could design. The same constructor tools could be used to rearrange the massive block walls, and like a sculptor working with soft clay, the matter manipulators carved away the stone and split open the Temple of Syrinx.

Oracle Fulcrum led his people as they surged inside. "This is the day that dreams begin."

—IX—

After the benevolent computers shut down and the paternal Great Face faded, abandoning the terrified Priests in the core chamber, Brothers Theo, Simon, and Adam were nearly catatonic. For centuries the Priests of Syrinx had ruled the people—but even the Priests relied on the great computers, and now they were thoroughly alone. They could not react to the emergency, could not solve the problem for themselves.

Father Brown could rely on no one but himself, but he could use these men for now. Taking charge, he ushered the other priests out of the core chamber. The three stumbled as they moved, their knees quaking. The Temple was a cacophony of chaos, which grated on Father Brown. Countless robed Priests ran around in panic inside the sealed structure, which was being bombarded from outside.

Tall synergy screens on the walls showed the turmoil in the streets, and the skies overhead were full of dreamships. The invaders were sweeping everything away without understanding, without the slightest grasp of who these poor people were. They needed someone to guide them, to think for them, to create a perfect world where all could be content ...

Sickened, Father Brown shook his head. Despite their grandiose

300

dreams of liberation, the Elder Race did not comprehend what Earth had become. The citizens had no ability to take care of themselves—independence had been bred out of them over the centuries. To grant them complete freedom was like giving a child sharp knives to play with!

The Elder Race thought they could simply open the floodgates of freedom, and the people would know what to do? Simply *telling* a person he was free did not *make* him free. And did the citizens even want that? Father Brown understood these people far better than the arrogant Oracles did.

With the armada of dreamships and their incomprehensible weaponry, he had no question that the invaders would succeed ... but he doubted they knew what they had done. A utopia did not create itself, and there were conflicting definitions of what constituted a perfect world.

The Red Star had fallen. The Solar Federation was doomed.

Father Brown made his decision. After the centuries of effort it had taken to create this contented world, he had another obligation. He placed his hands on the trembling shoulders of Brother Theo and Brother Adam. Dozens of Priests had gathered in the Great Hall, staring at the open empty air and praying for the computer god to reappear and give them instructions. Like the citizens they ruled, they could not think for themselves, either.

Father Brown spoke in a firm, commanding voice to Theo, Simon, and Adam. "Be strong—that is what you must do. Go and meet the Elder Race. It is your only chance. Make peace—they will accept you."

"But, you have to lead us!" cried Simon. "Please, Father Brown."

He shook his head. "I have another mission. It may not succeed, but I have to try. This world did not turn out the way I envisioned, but maybe there is a second chance."

Brother Adam's face formed a grim mask as he struggled to defeat the fear inside him. "If anyone can do it, Father, you can." Then he, Simon, and Adam marched forward, leading the lesser Priests to the grand archway as the walls of the Temple crumbled and fell. They went to meet the Elder Race.

After they had left, Father Brown retreated into the computer vault—his only chance. The heavy vault door slammed shut, protecting him, giving him time ... but he knew the Temple defenses would not last long against the invaders. He had to hurry.

Behind the engram-enhanced silicon walls, he ran his fingers along the circuit paths, tracing an emergency pattern no one else knew. He had planned for this ever since he began to fear what Earth might face. Now that the computers had shut down, he used the last flickers of energy to activate a code.

With a sound like a defeated sigh, a hidden access door slid open to reveal the secret vault that contained remnants of ancient technology considered far too dangerous for the average to see.

Earlier High Priests had locked all that equipment there, relics discovered by excavators as they rebuilt ruined sections of the city. In the past, citizens were fearful enough to surrender any such objects, but it was only a matter of time until someone decided to toy with them …

The forbidden technology of the dimensional gates had not been tested in countless years, and even Father Brown didn't understand it—thought amplifiers, resonance lenses, sensory prisms. He did know though, about the moonstone mirrors.

When the Elder Race left the world so long ago, all the dreamers had built countless dimensional gateways for their exodus. They had traveled to an alternate Earth, a place where they had apparently thrived for centuries.

Some of those moonstone portals remained, though, and now Father Brown stood before one deep in the secret vault, saw the faint pearlescent glow of its latent energy. The Priests of Syrinx had suppressed any further investigations, but according to the theories left behind, there were countless similar worlds. Infinite possibilities. Anywhere but here …

As the portal shimmered, Father Brown stared at it. He had to escape, had to take his knowledge with him, but he didn't dare go to the parallel world where the Elder Race had built its great civilization. He needed a fresh start. Instead, he adjusted the portal, found a random mirror image of different possibilities.

Father Brown had always been a man of firm convictions, untroubled by doubts, unwavering in his straightforward path. All answers were clear when one didn't bother with questions. Now, though, he paused to stare at the gateway that would take him away from this collapsing civilization. There would be no turning back.

It was his only chance.

Above him, behind the sealed door of the vault, he could hear pounding noises, then shouts as the invaders breached the chamber. They were coming. Father Brown could no longer wait.

Without looking back at the fallen Red Star, he stepped through the moonstone portal.

—X—

When he emerged on the other side, in another world, his great city was gone, and he saw no sign of the Great Temples or the geometrical dwelling units that sprawled as far as the eye could see. Instead, he stood on a rolling green hill looking down toward a village in a valley below—but he also saw fire and smoke. Many of the small quaint dwellings were burning. From where he stood, he heard distant shouts and screams, saw marauders charging through the streets while villagers evacuated in panic and ran into the hills.

Father Brown took shelter under a tree so no one would see him, and he watched, gathering information. He was surprised when a man, a woman, and two raggedy children crashed through the trees behind him. The refugee family stared in terror at his strange appearance, but even Father Brown in his Priest's robes was not nearly as terrifying as the marauders attacking the village. The mother gasped and snatched up her children, gathering them protectively while the man stood before them, ready to fight. "Who are you, sir?"

Father Brown raised his hands. "I'm just a visitor. I mean you no harm."

The man looked at him suspiciously, then jerked his gaze sideways, interrupted by the sharp icepick sounds of gunfire, the shouts and explosions from the village. He looked sickened and terrified. "You're not one of the bandits, then?"

"No … I don't think so," said Father Brown.

"They prey upon our village every year," said the woman. Tear tracks cleared lines down her soot-stained cheeks. "Many of us escape, and we spend months rebuilding. When we beg the nearby towns for help, they only see our weakness and then they steal our stored crops. It never ends."

The man's brief laugh had no humor. "Last year, the bandits

raided during fever season—and they also stole our sickness, so their numbers are smaller this year." He spat on the ground. "Not that it does us any good."

Father Brown was appalled to see the barbarism, the chaos. "It sounds terrible. Complete anarchy! Don't you have a leader to bring everyone together? To show you how to make the world an efficient place?"

The ragged, forlorn family looked at him, uncomprehending. The mother shook her head.

"It sounds like you could use some stability," said Father Brown. "What is the name of this land?"

The man frowned, wondering if the question was a trick, but one of the children piped up, "Albion. It's Albion."

Father Brown nodded. And the wheels began to turn like clockwork in his mind.

Greg Benford and I spent many months extrapolating a possible epic future of Siberia, with geopolitical forces in conflict, resources in question, and the colonization of the last great frontier on Earth.

As an offshoot of these plans, we came up with a grand scheme for cloning mammoths—an idea that's not so far-fetched today. In fact, several research teams are currently at work on the concept. And radical protest groups are already up in arms, writing scathing letters to the San Francisco Chronicle, science magazines, and other venues. Even some of the museum curators and scientists we talked to during our research for this story had knee-jerk distaste, resisting the very idea of bringing back an extinct species—even if early humans had wiped out that species in the first place.

"Mammoth Dawn" is only the prologue to a projected novel. Unfortunately, the reality of this concept is sweeping down upon us with the speed of a stampeding woolly herd. We released the novella, our full detailed outline for the proposed novel, and several technical articles about the process of cloning mammoths in the book Mammoth Dawn *(WordFire Press).*

MAMMOTH DAWN

(with Gregory Benford)

If only the protesters' intellect matched their verbal cleverness, Alex thought, the Helyx Corporation wouldn't have any problems at the gate.

It's Not Nice to Fool with Mother Nature! said one of the waving signs displayed on a securitycam window projected on the surface of his desk. The usual. Alex Pierce had stopped trying to understand the Evos' odd point of view, had ceased even being bemused by their antics. He had a company to run.

He relegated the securitycam image to the background and brought more important documents forward. Datascreens and email lists cluttered his table-sized desktop screen as much as memos and paper messages had once done.

Earlier that morning he'd woken up in Miami with a hangover. He'd downed three drinks too many at yet another fancy fundraiser dinner—this one to preempt birth defects through parental genetic screening. Before midday he had choppered back to the main lab administration offices in rural Montana. For a worldwide corporation, business hours lasted all day long, and it was always time for the boss to get back to work.

His wife Susan had stayed home on the ranch. She disliked black-tie functions like the one in Miami, though she could be devastating in a cocktail dress, the barest breath of jewels implying wealth far better than gaudiness did. But too often the diplomats and VIPs treated Alex as the only important face in the room, and Susan the gorgeous trophy wife rather than a talented scientist in her own right. She hated the attitude, and Alex had made appropriate excuses for her.

But Susan's real reason was that she wanted to stay with her mammoths.

As his company had grown from a fledgling startup with one biotech product—a symbiotic microorganism that could fend off strange *E. coli* in the human digestive system—to a corporate leviathan that spent most of its resources just figuring out how to receive and manage the enormous profits, Alex had learned to multi-process. While taking care of corporate details, answering vidmessages, and delegating responsibilities, a calm and meditative part of his mind was anticipating an evening of campfires and peace with his wife, out near the herd....

"We got another fence-jumper," Ralph Duncan said on the secure phone, interrupting a dozen separate trains of thought and delivering a problem of his own. "Got him cold."

Alex's autosecretary instantly knew this was important, captured the call, and transferred the security man's weathered image to the upper corner of the desk. "Remember that li'l hint we got on the acoustics? Tracked him in the woods up along the eastern ridgeline. Ambitious bastard."

Alex was glad to be interrupted from pharmaceutical statistics, Third World traveler health records—dull, even if they did point to continued success. "Another Evo type?"

"They don't carry some kinda ideology tag, Boss, but you can bet he was trying to get a look at the mammoths. Should I tell the sheriff?"

"No, he'll just process the guy, slap him on the wrist, and let him back out to cause more mischief." Alex rubbed his fingers over thin lips. "Usually only the hardcore ones try to get past the fences. How's he outfitted?"

"Pretty fancy. Overnight gear, one of those microbags for sleepin', videocam with close-up fittings. Five kilometers inside the fence, easy. No question about boundaries and jurisdictions." Ralph snorted.

By now, the questions came automatically to Alex. The ranch often had intruders. "No weapon?"

"Nope. Except for tryin' to run at first, gave us no trouble."

As he dealt with the conversation, Alex finished some routine computer work, forwarded several inquiries to Susan's mailbox, bumped a set of interview questions to his PR squad (who knew all the right answers anyway), and keyed out, using his thumbprint to secure. At no point did Ralph ever notice that he didn't have Alex's full attention.

"If you ask me, this guy wanted to be caught. Claims he knows you professionally." Ralph's sun-grizzled face showed just a hint of amusement. "His ID says Geoffrey Kinsman."

Now Alex paid attention. "Damn! I think I know him. Spelled with a G?"

"Yep."

"What's a good biologist doing with that bunch of Luddites?"

"Says he'll talk only to you, Boss."

Alex shut down the other operations in the office, signaling all his staff distributed around the world that he was not presently available. "Bring him to the Hospital, not here."

Ralph had an intuitive sense of Alex's moods, born of a decade's close collaboration. But now the security man seemed surprised. "Show and tell, Boss? For one of those clowns?"

"The Evos are always more afraid of what they imagine than what they actually see." He put on a pair of spex and tested the uplink as he headed out of the office, his boots clomping down the varnished wooden stairs, and out onto the plank porch. "Stall him for five, Ralph. Give me time to profile him."

When Helyx had purchased an isolated chunk of northern Montana, Alex kept the original ranch buildings, letting them fade and weather from bleached white to an ash gray like raw silver. The primary genetics labs were in the old pine-log barn, which Susan had dubbed the Pleistocene Hospital.

"Full database search," he subvocalized into the spex as he walked. "Summarize relevant information on Dr. Geoffrey Kinsman. Reference point: He was in my lab around fifteen years ago. Apply context filters."

With a big drive-in bay and concealed windows, the hospital barn looked like an equipment garage. Inside, the crisp antiseptic air mixed with the moist organic odors of feathers and fur, droppings and feed—a contrast to the smelly oil drums just outside on the loading dock.

Lounging in his jeans against the split rail that bounded the old barn, Alex read a data summary that scrolled across the spex. All he needed to know about Geoffrey Kinsman: a man with just a bit too much clout and education to dismiss as simply a misled Luddite, as Alex had always considered the Evos to be.

For years, Kinsman had associated with political activism, starting with Ruckus Society training camps, where bright-eyed kids learned street protest tactics. His molecular biology research had produced over a hundred papers, recently with an angle toward genetics and species preservation. Another "clean genes" guy. Unarmed, a routine lab type, Kinsman did not seem dangerous. Maybe that didn't include the threat of being bored to death.

Alex bit his lip in annoyance. He wished they had a network of sympathetic locals who would warn Helyx before a guy got this far in. He had endured the backwoods suspicions, had expected them because he'd grown up just over the Idaho border. For the first few years, the locals had given him a narrow-eyed appraisal. In fact, for a while an ugly rumor had spread that he was here to recruit locals as organ donors for sinister Helyx experiments.

But when his staff offered only day work and some well-paid farmhand jobs, the people were disappointed—until the area economy picked up and kept growing. Within a year Alex Pierce could walk into any bar and get his beer paid for, because Helyx Ranch pumped in a goodly share of the county's revenue.

Alex pursed his lips, pondering. A lot of the locals might agree with the protesters' views, even help them out a little. A bitter truth —he hadn't won the war of ideas even here, in home country. He knew these people, shared many of their gut responses. But he had not lived in their world, really lived in it, for a good long while. Ralph was the real thing—and looked it in his rough pants and boots as he came through the door with his captive.

The man walking next to him was a dapper, compact item, fresh from an upscale outfitter: olive green Gore-Tex jacket, trim all-weather leggings, a big hiker's watch with a global positioning readout. He looked as out of place as a chicken in church. A bit heavier than Alex remembered, but the tight mouth was the same.

Geoffrey Kinsman's voice was as hard and flat as a stove lid. "Dr.

Pierce." East Coast accent, mid-Atlantic state. He held out a hand, and Alex ignored it. "You don't remember me?"

"I remember. Just read the data squirt about you, Dr. Kinsman. All the good stuff." He decided to have some fun with him. "You seem to have strayed a bit out of your way."

"Might as well admit the obvious," Ralph growled, playing the tough cop. "You wanted to create some disturbance—give the Feds a pretext to come in here."

Kinsman glanced at the old security chief as if he were some kind of lab specimen. "You overestimate my powers."

"That's just what you did at that animal experimentation facility outside Topeka, five years ago," Alex said. It sometimes put these people off-balance if you could demonstrate up front that you knew all about them.

But Kinsman didn't even blink. "That was coincidence."

Ralph snorted, and Alex grinned. Kinsman was not going to be any trouble, he judged; he didn't even have a cover story. "We'll be fine, Ralph. Thank you." As the security man turned to leave, Alex scowled back at Kinsman. "So why, exactly, was it so important to break through my fences and trespass on my private property?"

The man allowed himself a small, dry chuckle, but his eyes were a brittle gray, like chips of slate, as he said, "To talk some sense into you. I consider that constructive, not destructive."

"Sense? Those people at the south gate have an excuse: they're ignorant. But we worked together, so I thought—"

"You didn't think twice about me when you published that paper, the one on mammoth genes."

"Right, you did some of the preliminary scans on the gene lines. A grad student for two years, then left."

Kinsman took on a self-righteous air. "I disagreed with the work, once I understood what you were doing."

"So what was your gripe? Was it because I 'didn't think twice' about you?"

"Neither of you even asked if I wanted my name on that paper."

Alex shook his head. "You were doing straightforward stuff. Not original. Sorry if we didn't acknowledge you—" He couldn't even remember for sure.

"Oh, there was a paragraph at the end, thanking me and a dozen others, sure."

Alex smiled slightly. "You wanted to be on the paper. Is that what this is about?"

"No, damn it!" But Kinsman's flushed face belied his words. "I just thought you'd listen to me because I was a lab grunt for you once. Maybe your money has insulated you from the arguments against this entire—"

Alex held up a hand, quick and decisive. "Already heard them. Before I took you on as a grad student, I had invented most of the arguments. Or my wife had. But we thought it through. Decided for ourselves."

Kinsman blinked, looking taken aback at Alex's bluntness. He must have had plenty of time to rehearse this confrontation while backpacking across Helyx wilderness property, Alex mused, but a lot of emotion churned in his face. There had been a lot of grad students in Alex's lab then, most of them doing routine tasks to get experience. Somehow this one had left little impression on him. But clearly that old, simple paper had been a big deal to Kinsman. Students normally didn't get their names on technical papers unless they did something creative, but Kinsman had apparently taken that irritating grain of sand and turned it into this pearl of a grudge. Alex had never been really good at judging people, but his years leading a stupendously successful company had sharpened what little skill he naturally had.

Nothing brings enemies out of the woodwork more effectively than success.

"Okay, let me talk some sense into *you*." Alex gestured toward the old oaks that towered near the barn and the ranch buildings. The immense, gnarled trees were majestic and stately—and full of birds. "Look over there, Dr. Kinsman. Beautiful birds, graceful. You should see them fly at sunset, like a cloud." Even without squinting, he could pick out a dozen nests in the branches, and the constant shifting, cooing, fluttering made the branches tremble.

"I didn't come here to look at birds, *Dr.* Pierce." He spat out the title.

Alex turned to him sharply. "You should. Once they blackened the skies; billions of them in North America when Columbus landed. But it was in their nature to nest in huge colonies, only in big stands of oaks or beeches, which made them easy prey. Over the centuries settlers cut down the oaks and beeches for firewood and lumber, or just to clear farmland. Hunters shot millions of those birds, usually for sport, though they shipped the carcasses to the cities by the barrelful."

Kinsman looked impatient, then startled. "Those are—"

"Passenger pigeons lay only one egg each spring. They couldn't possibly reproduce faster than they were slaughtered. It was genocide, pure and simple, *Dr.* Kinsman, perpetrated by human beings. The last passenger pigeon died in 1914 in the Cincinnati Zoo, and the species was extinct in a historical blink of an eye. Until Helyx brought them back." Alex couldn't keep the happy pride out of his voice.

Kinsman, though, looked disgusted to the point of being ill. "Extinction is Nature's way, Pierce—for whatever reason. You can congratulate yourself for the hubris of your genetic breakthroughs, but can you honestly say the world is a better place because you have brought back a ... pigeon?" He waved dismissively toward the oaks. As if at a signal, several of the birds took flight, ruby-throated, with lovely gray body feathers and long pointed tails. "Your means are dangerous, and your ends are utterly inconsequential. Pigeons!" The fire in Kinsman's eyes made Alex reconsider the wisdom of having sent his security chief away so quickly. "You're a big shot businessman—what possible market can there be for passenger pigeons. For zoos? Pets? *Meat?*"

"Market talk is what I feed the Board, but that doesn't even start to explain why I'm here." He allowed a small, self-deprecating smile. "I didn't want to go down in history as Dr. Diarrhea." Alex turned from the split-rail fence. "Come have a look. Maybe we can use a crowbar to open your mind."

Inside, the lab was a mix of cool high-tech surfaces and ancient woods, the barn's past never wholly banished. Consoles and elaborate digital diagnostics stood next to old feed cabinets, still useful for storage. High spotlights gave the scene an evenly lighted patina and crisp, conditioned air fought the old horsy smells and new disinfectants. Chrome countertops sat next to wooden fences and thick wire-mesh cages.

"Not many people get to see this, Dr. Kinsman," Alex said.

"Not many people should."

Why do I try? he thought. *If Kinsman wasn't a colleague ...*

Inside a shoulder-high pen stood two gawky-looking birds like giant chickens with stretched necks. They had mottled brown feathers, lizard-like feet, and towered nearly ten feet tall.

"This is our first mating pair of moas, a New Zealand bird that went extinct sometime in the 1600s." Elated notes crept into Alex's voice, but he saw no wonder in Kinsman's eyes. "We're currently in our third-generation retrograde development of the Tasmanian tiger, too. But the lack of a close sibling-species as well as general difficulties in dealing with the marsupial gestation process has caused some delays."

He glanced toward the set of thick doors and reinforced windows at the back of the Pleistocene Hospital. Kinsman looked suspiciously at the closed-off rooms ... but Alex didn't think the man was ready for that sight yet. "Other resurrected animals," he explained with an offhanded comment. "Look, I don't have time to show you everything. It's obvious you're more interested in proselytizing than in science."

A rotund bird higher than a man's knee waddled across the floor, looking comical, its black beak blunt and ugly, its eyes innocent. Two stubby wings betrayed the flightless nature of the bird, which moved at a rapid, though ungainly, clip. A tufted curlicue of feathers poked up like a pigtail from its rear. The bird prodded around in corners, pecked at imaginary insects, as if it had forgotten where its food dish was.

This time Kinsman stared. "*Dodos*, too?" The dapper man leaned forward and took out his pen, pointing it at Alex as if it were a symphony conductor's baton. "Where will you stop, Pierce? Do you intend to bring back smallpox as well? Or any number of vermin the world is better off without? Have you no respect for the natural order?"

Alex picked up the ungainly bird and carried it squawking to a bowl of grain. The dodo immediately forgot its annoyance and began to gobble the corn. "These birds lived quite nicely on the island of Mauritius until European sailors came and killed them for food. That wasn't so bad, but the sailors also let loose dogs, rats, and hogs, which ate the dodo's eggs. It took only a century or two for the entire species to be wiped out." He scratched the feathers on the turkey-sized bird. "What, exactly, is *natural* about that?"

Kinsman directed a condescending look at Alex Pierce—who captained a gigantic corporation, who had developed a cure for the digestive misery of billions—as if he were an ill-educated child. "You can't possibly predict the long-term consequences of your tampering. Forced breeding, gene selection, wombs implanted with embryos they were never meant to carry. Why must you *push* things so much?"

"Because I don't have time to waste," Alex said mildly. "Evolution can meander all it likes. We have calendars."

Kinsman sniffed, clicked his pen twice in a nervous gesture. "Mankind is part of the natural order, Pierce, the dominant species on Earth, while other species failed along the way."

"Sometimes with a little help from us. What's wrong with rectifying that?"

Kinsman tossed his pen onto a cluttered desk and actually clasped his hands together in a melodramatic beseeching gesture. "What makes extinction caused by human interference so different from extinction due to, say, a huge asteroid impact? Will you try to bring back dinosaurs next?" He scoffed. "Or woolly *mammoths*? I've heard what you have back in your valleys."

Alex maintained a noncommittal expression. "Rumors."

"Satellite photos."

Alex didn't respond, trying to hide his surprise that Kinsman and his protesters could have gotten such high-resolution images from the Feds.

Kinsman pressed his advantage. "I want to see them, Pierce."

Blocked from view by a thick stand of Ponderosa pines, the corral had once been used for breaking horses. But Helyx had reinforced the fences, added motion detectors and voltage zappers, and made the barricades much taller. As needed.

Inside the enclosure, Susan studied two of the first-generation hybrids, giving each one a standard monthly physical exam. Maybe Kinsman would be satisfied with this.

When she saw her husband pass through the double gate, Susan's face lit up. They had spoken via earlink after he'd arrived back from Miami, but both of them had been too absorbed with ranch duties to see each other before now. They would have plenty of time tonight, camping out under the stars, back where no one could find them....

Susan rang the old notes in him with a little breath, a flash of a smile. He had called those eyes "molasses brown" because when he looked into them he felt stuck and never wanted to look away. High cheekbones, luxuriant brown hair, a delicious set of curves artfully set off in a blue blouse atop trim black jeans. She greeted Alex with a broad smile, but when she saw Kinsman follow him into the corral, she immediately adopted a more businesslike expression.

"Susan, this is Geoffrey Kinsman. Remember, he was a grad student back—"

"Oh, yes. And now a member of our loyal opposition." Her voice was neutral, neither friendly nor antagonistic.

"I came to see your mammoths. I didn't know whether I could believe the appalling—"

Susan immediately clued in with just a glance at her husband. "Actually, these are 'mammophants.' Just a first-generation hybrid, still far from being an actual mammoth, Mr. Kinsman."

"Please, it's *Doctor* Kinsman. I got my degree at—"

"This one is Short Stuff," she continued without the slightest hesitation and stepped close to the oldest of the mixed-breeds, a docile gray-haired beast with rumpled skin and big eyes, a trunk shortened to a few feet, and no tail. "We used mammoth DNA from Siberia, inserted it into a female elephant's egg, and let the mother bring the baby to term with a lot of uterine monitoring."

Playfully, Susan reached up and slapped Short Stuff's rump, and the tall beast ambled a few feet, then stopped to munch from a pile of sage-green hay piled near a corrugated water trough. "And she's a sweetie."

Alex knew the details, had lived with them for a decade. Short Stuff was not a pure mammoth because she had spent twenty-two months in an Asian elephant's womb, sharing the chemical and hormonal bath evolved for elephants alone. But the womb had proved similar enough to a mammoth's, or the hybrid would have spontaneously aborted.

"We're learning the hard way that there's a critical conversation between the genes and the womb," Susan said. "Call it feminine knowledge. So we're still working to get the right dialog between the mammoth genes and the wombs of each new generation."

Indeed, Short Stuff's womb had turned out to be a much better approximation, and using the sperm of the first male, Middle Man, their offspring was even closer.

"You can sure see the original elephant genes showing through." Susan lifted Short Stuff's leathery left ear, as big as a blanket. "No woolly mammoth had this large an ear. It would lose too much heat in an Ice Age climate. Most of Short Stuff's body was designed for the tropics—she's got a hide that stands up under strong sun. Still, you can see the beginnings of hair, an extra coat to keep her warm. A step in the right direction."

She talked faster as Kinsman's frowning displeasure became more obvious. Susan moved to the other big animal in the corral, the first hybrid male. He snorted, curled his trunk, but she fearlessly thrust a hand into the sparse pelt beneath the massive mouth to reveal stubby, gray-brown shafts. "See Middle Man's tusks? Pretty short for now, but they'll grow longer than any elephant's."

Susan rubbed her hands along Middle Man's midsection, eliciting a pleased sort of grunt.

Kinsman ground his teeth—the first time Alex had ever seen anyone do that, outside of movies. "And what is the point of this nonsense animal? The pure species died out long ago, and your interbreeding process creates only a succession of polyglot monstrosities."

Susan gave him her patented I-don't-suffer-fools-gladly expression. "Exactly. Did you think species just jumped in one shot to a completely different form? That's why it's called *evolution*."

Kinsman eyed the two hairy elephants in the corral. "Evolution didn't make these forms—"

"Right. We did," Susan shot back. "Unlike evolution, we have a goal. Short Stuff and Middle Man are investments for the next generation."

Alex smiled; his wife was a better debater than he could ever be. And she wasn't giving away anything technical, either, trying to swamp Kinsman with pizzazz. He did not need to know how far the plan had already progressed.

Mammoth DNA was a heritage that belonged to all humanity—paid for with private money, part of the fortune Alex had earned as "Dr. Diarrhea." Early on, before he'd learned to keep quiet about Helyx's activities here, he and Susan had published a joint paper—

the one Kinsman had done some routine lab work on—showing that the difference between elephants and mammoths was only a few dozen critical loci. The media speculation *that* provoked taught them to keep their work quiet. Every journalist could see the potential, write a quick deep-think piece. But making the project happen was a career.

"You frighten me," Kinsman said, looking from Susan to Alex. "Both of you. Our environment is a vast and complicated system that adapts to changes through delicate checks and balances. Dodos and passenger pigeons and moas—and, yes, mammoths—were removed from Earth's equation long ago, and your meddling may well throw everything out of balance again."

"That's an awfully sophisticated argument for a bunch of protesters who usually can't come up with anything more pithy than 'It's not nice to fool with Mother Nature.'"

Kinsman dismissed his cohorts down at the south gate. "They're just afraid of genetic engineering on general principles. They don't need any deeper argument than that."

"No, I don't suppose they do. People like that have always used their ignorance as a weapon." *And often it turned to violence.*

Kinsman backed toward the gate, as if afraid to get any closer to the gentle hybrids. "Your work is immoral, even aside from the ethical issues. Introducing a big grazer into lands that cows and sheep have already depleted is sure to have a major impact on the environment."

"Helyx's track record speaks for itself. We're concerned about the environment—and it isn't just corporate bullshit either," Alex said with a sigh. Whatever hope he had harbored that a real biologist would be open to rational ideas faded as Kinsman's sour scowl deepened.

As a last shot, the man said, "You have to know that a lot of us in this world think what you're doing here is, at the very least, ugly." He flicked a disapproving glance at the furry mammophants wandering around the enclosure.

Alex could tell the discussion was over, and he knew Susan was already close to losing her cool. "I could tell you things—*ugly* things —that'd make your ears curl up in self-defense."

He remembered news images dating all the way back to the late twentieth century: Eco-terrorists burning fields of modified rice that would have grown in the alkaline soil and brackish water of the poorest Third World countries. Or ripping up experimental plantings of frost-resistant strawberries, like children throwing a tantrum. Later, assassinating a researcher who was developing a protozoan symbiote that would have enabled starving populations to break down cellulose and digest some forms of grass.

And if they were caught afterward, the violent protesters always seemed smug and self-justified! Thick-headed fools …

All of those things would have helped the human population, fed millions, improved the quality of life worldwide. And yet the rowdy rabble felt they were in a better position to decide what was best for the world than all the blue-ribbon panels of experts and all the United Nations committees. Yes, indeed, they sure seemed to have the best interests of humanity uppermost in their minds.

He pointedly nudged Kinsman through the gates of the corral before Susan could lash out at him, then used the direct-connect uplink in his spex to summon Ralph and a security escort. "It's time for you to go. You've had your say … I just wish you'd had your 'listen.'"

When they emerged from the dense pines around the corral, Ralph was already there to take him away.

It wasn't until later that Alex discovered Kinsman had left his pen behind inside the Pleistocene Hospital. Rather than hurrying to give it back to the educated Luddite—was that an oxymoron?—he tossed it into a desk drawer in disgust. He had better things to look forward to that evening.

Alex rode his strong black gelding uphill, stretching himself and enjoying the zest of at last getting away from the office, far away, with Susan and the young ranch hand Cassie Worth. Clement Valley was about as deep in the wilderness as he could go and still remain on his vast acreage.

After the irksome arguments and corporate busyness of the afternoon, this was heaven. He had spurned the convenience of using a company jeep; taking the horses felt more natural, more *real*. As the dense alders and ponderosa pines closed around the narrowing four-wheel-drive road, they rapidly left the log cabin lab buildings and the Pleistocene Hospital behind.

Cassie, the spunky, and at times incredibly earnest, young ranch hand, urged her horse into a trot ahead, anxious to get to the high overlook into the next valley. The young woman's long chestnut hair had been quickly woven into a thick practical braid that dangled beneath her white cowboy hat. Her face still retained a splash of youthful freckles, and her clear blue eyes held a fresh sense of wonder.

With good reason, he thought, *since she has seen miracles.*

But Alex and Susan did not hurry. Feeling anticipation build, they rode side by side, smelling the creaking saddles, the sweating horses, and the sweet sun-warmed pine sap. It had been a long time since they'd been so calm, though young Cassie's presence would dampen any amorous impulses in the sleeping bags out by the campfire. No matter; it was good just to be together.

While Susan watched approvingly, he had made a brave show of switching off his pager, but within half an hour the cloying weight of corporate responsibility forced him to turn it back on. When Susan wasn't looking, of course ...

Horse Valley was more lush now than it had been for millennia. Using Helyx profits, Alex had started this ranch by channeling mountain streams into the headlands above, so that his experts could use the moisture to grow the sedges that normally flourished only in tundra. Reflections of aspen shimmered in mirror puddles of water as he headed up the slope, relishing the crisp air. Purple poets always talked about the "forest primeval" and Alex couldn't get the phrase out of his mind. *That's how this is supposed to be.*

In low-lying swampy areas beside the path, giant ferns like horned and scaly monkeys' tails curled up, flourishing next to fluted flat-leaved hyacinth—ancient plants that had not grown naturally since the last ice age. As they rode past, he sniffed the mulchy smell, wondering if the resurrected plants were edible, if there might be a high-end niche market for, say, Jurassic Salads....

"Majestica is looking ready to deliver," Cassie called over her shoulder, slowing her mare so her two bosses could catch up. "I've gotten close enough three times in the last week to take readings, but Bullwinkle doesn't like it."

Alex smiled. "They trust you, Cassie." Forget the scientists and the so-called professional handlers; this young woman had a better knack with the big beasts than anyone else on the ranch.

Susan drew a deep, satisfied breath. "It'll be our first pureblood, after fifteen years."

"Think of it as an anniversary present," he said. "Without your grandiose dreams I would have spent all my research money on a cure for flatulence." The three horses splashed across a stream, climbing steadily now.

Susan laughed. "I still think you deserve the Nobel Prize."

"Relieving the world's diarrhea problems through genetic engineering makes one fabulously rich but earns no professional respect whatsoever."

Behind them, the view was stunning, a full mile of untouched wilderness. It felt odd to know that he owned very nearly everything within view, even from the highest vantage. Only in Montana was there enough land to tackle the really big projects that made his wife happy.

"After this, Alex, nobody will even bother remembering all the little things you did in your reckless youth."

Impatient with the two romantics, and smiling with anticipation, Cassie led them toward the top of the ridge. All around the valley, thick pine and aspen forests covered the hills. Cassie slowed her horse as they entered a rank of thoroughly stripped trees that showed long scraped gouges in the bark.

Susan was amazed, and concerned. "They're foraging all the way up here? They shouldn't be wandering so far afield." She urged her gray mare into the great field of sedges and sages so carefully arranged by innumerable days of gardening.

Cassie cocked her hat back with a wry smile. "Do you want to be the one to tell them where they can and can't go, ma'am?"

Alex made a mental note to see about putting a few sonic "discouragers" up here. He couldn't imagine what would happen if a stray happened to wander down the valley to within view of the protesters at the gate. Then he'd have to deal with the local sheriff, the Feds, a dozen regulatory agencies, and a host of tabloids....

As they emerged from the aspens, the girl's sweeping arm drew Alex's attention to the grassy lowland in the bowl of the valley. "See, they always come together at dusk. It's the best time to watch."

Their horses standing close together, the three of them looked down onto Clement Valley in the last light of afternoon. Susan could barely tear her dark eyes from the sight below, but she gave her husband a loving glance that said, *We did this, you and I.*

Alex stood transfixed by the slowly moving shapes before him. His company had been right to keep the media resolutely away from the valley, and here was the proof. You had to see the woolly mammoths for yourself.

Whenever he had a fresh glance at the herd, the beasts seemed like sailing ships. There was a stately glide to their passage as the great russet vessels crossed the flatness, each beast moving as though before steady winds. Only slowly did the mammoths tack and turn, ponderous yet inevitable.

As if Cassie had trained them to recognize her, the nearest behemoth raised its head and let out a long, soaring salute. The next took up the sound, and the next, and soon nearly three dozen massive beasts joined in the trumpeting call.

Alex felt an eerie shiver travel down the length of his spine. The strange, echoing song reached even deeper into his primal core, building in layer after layer, delving into bass notes seldom heard outside the cathedrals of Europe. Even when the haunting chorus faded into the soft sigh of a breeze among the shadowed pines, the three human interlopers remained still, afraid to move as if they had been the ones transported through time, not the mammoths.

"Humans haven't heard that call in ten thousand years," Susan said as she leaned over to kiss him. He was too overwhelmed to say anything at all.

With Cassie in the lead, sitting high on her roan mare, Alex and Susan rode down toward the mammoths in the last light of afternoon. The herd was accustomed to horses, and especially to the smell of the young ranch hand who tended them. Raised entirely without predators, the mammoths were unwary. Though his mare seemed a bit skittish, Alex did not feel threatened as he approached the magnificent woolly behemoths.

The sedge grasses were tall and resilient, grazed short and trampled flat especially around the muck of watering holes. Playing the Helyx CEO, Alex noted that at the grassy margins the cottonwood branches and even bitterbrush were being browsed down to nubs. He would have to speak to the tenders about keeping the food supply going so the animals didn't wander into the stands of trees bounding the meadows. Soon, the herd would outgrow this valley.

He made a mental note to look into buying even more land, maybe expanding the huge Helyx Ranch into adjacent valleys. The politics of doing that would be far worse than the economics; the perpetual gang of Evo demonstrators at the south gate would grow, joined by garden-variety environmentalists. Folks around here didn't look much to the future—or to the distant past, either, it seemed—and they didn't like change....

With the approach of the horses, the mammoths snorted and stirred. Bullwinkle, the big leader of the herd, hung his shaggy head and lowered long tusks as he gazed at the others. The mixed-bag of hairy elephants had a range of body types, each generation only a few years separated from the previous, and each one significantly woollier than either of the two hybrid mammophants Alex had allowed Geoffrey Kinsman to see.

Cassie halted her mare beside a tree completely stripped of leaves and half of its bark. "Best to tie up our horses here." She dismounted with the springy grace of a gymnast. "I prefer to walk among them."

"Aren't you afraid of getting stepped on?" Susan asked.

The ranch hand flipped her braid back between her shoulder blades and adjusted her hat. "No, ma'am. But I'm afraid for the horses."

The few stands of valley grass darkened to jade as the sun settled on the distant blue mountains. A nighthawk flitted with thin cries above the willows of a narrow creek that meandered through the meadow. Alex's eyes followed the hawk up toward the peaks that towered against a hard, cobalt sky already dotted with the fires of far suns. The light would fade fast, dark scarcely an hour away.

A perfect night to camp.

Cassie started ahead, glancing over her shoulder and resisting the impulse to leave the other two behind. Alex remembered when he had been that impatient, and that young—not so long ago. Though this entire project had sprung from his wife's dream decades ago,

Cassie Worth was the unrelenting factotum who supercharged the Helyx staff and never seemed to sleep. She ran down innumerable practical details about exotic animal husbandry, and she figured out the answers for herself when no alleged "expert" had a clue.

Alex reflected as he watched the young woman move swiftly through the herd. To think that she had just applied to Helyx out of the blue. No advanced degrees, just solid experience at UC Davis, a farm upbringing, and an ache to bring back to the world something long gone. Alex had noted more common sense in Cassie than in half of his own VPs and Division Heads. And she had a real rapport with the animals.

"Come on, you guys, I want to show them off, but I'll need to get us back up on the slope where I can set up camp for the night ... or did you change your minds again?" She turned her clear blue eyes to Alex—did he see a girlish crush there? He was abashedly reminded that he had canceled their plans three previous times for the usual "business reasons."

"Nothing's more important tonight." Alex reached over to stroke Susan's shoulder. "My wife and I are going to sleep out under the stars."

"Where I can hear my mammoths snore," Susan added.

They moved among the gigantic but gentle animals; it seemed to Alex as if he had wandered into a truck stop filled with living, hairy semis. The heavy air was laden with smells like hot oiled leather, old upholstery, musk and fur—stronger than the closeness of bison or penned cattle. But it was a wild musk, from thick and wiry hair grown to protect the beasts from the cold of an Ice Age.

Alex felt giddy.

It was a pure joy to watch Cassie in her element, like a child at a petting zoo. She led them from one large bulk to the next. Alex had never before seen so many of the beasts together in the valley. In a single glance he could see that each successive generation had fewer of the humped backs of African elephants. Instead, the younger hybrids' backs sloped down, the rich cinnamon-colored pelts thickened, and the males' tusks grew.

Closer and closer.

Cassie reached beneath the coat of the nearest hybrid and pulled up the coarse guard hair to reveal silky red under-wool. "It's so good now we should be able to leave them out all through next winter."

"Even in Montana's worst?" Alex asked, trying not to sound as if he was just protecting his investment.

"They'll love it," Susan said, smiling at the young woman.

"And they're getting interested in mating with each other now!" Cassie said, then lowered her voice as if embarrassed. "I follow them on the vidcams, and they really go at it. Just frisky play, so far. After all, they haven't reached adolescence yet. But the males are starting to herd the females—another sure sign."

Susan said softly, "We can't actually let them mate, though."

Cassie cried, "Why not? Just think—no more egg transfers, no sperm-sucking games to play." Her face wrinkled in disgust, and Alex didn't want to imagine the details of the mammophant sperm-harvesting operations.

Susan put an arm around Cassie. "We're careful with their genes. Select for mammoth aspects, weed out the elephant ones. Unchecked mating would scramble all that."

Cassie looked stricken. Plainly this had been her big announcement.

"But you're right," Susan hastily added. "Just like in nature. Desire is the only sure diagnostic." She gave her husband a quick, sultry glance. His breath caught. "These animals know, right down in their hearts—which by the way are bigger than a human head, bigger even than Alex's!—that they are worth making more of."

He hugged her. "And so we'll make more." *Some people buy diamonds for their wives ... I clone mammoths.*

Cassie made quick jabs at nearby shapes, showing off as she quickly recited the names of the other hybrids. "Those two are Rachel and Napoleon—the shorter ones are always the worst—and Angel Pie."

Alex was amazed she could identify the individual herd members so easily. The Helyx geneticists had used five to ten elephants for each step of the process, because it took twelve years for any one of the hybrids to mature to fertility. And some interbreeding attempts spontaneously aborted, nature's editing.

Cassie led them unerringly to a huffing female, her big eyes casting a calm gaze down at the small humans. Long breaths steamed in the cooling air as dew condensed on the rocks and trampled grass. "Here, Majestica is at term and already showing signs of labor. Everything's normal, as far as I can tell. She's been in labor for about a week already."

"I can't imagine being in labor for a week," Susan said.

And the big female's gestation period had already taken nearly two years. "Mammoths and elephants aren't in much of a hurry about these things," Alex said.

Actually, the gestation period had varied with each hybrid generation, as the offspring approached pure mammoth stock. According to her continuing researches into the original genome, using numerous fourth-order projections with hypercomputers inside the pine-walled stable building, Susan was convinced that the mammoth gestation time in the Pleistocene would have been longer than a modern elephant's twenty-two months. One of the earlier female hybrids, Alexandria, had carried her baby for twenty-three months.

"We're converging toward the mammoth pattern in the ancient wild, I bet," Susan said.

Alex smiled wryly. Given her anxious attention to all aspects of the projects, his wife probably would have preferred to keep the pregnant Majestica in a separate corral back at the Pleistocene Hospital, with a whole bank of real-time blood-test gear, round-the-clock technicians, and a full array of instrumentation and diagnostics surrounding her pregnant bulk.

However, these creatures needed to bear their young naturally, in the wild, and Cassie Worth had seen more live births among ranch stock than any of Helyx's experts. She was ready.

But no one alive had ever seen the birth of a real woolly mammoth.

The smoke of green branches and dry wood wafted up from the campfire, crackling with a pungent, sweet bitterness. Alex breathed deeply, smelling the heady primal scent. Hidden in the gathering darkness, insects and night birds set up a simmering background music that seemed to come from a different time altogether.

Below them in the valley, under the light of the waxing moon and a billion stars in transparent Montana air, the herd of elephant-mammoth hybrids settled down for the night. Many of the big dark shapes still moved about restlessly. While some slept like mounds of dirt near the watering hole, others paced around, munching on sedge grass. Eerily, some of the mammoths on the fringe looked as if they were keeping watch.

Cassie busied herself, happy to be out camping, much more comfortable here within sight of her mammoths than up around the administration buildings. She never tried to understand the protesters, preferring to ignore them by staying far from the gate. "People always find something to complain about, especially when somebody else is successful," she had said once.

The young woman had outdone herself with the fire, the bedrolls, the childishly simple dinner of hot dogs roasted on twigs over the flames, a speckled blue-enamel coffee pot hung over the coals. All they needed was marshmallows (and Alex wouldn't have been surprised if Cassie had them stashed in her saddlebags). A perfect evening, in every detail.

Helyx could have provided the most sophisticated camp equipment, thermal chargers for foodpacks, heated sleeping bags and damp-resistant tents. Alex could have assigned workers to set up comfort-weave tents, groom the clearing, erect tables, string lanterns, even prepare a gourmet meal.

But this was better, much better.

"When do we start singing 'Kum-bay-ya'?" Alex said with a grin to his wife.

"I have a strummerpack," she answered, calling his bluff.

Alex's implanted pager tingled, and he recognized the source. He reached up, touching a contact point. "What's the trouble, Ralph?"

Susan frowned at him, mouthed the words, *I thought you turned that off?*

"Can't figure, Boss." His usually casual voice now sounded pinched with concern. "We're getting pinged by microwaves. Somebody's interrogating a passive receiver. Must be located somewhere around the ranch buildings."

"Not one of ours?"

"No chance. Just a simple incoming pulse from some airplane, flying pretty high. Don't think anybody could get much from that, maybe just a location marker. The pulse could be hitting some tiny receiver that shoots it back with a li'l information attached, I'd guess. Not powerful enough for us to track down where it is, though."

"Probably some new gear brought in by the demonstrators at the gate," Alex suggested. He didn't need a new technical puzzle to ruin his jealously planned evening.

"Could be, Boss. Those Evo types have plenty to spend on new toys."

"Keep on it." He disengaged the pagerlink, saw both Cassie and Susan staring at him with concern. He made a placating gesture but didn't volunteer any details. The ranch hand would assume it was yet another corporate emergency such as had canceled their first three outings; Susan, though, could read his expression much better. Her molasses-brown eyes trapped him again, looking like bottomless wells in the smoky campfire shadows.

He leaned against Susan as they both stared into the throbbing orange and yellow embers. Their clothes smelled of sweat mixed with the musk of mammoths. Alex preferred this sharp but resonant aroma to the infrequent, expensive perfumes his wife felt obligated to wear at ecological fundraisers—like the recent one she'd skipped in Miami.

Under the stars, Alex helped with the bedding down chores, glad for the chance to get his hands dirty rather than just pound on a computer keyboard all day. It felt good, and safe, to be out here, "just like a real person."

The crackling wood made him think of the prehistoric hunters, Cro-Magnon warriors who had tracked herds like this using spears and pits and cliffs to kill the giant animals for food, fur, and ivory.

Like the restored bison on the Great Plains, Susan's dream-experiment might turn out to be so wildly successful that large numbers of these once-extinct creatures could roam the open Montana range. They might wander north into Saskatchewan and Alberta, heading up toward the subarctic regions for which their huge bodies were designed.

He had been so focused on working one generation after

another, converging toward a full-blood woolly mammoth, that he had not let his mind wander far into future possibilities.

"Maybe one day we'll have a large herd of mammoths that breed true and reproduce in the wild." He ran fingers over Susan's hair, recalling Kinsman's concern (one of his few legitimate ones) about the impact a sizable group of such huge grazers would have on the landscape and environment. What if they had to thin the herd? "Can you imagine if we had enough of them that we could even sponsor a good old-fashioned mammoth hunt?"

Cassie, very protective of the animals, glared across the fire at him. "What! Use guns on my mammoths?" She had been working here only two years, but the mammoths were *hers*. "Not unless you play fair." The girl's firm lips curled into a devilish grin on her freckled face. "Dress your big-game hunters in furs, then send them out with stone axes and sapling spears. Pleistocene rules. I don't think you'd get many takers."

"Not me," Susan said. "Not for all the testosterone in the world."

Alex returned a noncommittal smile. He did not argue, but he knew both women were wrong. Over the years, he had encountered any number of too rich, too bored, dot-com millionaires or genetics patent holders—people who had delusions of immortality and an overblown sense of necessary machismo.

Even with Pleistocene rules, Alex knew he could find plenty of takers....

As he bedded down next to Susan, the moon continued to rise, spilling silver light. Even here, as isolated as one could be in the continental US, he felt as if he were under a spotlight. He couldn't sleep, and he knew Susan was awake and thinking beside him.

Below, the mammoths sounded restless. Snuffles and loud snorts rippled through the big animals. Most of them seemed awake. On the other side of the fire, young Cassie sat alone, her knees drawn up to her chin as she stared down into the valley, reflecting the animals' uneasiness.

Alex couldn't imagine what possible threats or predators could worry the gigantic prehistoric beasts this deep within ranch property. "Are they like this every night?"

Impishly, Cassie raised her eyebrows. "I *do* have quarters of my own back in the complex, Dr. Pierce. Sleeping outdoors is a treat for me, too."

A bright meteor streaked overhead, low and horizontal, like a rocket on the Fourth of July. It came over the line of trees on the ridge, flying hot, traveling with a speed and deadly accuracy that surpassed any shooting star.

Make a wish …

Susan was already on her feet, leaping out of the blankets on the damp ground. "It's heading toward the lab complex!"

The trail of fire faded into orange against midnight blue, and the incandescent arrow struck the valley behind them with a bright flash. The main Helyx compound. A muffled *whump*.

As Alex lurched to his feet, the implanted pager tingled again. "Boss, we've been hit down here. Somebody sent in a mini-cruise, I'd say. Hit the pines close to the Hospital … still trying to assess the damage."

"A mini-what?" Alex subvocalized, and his words went back to Ralph.

"Backpack-sized cruise missile, Boss. Short-range, with a nose full of high explosive. A man can carry one a fair way, then launch it from a rack."

Susan was already racing for her horse while Alex paused to get an update. "I'm going there!" she shouted and swung herself up bareback. "Short Stuff and Middle Man are still in the corral."

"Wait! You can't do anything—"

"Just work things out with Ralph," she called over her shoulder, then raced her horse down the four-wheel-drive road and disappeared into the shadowed trees. He had never seen her ride like that before.

Reacting on instinct, Cassie was at their supply packs. She withdrew the two shotguns she had carried with them, ostensibly for protection against coyotes or bears.

Alex didn't need to think hard about who might have done such a thing. "Kinsman was a decoy," he said to Ralph. "Him and his supposedly reasonable discussion, he was just a plant to get inside. But how could they target the hospital in the dark and from so far away?"

"I'm willing to bet they targeted this place with those microwave echoes I keep hearing. If Kinsman planted some sort of passive echo locator—"

"His pen! Damn, I didn't even think! He left it on purpose. They could have targeted from that. I'm packing up Cassie, and we'll be right down there."

Before Alex could switch off, the security chief said, "Wait—that's gunfire. Jesus, those bastards are coming in from the south gate!" Ralph's voice strayed for a moment as he barked orders to a security crew, who scrambled in response. "The Hospital's in flames, Boss. We're sending people in to try and rescue the animals."

"Keep yourself safe," Alex barked. "Susan's already on her way." He thought of the two adult mammophants in the corral, the wonderful dodos and moas, all the exotic and frightening animals he kept in the solid-wall pens in the back of the Hospital. And all of his people. He prayed his wife would be safer down there with Ralph and his crew than up here. "We're coming in—"

Another thin patter of popgun shots rang out. Alex thought he was getting Ralph's background noise until Cassie cried, "Just below us!"

"Ralph, we've got intruders up here, too."

"Clement Valley! Jesus, do you want me to send a—"

"You just do your job there. And watch Susan's back, dammit."

He shut down his link and studied the shadowy trees. Another few shots, yes, nearby. One of the mammoths bellowed in surprise, or perhaps pain, sounding like a squeaky cannon.

"Hey!" Cassie tossed Alex one of the shotguns, and he caught it instinctively. The weapon felt hard and cold and strange in his hand. She looked at him with an anguished face. "Maybe that missile hitting the Hospital was just to get our forces away—so they could come up here and kill my mammoths." She swung herself up onto her already frightened mare and bent low, snatching the tether rope. "I'm going down to the herd."

The gunshots came faster as she rode hard down into the valley.

"Wait!" Alex called after her—pointlessly—then got his butt in gear.

He mounted his own gelding and followed her into the darkness. Here he was, the head of a gigantic international corporation—and his wife and a young girl had both jumped into action while he stood around and talked to himself.

The horses were already uneasy with the smell of the mammoths, and the pattering gunfire spooked his mount even more. He caught up to the young ranch hand as she tried to see down into the darkness. "You leave the mammoths alone!"

"Quiet!" he urged, fearing the shadowy attackers might target Cassie instead of the animals.

Sharp, flat shots from their left.

Alex saw dim shapes running, stalking closer, as if intimidated by coming so close to the prehistoric beasts. Simple rifles would have little effect on a woolly mammoth, he thought—just before another round of muffled percussive bangs.

A few seconds, then distant explosions came from the open valley floor.

"Grenade launchers."

"You bastards!" Cassie screamed.

"Hush! They don't know we're up here." He and the young ranch hand were still on a slope above the trees, a hundred meters from the open grassland. They urged their horses closer. It was quiet for a moment, a deathly stillness.

The mammoths churned about, grunting, drawing closer like covered wagons circling against a Comanche attack. Amazingly, acting on instinct, the bigger bulls formed outer ranks, clearly to protect the rest of the herd. The alpha male, Bullwinkle, with its huge tusks and russet fur, snorted and moved forward like a locomotive, looking for an enemy.

No sign of the shadowy figures, but the fringe forests offered plenty of cover.

Alex knew that Cassie's first thought was for Majestica, the pregnant female about to give birth to the first pure mammoth. They rode toward her, and Alex prayed the beasts could tell the difference between friendly humans and deadly ones.

Abruptly, scarlet fireballs burst a hundred meters away ... and another right on top of them. One of the wild grenades struck Majestica between the shoulders, and the impact knocked even the giant female battleship flat to the ground, her upper body cratered with ragged, flash burn wounds.

Cassie screamed. She threw herself off her horse and raced to the fallen pregnant female.

Alex waved his shotgun around, then took a few high potshots, hoping the retaliatory gunfire would at least stall the attackers, send them scrambling for cover. But it was a pitiful gesture at this range. None of the terrorists came out of the tree line.

Gunshots rang out and ineffectual bullets peppered the mammoth-elephant hybrids, sending them trumpeting into a frenzy. Some charged, stopped, trumpeted. But the big male Bullwinkle thundered into the night, toward the attackers hiding in the trees.

Alex dismounted and came up beside a determined but weeping Cassie. His heart wrenched, knowing they had all been betrayed. The young woman impatiently swiped tears from her eyes and got to work. "Damn, Dr. Pierce—I don't have the equipment for this!"

Back in the forest, startled shouts turned to shrieks. Alex could well imagine the giant bull trampling the bastards into paste on the ground. Bullwinkle hooted, a powerful bellow that brought more shrill screams. A grenade burst near the beast, then the big mammoth was into the trees, smashing branches, splintering trunks, following the panicked outcries.

More screams. He did not think further about what Bullwinkle was doing. He could see only the pregnant mammoth's blood shining dark and wet in the moonlight. "Don't worry. I'll help," he said to Cassie. Corporate CEO bullshit, but it seemed to be what she needed to hear. He knelt beside her, trying to anticipate what the young woman was trying to do. She worked with utter concentration, adrenaline, and desperation, staving off panic.

As he tore off his shirt and wadded it up into a large pad—nowhere near enough, he saw, as he pressed it into the gaping wound—he heard a faint sound and looked around. Other mammoth hybrids bellowed, but the gunfire had halted for the moment. Bullwinkle's work?

The whispery sound of feet in the sedge grasses came nearer. Cassie didn't notice it. Bare-chested, Alex backed away from the dying animal, leaving his shirt to soak up a gusher of blood. He smelled gunpowder and meat. "They're coming back," he said. Grabbing his shotgun from the trampled ground, he moved as quietly as he could around Majestica's massive bulk.

"Keep them the hell away from my mammoths," Cassie said, her voice thin. She didn't even look up from Majestica.

Alex jacked a shell into the shotgun, hoping the flat *clack-click* sound would be enough of a deterrent. *Never.* Halfway around the heaving beast, he crouched down, looking across the moonlit expanse.

He cursed himself as much as the fanatics. He had underestimated their dedication, dismissing them entirely. He had scoffed at their mindset, never giving them credit for a zeal that would push them beyond theoretical protests. How could they be so *vehement*? There was a long, precarious bridge between waving signs and launching missiles, but Kinsman and his Evos had crossed it.

He'd considered the Luddites to be quaint, backward, even silly. Now they had proved deadly. Causes had always attracted violent crusaders whose actions seemed inexplicably extreme to most people—pro-lifers shooting abortion doctors, environmentalists "protecting the Arizona desert" by setting fire to luxury homes. Could any ends justify such means?

The Evo crusaders came out of the trees, hunched over as they emerged from the protective shadows. They were competent enough, moving quickly, not talking. But Alex saw the reflection of their eyes as they covered the last twenty meters. Three that he could see, two headed directly this way, weapons ready ... thinking they had already won.

He raised the shotgun and a lot of thoughts ran through his mind. It was easy enough to think you could shoot at an enemy, someone with a grease-blackened face and cradling a grenade launcher, pistol strapped at his waist. But when it was a kid of maybe twenty ...

The kid raised an arm to his comrades, who immediately squatted and aimed—at Majestica. And Cassie! They knew their target. They knew exactly what they intended to shoot.

And Alex had no time left for doubt. Executives, he often said to others, were people who could make decisions on time. Well, here was one. He shot the kid with a spray of pellets. He hit him in the legs, but square on.

Alex did not let himself hear the screaming as he jacked the next shell in, sighted on a man who had half-risen to his feet and was swinging a long-barreled weapon toward Alex. "Cassie, get down!" he yelled, then sighted and squeezed off the round. The feel of the gun was as natural as when he'd potted away at clay pigeons on weekends, long ago.

Now the third Evo, a woman—but she was already running away. He let the terrorist take three more strides to be sure she was out of lethal range. The blast of pellets against her shoulders and backpack did not knock her down, but she cried out, and ran even faster in a headlong stagger back toward the trees.

The first kid was yelling, rolling around with his bloody-hamburger legs drawn up to his chest. The second man lay still; Alex didn't even know where he'd hit the terrorist. The woman made it to the trees, where Bullwinkle was still crashing around. Alex kept down—the Evos had plenty of distance weapons and would be looking toward the source of his shots.

"Dr. Pierce! I need your help here!" Cassie sounded closer to panic than he had ever heard her.

Slinging the shotgun low, ready to spin around and open fire again into the night, Alex scrambled back around the dying Majestica.

Susan rode hard, and her horse was hot, its mouth foaming as she careened down the bumpy jeep road. She could see the darkness of trees and night blended with probing beams of hard white surveillance lights ahead.

She and Alex had always talked about beefing up security in an apron covering the entire approach from the south gate. When the protesters had settled in, they'd brought their own lights, as well as coolers of food and drink, so they could squat down and begin chants and drum beating in a general disruptive "people power" party. They kept it up until the early hours, youthful idealism uniting with the universal instinct to party. Annoying, certainly, and frustrating—but nothing to be taken seriously.

That had been their biggest mistake.

Occasionally, those little protests had only been a distraction, a cover for one or two Evos to slip past the fencing and guard stations in the dark. Once inside, though, they had no good idea which targets to go for, what vandalism to accomplish. Inept commandos, they generally blundered into staff housing or maintenance sheds, which had been deliberately disguised to look like laboratories and stables.

But now, the log-fronted Pleistocene Hospital was on fire. They had struck directly to the heart of the retrograde evolution project.

"Damn you," she said. "Damn you all." She kicked her horse, riding harder.

The tall pines surrounding the corral had become torches in the night, crackling resinous flames. From inside the high reinforced fences she heard a roar, an indescribable screaming cry that sounded like nothing human. Short Stuff and Middle Man, the first two mammophant hybrids, were still in there, far from the safety of the rest of their herd ... brought back to the ranch buildings for regular health monitoring.

Susan dismounted from her gray mare before the horse had even come to a stop. She hit the ground running and, frightened by the noise and the smoke, the exhausted mare trotted away in confusion. The fire from the Ponderosa pines had already descended to the corral fence. Susan slammed through the gate, calling out to the two oldest mammophants.

Middle Man had backed to the far corner, away from the burning trees, away from the light. The big male trumpeted a sound like anguish, obviously frightened and confused. He bled from several wounds in his thick hide, but the injuries seemed relatively minor. Susan didn't even stop to consider whether Middle Man might charge her.

In the center of the trampled enclosure lay Short Stuff, collapsed to the ground like a defeated calf in a rodeo spectacle. High-powered gunshots had blasted both of her forelegs, ripping gouges in muscle and bone until the female hybrid had crashed. Short Stuff chuffed and hooted as she struggled on the grass, her legs bloody and useless appendages.

In shock, revulsion, and helplessness, Susan swayed backward, grabbed for the corral fence to support herself, but missed. Watery-kneed, she sank down, and froze, utterly unable to do anything. Short Stuff trumpeted again in unspeakable pain.

Ralph Duncan strode into the corral, swinging his head from side to side, taking in details. His eyes had always looked world-wise, as if they'd already seen everything, but now his face had a disgusted horror. "God damn! God *damn*!"

He strode forward like an avenger, holding the powerful rifle at his side. Susan made a strangled sound, and he whirled, ready to shoot, but when he recognized her, his expression instantly changed. "Miz Pierce!"

Short Stuff let out another hollow, trumpeting call. Ralph's expression hardened, and he turned away from Susan, ignoring her. Without hesitation, he marched up to the writhing, wounded mammophant, pushed the barrel of his rifle up against the base of Short Stuff's massive skull, and pulled the trigger. The hybrid groaned and slumped. Ralph shot her again, then turned back to Susan. His face was ruddy and murderous. "God damn it!"

Shaking, Susan pushed back to her feet, then grabbed the corral fence and vomited. More shouts and gunshots came from the main lab complex. Through the fence and the trees she could see flames shooting from the admin building. She coughed and spat. "How many are there? What—"

He took her arm and led her out the gate. "Middle Man's fine for now. I've got security troops split between defending the ranch and trying to fight the fires." He touched his earpiece, listened, then shouted, "Dammit, don't wait for the sheriff! Just move on it!"

Susan heard the distant patter of gunfire, military-style commands, and the frenzied shouts of shadowy attackers. They could have broken through the fences anywhere. Were these the same protesters that had innocuously waved their signs and posed for the TV cameras? Could it all have been a feint, a ploy to let Helyx security believe the Evos were ineffectual whiners and bored activists in search of a cause ... when all the while they were planning this brutal strike as soon as they could get a man inside?

She saw birds fluttering in the trees, the passenger pigeons disturbed from their nests in the big oaks. "I'm going to the Hospital!" She heard sounds that could only be giant moas squawking in panic. "Ralph, get those fires put out!"

As she ran toward the Hospital, Ralph yelled louder into his voice pickup. On one side of the main admin building, a few men had set up a hose and were spraying the yellow flames on the log walls, but fiery fingers already crept along the roof.

Susan didn't give a damn about the computers and office

furniture inside. She ran toward the Hospital itself where all the retrograde hybrids were kept, her life's work, the maturing ambassadors of species long extinct. Why would anybody want to harm them?

Probably the same people who break into cancer-research centers and "liberate" all the experimental animals, she thought. *I guess they don't see the contradiction.*

Out in the Hospital yard, she saw tall, ostrichlike moas set free from their cages, wandering around in terrified confusion. Brown feathers ruffled, serpentine necks swiveling about, horny beaks open with hissing squawks, they kicked up dirt with lizardlike feet and pecked at any person who came close. Ungainly dodos scrambled about like overgrown drunken chickens, honking in fright. Susan heard other animals scream and yowl from within the Hospital itself. Smoke oozed through several broken windows, growing thicker, blacker.

Just then a man with a prim face and dapper-looking clothes stepped across the porch holding a revolver in his hand. Geoffrey Kinsman. Like a grim executioner, he pointed at the dodos and methodically shot them all, moving from one to the next to the next.

Though armed with nothing but her anger, Susan raced toward him. Other protesters ran past Kinsman into the lab building, not willing to simply let the fire do its work.

Kinsman turned toward the closest frightened moa, putting three bullets through its long neck. The giant bird toppled like a fallen tree. Not even pausing to reflect on his handiwork, the man stalked toward the smashed-open door of the Hospital and vanished inside.

Susan screamed in outrage, but Kinsman didn't even notice her.

After stepping over the shattered carcasses of the magnificent lost birds, she barged into the main laboratory. Evos were overturning desks, smashing computers, dumping animal feed on the floor in a wild frenzy, like capering cannibals celebrating the arrival of a boatload of missionaries. These crusaders had no organization, no plan, just chaos.

Dressed in her jeans and camping clothes, Susan entered the lab, smelling the fire and spilled chemicals, the blood and nose-tingling gun smoke.

In the harsh, stinging smoke she saw Geoffrey Kinsman, proud slayer of helpless dodos and moas, trotting from cage to cage, shooting every creature inside. Fast, methodical, intent.

Susan's eyes burned with disgust. Ducking through the smoky light, she went to the cages on the other side, past lab furniture, desks, equipment racks. She threw open cage doors and coops, chasing the dodos, moas, and other hybrids out, giving them a chance. Squawking and hissing, the marvelous creatures ran, fleeing the fire, fleeing the gunshots.

There, dammit! The chaos grew. Shouting and gunshots echoed from outside. She heard a shrill whistle, a bullhorn. A helicopter circling.

Grinning, a blond-haired, clean-shaven man ran past her holding a long shovel, battering file cabinets, smashing beakers, computer screens, even ceramic coffee cups. He took a swipe at a waddling dodo, missed, and Susan grabbed the shovel handle, wrenching it out of his grip.

The man shrugged, then toppled a heavy laser-ROM storage rack, scattering the prismatic platters like Christmas ornaments. He snatched up a crowbar some other protester had dropped.

From nearby came the sound of a window smashing. More strangers ran in through the Hospital door, carrying weapons.

When his pistol was empty, Kinsman took a repeater assault rifle from one of the Evos, checked that it was loaded. Then he looked up and saw Susan. Recognized her.

"Damn you!" she said, raising the shovel as if it was a match for his rifle.

Behind her, the reckless blond Evo grabbed the closed doors of the larger pens at the back of the laboratory. The barricaded, reinforced rooms.

Kinsman hesitated with his rifle, smug with self-justification. "This has to be done."

With a deft twist the blond Evo pried open the lock. He must have expected nothing more than another awkward-looking bird. He held his crowbar loosely in one hand, as if ready to bash a few more animals.

And a saber-tooth cat lunged out at him, already maddened by the fire and the noise.

The big panther's front fangs gleamed, as long as scimitars. It reared up to embrace the man and with a throaty growl it bore him down, muscles moving like liquid beneath its mottled, long-furred coat. The Evo screamed as the panther/sabre-tooth hybrid tore open his chest, raising long curved fangs and plunging once, twice, three times.

Susan managed to shout "No!"—just as a panicked Kinsman opened fire.

On the sedge grass, trampled and bloodstained, Cassie leaned over the gasping, quivering hulk of the fallen Majestica. The female almost-mammoth panted and shuddered, her body core ripped open by the grenades.

"She's dying." Cassie looked up at Alex, her eyes wide and pleading, as if somehow this important corporate executive could do something.

"Yeah," he said uselessly.

She seemed to be in a daze, saw the shotgun slung low in his hand. "You shot at the Evos?"

"Forget them."

Majestica's body heaved and clenched and trembled in spasmodic labor—dying, but also following a biological imperative. Alex heard a snorting and pounding sound and held up his shotgun, ready to defend them against a continued Evo attack—but he saw only the huge head and long curved tusks of the angry Bullwinkle. The large mammoth stomped on the ground, thrashed his shortened trunk.

In the stark, silvery moonlight Alex saw a few flecks of black blood peppering the shaggy fur, minor wounds from gunshots. He had expected to see the bull's long ivory spears coated with gore, his front feet splattered with the blood of crushed humans. But Alex heard the Evos still screaming and crashing away into the night as they fled up the valley.

The bull mammoth had let them live. Bullwinkle could easily have trampled every one into the ground. Instead, he had just driven them off and turned back to come here. At the moment, Alex himself didn't feel so civilized.

Lumbering close to Majestica, the shaggy bull sniffed, quested with his hairy trunk. Bullwinkle watched with round, wise eyes as

Cassie felt the pregnant female's heaving belly, her hands exploring the quivering muscle and tough hide.

She drew her long hunting knife.

The other hybrids milled about nearby, circling and snorting, some trumpeting their pain, all clearly agitated. One of the youngest hybrids waded out to the middle of the muddy watering hole and raised its trunk high as it honked into the night.

The Evos had gone away, their destruction accomplished, leaving pain in their wake. *Making their savage point.* Alex knew he should call Ralph and his security men, bring them out here in Helyx choppers to run the terrorists into the ground, apprehend them and haul them off for Federal prosecution.

But as he knelt beside a blood-streaked Cassie, he didn't feel that was important enough right now.

The pregnant female had closed her intelligent eyes in wrinkles of dark skin, blinking only occasionally. Majestica's breath was slow and deep, a bass-noted wheezing, accompanied by a bubbly wet sound of blood and air oozing from large holes in her massive torso.

Majestica's pelt gleamed, glossy and moist. A heavy musk mixed with the metallic sourness of blood rose from the laboring mountain. The female's pelvis was tilted, her womb clenching as she used the last of her energies to squeeze.

A charge of tension permeated the air, a slow silent sense of gathering energies ... of time contracting down to a completion.

Cassie pressed her hand against the distended belly. The abdominal muscles shuddered, but Majestica was clearly dying in the moonlight. Even Alex could see that. She wouldn't last long enough to give birth, and the purebred infant woolly mammoth would die inside the womb.

He knew that young Cassie had needed to sacrifice mother animals before, delivering their young by Cesarean. It was a part of ranch life when there were a lot of animals to herd and tend. In her hesitation now, he read that Cassie didn't know if her muscles and her resolve and her knife edge would be up to the task she now faced.

Ralph's hoarse voice chirped in Alex's ear, with words so devastating that Alex could spare no attention for what the young ranch hand was about to do. "Boss, you'd better get back here." The old security chief paused, as if gathering courage. "It's Susan. Get back here now."

Cassie barely looked up as Alex ran to his horse.

Sobbing, she raised her long knife high, hesitated, then plunged it deep.

When Alex rode up to the main Helyx complex, two of the ranch buildings were engulfed in flame. Fire crackled and roared, clean woodsmoke mixed with the foul stench of burning electrical wires, chemicals, and plastics.

He called for Ralph, then he saw the security men dragging bodies out onto the lawn in front of the Pleistocene Hospital. His stomach lurched.

Alex had underestimated the Evos completely, the intensity of their gut-level resistance to what he was doing. And Kinsman himself, a former colleague, was someone who should have known better. Alex had rolled his eyes at the silly signs, foolishly dismissed the objections of people he considered Luddites. "It's not nice to fool with Mother Nature."

Re-creating the mammoths had aroused such a passion, such a sense of wonder in his wife—but he had never considered that it might engender equal and opposite emotions in her detractors.

He called for Ralph again, but his voice broke as he stumbled across the yard. The rangy old man jogged up to him, feverish, his leathery face fallen in despair. He threw himself on Alex, both arms around his shoulders. Alex went weak with dread.

"Where is she?" he croaked, but he could tell from the stiffness in the security chief's muscles that he was already too late. "Where is she!"

Ralph staggered back. Without a word he walked with Alex toward the burning Pleistocene Hospital. In the acrid yellow glow, a few surviving animals ran about in panic. Passenger pigeons squawked from the oak trees. Others fluttered across the night sky, escaped from burning nests. Bloody mounds of feathers on the grass marked the slaughtered dodos and moas. *Extinct again.*

He took a few steps, choked on acrid smoke, turned.

Susan lay outside on the ground where Ralph had carried her.

She had a crumpled, broken look, he thought abstractedly. That was when the fog began to wrap itself around him, dulling the clamor, shrouding the world in a ghostlike slowness. He shook his head, but the fog remained. His field of view telescoped away and he staggered. He reached out to steady himself on a beam and his hand felt nothing. Sour air rasped into his lungs. The iron taste of blood told him he had bitten his tongue. And the soft fingers of fog thickened.

The feathers of ancient birds fluttered around her like a halo, catching the glow of hot white security spotlights. Her flannel shirt had soaked up the crimson blood. She lay, waxen, lifeless. He did not count the gunshot wounds.

In the background he barely heard Ralph's security men shouting. Ranch workers, in shock and keeping themselves moving with forced activity, braved the inferno of the lab to rescue a few remaining experimental animals from their cages. To salvage some of the records. To preserve cellular specimens. Sometime in the distant future, he would probably thank them.

None of that mattered now.

He tried to take two steps toward Susan, but his muscles disobeyed. His knees buckled, weak and watery. Alex collapsed, sitting on the rough ground. Close enough to see her, but she would never again be close enough to touch.

An empty man rode back out to Clement Valley. The cool night air brushed at his face, but he did not feel it. The east brimmed with a pale glow, but he did not see it. The soft fog fingers were still there in his head. He shook it.

He found Cassie, her shirt and braided hair and jeans soaked with dark wetness. When he saw the blood, he had a sudden fear that she too had been shot. But she got up on unsteady legs, looking utterly exhausted in the beam of his flashlight.

Then Alex saw the small creature, like a newborn elephant but covered with matted wet fur. It stood already. About the size of a riding lawn mower. The baby mammoth moved on wobbly legs slick with its mother's fluids—aware and healthy. Somber eyes accepted him in a mute communion.

Alex drew a deep breath. A mammoth, the first purebred ambassador from that extinct species, arriving on this night of smoke and blood.

He felt a trickle of amazement through his shell of despair. Though its mother had been murdered by attackers, this fourth-generation offspring had been successfully delivered alive.

In spite of all this. Thanks to Cassie.

"It's a start," she said. Her large, wonder-filled eyes stared at Alex as he touched the thick reddish fur on the young mammoth's sturdy shoulders. He knew he should tell her about Susan, but he wasn't ready to deal with the questions ... or the sympathy. He couldn't think of anything to say.

"I want to name him Adam," she continued. "Seems appropriate."

The rest of the herd huddled together in the naked night, while Bullwinkle stood near Majestica's carcass. He twitched his trunk, snorting steam plumes in the waning moonlight. Alex imagined the big bull was as anguished at losing his mate as he himself was over Susan. He heard a low, guttural note in its sighs and wheezes that had not been there before.

He turned away. Shared grief was little comfort.

The big animals clustered together, calmer now, as light seeped into the valley. Tall, powerful, magnificent. Back from extinction. Distantly, hollowly, a part of Alex thought that the throwback Evos were a portion of humanity that might be better off extinct. Not these creatures. Not these strong and wonderful miracles that his wife had brought forth from dreams.

Alex stood among the herd and looked at young Cassie, seeing her resolve undampened. She was saying something, but he could not hear, somehow.

In Susan's memory, he promised himself that he would carry on this project. Even though he might have to move to the ends of the Earth, where he and the mammoths could be safe ...

Somehow.

Adam tottered off toward the herd. It waddled in the grass, lit by thin rays of sun, bleached of all color. Bullwinkle saw the small moving thing and sent a blaring trumpet salute. The herd answered with a chorus of bellows and huffs.

In this moment Alex felt his own life slip into insignificance, one more mote beneath the hard stars. One more member of a newcomer species, a mere vessel. His best work lay forever in the past now, but he could still make some difference.

The fog around him cleared, just a bit, letting in the glow of the east. Susan could live only through these creatures, through her work. He would have to speak and care and fight for his wife's memory, too, and for all of her legacy, living and dead.

Clouds were moving in, he noticed absently. It was a shrouded dawn, though it could turn bright.

I am a member of the Science Fiction Advisory Council for XPRIZE, serving with many well-known visionaries and futurists. In a partnership with Japanese airline ANA, XPRIZE asked its science fiction writers to each create a story about a specific passenger in a specific seat on an ANA jet that somehow jumps twenty years in the future.

The aim was for us to showcase marvelous changes that might be possible in the next twenty years.

Then I learned that my very close friend Neil Peart had been diagnosed with terminal brain cancer. Reeling from that news, and the last few years I spent with him, I had to write this story.

TERMINAL

Turbulence didn't bother her—Magdalene Cross had enough going on in her mind. Her thoughts and memories, which had once been so organized, were now as scrambled as unpredictable air currents high over the Pacific.

It was 4:30 in the morning, but on the long overseas flight from Tokyo to San Francisco the string of time zones made the hour meaningless. Magdalene couldn't sleep, and she couldn't concentrate. The anti-seizure meds always made her feel dopey but not sleepy, the worst of both worlds. More drugs treated her dizziness and nausea, and several varieties of potent pain meds battled the mind-shattering headaches that would be her constant companion until the end.

Magdalene would rather have been with her family in her last days, but she feared she had waited too long for the flight home. Always cutting it close …

Throughout her career, Magdalene had prided herself on her punctuality, meeting every deadline, arriving just in time so as to waste not a minute. Thirty-five years as a corporate executive managing projects, leading research teams, jockeying for government grants, overseeing university hospitals, receiving awards for her landmark work on breast cancer research. Everyone in the field knew that she had helped shepherd tremendous progress toward a cure. That had been her passion.

Oh, the cruel irony!

The Boeing 777 twitched and jumped, and Magdalene blinked as she saw a strange underlying *ripple* go through the air, but the distortion faded away. She often experienced vision problems, halos, ghost images.

She found her purse in the little alcove near her window seat and removed her pill case. God, it was like a portable pharmacy! She took two OxyContin and waited for them to work, knowing they would only make her feel more fuzzy and disconnected. But it was better than the pain.

With all of her meetings and appearances throughout her career, Magdalene knew how to be comfortable aboard the ANA flight. Her window seat was spacious enough and the tray table gave her room to put together one of her jigsaw puzzles, a small one. Alas, small ones—ridiculously simple ones—were all she could do these days. It was embarrassing and sad.

Taking a plastic zip bag from her purse, she spilled out the colorful cardboard pieces onto the tray table. Twenty-five large pieces with prominent curves and protrusions designed to challenge a four-year-old. Working through the process meticulously, Magdalene turned each jigsaw puzzle piece face up, looked at the colorful printing. It would be a smiling cartoon figure, a happy rabbit. The twenty-five pieces were scattered at random, and she felt a moment of panic as she looked down at them. The colors and broken artwork made no sense. How would those pieces fit together?

Magdalene felt the floating sensation of the opiates kicking in, and she made herself consider the puzzle like a large project that she had once managed, step-by-step. She could do this. She sorted the edge pieces using her fingers to feel the smooth straight side, because the tactile addition helped make the pieces fit together mentally. A wave of nausea rippled through her, and she paused, waiting for it to pass.

Then she began to align the edge pieces, looking in dismay at the swatches of color, trying to understand the order. Slowly trying one after another in an organized fashion, she lined them up.

During the months of treatment in Tokyo, she would spend hours at a table in her room working on jigsaw puzzles until they became too disheartening. The puzzles were meant to be a distraction from the rigors of chemotherapy supplemented with targeted radiation. It was a new experimental procedure available only in Japan, not authorized for use in the United States. "Aggressive yet promising" the research papers had stated, offered to only a select few patients, but she was *Magdalene Cross*, and she had connections, many friends in the research field. And she had no other chance.

She'd always known the treatment was a gamble, and it would take six months, perhaps the last six months of her life. She clung to hope, clung to her faith in science and medical research, knowing that these colleagues wouldn't let her down. And they hadn't let her down; the treatment hadn't let her down. Her body had. Her brain had.

And now she was racing home—yes, *racing* was the proper term, because the ticking countdown inside her body had nearly reached zero. She just wanted to see her daughter Candace and her five-year-old grandchild Aspen, a beautiful little girl.

With a brief glimmer of clarity, or by coincidence, Magdalene found two pieces that aligned and interlocked. Then a corner, and then another piece. She took advantage of her mental momentum and finally had the small puzzle framed, which gave her an absurd sense of triumph. Jigsaw puzzles had been her hobby, and she remembered putting together large ones, masterclass puzzles, two thousand pieces, five thousand pieces. Once she had even completed a maddening exercise of an entirely white puzzle. Now, she looked down at the cute happy rabbit and couldn't figure out where his ears went.

"It's that one," said the man in the seat next to her. He had been friendly, even though she clearly didn't want conversation. "This one right here." He picked up a piece and slipped it into place. The intrusion angered her, but she couldn't express herself.

"I … I'm fine." She picked up another piece and stared at it, defensively, but it was just a gap in her hand.

The too-friendly man smiled and opened his mouth to say something, but his expression froze. "Oh, I'm so sorry! I saw the meds, and I didn't think. Is it Alzheimer's?" He blushed as he realized he'd dug his hole even deeper. "Never mind. It's none of my business."

Previously, when she traveled in business class, people had clear boundaries of privacy, and in Japan she had grown accustomed to a more reticent culture. But now she was flying home in coach, and this man was obviously a tourist, well-meaning, but he didn't play by the same rules.

Not Alzheimer's, you idiot! she wanted to say, but the words were as elusive as the pieces of the jigsaw puzzle. Her thoughts had been shoved aside by the thing growing there. *Glioma.* Yes, that was the word! But she couldn't make it come out of her mouth. A particularly aggressive tumor growing inside her brain, stealing her thoughts, infesting her gray matter like an annoying pop song that you couldn't get out of your head. But this cancer song was deadly. The aggressive experimental Tokyo treatment hadn't helped, hadn't prolonged her life. It had only taken six months away from her, probably the last six months. She would have been better off staying home and giving little Aspen memories of her grandmother.

Embarrassed by his faux pas, the man in the adjacent seat pulled a sleep mask over his eyes and snuggled down, withdrawing into a belated sense of privacy. With a sigh of relief, Magdalene turned back to her unfinished puzzle.

The plane was dark, many of the passengers asleep. The seatbelt light went off, and the captain announced something over the garbled loudspeaker about being past the unexpected turbulence, but Magdalene was too focused on her challenge. The happy rabbit slowly took shape one piece at a time, and within an hour, she had managed to finish it. In the meantime, she had taken more anti-nausea drugs and one more pain pill. As they approached San Francisco, she was drifting and detached, but in a lost, seasick way rather than pleasant euphoria.

When the flight attendants came around and the cabin lights flickered back on, she declined breakfast, even coffee. Magdalene didn't think she could keep any food down. Sparkles of thoughts and pain jittered inside her mind, as if the uninvited glioma was doing a victory dance.

As ANA Flight 008 came in for a landing, Magdalene picked up a tension among the crew. The flight attendants looked concerned, talked in low voices with one another. The captain made more announcements than usual about "inconvenience" and "representatives meeting everyone at the gates," as well as the always-alarming "please remain calm."

The man in the adjacent seat fidgeted, sweating. He looked over at her as if seeking comfort, then flushed in embarrassment again, but he didn't turn away. "You think something's wrong?"

You mean with the world in general? she thought. *Or the plane? Or with me? I can sure as hell tell you the answer to the last one.* But Magdalene just shook her head and leaned back. What a colossal irony if the plane were to crash on her way home, when she only had months, weeks, even days left. Almost as ironic that one of the greatest breast cancer advocates was struck down by a *brain* tumor.

The 777 landed safely, and the worry seemed to be about something entirely different. The passengers picked up on the uneasiness, and they were disturbed, some curious, some afraid, and the flight attendants didn't look any better. The 81 passengers rummaged through overhead bins, grabbed their carry-ons, crowded the aisles in a rush to disembark. Magdalene's clueless companion hurried to join the flow, but since she was in a window seat she was in no hurry. All of her meds had kicked in now, many of the drugs clashing with each other. Her body was like a pharmaceutical puppet, her mind a marionette controlled by the insidious tumor.

The crew knew about her medical condition; she had filed papers, included her medical records. She was too touch and go, traveling alone, and airlines didn't like the PR debacle of someone dying on their plane. The flight attendants had discreetly watched over her, and they were supposed to see that she exited the plane safely. Once she got into the terminal and met Candace and her granddaughter, then she wouldn't be ANA's responsibility any more.

As the cabin emptied, she waited for someone to come and escort her. But as the flight attendants did their best to herd everyone into the terminal, Magdalene realized they must have forgotten about her special needs. The worried-looking crew wanted to get off the plane as quickly as possible.

When she decided that she was on her own, Magdalene got up to make her own way. She'd survived the horrific chemo and radiation in Tokyo, endured the long overseas flight, the odd turbulence; she could certainly make it just a few more minutes off the plane into the terminal, through customs and immigration ... and to Candace and Aspen just outside of security. She imagined how the girl would jump up and down, calling out "Grandma, Grandma!"

She took her purse, which contained her meds and the few things she clung to, mostly digital photographs, reminder notes she made to herself, and a painstaking letter she had written to her daughter in her last days in the Tokyo hospital. Magdalene wanted to say so many things, to say goodbye, to leave a legacy for her granddaughter. But the words just wouldn't come. Simple communication eluded her, brought her to tears as she struggled with the slippery but simple concepts. After she exhausted herself, poured out everything she could think of, Magdalene saw she had written only two paragraphs, and then she cried even more....

She stood and gripped the seat back, wavering, feeling her legs turn to shaky jelly. Her balance looped around like a drunken bumblebee. The aisles were starting to clear, and Magdalene tottered out. One step. Another step. Moving forward, passing one row of seats, then another, then the next section. Reaching business class was one little victory, and the door and the jetway was another. The flight attendant at the door seemed pale, parroting her usual "Thank you, have a nice day," but her voice wavered.

Magdalene might have been curious about what was wrong, but her brain was so full of the glioma that she had no room for questions. She could only concentrate on moving, her vision focused down to a tunnel as she gripped the railing, trudged up the jetway. The pain in her head was like an enthusiastic street drummer banging away on overturned plastic tubs. The tumor seemed to be taking a victory lap.

Magdalene refused to let it win. Just a little farther ...

When she emerged into the terminal she saw a milling crowd, the passengers from Flight 008 being corralled, held back. She saw security troops, but their uniforms looked odd, of a more futuristic design. The décor in the San Francisco airport looked different. Ad displays on the walls were interactive, intrusive holograms that stepped in front of potential customers rather than a more easily ignored poster. She kept walking among her fellow passengers because she didn't dare stop moving her legs, although the black static around her vision swirled and darkened, while the pounding in her head grew to a deafening roar.

Over a loudspeaker, an androgynous voice said, "Passengers

from Flight 008, please remain until we can assess the situation." His words faded in and out like an AM radio station in a car driving in the desert. Magdalene had done that once when she was in her early twenties, a free spirit exploring the country on her own … "Everyone seems to be fine … no ill effects." The next words made even less sense, and she blamed it on the brain tumor. "… time ripple."

"… skipped forward entirely."

"… 2037."

Her brain fired one last series of explosive pains like the grand finale of the fireworks from last Fourth of July, when she, Candace, and Aspen sat on a blanket on the grass in a county park watching the show. Magdalene had known of her terminal cancer then, had been convinced that would be her last Independence Day celebration. Her last …

Her body finally surrendered. She collapsed, sprawling forward, the world spinning, contracting down to a pinpoint that was a whirlpool of colors, memories, and unexpressed thoughts. People shouted, some backing away from her, others pressing closer. Within a moment, medical teams closed in, uniformed med techs bending over her with scanning apparatus, strange interactive devices. Touchpads were applied to her neck, her cheek.

How did they get here so fast? Were the med teams already at the gate?

"Must be an aftereffect of the time ripple," said a woman doctor, studying her screen. "Better quarantine all passengers. Quick, run a scan!"

"We need to get her into the medical suite, just at the end of the terminal," said the young med tech beside her. "But we have to start from baselines. We don't know what the effects of the distortion could be."

"Baseline …" Magdalene croaked, amazed that she had found the word. "It's not any effects … of whatever. It's brain cancer. My records … aboard the plane." Somehow she made herself keep speaking, though she had to force each word out of her mouth. This was important. "Glioma … terminal. Nothing you can do."

Startled, the medical techs looked quickly at one another. Magdalene could barely keep her eyes open, but the darkness behind her closed eyelids was even more frightening. She felt fumbling hands on her. Someone withdrew the boarding pass sticking out of her purse, found her seat number, identified her name.

"It's Magdalene Cross! Remember, she was on the passenger manifest," said the woman doctor. "It is brain cancer. Terminal glioma."

Magdalene couldn't quite parse the woman's words, couldn't understand her expression. The doctor seemed *delighted*, and the young tech beside her started laughing. "Brain cancer! You mean it's only brain cancer?" He seemed relieved.

Someone else said, "No reason to believe her collapse was caused by the time distortion."

"Brain cancer," Magdalene said. They didn't seem to understand. "Terminal."

"We know, we know," said the female doctor. "Don't worry about it. The airport's medical suite has all of the necessary microsurgical apparatus and the avatar hookup. For you, we'll get one of the very best neurospecialists. I think he's in Bangkok right now, but he can hook up via avatar and perform the surgery. You'll be just fine, Dr. Cross. Nothing to worry about."

As she finally blacked out, probably for the last time, Magdalene thought the words were the cruelest hallucination of all.

When she awoke, her thoughts were clear. Her head throbbed, but not in pain; rather, it seemed more a fuzziness, a confusion, not the same sludge of drug sensations from her anti-seizure meds, her anti-nausea meds, her painkillers.

She focused on her surroundings, a small room with a lush pristine forest and blue skies projected on the walls and ceiling. Monitoring devices were connected to her, but without wires or cables; she felt something attached to her head. This was nothing like the horror of tubes, electrodes, beeping pumps and monitors during the treatment in Tokyo.

The young woman sitting at her bedside was beautiful, around twenty-five. Her expression filled with warmth and genuine concern, not the typical bedside manner with which Magdalene had become so familiar.

In a voice filled with wonder, surprised that the words came easily, smoothly, she said, "I'm alive—that's one thing at least."

The young woman chuckled. "You'll be alive for a long while, Grandma. The brain cancer is gone, and you just need time to recover—and to adjust, I suppose. We all need time to adjust." She reached forward to squeeze Magdalene's shoulder. "I still can't believe it!"

"You called me Grandma. What on Earth …"

"I know you don't recognize me. I'm Aspen." She seemed to be holding a delicious, exciting secret. "The last time you saw me was when we watched the fireworks. You must remember it?" When Magdalene didn't immediately answer, the young woman's eyes narrowed with concern. "The neurosurgeon said that some memories might be gone because the glioma was extremely large and pervasive. Please tell me you remember the fireworks in the park!"

"Of course I remember," Magdalene said. "That was with my daughter and granddaughter just last year, Fourth of July."

"It's 2037, Grandma. Your plane skipped forward twenty years in time. ANA Flight 008 vanished in June 2017, and we all thought it had gone down in the Pacific without a trace. It's been two decades!" Aspen shook her head. "Mom and I were sure we'd never see you again."

"Your mother …" Magdalene still couldn't understand, trying to decide which was more fantastic—that she had somehow time jumped into the future, or that her brain cancer had been cured. "Where am I? Where's Candace?"

"She's in Antarctica, but she's on her way. Within the hour, she'll take a SpaceX suborbital flight to San Francisco. But I'm here now."

"Where?" Magdalene asked.

"Still in the terminal facility. They were able to perform the surgery right here. It's a small medical suite, but they can take care of emergencies."

"My brain cancer—major surgery, minimum, but the tumor was inoperable." She took a moment to realize, and marvel at, how easily the thoughts came now, how articulate she sounded. "It was of moderate size, but the location …"

"Every basic medical facility has the right remote equipment." Aspen smiled, and her eyes glimmered with tears. "Remember laparoscopic surgery from back in your day? This is the same thing, only orders of magnitude smaller, a tiny probe, drill, and extraction tube inserted right between your eyes." She reached out to touch a bandage across the base of Magdalene's nose.

"The robotic surgical arms were guided by avatar. And because of who you are—who you were twenty years ago—all the cancer researchers remember you. You're revered! The world's foremost microglial surgeon used the avatar linkage, and he performed the surgery from his clinic in Bangkok. He neutralized the tumor, killed and extracted the key mass bit by bit through the microtube— delicate but efficient. Then he repaired as much of the tissue as he could. You're fine, Grandma. You can go home with us by the end of the day. Mother's suborbital will be here by then."

Magdalene had to close her eyes. This was a complex jigsaw puzzle of unbelievable facts and preposterous claims that she simply could not assemble, no matter how she looked at the pieces, turned them, rearranged them. She let out a sigh and concentrated on something more comprehensible. "You're so beautiful. You grew up well. I wrote you and your mother a ... letter. It was in my purse."

Aspen looked serious. "A goodbye letter doesn't matter anymore. You're here. There have been a great deal of changes and progress in the twenty years you've been gone, incredible advances in minimally invasive surgery, in cancer treatment, in medical avatars."

Magdalene remembered what the medical techs had said after she collapsed in the terminal. They laughed, relieved that she "only" had brain cancer. She tried to put the pieces together. "So removing a brain tumor is nothing more complicated than getting a filling at the dentist?"

Aspen leaned closer, amused. "A cavity filled at the dentist? Oh, Grandma, we have vaccines against tooth decay. Drilling holes in your teeth and filling them with metal is as outdated as drilling holes in your skull to treat a brain tumor."

Filled with wonder instead of dread, Magdalene reached out and spread her fingers, extending her hand toward Aspen. "I look forward to hearing all about it ... and all about you and your life." She slipped her fingers into her *grown* granddaughter's hand. She clasped tight, and the pieces fit, slipping perfectly into place.

PREVIOUS PUBLICATION INFORMATION

"2113," copyright © 2016 WordFire, Inc., first published in *2113, Stories Inspired by the Music of RUSH*, ed. Kevin J. Anderson and John McFetridge, ECW Press.

"The Bistro of Alternate Realities," copyright © 2004 WordFire, Inc., first published in *Analog*, June 2004.

"Carrier," copyright © 1985, WordFire, Inc., first published in *Stardate 5/6* , March/April 1985.

"Combat Experience" © 2017 WordFire, Inc. First published in *Brothers in Arms: Stories Inspired by Richard Matheson's Beardless Warriors*, ed. Barry Hoffman and R.C. Matheson, Gauntlet Press, 2017.

"Escape Hatch" © 2014 WordFire, Inc. First published in *Five by Five 3: Target Zone*, ed. Kevin J. Anderson, WordFire Press, 2014.

"Good Old Days," copyright © 2007, WordFire, Inc., first published in *The Future We Wish We Had*, ed. Martin H. Greenberg and Rebecca Lickiss, DAW Books, 2007.

"Hunting Harkonnens," copyright © 2002 Herbert Properties LLC, originally appeared as a promotional booklet released by Tor Books, 2002.

"If I Fell, Would I Fall?," copyright © 1988, WordFire, Inc. and Doug Beason, first published in *Amazing Stories*, September 1988.

"An Innocent Presumption," copyright © 2003 WordFire, Inc., first published in *The Silver Gryphon*, ed. Gary Turner and Marty Halpern, Golden Gryphon, 2003.

"Mating Ritual," copyright © 1987, WordFire, Inc., first published in *Etchings & Odysseys 10*, 1987.

"Mammoth Dawn" with Gregory Benford © 2002 WordFire, Inc. and Gregory Benford. First published in *Analog*, July/August 2002.

"Paradox & Greenblatt, Attorneys at Law" © 2005 WordFire, Inc. First published in *Analog*, September 2005.

"Prisoner of War" © 2000 WordFire, Inc. First published in *The Outer Limits: Armageddon Dreams*, ed. Kevin J. Anderson, BSV Publish- ing, 2000.

"Ruins of Memory," copyright © 2023, WordFire, Inc., first published in *Stories of the Reconvergence*, ed. Angie Hodapp and Joshua Viola, Hex Publishers, 2023.

ABOUT THE AUTHOR

Kevin J. Anderson has published more than 180 books, 58 of which have been national or international bestsellers. He has 24 million copies in print in 34 languages.

He has written numerous novels in the Star Wars, X-Files, and Dune universes, as well as the unique Clockwork Angels steampunk trilogy with legendary Rush drummer Neil Peart. His original works include the Saga of Seven Suns series, the Wake the Dragon and Terra Incognita fantasy trilogies, the humorous Dan Shamble, Zombie P.I. series and the Dragon Business series.

He has edited numerous anthologies, written comics and games, and the lyrics to two rock CDs as companions to his Terra Incognita trilogy.

Anderson is the director of the graduate program in Publishing at Western Colorado University, and he and his wife Rebecca Moesta are the publishers of WordFire Press.

www.ingramcontent.com/pod-product-compliance
Lightning Source LLC
Chambersburg PA
CBHW050507110726
47899CB00005B/1365